Praise for the novels of Alison Packard

"I liked everything about this book.... I hope readers pick this up. I think they'll be thrilled with the adult romance. It's one of my favorite books of the year."
—*Dear Author* on *The Winning Season*, recommended read

"I pretty much liked everything about Matt and Kelly's story.... This romance really worked for me and I will definitely be recommending."
—*FictionVixen.com* on *The Winning Season*

"I absolutely adored this book, it was so fun and sexy and everything I love about romance."
—*The Book Pushers* on *The Winning Season*

"*Love in the Afternoon* is enjoyable, interesting and charming.... Highly readable."
—*Romance Around the Corner*

"I think that this may be my favorite debut novel of 2012! Anyone who likes Jill Shalvis, Carly Phillips, Susan Mallery or Victoria Dahl will probably fall in love with this book as much as I did."
—*The Book Pushers* on *Love in the Afternoon*

"A fun, sweet, easy read.... I really enjoyed myself while reading this one."
—*FictionVixen.com* on *Love in the Afternoon*

Also available from Alison Packard and Carina Press

Love in the Afternoon
A Christmas for Carrie
Catching Heat
Breaking His Rules
Stealing Second

THE Winning SEASON

ALISON PACKARD

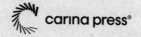

carina press®

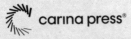

carina press®

ISBN-13: 978-0-373-00319-8

Recycling programs
for this product may
not exist in your area.

The Winning Season

Copyright © 2013 by Alison Packard

www.CarinaPress.com

Printed in U.S.A.

This one's for you, Dad. I miss you

THE
Winning
SEASON

ONE

"Hey, Maxwell, rumor has it you like it hard and fast."

Kelly Maxwell tightened her batting glove around her wrist and gave the opposing team's smart-ass catcher a smirk. "Actually, I like it slow and delivered with finesse. Something you know nothing about." She pulled her favorite bat out from under her arm and stepped up to home plate. "Rumor has it," she added with a grin.

"Come on, Kel. Get a hit." The feminine voice belonged to her roommate, Stacia Lindstrom, who, while not on Kelly's coed softball team, occasionally tagged along to—in her words—supply moral support to the team. In reality, though, the only reason Stacia bothered to show up was to meet hot guys.

"Who's your friend?" the catcher, Kevin, an investment banker who worked in the financial district, asked after casting a lingering glance at Stacia, who, despite the cool San Francisco summer evening, wore a skimpy top that left little to the imagination.

"Out of your league," she said, getting into her batting stance as Kevin crouched down behind home plate.

"Ouch. Seriously, can you introduce us?"

"I'm not a matchmaker." Kelly looked at the pitcher and met her hard stare. Not intimidated, she continued, "But if you're interested, we usually head over to Kamu's after the game."

"Thanks for the tip. I owe you."

"Don't mention it," she said as the pitcher went into her windup and delivered. The trajectory of the ball looked high so she took the pitch. She had a good eye—the umpire standing behind them called it a ball.

"By the way, I'm going yard tonight," she said after digging the toe of her spikes into the dirt and then smoothing it out. There was no particular reason for doing this. It was just a part of her at-bat ritual. A ritual she had performed since she was a kid playing in the peewee league. Even back then she took the game seriously.

"Still as cocky as ever, I see." Kevin glanced at her after he threw the ball back to the pitcher. Through his catcher's mask she could see the amused glint in his eyes. "No one's hit a home run off Beth so far this season."

Recognizing a challenge when she heard one, Kelly shot him a confident grin. "There's a first time for everything."

Two hours, three hits and one home run later, Kelly sat among her teammates at Kamu's Tavern enjoying the sweet taste of victory. Sipping her beer, she watched—bemused—as Kevin tried his best to get Stacia's phone number.

Stacia was to men what catnip was to cats. In a word: *irresistible*. The proof of that was Kevin wasn't the only guy from the opposing team who'd shown up at the restaurant after being annihilated on the baseball diamond this evening.

"I see your roomie is fending them off once again." Kelly shifted in her chair as her team's pitcher, and her coworker, Angie DeMarco, sat next to her. "I hate her." Angie wrinkled her pert nose.

"Would it make you feel better if I told you she snores so loud I can hear her from my bedroom?"

"Extremely," Angie said with a devilish grin. "I'd hate to think she's as perfect as she looks." The remark made Kelly smile. With long dark spirals of hair most women would kill for, and bright blue eyes, Angie wasn't any less attractive than Stacia.

A chorus of boos erupted at the bar. Both she and Angie turned to look behind them at the flat-screen television mounted on the wall over two rows of lighted shelves that held a variety of liquor bottles. "Damn it," Kelly muttered, looking at the box score on the screen. "The Dodgers won again."

"It figures they'd get hot while we're in a slump." Angie lifted her beer. "They got rid of Scanlon and started winning. We got him and started losing." She tipped the bottle to her lips and took a sip.

Kelly didn't want to agree, but that's exactly what had happened. The minute the Blaze had lost their catcher, Rick Taylor, for the rest of the season, and the Dodgers had unloaded their troublemaking bad boy, Matt Scanlon, the Blaze had been in a tailspin. The combination of losing Rick, who was a shoo-in for rookie of the year, and getting a player whose best days just might be behind him had cast a pall over the clubhouse that hadn't lifted yet.

"But on the bright side," Angie said, "his jersey is selling like hotcakes." Angie worked in the accounting division so she would know this. "The women love him, and the men want to be him."

"Not all women love him," Kelly said darkly.

No one at work, including Angie, who was her best friend, knew that she and Matt had met a few weeks be-

fore he'd been traded from L.A. to San Francisco. Nor
would they ever know. She wasn't about to repeat the insults he'd hurled at her, or reveal that she'd given just as
good as she'd got. The only satisfying thing about their
heated exchange was she'd managed to get in a final
parting shot that had left his jaw on the table. Not her
proudest moment, but the arrogant bastard had started
it and deserved every bit of her ire.

"Is he still refusing to give interviews?" Angie asked.

"Yes." Kelly's jovial mood took a turn for the worse.
That's what usually happened when she thought about
Matt. The jerk knew it was her job to schedule his interviews and had told her adamantly he wasn't talking
to anyone. His exact words were "I'm here to play ball,
not spill my guts to a bunch of damn reporters."

That was rich coming from a guy who'd spent the
past year partying, setting a new record for being ejected
from games, and pretty much nailing anything in a skirt.

Now he wanted to keep a low profile?

If he wasn't her problem, she'd probably find it amus-
ing.

As the senior media relations coordinator for the San
Francisco Blaze Major League Baseball team, it was
her job to handle all aspects of public relations for the
team. There were days when she felt like a babysitter to
a bunch of six-year-olds, but she had landed her dream
job and truly enjoyed coming to work every day. Or at
least she had until Matt Scanlon arrived on the scene.

"We're here to celebrate our victory." She lifted her
beer. "Not talk about that pain in the ass."

Angie laughed. "I'll drink to that."

"You're starting tomorrow."

Matt Scanlon looked up from the notes he'd been

studying and watched J.T. Sawyer head toward him. J.T. had just come from the showers and had one towel wrapped around his waist and another looped around his neck.

"I heard," Matt said. Closing the binder, he rose from the slatted bench in front of his locker and pulled his gym bag from the alcove. "Morgan told me before he went home." He shoved the binder into the bag and zipped it.

"It had to happen." J.T. halted in front of his locker, two down from Matt's. "That's why they brought you here."

J.T.'s voice held no rancor, which was surprising because until the Blaze had bought out Matt's contract with the Dodgers, J.T. had finally gotten the chance to be a starter. Now he was back to being number two and yet the guy seemed to hold no ill will toward Matt at all.

"I guess they figure you've had enough time to get to know our pitchers," J.T. continued as he pulled out a deodorant stick and quickly applied it.

"I suppose so." He'd gotten to know them, all right. Most of them hated his guts.

"You wanna grab a beer?"

J.T.'s impromptu invitation was the first one he had received since he'd joined the team. A bit surprised, he nodded. "Sounds good."

"There's a place not too far from our building. Kamu's. Have you been there yet?"

J.T. lived in the same building Matt did, just across the street from the team's ballpark in the area of the city generally referred to as SoMa, or South of Market Street. Several of his teammates who resided in other cities also rented condos or apartments near Blaze Field during the season. It was easier getting to and from work that way.

"No. But I've gone past it on my morning run."

"I think you'll like it." J.T. pulled the towel from his neck. "The owner's been a Blaze fan since the seventies. It's the one place around here where we can go and have a beer or a meal in peace. The owner makes no bones about throwing out anyone who gives the players a hard time. Plus, he's got a shitload of memorabilia. It's fucking awesome."

If Matt were a Blaze fan he'd be thrilled to see the team's memorabilia. But he wasn't. He was a Dodgers fan and had been since he was old enough to swing a bat. Now he was playing for the rival team he'd hated and ridiculed his whole life.

There was no doubt about it. He'd fucked up his life— royally.

Not long after he and J.T. left the clubhouse, Matt sat at the bar with a beer in front of him, watching the highlights from the day's games on one of the flat screens mounted above the bar. Like most sports-related establishments, Kamu's featured a gleaming mahogany bar with comfortable leather-padded stools as well as a number of television sets located in strategic positions for optimum viewing from either the bar or the adjoining restaurant. Framed photographs of Blaze players past and present hung on the walls, and when he and J.T. walked in, he'd noticed a custom-made cabinet that housed autographed baseballs near the entrance. It was a baseball fan's paradise.

Today had been a rare off day for the Blaze but several other teams had played. His former team, for one. He watched the footage of the Dodgers beating the

Braves, but because his loyalty had been in question ever since he got to San Francisco he forced himself to remain impassive.

He was anything but.

Starting a few days after he'd been traded, the Dodgers had embarked on a winning streak that had catapulted them into first place in the division. Conversely, the day he'd donned a Blaze uniform, the Blaze had lost enough games to drop out of first place and into second, tied with the Padres.

Taking a long pull of his beer, he half listened to J.T. talk to the bartender. He heard Rick Taylor's name mentioned, and for the first time in his life knew what it was like to play in someone else's shadow. What was even more messed up was that Rick Taylor was a damn rookie.

The best rookie catcher to come along—well—since Matt himself. Not that he was bragging or anything. After all, he did have the National League rookie of the year award to prove it. Until his motorcycle accident, Taylor was a shoo-in for that same award. By all accounts, Taylor was a decent kid from Texas who had earned the respect of his teammates with his strong worth ethic and solid leadership.

Now the team was floundering without him.

A light tap on his shoulder pulled him from his thoughts. He turned to find a stunning blonde sliding onto the stool next to him.

"You're Matt Scanlon," she said, flashing a wide smile. Her eyes were sky-blue and her breasts impressive. She looked like a centerfold model—exactly the type of woman he went for. Or she would be if she wasn't looking for a relationship. He liked to keep things casual. And by casual, he meant sex with no strings attached.

"And you are?" he asked, angling away from J.T. to give her his full attention.

"Stacia Lindstrom." She tilted her head and gave him a practiced smile. "I don't usually approach men I don't know, but I've heard so much about you that I had to come over and say hi."

"I'm flattered." He'd heard that line before and had, many times, used it to his advantage. It was amazing the number of women who chased ballplayers. Some just wanted to score with a professional athlete, while others were looking for more. Specifically, to sit in that special section in the ballpark where the players' wives and girlfriends sat.

"How do you like San Francisco so far?" she asked.

"I haven't had a chance to see much of it yet."

Stacia's smile turned suggestive. "I'd be happy to show you the sights."

Matt had a pretty good idea what sights she meant and the thought wasn't unappealing. He cast a quick glance at her amazing rack. "Can I buy you a drink?"

After thirty minutes Matt had a good idea of where he'd be spending the night—or at least a portion of it. And he was looking forward to it. He hadn't gotten laid since he'd left L.A. and needed to release some tension. Sex between two consenting adults who knew the score was the way to go. He didn't have time for a relationship, and after the year he'd had, he didn't think he could deal with the emotional baggage that came along with one. All he wanted was uncomplicated sex.

Excusing himself from the bar, he left Stacia with J.T. and headed for the restroom. There was recognition in several people's eyes but no one said a word to him. Just like the team, the fans in San Francisco treated him warily. In L.A. he'd been the toast of the town, but here he was persona non grata.

Rounding a corner, he headed down a short corridor decorated with Blaze memorabilia. As he approached the men's room, the women's restroom door opened and the woman who emerged caused him to stop cold.

Shit.

Kelly Maxwell's eyes narrowed and her expression hardened the moment she saw him. He recognized the look—it was the same one he got whenever they crossed paths.

"What are you doing here?" she asked in her husky voice that reminded him at lot of the actress Demi Moore. When he'd met her in L.A. a few weeks ago it was the first thing he'd noticed about her. That and the fact she was an Amazon.

"Having a beer," he said, quickly taking in her grime-covered baseball uniform. The word *Panthers* was emblazoned across her chest and she had a baseball cap turned backward on her head. Her cheek was lightly streaked with dirt, and although she'd just come from the restroom she hadn't bothered to wipe it off.

She was the antithesis of everything he found attractive in a woman.

Obviously, she found him just as unattractive. Her whiskey-colored eyes looked at him like he was lower than pond scum. Not the typical reaction he got from women, but then Kelly Maxwell was anything but typical.

"I hear you're starting tomorrow." She folded her arms across her chest. He noticed a scrape on her forearm and assumed she'd gotten it from the game she'd apparently played tonight. "The Brewers have been on a hot streak. Please tell me you've done your homework and studied their hitters. Or have you been spending your free time partying it up like you have all season long?"

As always, he bristled at the disdainful tone of her voice. "Are you fucking kidding me?" He glared at her. "I've been in the National League for eight years. I know who can't lay off the first pitch, who's a sucker for a hanging curve and who I can rattle with a well-timed insult about their mother."

Damn the woman. From the first moment he'd met her she'd been able to make him lose his cool.

Kelly's lips twitched with amusement. "I was just asking. You really shouldn't be so defensive. It's not my fault your sorry ass got traded. I warned you it would happen, remember?"

He fixed her with a hard stare, and like that night in L.A., she didn't flinch and she didn't back down. *God, she was infuriating.* The air grew taut between them.

"Oh, I remember." She was tall—six foot at least. He was an inch above that. There weren't many women who could meet his gaze levelly. But she did. "You've got quite a mouth on you. That's not an attractive quality in a woman."

"Like I give a fuck what you think." Kelly's eyes flashed with fire. "And I couldn't care less what you find attractive in a woman. Judging by your choice of companions for the past year, I'm sure it's not brains."

"Nice language."

"Yeah, I swear. So what?" Unfolding her arms, she got right into his face—so close he could see the golden flecks in her eyes. "You men and your double standards. It's okay for you to cuss, spit and scratch your balls but if a woman swears it's a big deal." She let out a sound that bordered on a snort. "Give me a break."

"I'm just saying…" He grinned. He'd gotten a rise out of her and derived great satisfaction from doing so. "If you want to catch a man you won't do it cursing like a sailor and not hitting the showers before you show yourself in public. You smell like a locker room."

Her eyes widened and then narrowed with anger. "My whole team is here, you ass. We came here after the game. It's a ritual. I'm not at Kamu's to catch a man."

"That's obvious." He brushed by her and headed for the men's room. As the door shut behind him he was pretty sure he heard the word *bastard* and couldn't help but chuckle.

Score one for him.

THE HOT SHOWER had been heaven. Pure heaven.

Too bad it didn't wash away the foul mood I'm in, Kelly thought as she left the bathroom and walked naked into her bedroom. The condo she shared with Stacia had two master suites, both with their own bathrooms. It was perfect for a roommate situation and she still couldn't believe she'd lucked into it. It was located a block and a half from Blaze Field. A similar unit had just sold for more money than she'd ever make in her lifetime, but Stacia's godfather, who was filthy rich, had taken a consulting job in London and would be there for at least three years. He'd sublet the place to Stacia and, luckily, her acquaintance from high school had wanted a roommate to look after the place when she was away. Stacia worked as a flight attendant for a transatlantic airline and was sometimes gone for long stretches at a time.

Passing by the full-length mirror, she paused and

studied her reflection. There was a time when mirrors had been her mortal enemy. But not so much anymore. She'd battled her personal demons and, for the most part, had vanquished them.

Turning from the mirror, she moved to the dresser and tried to push Matt Scanlon's irritating image from her mind. It didn't work.

The man was an arrogant prick and had been since the day she'd met him. Only then he hadn't been her problem. He'd been the Dodgers' problem. With amazing clarity she remembered her sister, Kayla, asking her what she would do if Matt got traded to the Blaze. She also remembered her response.

Lose her mind.

And boy had she lost it. The man pushed her buttons in all the wrong ways. She didn't know what was worse: that he irritated the hell out of her, or that he looked so damn hot doing it.

Matt Scanlon was the poster boy for chiseled good looks. He resembled a golden-skinned pirate with his coal-black eyes, strong jaw, firm lips and darker-than-midnight hair. His handsome features were designed to make women swoon with lust and had graced hundreds of magazine covers over the years. Not surprisingly, in the past year his bad-boy behavior had landed him in the tabloids as well as the sports magazines. According to the gossip rags, he'd been spotted on the town with models, starlets and even a few strippers. Not that she actually bought those trashy tabloids, but she'd been known to read them in the grocery store checkout line.

Didn't everyone?

After putting on her usual sleep attire of boy-cut shorts and a tank top, Kelly left her room and headed for the kitchen. She spied Stacia's purse on the sleek black modular couch, surprised she was home. She hadn't seen her roommate since Stacia had given Kevin the brush-off at Kamu's. She had, however, received a text from Stacia telling her to go home without her. That usually meant Stacia had hooked up with someone.

Knowing of her roommate's prolific sex life, there was no doubt in her mind that, right now, Stacia had some poor besotted fool in her bedroom where she would show him a headboard-slamming good time and then send him on his way. That was how Stacia rolled. Casual sex was her specialty. Or it would be until she snagged a rich husband. Sadly, that was Stacia's goal in life.

Walking into the kitchen, she stopped dead in her tracks when she saw that Stacia had some guy pressed up against the edge of the quartz countertop. The mystery man's hands dug into Stacia's ass as they engaged in a pretty steamy kiss.

Damn it. That bottle of water she'd wanted would have to wait.

She took a step backward. Then another. She was nearly out of the kitchen when her heel hit the tile floor and something sharp dug into her skin. "Son of a bitch," she exclaimed as she lost her balance and, with arms flailing, almost fell over. Righting herself, she looked up and smack-dab into the eyes of the last man she'd expected to see.

Matt Scanlon.

TWO

WITH HIS HANDS still cupping Stacia's delectable ass, Matt stared at Kelly Maxwell's stunned face and felt like he'd been doused with a giant bucket of ice-cold water.

She was the roommate?

Of course she was. Because that's exactly how his life had been going lately.

"Sorry, Kel," Stacia said, twisting around in his arms. Of the three of them, Stacia seemed the least surprised. "Did we wake you up?"

For a moment Matt wondered if Kelly was going to speak at all. She stood mutely in the doorway like the proverbial deer caught in headlights. When her gaze lowered, he was reminded of exactly where his hands were. He let go of Stacia's shapely posterior, and because he knew it would piss Kelly off, he grinned.

He was right. She pinned him with a hard stare.

"I was awake." She moved to the refrigerator and jerked open the door.

Stacia eased away from him and shot him an apologetic look and a shrug.

"I came out to get some water." Kelly pulled a plastic bottle from the refrigerator and then closed the door.

As she twisted off the cap, Matt couldn't help but notice her nipples, taut against the fabric of her snug pink tank top. Then he noticed her legs—a mile long and,

while muscular, were smooth and shapely. And then he
noticed he was noticing and that pissed *him* off.

"You know Matt, right?" Stacia asked.

"Yes, and it appears you know him too."

"He's nothing at all like you described," Stacia said,
implying that whatever Kelly had said wasn't flattering.

Kelly opened her mouth but then clamped it shut.
He could see a flicker of irritation in her eyes but it was
gone quickly.

"I'm going to bed," she said, looking from Stacia to
him. "Enjoy your evening."

Unable to resist, Matt grinned again. "I'm sure we
will."

For several long seconds Kelly held his gaze. Judging
by the tightness of her jaw and the steeliness in her eyes,
it was killing her not to say anything. But just like in the
clubhouse, or in the administrative offices at the ballpark, she kept her cool when other people were around.

"Good night," she said and then turned to leave.
When she did, he noticed one more thing about Kelly
Maxwell.

She had a spectacular ass.

Until he felt Stacia's hand on his arm, he'd almost forgotten she was there. He turned to look at her. "Sorry
about that," she said with an apologetic smile. "I guess
we should have gone straight to the bedroom."

Thank God they hadn't. The last thing he wanted
to do was have sex while under the same roof as that
she-devil, Kelly Maxwell. Now that he knew she was
Stacia's roommate there was no way in hell he was staying. It was too fucking weird. No matter how impressive
Stacia's body was.

He glanced at his watch. "It's late," he said and felt a

twinge of guilt when disappointment flickered in Stacia's eyes and her smile faded. "I've got to get to the ballpark early tomorrow. Maybe another time?"

"I'd like that." Stacia's smile returned full force.

During the ten minutes it took him to walk from Kelly and Stacia's building to his, Matt couldn't help but think of the night in L.A. when he'd first met Kelly. If he'd apologized to her for his boorish behavior that night she might not be riding his ass so hard now. Ironically, he'd intended to do just that the minute he got to San Francisco, but before he could get the words out she'd shut him down with some caustic remark about the trade and that's all it took—his good intentions had flown right out the window. They'd been sparring ever since.

After letting himself into the condo, he tossed his keys on the glass-topped coffee table and moved to the big picture window in the living room. The condo, while stark and utilitarian, had a spectacular view of the ballpark built on the edge of the bay. He wished he could appreciate it, but looking at it only reminded him of how badly he'd trashed his life.

Turning from the view that mocked him, he caught a glimpse of the framed photograph he'd placed on the mantel above the fireplace. His heart constricted as he gazed at an image frozen in time. That's all he had left now. Frozen images.

Moving toward the fireplace, he picked up the baseball next to the picture and stared at the colorful crayon markings on it. The pain that knifed through him was sharp—even now.

Contrary to popular belief, time did not heal all wounds.

THE NEXT MORNING, Kelly sat at her desk typing a press release regarding the latest medical status of Rick Taylor when her summer intern, Alexis, knocked on her semi-open office door and walked in.

"You wanted to see me?"

Kelly turned from her computer and smiled at the young blonde. "Did you post the information about the wives' charity softball game on our website?"

"First thing this morning," Alexis said. "I've also been tweeting about it."

"Good thinking. Our Twitter account has picked up quite a few followers in the past few weeks."

"Because of Matt Scanlon."

Observing the dreamy expression on Alexis's face, Kelly scowled. But hell, she couldn't take her bad mood out on her intern, so instead, she forced a smile. "Whatever the reason, you're doing a good job. Keep it up."

"Thanks. I'll do my best." Alexis beamed at her. "Is there anything else you need?"

She was tempted to ask Alexis to go to the clubhouse and direct Matt to speak with the local sportscaster who was hounding her for an interview. But dealing with the players was her job, and as much as she loathed talking to the Neanderthal (as she occasionally referred to him), she would grit her teeth and do it herself.

"Check to see if those press credentials I okayed are ready." Kelly leaned back in her chair and studied Alexis. "Have you lost weight?"

"Almost eight pounds." Alexis grinned, her eyes alighting with pleasure. "I've been following a low-carb, high-protein diet."

Kelly was familiar with the plan, having been on every diet known to mankind. Looking at Alexis, she wouldn't classify her as obese—a lot of girls put on a few extra pounds in college. But in a society where anything above a size six was considered fat, Alexis, like a lot of young women, was under a lot of pressure to be thin.

For a moment, she considered relating her own experience with dieting but decided against it. Just because Alexis wanted to drop a few pounds didn't mean she had an eating disorder.

"You look great," she said and left it at that. She'd learned a hard lesson about focusing solely on her weight and didn't want that to be the only thing Alexis thought was important in her life. "Again, I'm very pleased with all the work you've been doing."

Alexis's round face suffused with color. "Thanks. I really like working here."

After the girl left, Kelly finished the press release and emailed it to the public information manager. Then, knowing she couldn't put it off any longer, she left her office for the clubhouse.

With almost a year on the job under her belt, the clubhouse was old hat to her now. Not the case during her first month with the team. Back then she didn't know where to look because all around her were men in various stages of undress. She'd never been the shy type, but for a while all she'd done was stare at the floor, or the ceiling, to keep her eyes from gravitating to a certain part of their anatomy.

It didn't matter, though. The players didn't notice her. Not then, and not now. Due to the growing number of female sports reporters covering Major League Baseball, the novelty of the opposite sex in the clubhouse had worn off.

They considered her one of the guys anyway. She was

taller than a number of them, and she never wore anything other than pants, conservative blouses and blazers to work. She saved dresses and skirts for her off hours. Downplaying her femininity was a conscious decision—she wanted to be taken seriously.

After entering the clubhouse, Kelly waved at a couple of players who were watching the big-screen television in the lounge that adjoined the locker room. She couldn't help but smile—the channel was tuned to their favorite soap opera, *A New Dawn*. Her sister, Kayla, and Kayla's boyfriend, Sean Barrett, were both on the show. Life had imitated art when they'd fallen in love, just as their characters, Jared and Shay, had on the show.

When she reached the locker room, she found Dave Rizzo, San Francisco's star pitcher, holding court as usual. Rizzo was a two-time Cy Young winner and had the ego that went along with the prestigious award. A lot of the players looked up to him and blindly followed his lead. Rizzo wasn't happy that Matt had been picked up by the Blaze and was pretty vocal about it to anyone who would listen. The result was most of the players had been giving Matt a wide berth.

Rizzo acknowledged her with a nod and then continued speaking to his rapt followers. Kelly bypassed Rizzo and his entourage and headed straight for J.T. Sawyer, the team's backup catcher, who was sitting on the bench in front of his locker.

"Have you seen Scanlon?" she asked when J.T. glanced up from his cell phone. She'd interrupted him mid-text but he didn't seem perturbed. His hazel eyes were friendly as she halted near the bench.

"He's in the conference room watching film," J.T. replied and resumed his texting.

"Thanks."

When she reached the conference room the door was closed. She stopped and took a deep, cleansing breath. She had to get Matt to agree to start doing interviews. Despite his behavior the past year, he was still one of the most popular ballplayers in the league and the trade was still big news. Everyone wanted to interview him but he wasn't having any of it. If she didn't get him to talk soon her boss was going to call her into her office and read her the riot act. That was the last thing she needed.

Matt didn't hear her enter the room. He sat in one of the chairs at the end of the long oblong table and in front of the flat-panel television screen, watching a series of at bats by the team the Blaze were facing tonight—the Milwaukee Brewers.

The sight of his broad shoulders took her back to last night when she'd interrupted him and Stacia in the kitchen. She'd been shocked to see him, but then wondered why. Stacia had wanted to land a professional ballplayer ever since they'd become roommates, and Matt Scanlon was, by all accounts, a man whore. They were made for each other.

Kelly had never been bothered by Stacia's choice of sexual partners but she was now. The thought of her roommate and Matt doing it in the next room was gross. They'd just met that night, for Pete's sake. She wasn't a prude, but hell, where was the romance in that?

Thank God they'd been quiet. After she'd left them in the kitchen she hadn't heard another peep out of them. This morning, when she'd left for the ballpark, Stacia's bedroom door was closed and there was no evidence that Matt was still there.

If the past was any indication, he would contact Stacia again. Every guy who slept with her always tried to come back for more—evidently Stacia was blessed with super powers in the sack. While her conquests were usually one-nighters, Kelly would bet her next paycheck that Stacia would jump at the chance to see Matt again. He was rich, successful, and hotter than hell.

Who wouldn't hit that?

Her, for one. Yeah, he was hot and all, but he was an ass. An ass she would have to convince to start doing interviews ASAP or Katherine, her boss and senior vice president of communications, would have a stroke. And because of that, she was going to have to change her tactics.

Why couldn't she be as nice as her sister? *Hell*, she'd settle for being half as sweet as Kayla. It might be the only thing that could get Matt to see things her way.

She closed the door behind her. "Do you have a minute?"

Matt swiveled around in the chair, a frown marring his handsome face.

So far, not good.

"This is about the interviews, right?" He reached for the remote and turned off the television.

"I'm not backing off."

He sighed. "I told you. No interviews." He set the remote on the table and leaned back in the chair. His gray T-shirt was molded to his body and for a moment she was distracted by the sight of his powerful physique. She shook it off and got back to the matter at hand.

"You do know that talking to the media is part of your job, don't you?"

"This isn't my first rodeo, Kelly." His voice was tinged with exasperation as he ran a hand through his wavy hair. "I'm well aware of my obligations."

"Then why do you keep putting me off?"

"Because I can't afford to be distracted right now." He rose from the chair and ejected the disc from the DVD player. "And truthfully, there's nothing I have to say that's particularly interesting."

"The media and the fans disagree." She watched him place the disc in its plastic holder. "They want to know how you feel about the trade, and how the transition is going."

He looked up from the DVD, his eyes enigmatic. "That may be, but I'm not ready to talk. When I am I'll let you know."

His dismissive tone irked her and, as usual, set her off. "You had no problem shooting your mouth off before the All-Star break. Hell, I got a dose of it that night at the restaurant with Sean and Kayla. And suddenly, now, you decide to clam up?"

"About that night," he began.

"What about it? Are you finally going to admit you were out of line? Because you were, you know. You were *way* out of line."

His eyes narrowed. "And you weren't?"

"I was provoked." She glared at him. "You called me beefy and then insinuated a woman my size had to be gay."

"There's nothing wrong with being gay."

"I agree. I live in San Francisco. I think it's safe to say that more than half the men in the city are gay. And that statistic doesn't bode well for us straight women, I can tell you that right now."

Matt's lips twitched in amusement. "Sorry."

"Don't be. I do just fine." Which was a bit of a lie.

She hadn't been on a date in months. But he didn't need to know that.

"I'm sure you do. Especially in that outfit you were wearing last night."

She clenched her fists. *Jeez*, he was infuriating. "I was there with my softball team. All of us were wearing our uniforms."

He gave her a slow grin tinged with a hint of wickedness. "I wasn't talking about your uniform."

"Then what the hell are you…" Her cheeks started to burn. "I wasn't expecting to see anyone," she paused, "but there you were, practically having sex with my roommate in the kitchen."

"We weren't having sex."

"You would have if I hadn't walked in." Her voice sounded shrill and, to her chagrin, jealous. She pressed her lips together to keep any more idiotic words from coming out of her mouth.

She wasn't jealous. Not in the slightest.

"But you did walk in." He moved toward her. "And we didn't have sex."

"You didn't stay?" she asked, surprised. He halted in front of her. Thank God she was almost as tall as him. If she was any shorter she'd feel at a distinct disadvantage, and he was one man she didn't want to feel at a disadvantage with.

"No."

"Why?" Something was off. He and Stacia had been hot and heavy when she'd walked in, and Stacia was more than willing. That was an undisputed fact.

Matt shrugged. "I remembered I had to get up early." He held up the DVD. "Hitters to study and all that."

"Oh."

Oh? That was all she had?

Pathetic.

Meeting his gaze, she was suddenly aware of his cologne. It was a warm spicy scent that made her lightheaded. This was *so* not good.

"Trevor Jackson, the sportscaster from KGO, has requested an interview," she said and resisted the urge to step back. The sheer male power he exuded was doing things to her body that she hadn't felt in a really long time. "I told him it was a go."

Matt's eyes flickered with annoyance. "I'm not doing it."

"Pretty soon it won't be me asking. It'll be Doug. And it won't be a request." That she had to resort to using the general manager to get him to capitulate pissed her off. It made her sound ineffectual and weak—two things she couldn't afford to be in the male-dominated environment she worked in.

"I can handle the GM." Matt scowled. "And I'll start doing interviews when I'm damn well ready to."

"You really are an ass, you know that?" So much for changing tactics; he was basically forcing her to be rude.

"Maybe, but I'm not doing any interviews." He brushed past her before she could think of a suitable retort and left her standing in the conference room alone.

Damn him.

AN HOUR LATER, Matt was in the Blaze's state-of-the-art gym using one of the many elliptical machines. He preferred to run to get his cardio in but he'd come straight to the ballpark this morning to study film and had forgone it.

Next to him, J.T. was sweating profusely on a similar elliptical and staring at the big-screen television mounted on the wall opposite them. It was tuned to the sports channel. Matt was watching it too, but he wasn't paying much attention to it. He had his headphones on, listening to his favorite playlist and thinking, for some ungodly reason, about Kelly Maxwell.

For a few minutes in the conference room she'd actually been civil. But then she'd gotten her panties in a twist—again—when he'd refused to do the interview she'd set up. The woman was tenacious, he'd give her that. She was just doing her job—a job coveted by many and one she wouldn't want to lose. He was under no illusion that she was going to stop breathing down his neck about the media anytime soon.

At some point he'd have to give in. Part of every ballplayer's job was dealing with reporters. Hell, these days most of the teams gave classes on how to handle the media. He'd been dealing with them for eight years and until last year he'd gotten pretty good press. Now all he wanted to do was keep a low profile and try to fix the mess he'd made of his life.

He couldn't tell Kelly his reasons for laying low. Only his best friend knew why he'd gone off the deep end and sabotaged his career. He never wanted the press to know anything about the hell he'd been through. He'd lived through it once, he didn't want to relive it over and over and have everybody and their damn brother talking about it.

A slap on his arm jolted him from his thoughts. He looked over at J.T. and pulled off his headphones so they rested on his neck.

"What did Maxwell want with you?" J.T. asked, wiping his sweaty brow with the back of his hand.

Matt hit the incline button on his machine to move it to the next level and kept up his pace. Getting back into shape was his top priority. Too much partying for the past year had taken its toll. He was still as fit as most of the guys on the team but that wasn't good enough. He wanted to play for as long as he could and that meant being in the best shape possible.

"The usual. She wants me to do some interviews." He drew in a deep breath, then exhaled. "What's the deal with her? How long has she worked for the team?"

"About a year," J.T. said. "You know who her sister is, right?"

"Kayla Maxwell. The actress." He didn't tell J.T. that he'd met Kayla, or that his best friend, Sean Barrett, was involved with her. A lot of ballplayers watched the soap opera they were on and he'd learned a long time ago that if he mentioned Sean was his friend they all wanted to know what was going to happen on the show.

"They look nothing alike." J.T. reached for his water bottle and squirted the liquid into his mouth.

"There's a bit of a resemblance."

They both had dark hair, a heart-shaped face and a voluptuous mouth. Unlike Kayla, Kelly had blond highlights in her hair. Although why he'd noticed was beyond him. At work, her long, thick mane was usually pulled back in a ponytail. The only time he'd seen it down was last night when she'd interrupted him and Stacia in the kitchen. He'd seen a lot more of her last night than he'd ever seen before and it was disconcerting—to say the least—that he couldn't seem to get the image of her standing in the kitchen doorway wearing almost nothing out of his head.

"Resemblance?" J.T.'s expression was incredulous. "Kayla Maxwell is hotter than hell. I wonder if one of them is adopted."

"I doubt it." Matt reached for the towel hanging on the rack in front of him and wiped his face.

"Dude, they're as different as night and day. Kelly is huge compared to her sister."

"She's athletic."

"She's freakishly tall," J.T. countered. "And she has no shape. She looks like a box."

Matt had thought the same thing—until he'd seen her almost naked last night. The clothes she wore to work did nothing to accentuate her statuesque body. Still, while she wasn't overweight, she wasn't the type of woman he usually went for. His type was blonde and petite.

"I think you're pissed because she's taller than you." Matt grinned when J.T. snorted and gave him a pained look. "What are you, like, five-eight?"

"Five-ten," J.T. shot back with a scowl. "And she's not taller than me."

"She's almost as tall as I am and I'm six-one."

"Catchers don't need to be tall," J.T. pointed out. "In fact, the taller you are the worse it is on your knees."

"Yeah, that's what all the short catchers say."

"Bite me, Scanlon," J.T. said with a good-natured grin and then turned his attention back to the television.

Matt laughed. Maybe things wouldn't be so bad in San Francisco, after all. At least one guy on the team didn't seem to think he was a fuckup.

Now he just had to prove it to everyone else. Including himself.

THREE

JULY IN SAN FRANCISCO was unpredictable. One day it could be gloriously warm, and the next, so cold a person could be forgiven for believing they were in Alaska.

Unfortunately, tonight was one of those Alaskan-like nights. Hunkered down in her seat, Kelly hugged her Blaze sweatshirt to her body in an effort to keep warm. As a front office employee she had access to one of the ballpark's luxury boxes but she rarely took advantage of the perk. She preferred to watch a ball game as close to the action as possible.

The reason for that was sitting next to her. Her father, John Maxwell.

Her dad was a sports enthusiast. He loved all sports, but baseball was his passion. He'd grown up in San Francisco and while he now called the East Bay home, he would forevermore be a Blaze fan. He'd passed on his love of sports to both her and her sister. Some of her best times had been spent with her dad watching baseball games. There was nothing like the smell of peanuts and cotton candy, or the sweet sound of the crowd cheering when one of the Blaze players hit a dinger into the cove.

They sat in the first row, right behind the Blaze dugout where they had an excellent view of the diamond and the Blaze players as they trotted on and off the field each inning.

Usually Kelly didn't pay that much attention to them.

After all, she saw them nearly every day when the Blaze played at home, and she often traveled with them on the road. But tonight her attention was riveted on Matt. Each time he left the dugout she couldn't help but watch him.

Used to seeing her sitting with her dad in his season ticket seats, several of the players had acknowledged her with nods throughout the game. But if Matt had seen her he hadn't let on. In fact, he'd barely looked at the crowd—he seemed wholly focused on the game. It was his first start since he'd been traded to the Blaze, and every fan in the ballpark was, no doubt, wondering the same thing she was. Would he continue the same bad-boy behavior that had gotten him traded from the Dodgers?

The Blaze led by three runs in the top of the eighth inning and, so far, he'd kept his cool. There had been no outbursts, no challenging the umpire, and when a pitch came within a hair of hitting him, his only reaction was a long hard stare directed toward the Brewers pitcher.

But the game wasn't over yet. A few weeks before he'd been traded, he'd erupted in the ninth inning over a bad call and was ejected with only one out left in the game.

"Scanlon's calling a good game," her father commented. He cracked a peanut shell between his fingers and popped the nut into his mouth.

"He's been working with the pitchers since he got here." Glancing at her dad, she had to smile at the picture he made. With his black Blaze cap turned backward on his head and his baggy Blaze sweatshirt zipped up to his chin, he resembled an overgrown kid. "And he's been in the league long enough to know the hitters."

"He's a helluva catcher. Or at least he was until last

year." John shook his head. "For the life of me, I can't understand why he went off the deep end."

Kelly had been pondering that herself. "I don't know, Dad. It's a mystery to everyone."

A mystery the media and baseball fans had been speculating about for a year now. It was as if one day, out of the blue, Matt Scanlon, the poster boy for model behavior on and off the field, had done a complete one-eighty. There was no apparent reason for it—at least no reason that had ever come to light.

"Is he still giving you a hard time about the interviews?"

She grimaced. "He won't budge."

John reached into the red-and-white-striped bag nestled on his lap and pulled out another handful of peanuts. "The GM is probably giving him time to get settled in before he forces the issue. After all, he's been a star since his rookie year. That's garnering him a little leniency."

"Perhaps. But I'm not giving up." Kelly turned her attention to the field. She fixed her gaze on Matt. He was crouched behind the plate waiting for the pitch from Rizzo. She'd noticed that each at bat was taking quite a bit of time. Matt had trotted to the mound several times since the first inning, more than likely to address the fact that Rizzo was shaking off a lot of his pitch calls.

The position of catcher was—arguably—the toughest in baseball. A Major League catcher, much like an NFL quarterback, had to know what was going on at all times. Besides calling plays, he also had to do everything in his power to keep hitters off balance. The latter included knowing a hitter's weaknesses. Did he always swing at the first pitch? Was he fooled by a hanging curve ball? Was he rattled by trash talk, complete silence or the stink eye? Each player was different; the mark of a great catcher was the ability to know and exploit each hitter's vulnerabilities.

Despite his recent behavior, Matt was a great catcher. Granted, his stats were lower this year than in previous years. But if he got his shit together there was no reason he couldn't return to his former glory. For the sake of the team, Kelly hoped he would concentrate on baseball and not pick up in San Francisco where he'd left off in L.A.

The vibrating of her phone startled her. She reached into the pocket of her sweatshirt to pull it out and glanced at the caller ID. Why would Jill Taylor, the wife of the Blaze's injured rookie catcher, be calling her this late? It was two hours later in Texas, which meant it was almost ten-thirty there.

"Hey, Jill." She put a finger in her other ear to drown out the noise of the fans around her. "What's up?"

"I need a favor," Jill said in her soft Texas twang.

"Name it." Jill probably needed a ride from the airport tomorrow afternoon. She was flying in to compete in the wives' charity game. She'd committed to it before Rick had been injured and was still planning on participating even though Rick was recuperating in the small town near Austin where he and Jill lived during the off season.

"I need you to get a sub for me in the charity game on Thursday."

"A sub?" Kelly watched the Brewers outfielder take a cut at Rizzo's slider. He missed it and the crowd roared. "Why?"

"I found out today that I'm pregnant."

"That's great. Congratulations," she said, genuinely happy for her.

"I hate doin' this to y'all and I know I'm probably worrying for nothing, but I can't help it. My mama had a few miscarriages before she had me and, well, I don't want to take any chances."

"I totally understand." She mentally reviewed the list of wives who'd taken a pass on the game. Although they didn't want to play, they still participated by doing interviews with the local media to help promote the charity they'd chosen for this year's game. It was a long shot, but maybe she could cajole one of them into playing. "Don't worry about it, we'll find someone."

Jill breathed a sigh of relief. "You're a sweetheart. Thank you so much."

"You're welcome." Kelly wasn't used to being referred to as a sweetheart and wasn't sure she liked it. The last thing she wanted to be perceived as was soft. "Take care of yourself. I'm sure we'll be in touch as Rick's rehab progresses."

After she and Jill had said their goodbyes, she shoved her phone into her pocket just as Rizzo started his windup. The pitch was a fastball. The batter swung and connected with a loud crack. The ball popped up high in the sky. Immediately, Matt tore off his catcher's mask and sprinted toward the Blaze dugout while looking up to track the ball. He'd almost reached the dugout and, for a second, Kelly thought he might actually dive into it trying to make the catch. Instead he stopped short, reached out with his glove and effortlessly caught the ball. The crowd cheered loudly, eager for the team to end their losing streak. They were one inning away from getting their wish.

Matt lowered his glove, pulled the ball from it and tossed it to a young girl sitting a few seats to Kelly's right. The youngster caught it and squealed excitedly as she showed it to her parents. Glancing from the girl to Matt, she was surprised to see a smile on his face. It wasn't the infuriating grin he'd given her when she'd interrupted him and Stacia in the kitchen. It was the megawatt smile that had graced the cover of *People* magazine when he'd been voted the sexiest athlete on the planet. An honor bestowed on him on more than one occasion.

The planet thing was a stretch. She'd give him sexiest athlete in Major League Baseball, though. She didn't like the jerk one bit, but she had to admit, he was gorgeous. Not that she went for guys like him, because she didn't. He probably spent more time in front of the mirror than she did.

The out ended the top half of the inning and as the rest of the team trotted toward the dugout, Matt turned his head and their eyes met with a force that sent a lick of heat through her body. Stunned at her reaction, she tried to look away but couldn't. It wasn't until the bat boy handed him his catcher's mask that he finally broke eye contact and then disappeared into the dugout with the rest of the team.

Blinking, she glanced up at the huge electronic screen high above centerfield and watched as they replayed Matt's catch. The picture froze on that dazzling smile of his. Somewhere behind her a woman yelled, "I'd do him." The fans around her laughed, and then another woman yelled, "Get in line, honey." That sexy grin had just won over half the stadium.

Damn him.

MATT PULLED HIS batting helmet from the bat cubbyhole near the dugout steps and shot a glance at Dave Rizzo.

The asshole had a towel draped over his bald head and was talking with Trey Gentry, another starting pitcher. They were probably talking about how Rizzo had been shaking off his pitch calls all night. Slapping the helmet on his head, Matt grabbed his bat and followed Marquis Lopes, the team's shortstop, out of the dugout. While Lopes went straight to the batter's box, Matt headed for the on-deck circle. He exhaled, surprised he couldn't see his breath—it was a damn cold night.

Securing the bat under his arm, he pulled on his batting glove and scanned the field. He had to admit, Blaze Field was a premiere ballpark. For one thing, the outfield was real grass, not that fake shit some ballparks had that looked like the tacky carpet in his uncle's basement.

The stadium wasn't huge, but it did seat approximately fifty thousand fans, and because of the intimacy of the design, even the fans in the bleacher seats had a great view of the game. The brick walls in the outfield gave it an old-fashioned feel, and there were two iconic San Francisco cable cars parked on the mezzanine occupied by food vendors.

The vibe of the ballpark was much different than Dodger Stadium. The fans were a lot less rowdy, and so far, no fights had broken out—at least none he'd seen anyway. Less rowdy didn't mean less passionate, though. The fans loved the Blaze and although the team had been on a losing streak, the game was sold out.

Tonight the fans had something to cheer about. It was the bottom of the eighth and the Blaze led the Brewers by a score of five to three.

While he'd never been one to let his nerves get the better of him, he'd be lying if he said he hadn't been apprehensive about his first start. All eyes were on him and he knew what they were thinking, and what they were expecting.

He wasn't going to give it to them.

Lopes took a pitch; it was called a ball. The fans cheered. Matt pulled his bat from under his arm and began to take a few practice swings. Over the hum of the crowd he heard a few jeers directed at him but ignored them. After eight years, and playing in virtually every ballpark in the league, he'd gotten used to it. It was when he'd begun to hear them in Dodger Stadium, from the fans who had always adored him, that it stung.

After a few swings, he rested his bat on his shoulder and was unable to resist glancing toward the dugout. He'd seen Kelly sitting in the first row right after the national anthem. The guy sitting next to her was older— probably in his fifties. It was evident by her wide smile and her body language that the man was important to her. A lot of women went for older guys but he didn't figure Kelly to be one of them.

He thought back to their first heated exchange in Los Angeles. He'd acted like a jerk and couldn't blame her for her explosive reaction. The fact was he'd gotten used to women throwing themselves at him—it happened whenever he was out in public. In the past year he'd taken advantage of that particular perk quite frequently.

But that night in the restaurant, when he'd sat next to Kelly, it was evident she wasn't one of his adoring fans. It had ticked him off and, consequently, he'd proceeded to do everything in his power to antagonize her. He was embarrassed now that he'd gotten such a kick out of it. Or at least he had until she'd eviscerated him with her sharp tongue. And just as she'd predicted that night, the Dodgers had traded him not long after.

The crack of the bat jolted him from his thoughts. He turned to see Lopes hustling to first after hitting a grounder between first and second base. As he trudged to the plate, his name was announced over the loudspeakers and he was surprised when the cheers outweighed the boos. So far tonight, he'd gotten one hit and had thrown out two runners trying to steal second base. It wasn't much, but then he knew the minute he'd stepped into the Blaze clubhouse that the road to redemption wouldn't be an easy one.

COMPRESSING HER LIPS into a grim line, Kelly watched Matt brusquely wave off the reporters who had descended like locusts around his locker. He turned his back on them and rubbed his wet hair with a towel until they gravitated to Marquis Lopes, whose locker was in between Matt's and J.T.'s.

The mood in the clubhouse was upbeat. The Blaze had taken the first game of the three-game series and had finally ended their losing streak. Matt had played a good game, but evidently it wasn't good enough for him to break his silence with the media. Staring at his back, she couldn't help but notice the play of his powerful muscles as he dried his hair. Another towel was slung low around his hips and for one brief moment she allowed herself to imagine what was underneath it.

A sharp tap on her shoulder startled her. She turned to find Trevor Jackson, a reporter from KGO, standing next to her.

"What's the status on my interview with Scanlon?" he asked as politely as a man could after being put off as many times as she'd put him off.

"I'm working on it, Trevor." She gave him an encouraging smile she hoped would buy her a little more time. "Can you give me another day or two? He's not talking to anyone right now, but I promise you'll get first crack at him."

Trevor was a former MLB player who'd grown up in the Bay Area. After retiring, he'd gone into broadcasting and was the lead sports reporter for a local television station. He also had his own show on a popular sports-only radio channel.

Trevor's eyes narrowed. "Are you yanking my chain, Maxwell? I heard Jim Rome is trying to get him on his show."

"I haven't spoken to Mr. Rome's people," Kelly assured him, although she couldn't say for sure that Jim Rome hadn't contacted Matt's agent. Still, all interviews had to be approved by her, so if the popular sports talk radio host was trying to get Matt on his show, she would hear about it. She gave Trevor a placating smile. "Have I ever let you down?"

"Not yet." Trevor shot Matt a cursory glance. "Two days." His tone was ominous. "If I don't hear from you I'm going to the GM." After giving her a reproving stare, he turned and headed for Dave Rizzo's locker.

Annoyed, she looked back at Matt and had to stifle a gasp when he pulled the towel from his hips and revealed the most perfect ass she'd ever seen in her life. A distinct warmth flooded between her legs as, mesmerized, she watched him pull on a pair of white briefs.

Like a voyeur, she let her gaze roam over him. His body was magnificent—powerful muscles shaped his long legs and strong thighs. When he reached for the jeans in his locker, his sculpted muscles flexed with the flow of his movements.

Swallowing hard, she forced herself to turn away. The throbbing of her pulse, along with thick beat of awareness in her blood, reminded her of how long it had been since she'd been with a man. It was obviously too damn long if Matt Scanlon could elicit this kind of reaction in her.

Kelly checked her watch and remembered that her dad was waiting for her at Kamu's. Not giving the Neanderthal another glance, she headed for the clubhouse exit.

KAMU'S WASN'T BUSY. Matt assumed it was because the game had been over for a while, and also because it was a weeknight. He hadn't planned on stopping by, but he was hungry and didn't have much in the way of food at his place. Kamu's takeout seemed like the perfect solution until he could stock up.

After placing his order at the to-go window near the entrance, he headed to the bar to wait for his food. He spied an empty bar stool and slid onto it. The man next to him was wearing a Blaze cap turned backward on his head and was watching Blaze highlights on one of the flat panels.

The bartender approached and asked him if he wanted anything. He shook his head and told him he was waiting for takeout. The guy nodded and said "good game" before moving to the other end of the bar. The exchange caught the attention of the man next to him. Matt felt the stranger's eyes on him and turned to meet his friendly gaze.

"He's right. You called a good game tonight."

"Thanks. I appreciate it." The guy looked familiar, but he wasn't sure why. "Were you there?"

"I try to make all the home games if I can." The man

lifted his beer and took a sip. "Must be tough playing for a team you don't like all that much." Matt stared at him, not quite sure how to respond. The man put down his beer and grinned. "I follow baseball pretty closely. And you've been nothing but vocal about the Blaze in the past."

"That's true," Matt admitted. "But I'm here now." He wanted to add that his loyalty was to San Francisco but the words wouldn't come. He didn't feel that way. At least not yet. The trade still stung.

A smile creased the man's face. "Very politically correct of you. It's probably good you're not doing interviews right now."

"I just want to play ball." He turned his attention to the television. Why did anyone give a shit about what he had to say anyway?

"I get that," the man said in a solemn tone. Matt turned again to meet his shrewd gaze. "There are times when a man has to prove his mettle."

"Are you a reporter?" Matt asked. He had the balls of one, that was for sure. No question was off-limits to them. Which was why he wasn't talking to them.

The man let out a short laugh. "Hell, no. I'm a pharmacist."

He'd never met a pharmacist before. "You like doing that?"

"It's a living," he replied in a matter-of-fact tone. Matt studied him. The guy was probably around fifty. It was hard to tell how tall he was, but he appeared to be in decent shape for his age. "I played baseball in college and hoped to make it my career but I tore up my knee. Going to the show was out of the question after that."

"I'm sorry."

The man waved his hand. "Don't be. I'm over it." He grinned good-naturedly. "I wouldn't trade my life for anything. I've got a great family and season tickets. I can't ask for more than that."

"Sounds like you've got it all," Matt said, feeling a slight twinge of envy.

"I do." He glanced at the watch on his wrist. "I do believe my daughter has stood me up. I'll give her five more minutes and then I'm heading for home." Glancing up from his watch, the man's eyes brightened. "Ah, there she is."

Matt turned on his stool and got the shock of his life when he saw Kelly walking toward them. Now he knew why the guy had seemed familiar. He was the man she'd been sitting next to at the game. Her wide smile faltered when she noticed him seated next to her father.

"Sorry I'm late." She came to a halt just behind them. "One of the players cornered me before I could get out of the clubhouse." She looked from her father to him and it was obvious by her annoyed expression she wasn't happy to see him. "What are you doing here?"

"Talking to your father. It's been enlightening," he shot back just to rile her. It worked. Her eyes darkened. Suppressing a satisfied smile, he turned to Kelly's father. "I didn't get your name."

"It's John," she answered for her father. "What were you two talking about?" She directed the question to John Maxwell.

"This and that," John said with a shrug. "I was about to invite Matt to eat with us. He probably doesn't know a lot of people being new here in the Bay Area."

"I'm sure Matt has other plans." Kelly fixed him with a hard stare that spoke volumes. "Don't you?"

"I just ordered takeout," Matt said, and then couldn't help himself. "But I could stay here and eat it with you and your dad."

"Great. Let's get a table," John said, seemingly unaware of the tension between them. Matt met Kelly's furious gaze and grinned.

Score another one for him.

FOUR

"NO KIDDING?" MATT EXCLAIMED. "You're restoring a '68 Chevelle?"

Kelly looked up from her pasta. *Oh hell.* The rapt expression on Matt's face could mean only one thing. He was a car freak just like her father. The father who was a little too chummy with Matt Scanlon for her liking.

"Originally, I had my eye on a '69 Corvette, but when I saw the Chevelle, I couldn't resist," her father said, picking up a French fry and dragging it through the large pool of ketchup on his plate. Next to her mom and baseball, classic cars were John Maxwell's other great love.

"Four doors or two?"

"Two-door hard-top coupe. With the semi-fastback flowing roofline."

"Sweet," Matt said appreciatively. "What color is she?"

"She?" Kelly interjected. "It's a *car*, people."

Both her father and Matt looked at her as if she'd just declared the moon landing was a hoax. Now if Kayla was here, she'd totally be into this car stuff. Her sister had spent as many hours in the garage with their father as Kelly had spent at baseball games with him.

"*Her* color is the original Matador Red," John said to Matt with an emphasis on the "her." "I'll have her repainted that same color when I'm finished." He popped the fry into his mouth.

"Those coupes are hard to come by." Matt set his fork on his plate. "Chevrolet only made about 60,000 of them that year."

Kelly picked up her water and took a sip. What she really needed was a stiff drink. Watching Matt charm her father was sickening. The only reason he'd joined them was because he knew it would irk her.

"Do you think you'll be able to get a substitute for the charity game on Thursday?" Her father, who was sitting to her left, finally changed the subject. *Thank God.* Any more car talk and she might very well go insane.

"I've got a couple of possibilities. I hear Trey Gentry's got a new girlfriend. I might hit her up."

"What charity game?" Matt asked. The waitress had brought him his take-out order, then had come back with a plate when he told her he'd decided to stay. Since then she'd returned to the table several times to check on his water glass. By the way the attractive redhead was ogling him it was pretty obvious she was hoping for more than just a big tip. Oddly, though, other than thanking her politely, he wasn't showing any interest.

"The annual softball game between the wives and girlfriends of the Blaze and the Oakland A's," she told him. "The proceeds go to a different charity every year."

"Oh, a powder puff game."

"Most of the wives take it pretty seriously. They don't like to lose."

"You never liked losing either," her dad reminded her.

He was right about that. She'd been born with a competitive streak. "I still don't."

John chuckled. "She gets that from me," he said proudly. "Right, Peanut?"

"Dad!" Kelly's face grew hot. *Great. Just great.* The

last thing she wanted was anyone—especially Matt—to know her childhood nickname. It would probably be all over the clubhouse by tomorrow afternoon. He would surely love to share this little nugget with J.T.—since they seemed to have become friends. Then, of course, J.T. would share it with someone else, and so on, and so on. By all that was holy, if one person dared to call her Peanut tomorrow she was going to hunt Scanlon down and throttle him.

"Peanut?" Matt's dark brows arched in amusement.

Oh yeah, he was *so* going to tell. Ever since they'd met in L.A. he'd had it in for her.

"Sorry." Her father at least had the decency to look contrite. "I know you hate that."

"I didn't mind it when I was five, but I'm thirty, Dad."

"I'll try to remember that." He gave her a mischievous wink. "Can I help it if I still think of you and Kayla as my little girls?" Turning his attention to Matt, he continued, "When you two have children you'll know exactly what I'm talking about."

Glancing at Matt, she saw his smile fade and the color drain from his face. He reached for his water glass and took a long drink.

"He didn't mean you and I are going to have kids," she said quickly, "together." *Jeez, was the thought so repugnant it made him ill?* "Honestly, if you and I were the last two people on earth the human population would die out."

She waited, but he said nothing. *Zip. Zilch. Nada.* Where was the snappy retort or stinging barb? Was he losing his touch? It wasn't like him to let her get the last word in. He put his glass down and met her gaze. His dark eyes didn't have a trace of their usual amuse-

ment, smugness or disdain. Instead they looked sad…
haunted almost. She wondered why and then chastised
herself for caring.

"What's the charity this year?" John asked after giving her a disapproving frown. Fine, so that last remark
might have been uncalled for. But her dad had no clue
how rude Matt had been to her. Especially the night
they'd met.

"It's the Wishes Do Come True program."

John nodded with approval. "Good organization."

"What do they do?" Matt asked. A bit of color had
returned to his face and the sadness she'd glimpsed in
his eyes was gone.

"They grant wishes for sick children." She laid her
fork on her plate.

"The Blaze have always been very active in the community." John picked up another French fry. "I imagine
the Dodgers are as well."

"Yes." Matt nodded. "I was involved with a few chari-
ties in L.A."

"If you're looking for something up here to support,"
Kelly said, "the Wishes Do Come True program might
be worth considering."

"Maybe." Matt regarded her with enigmatic eyes. "I'll
have to think about it."

"I'm not pressuring you, or anything."

"That's a first." Now *that* was more like it. He was
back to his sardonic self.

"It doesn't apply to interviews, though," she clarified
just in case he thought she was going soft on him. There
was no chance of that, not when she was still trying to
prove herself to her boss. "I'm still going to ride your
ass about those."

"Good thing your mother isn't here." John grinned. "You know how she feels about you swearing."

"All I said was ass, Dad. That's not really swearing."

Her father favored her with a pointed stare. "You and I both know you swear like a sailor."

"I can vouch for that," Matt chimed in and followed it up with a lazy smile that made her insides flutter. Her mind flashed to the locker room when he'd pulled his towel off and she'd caught a glimpse of his sculpted body. *Why the hell did he have to be so damn hot?*

"In my defense, I swear a lot less than I did in college." She put her hand on her father's forearm. "Remember when I got thrown out of that game with Santa Clara?"

John laughed. "Boy, do I. I don't think I've ever seen you that angry. I couldn't believe the words coming out of your mouth. And I couldn't blame you. That was one of the cleanest picks I've ever seen. That girl was out by a mile."

"I know. I was absolutely livid." She met Matt's inquisitive gaze. "I had a streak going that season. I'd thrown out seven players in a row trying to steal second or third base."

"That's some streak. I'd be pissed too." He leaned back in his chair. The white cotton shirt he wore was unbuttoned at the collar and revealed his bronzed skin. "Did you get tossed because of the swearing, or did something else happen?"

"Oh, something else happened all right," her father said before she could reply. "And it wasn't pretty."

Matt's eyes flickered with interest. "I can't wait to hear this."

"Things got a little carried away," she admitted with

more embarrassment now than she'd felt at the time. But she'd been young and hot-tempered. Now she was just hot-tempered. "I didn't mean to throw the first punch. And I certainly didn't think the benches would clear."

"You started a brawl?" His expression was one of astonishment.

"She did." Her father nodded. "And was suspended for two games."

"But I learned my lesson. It never happened again no matter how ticked off I got. We lost one of the games I missed and it cost us. We didn't win our division."

Her father covered her hand with his. "And you apologized publically. I was proud of you for that," he said and gave her hand a gentle pat.

"Yes, well." She cleared her throat, conscious of Matt's eyes on her. "It was the right thing to do." She grinned. "But I was still pissed my streak was broken."

"Spoken like a true competitor," Matt said. Was that a hint of admiration in his dark eyes? No. It couldn't be. Matt Scanlon didn't admire anything about her. And never would.

THERE WAS ONE thing about San Francisco Matt didn't think he'd ever get used to—the weather. He remembered some old quote about the coldest winter someone ever spent was a summer in San Francisco. Whoever said it wasn't joking.

"Matt, it was a pleasure." Matt withdrew his hand from the warmth of his jacket pocket to shake John Maxwell's outstretched hand. "Maybe we can do this again."

"I'd like that." He glanced at Kelly. She was wearing a Blaze sweatshirt and had her arms wrapped around her midriff as if hugging it to her body would somehow warm her. Her cheeks were tinged with pink from the chilly night air, and wisps of her hair had escaped from her ponytail and lifted in the light breeze that had drifted in from the bay. She didn't seem quite as intense as she did when she was pestering him about interviews. In the presence of her father, she was softer, more approachable.

"Maybe you can come by the house during your next home stand and check out the Chevelle," John suggested as he zipped his black Blaze sweatshirt all the way to his chin. "Pleasanton isn't that far from the city."

Kelly's brow furrowed. "Dad, I'm sure Matt isn't interested in seeing your car."

"Not true. I'd love to see it," he said quickly. And not just to rile Kelly. The Chevelle was a classic. He'd been dying to see it ever since John had told him about it. Next to baseball, surfing and women, cars were his favorite subject. "We have a ten-day home stand in early August. I'll get your number from Kelly and give you a call."

"Sounds like a plan." John put his arm around his daughter and hugged her. "How about I walk you home before I catch the light rail to the BART station?"

"I live up the block, remember?" she said with a smile. Her affection for her father was obvious. "And it's getting late. You have to work tomorrow."

"I'll see she gets home, John," Matt said, ignoring Kelly's frown. "I live nearby."

"*Hello.* I'm an adult." She looked from him to her father. "I can get home by myself."

John put his hands on her shoulders. "Humor me. Okay, Peanut?"

Matt bit back a laugh as Kelly rolled her eyes. "Dad."

"Sorry." John grinned. "Just let Matt walk you to your building. It'll make your old man happy."

"You're not old." Kelly leaned forward to kiss his cheek. "I love you, Dad," she said softly. "Give Mom a hug for me and tell her I'll see her soon."

"Will do." John turned to him. "I know you've still got Dodger blue flowing in those veins of yours, but the Blaze will grow on you." He winked. "If you give us a chance."

"I'll do my best."

John gave him a nod of approval. "That's all anyone can ask." He glanced behind him. "There's the train. I'd better go."

"Bye, Dad," Kelly called after him as he stepped off the curb and crossed King Street. After John disappeared from sight, she turned back to him. The soft expression was gone but at least she wasn't looking at him like she wanted to knock his block off—like she usually did. "You don't have to walk me home."

"Yes. I do. I promised your dad."

"He won't know."

"I will."

She studied him thoughtfully for a few seconds. Under the streetlights, her whiskey eyes appeared darker. Almost as dark as his own. "Okay, then. Let's go."

Side by side, they walked past Kamu's entrance and up 2nd Street not talking. "You must like living so close to work," he said, finally breaking the silence.

"I do." She reached up to brush an errant lock of hair behind her ear. "I walk just about everywhere."

"Do you even own a car?"

"Yes."

"I like your dad."

"He likes you too," she said grudgingly.

"That bugs you, doesn't it?" Matt glimpsed a lone jogger heading their way and moved closer to Kelly to let the guy pass. His shoulder brushed hers; she shifted to her right to break the contact. The move reminded him of the night they'd met. Her body language that night made it clear she didn't care for him. Obviously, that hadn't changed. It bothered him but he wasn't sure why. It wasn't like he cared what Kelly thought about him. What anyone thought about him hadn't mattered in a very long time.

"He doesn't know how you talked to me in L.A." They stopped in front of her brick building. "If he did, he wouldn't have been so friendly."

"You gave as good as you got," he reminded her. "I have a feeling your father wouldn't have been surprised by *your* language that night."

Her eyes narrowed. "You started it."

"That's debatable."

"I think I'll go inside before I say something I'll regret." She reached into her purse and pulled out her keys. "Thank you for walking me home."

"You're welcome."

She turned toward the glass double door entrance, but then halted to look back at him. "About that interview with Trevor Jackson—"

"It's not happening," he cut her off more brusquely than he'd intended. "I have nothing to say to anyone right now. Why can't you get that through that thick head of yours?"

Her jaw tightened as her eyes flashed with fire. "You know, for a minute there, I thought I might have been wrong about you. But I wasn't. You *are* an ass." She spun around and jerked open the door.

He watched her stalk through the lobby and punch the call button for the elevator. She didn't look at him and several seconds later stepped into the elevator.

Running a hand through his hair, he turned and headed toward King Street. He tried to ignore the little voice inside of him telling him he was the ass she claimed him to be but he couldn't drown it out. He'd been acting like a prick ever since he'd met Kelly Maxwell. Wait, that wasn't quite true. His behavior had been reprehensible for almost a year—it just took that night in L.A. for him to realize it.

KELLY THREW HER purse on her bed and stripped off her Blaze sweatshirt. Even though she'd just finished dinner she had an overwhelming urge to go to the kitchen and stuff her face. It was always like this. At first, her eating disorder had been about her body, but somewhere along the line it became about emotions she didn't know how to deal with. Instead of dealing with her feelings she began to numb them with food. It worked for as long as she was eating, but afterward, when she was so full she felt like she'd burst, the feelings she'd been trying to ignore were still there, unresolved. And what she was left with was the guilt and shame of being so weak.

The good thing was she now recognized her pattern. The bad thing was it would never go away. She would always have to deal with it. It was as much a sickness as alcoholism or drug abuse.

She needed a distraction that didn't involve food yet would calm the edginess Matt always seemed to evoke within her.

Quickly, she slipped off her shoes, shed her clothes and moved to the bathroom. After turning on the shower faucet, she pulled the elastic band from her hair and tossed it on the marble vanity before stepping into the shower stall and closing the glass door behind her.

The hot pulsating stream of water cascaded down her body but it didn't relax her. Leaning back, she let the water soak her hair and tried to get Matt Scanlon out of her head. But it was impossible. The man was infuriating and had been from the moment she'd laid eyes on him.

It had been less than a month ago, yet it seemed like yesterday.

That day had started marvelously. Although traveling with the Blaze on their four-day road trip to L.A., she'd decided to stay with her sister, Kayla, rather than at the hotel with the team. She'd been looking forward to the trip not only because she missed her sister, but because she wanted to meet the man Kayla was dating. Her costar on *A New Dawn*, Sean Barrett.

She'd liked Sean immediately. He was a nice guy and even hotter in person than he was on TV. It was obvious he was head over heels for Kayla, and the feeling was mutual. Kelly had never seen her sister happier. They'd spent the first day at Dodger Stadium where the Blaze had beaten the Dodgers handily. After the game, she and Kayla had gone back to Kayla's house to change clothes and then Sean picked them up for a night on the town.

They'd gone to dinner at The Sky Room in Long Beach. It was all downhill from there.

"Should we wait, or go ahead and order?" Kayla asked Sean.

Turning from the lovely view of Long Beach Harbor, Kelly asked, "Wait for what?"

"I invited my friend Matt to join us." Sean reached for his glass of wine. "But he probably had some media obligations after the game. I'm sure he'll be here shortly, though."

"Media?" Her initial thought was his friend Matt was also an actor, but it didn't take long for her to put two and two together as soon as the "after the game" portion of Sean's comment registered. "Is your friend Matt Scanlon?"

"Yes." He set his glass on the table.

Kelly compressed her lips to keep from saying something she might regret. Scanlon's downward spiral had been well documented by the media for well over a year. The once admired catcher was now a tabloid staple and had been thrown out of more games in the past three months than he had in his entire career. That train wreck was joining them for dinner? Wasn't that just peachy?

She knew the exact moment he'd entered the restaurant. The noise level in the room heightened, and across the table she saw the look of recognition in Sean's green eyes.

"Sorry I'm late," Matt said when he reached the table. Out of the corner of her eye she caught the frank appreciation in his gaze when he looked at her sister. Sean noticed it too. He lifted his arm and draped it over Kayla's shoulders possessively. "It's nice to finally meet you, Kayla," he said smoothly as he pulled his chair out and sat next to her while still ogling Kayla. Kelly shifted in her chair, leaning slightly away from him. She didn't like him already. "I'm a big fan of your work," he added.

"Thank you," Kayla replied politely and glanced at her. "This is my sister, Kelly."

Matt gave her a cursory nod. "Nice to meet you." His

tone was perfunctory, his gaze dismissive. After a quick perusal, she'd been assessed and found lacking.

Irritated, she pasted a fake smile on her face. "Same here," she murmured, immediately aware of his scent, a blend of soap, shampoo and expensive cologne. It traveled along her nerve endings and filled her with sexual awareness.

Damn him.

Matt turned his attention to Kayla. "Did you enjoy the game?"

"Yes. We had great seats right behind the dugout."

Kelly picked up her wineglass and couldn't resist saying, "And our team won. It doesn't get much better than that." She sipped her wine. If he expected her to suck up to him like most women, he had another think coming.

"You're Blaze fans?" His expression was one of such shock it was all she could do not to laugh. Of course, he would think the sun rose and set on his precious Dodgers.

"Since birth," Kelly said as she set her glass back on the table. "Right, Kay?" she asked her sister. As Kayla nodded, she continued confidently, "One down, three to go."

"You're not sweeping us." Matt leaned back in his chair and fixed her with a hard stare. "You got lucky today."

Kelly shrugged. "Rizzo's pitching tomorrow. And as I recall, you struck out three times the last time you faced him."

He scowled. "Rizzo's an overrated punk."

"Dave Rizzo's won the Cy Young award two times," she countered. "And when the phrase *overrated punk* is used, he's not the man who comes to mind." The air became thick with tension as their eyes clashed.

Take that, asshole.

"The band is amazing," Kayla said, breaking the taut silence. "There aren't many restaurants like this anymore." She glanced around the room. "And with this Art Deco décor it's almost like we've stepped back in time."

"Would you like to dance?" Sean asked Kayla.

Oh shit. The last thing she wanted was for Sean and Kayla to leave her alone with Matt.

Kayla's eyes lit up. "I'd love to." She looked at Kelly and then Matt. "You don't mind if we leave you for a few minutes, do you?"

"No," Kelly said, giving Matt a wary glance. "We'll be fine."

As soon as Sean and Kayla left the table, he turned to her, his dark eyes blazing. "Were you calling me a punk?"

She shrugged. "If the shoe fits…"

"You're nothing like your sister," he said harshly. "Are you gay?"

"What?" She stared at him with amazement.

"It's a simple question," Matt said, his expression filled with contempt. "You're quite the Amazon. Admit it. Beefy chicks like you are into women, right?"

Kelly clenched her fists, tamping down the urge to punch him. "My sexual preference is none of your business. But *yours* is everyone's business, isn't it?"

"What the hell is that supposed to mean?"

"Well, according to the tabloids, you're quite fond of strippers and porn stars."

"Don't believe everything you read," he said tersely and pushed his chair back.

"Leaving so soon?" Her heart pounded as she met his angry gaze. "What's the matter? Can't take the heat, so you're getting out of the kitchen?"

"Baby, I can handle anything you can dish out." Matt's smile was smug. He glanced over his shoulder toward the blonde hostess near the entrance. "But I'd rather spend the evening with a real woman."

Kelly snorted derisively. "She's minor league, Scanlon. But since that's where you're headed, she's probably just your speed."

"You really are a bitch, aren't you?" he shot back, not bothering to lower his voice or conceal his animosity.

"Hey, I call them like I see them. And what I see is a once great player embarrassing himself and his teammates on a daily basis. The Dodgers are either going to trade your sorry ass, or send you back to triple A."

Matt leaned toward her, his face inches from hers. The tension between them was palpable. "Fuck you," he said in a low controlled voice.

"Fuck me?" She smiled sweetly even though her pulse was racing full throttle through her veins. "You should be so lucky."

FIVE

SHAKING OFF THE memory of that night in L.A., Kelly turned off the water and stepped out of the shower. She dried herself with a fluffy towel and then plugged in the hair dryer and blew out her hair.

Minutes later, she was lying in bed but sleep was elusive. She couldn't stop thinking about Matt. Tonight she'd glimpsed a different side of him. A side she liked. At dinner with her father, his demeanor had been pleasant, friendly even. It reminded her of the interviews she'd seen of him before he'd gone off the deep end. In them he was personable, humorous and humble.

What the hell had happened to him?

The musical ring tone of her cell phone cut through the silence. She glanced at the clock on her nightstand as she reached for it. It was just after eleven. Who would be calling this late?

She didn't recognize the number on the caller ID but she had to answer it. All the players and coaches had her cell phone number in case they needed to reach her. She prayed that one of them hadn't gotten pulled over for drunk driving again. That was all she needed. The last thing she wanted was to get out of her warm bed and post bail. Been there, done that, bought the T-shirt.

"Hello?"

"I know it's late, but I took a chance you'd still be up." It was Matt. Her heart skipped a beat.

"Is everything all right?" she asked, automatically shifting into PR mode. What trouble could he have gotten into in the ten minutes it took for him to walk from her place to his?

After a brief silence, he said, "I shouldn't have snapped at you like that." He paused. "You know, outside your building."

She rolled to her back and stared at the ceiling. Moonlight filtered in from the blinds, bathing the room in a warm soft glow.

"Does that mean you'll do the interview with Trevor Jackson?"

"No."

Damn it. She should have known better. So much for getting her hopes up. "Can I ask you a question?"

"Sure."

"If it was anyone but me asking, would you do it?"

"No. I still wouldn't do it."

That made her feel marginally better. For a while there she'd thought it was personal. "You have to know I'm going to keep after you about these interviews. It's my job."

"I'll keep saying no."

"I'll wear you down." She smiled. "I'm tenacious like that."

"I've figured that out. By the way, in case you're worried, your secret is safe with me."

"What secret?" she asked with trepidation. Did he know about her eating disorder? He couldn't, could he? No one knew except her family.

"I think you know." Amusement edged his voice. "Peanut."

Her cheeks grew warm. "How do I know I can trust you to keep your mouth shut?"

"You don't."

"You could hold it over my head. To get me to stop bugging you about those interviews."

"I could. But I won't."

"Why?"

"I have my reasons," he said and then chuckled. "G'night, Kelly."

Before she could reply she heard the decisive click that indicated he'd hung up. Rolling to her side, she put her phone on the nightstand. That had to be a record. They'd actually had a conversation without biting each other's heads off. Who knew?

Pulling the blanket over her shoulders, she smiled. He didn't know it yet, but he was going to do that interview with Trevor Jackson. Now she just had to figure out how she was going to make it happen.

THE NEXT MORNING, Matt walked into the clubhouse and headed for the locker room. As he passed by the lounge he saw Dave Rizzo and Trey Gentry sitting together at one of the round tables farthest from the big-screen television. Gentry was pitching tonight and, not wanting any of the same bullshit Rizzo had pulled the previous night, he detoured inside. He was done tiptoeing around his new teammates. He understood why they didn't want him on the team. He'd been the enemy for so long it was probably hard for them to see him as anything but. And as much as he'd hated coming to San Francisco, he was here. The Blaze was his team now. At least until Rick Taylor came back.

As he approached the table they stopped talking and

looked up at him—Rizzo with undisguised dislike and Gentry with guarded curiosity. Gentry was a rookie, and from what Matt had seen, he was a good guy despite his hero worship of Rizzo.

Dave Rizzo leaned back in his chair with a smug expression on his sun-weathered face. He'd been in the league two years less than Matt and they'd had their share of run-ins over the years. The guy was a helluva pitcher but, unfortunately, he was a grade-A asshole. "What's your problem, Scanlon? You look like someone kicked you in the nuts." Rizzo shot Gentry an amused smirk. Gentry was smart enough not to grin back.

"You're my problem." He fixed Rizzo with his patented stink eye. He'd perfected it over the years and had intimidated many of his opponents with it.

"Me? What'd I do?" Rizzo's eyes widened with mock innocence.

"Don't fuck with me," Matt snapped. "If you pull that shit the next time you pitch I'll leave you on the mound twisting in the wind."

Rizzo shot him a confident grin. "I doubt that."

"You shouldn't." He put his hands on his hips and glared at him. "What you know about the hitters in this league couldn't fill a shot glass. And if you start questioning my calls again you'll find out just how much I know about them because they'll be hitting jacks off you all night. Or at least until Morgan pulls you out of the game." He stared pointedly at Gentry. "The same goes for you too, rookie. I know what I'm doing. Don't make me come out to the mound as many times as I did last night."

"You're full of shit," Rizzo said with a sneer. "The Dodgers kicked your ass to the curb and we had to take you because Taylor's out for the rest of the year. None of us want you here, Scanlon."

"I'm here, so deal with it. And you know what? I don't give a fuck what you think about me. I'm here to play and I'm here to win. If you cross me or question my pitch calls again, I'll make you pay." He paused to give Gentry a look of warning. "You want to test me? Go right ahead. I can be your best friend out there, or your worst enemy. It's your decision."

Matt shot Rizzo one more hard look and then turned and left the lounge. He walked into the locker room and stopped short when he saw Kelly talking to J.T. in front of J.T.'s locker. As usual, she was wearing her standard attire of dark pants and a baggy blazer. Her hair was again pulled back into a ponytail and for some insane reason, he itched to pull the band from her hair so he see it cascade over her shoulders like it had when she'd interrupted him and Stacia in her kitchen.

What the hell? First, he'd called to apologize to her last night, and now he was thinking about her hair. *Jesus.* She wasn't even his type. He preferred petite blondes, not statuesque brunettes with mesmerizing eyes and legs that went on for days.

Resuming his stride, he moved toward her and J.T. She gave him a nod as he walked past them and to his locker.

"Come on, J.T.," Matt heard Kelly say pleadingly. "Isn't there anyone you know who could play in the charity game tomorrow? What about a sister? For the love of God, do you have a sister?"

"Nope," J.T. replied. "Three brothers. Sorry."

"Damn it to hell," she muttered. Her smooth forehead wrinkled with a frown. "This is not good."

"Did you ask Gentry?" Matt asked as he began to unbutton his shirt. "He's in the lounge with Rizzo."

Kelly met his gaze, her expression glum. "I struck out. He said it's not serious and he doesn't want to ask her to be in the game. He says it might give her ideas."

J.T. laughed. "Which means she's just a booty call. Only she doesn't know that yet."

"Great. Because he can't commit, I'm one player short for tomorrow's game." She put two fingers to her temples and rubbed. "Maybe I can get Angie to do it."

"Angie DeMarco? From accounting?" J.T. asked. Matt noted the gleam in J.T.'s eyes. Interesting.

She nodded. "She's on my coed team."

"Really?" J.T. asked. "I didn't know you guys played softball." He paused. "Maybe you should play, Maxwell."

"Oh no." She put her hand up and shook her head. "I couldn't."

Matt pulled his shirt off. "Why not?" he asked and then hung it on a peg in his locker. "It's for charity." He turned to find Kelly staring at him, her face flushed. "Are you all right?"

"I—I'm fine," she said, quickly averting her eyes. "I'm not a wife or a girlfriend. I can't play."

"Neither is Angie," J.T. pointed out. "Wait. She's not dating anyone on the team, is she?"

"No." She sighed. "She has a strict policy against dating ballplayers."

"Why?" Matt asked, again noting J.T.'s interest in all things Angie.

"I'm really not sure," Kelly said and then groaned. "Damn it. I just remembered she's off on Thursday to help her mother paint her house."

"Looks like you'll have to take one for the team, Maxwell." Matt grinned. "Come on, show us those mad soft-ball skills you claim to possess."

"Yeah. We don't want the A's wives to beat our girls," J.T. chimed in. "With you we've got a chance to kick their asses. They beat us last year. It was ugly."

"No." Her tone was vehement.

"Why not?" Matt asked.

"I prefer to remain behind the scenes. Softball is something I do on my own time."

"The team needs you." J.T. put his hands on his hips and gave her a pleading look. "Don't let us down."

"No. That's my final answer," she said firmly and turned to leave.

"If you play I'll do the interview with Trevor Jackson." The words were out of Matt's mouth before he could stop them. Kelly froze in her tracks and slowly turned around.

"Are you serious?" She searched his face warily.

"Yep. I'll do one interview if you play in the charity game."

Indecision flashed in her eyes but then she nodded. "Okay." She cocked her head. "You won't change your mind at the last minute, will you?"

"No. I give you my word." He lifted his hand and made a cross over his chest with his finger. A luminous smile lit her face and caused Matt's breath to hitch. "I'll do it before the game," he said, unable to tear his gaze from her.

"I'll call Trevor," she said and looked at J.T. "Those A's wives are toast." She grinned, then turned and left the locker room.

J.T. let out a short laugh. "I think you just got played."

"You think?" Matt asked before turning to his locker.

"I have to do interviews eventually. At least I'm doing something to help the team."

"You know, Maxwell's okay." J.T. sat down in front of his locker to unlace his shoes. "I might have to check out one of her softball games."

Matt held his tongue. J.T. was so transparent it wasn't even funny. The guy had women panting after him like rabid dogs yet the minute he'd learned that Angie De-Marco played on Kelly's coed team suddenly he was interested in going to a game?

"I'll go with you," he said and when J.T. shot him a quizzical look, he shrugged. "It beats staying home and watching reruns."

ON THURSDAY MORNING, Kelly headed for the ladies' room just down the hall from her office carrying the replica Blaze uniform she'd be wearing in the charity softball game.

They were slated to start at ten-thirty, five hours before the Blaze played the final game in their series with Milwaukee. Since it was for charity, the game only went five innings and whoever was ahead at that point was declared the winner. All tickets purchased for the charity game went to the Wishes Do Come True program and several of the youngsters well enough to attend were able to get in free of charge.

As she passed by her boss's office, she glanced inside. Katherine was talking to Tom Morgan, the Blaze manager. Neither of them looked happy but then again the word on the street was they'd never gotten along. Whatever it was, it couldn't be about Matt not doing interviews. Finally, she'd been able to report that Matt had agreed to talk with Trevor Jackson. In fact, they were taping in the media room right now.

Funny how that had worked out. She hadn't gone into the locker room with a plan but somehow she'd walked out with him agreeing to an interview. How that had happened she still didn't know. The second Matt had started to undress, she couldn't think straight. As it turned out, all she had to do was agree to play softball with a bunch of the players' wives and girlfriends.

Piece of cake.

Pleased with the entire situation, she pushed open the bathroom door and cringed at the sound of someone retching. Concerned, she walked in and let the door close behind her.

"Hello?" She halted in front of the double sinks. "Do you need anything?" There was silence and then the toilet flushed. Seconds later, the stall door opened and her intern Alexis emerged. Her face was red and her eyes were bloodshot. "Are you all right?" she asked as Alexis moved to the sink and turned on the water.

"I'm fine." Alexis avoided her gaze in the mirror and bent over to splash water on her face.

"Are you sure? Maybe you're getting the flu." Kelly hung her uniform on a hook next to the full-length mirror opposite the vanity and moved back to the sink. When Alexis straightened, she pressed her hand to the girl's forehead. Her skin was cool to the touch. "You don't feel like you have a temperature."

"I'm fine." Alexis turned to pull a paper towel from the dispenser and dried her hands. "It might have been the eggs I ate for breakfast." Still not meeting Kelly's gaze, Alexis threw the towel into the waste dispenser and brushed past her. "I'll go check to make sure everything's ready for the game," she said as she opened the door.

"Okay." Kelly stared at the door a few seconds before retrieving her uniform and going into the larger of the two stalls to change. As she stripped off her clothes, she couldn't help but wonder if Alexis was purging. Was she suspicious because of her own issues? Maybe Alexis really had eaten some bad eggs. She hoped that's all it was. Bingeing and purging was a hard habit to break. No one knew that better than she did.

Thirty minutes later, Kelly surveyed her team and wanted to cry. With one exception, not one of the women looked like they knew how to hold a bat, much less throw a ball. She moved to the bottom stair of the dugout, put her fingers to her lips and blew out a loud whistle to quiet their chatter. For better or worse, today, she was their leader.

"Okay, ladies." She took in their made-up faces and perfectly coiffed hair and tried to muster up a smile. "Any of you ever play ball before?"

A couple of hands rose in the air.

"In high school," Dave Rizzo's wife said. Chantal Rizzo was a blonde—bottle blonde, not natural. There was no way that shade of platinum existed in nature. Chantal had also taken the liberty of tying the ends of her Blaze jersey into a knot under her breasts so that her tanned and taut midriff was exposed. Kelly frowned. She'd have to deal with that before Chantal took the field. This was a charitable event and children would be present.

"What position did you play?"

"First base."

"Then you'll play first base today. Do any of you run

or jog?" Three more hands went up. "Okay, you three take the outfield." Since they probably couldn't catch a softball to save their lives, they could run for them.

"I can play shortstop," Marquis Lopes's girlfriend said shyly from the far end of the dugout.

Kelly nodded. "The position is yours." Looking around, she pointed at one particularly well-endowed wife who apparently thought it was cute to wear her baseball cap sideways on her head. "Third base." She fixed her gaze on another wife. "Second base for you." She put her hands on her hips. "I'll catch, and…" Kelly met the eyes of the only woman in the bunch she knew for sure had any athletic ability at all and said, "Sheila, you're pitching."

Sheila Morgan, Tom Morgan's sister, grinned. "I've been practicing. Those girls beat us bad last year. I'll be damned if they'll do it again this year."

A chorus of squealing cheers spontaneously erupted. Kelly shook her head. It was going to be a long five innings.

"This is sad," J.T., who was sitting next to him, said just before the bottom of the last inning. "Kelly's gotten on base every at bat but not one of our other players can get a hit.

"I'm surprised Sheila hasn't gotten a hit or two," Matt commented. "She's a damn good pitcher."

"So is the A's pitcher." J.T. reached under his seat and grabbed a large bottle of water. "She's definitely played before." He twisted off the cap and took several long gulps. "I'm surprised the score is only two-zip," he said a few seconds later.

Stretching his legs out in front of him, Matt couldn't

get over the change in the weather. The past two days had been overcast and chilly. Today, however, was beautiful. The temperature was in the mid-70s and there wasn't a cloud in the sky. Hopefully, the warmer weather would hold for their game later on.

Matt scanned the ballpark as the teams changed sides. It wasn't packed like it was for the Blaze games. Only the lower sections between first and third bases were filled. The section he was in, just behind the Blaze dugout, had been reserved for Blaze players and the kids from the charity. After the game the players would mingle with the kids and the fans. They'd sign autographs, take pictures, that kind of thing. And while he believed wholeheartedly in the cause, he'd made it a point this past year to avoid any charitable events associated with children. But today he had no choice, he'd just have to do his best to get through it.

"Good game last night," J.T. remarked. "Gentry was solid. And you didn't have to go to the mound as much as you did when Rizzo pitched."

Matt shifted in his seat, inhaling the aroma of cotton candy that wafted in the air. "I'm just glad we won. But we're still trailing the Dodgers and the Padres."

The Blaze game announcer's melodic voice came over the P.A. system. "Now batting is Chantal Rizzo."

J.T. elbowed him in the side as Chantal sashayed to the plate. "I'll bet the carpet doesn't match the drapes."

Matt chuckled. Rizzo's wife was definitely not a natural blonde. She was attractive, though. If you liked that type. Actually, he did like that type. Or he had. But looking at Chantal, he felt nothing. Not even a glimmer of interest.

Chantal swung at the first pitch and hit a blooper

that trickled toward third base. With a loud squeal, she dropped her bat and took off toward first base. The pitcher fielded it and threw it to first. Chantal would have been out but, as luck would have it, the ball passed through the legs of the woman on first base. Chantal, seeing her chance, rounded first and ran to second base. When she got there safely, she jumped up and down like the cheerleader she'd probably been. The crowd clapped and whistled enthusiastically, thrilled to see someone other than Kelly get a hit.

As the announcer said her name, Sheila Morgan trotted out of the dugout, eager to get to the plate. She took her stance, waited and then took the first pitch; it was called a strike. She took the next pitch; it was a ball. When the third pitch was delivered, she swung and connected. The ball sailed over the pitcher and right at the woman playing second base. She put her glove up, but the ball glanced off the top webbing and fell directly behind her. Chantal wisely stayed put on second and Sheila made it to first base without a problem.

"Hey, maybe we have a shot." J.T. leaned forward in his seat and clapped as Kelly emerged from the dugout. "Yo, Maxwell. Knock one into the cove," he yelled through cupped hands.

Kelly must have heard him; she turned and scanned the crowd. She grinned, gave J.T. a thumbs-up and then walked to the plate. When the announcer said her name, the fans cheered. They'd seen her get two hits already and were hoping that, somehow, she could pull out a win for the team.

Matt leaned forward, as hyped as the spectators around him. The snug uniform she wore showed off the curves she hid so well under her loose work clothes.

Her body was fit and strong. Every move she'd made on the field today had showcased her athletic ability. There was a confidence about her that surprised him. She played like she loved the game. He knew the feeling. He'd played that same way until last year.

The crowd went silent as Kelly waited for the pitch. The pitcher went into her windup and let loose a fastball. Kelly took the pitch and then stepped out of the batter's box after the umpire called it a strike. The crowd remained mute as she resumed her place at the plate, her eyes focused on the pitcher. She swung at the next pitch. It nicked her bat and sailed back into the stands. A foul ball and strike two.

"This is nerve-racking," J.T. muttered. "If she strikes out the game is over. There's no way any of those other women can get a hit."

"You're right about that." Matt focused on Kelly. She stepped back into the batter's box, smoothed the dirt with the toe of her cleat, and took her stance. A seagull cawed noisily as it flew over the stadium. As Blaze Field was right next to the bay, gulls were plentiful and, at times, damn annoying. "Come on, Kelly," he murmured under his breath. "Win this fucking game."

The pitcher went into her windup and delivered a perfect fastball. Kelly swung and the sound of it hitting the sweet spot on her bat was loud. The ball shot into left field. It was low but had some speed. Everyone, including Matt, jumped up from their seats to watch it. The left fielder sprinted toward the wall and made a valiant effort to jump and catch it, but the ball went over her head and hit the dirt just past the grassy area. It rolled toward the wall. The left fielder tried to pick it up, but dropped it. The crowd roared.

He looked back at the diamond. Chantal had already crossed home plate. Sheila was sprinting from third and made it easily. The left fielder finally picked up the ball and fired it back to the infield. As Kelly rounded third base, the ball was heading for the catcher. They were neck in neck as she dove to the ground, face-first, and slid into home plate just as the catcher caught the ball and made the tag on Kelly's shoulder. All eyes were on the umpire.

"Safe!" he yelled with his arms outstretched.

The small crowd in the stadium went nuts, screaming with excitement. J.T. slapped him on the back. "Hell, yeah," he said with a grin on his face.

On the field, the Blaze wives and girlfriends had cleared the dugout. They were on the field screaming and hugging each other. Sheila and Chantal helped Kelly up and engulfed her in a group hug. Kelly's batting helmet was on the ground as her teammates rallied around her, delirious with the thrill of victory.

Over their heads, Kelly looked toward the dugout. Their eyes locked and the pure joy on her face ignited a spike of heat low in his gut. He stared at her, stunned.

Just when the hell had Kelly Maxwell turned into the most beautiful woman he'd ever laid eyes on?

SIX

AFTER POSING FOR a few publicity photos with the A's wives and girlfriends, Kelly left the Blaze women in all their victorious giddiness to attend to her other duties. The game was over but there was still work to be done. Shortly, Katherine would present the check to the director of the Wishes Do Come True organization, and immediately afterward a drawing would be held in which the winner—one of the children from the program—would get to have lunch with his or her favorite Blaze player at a nearby restaurant of their choosing.

Right now the Blaze players were on the field. For the past half hour they'd posed for pictures, signed autographs and talked to the kids. This particular event was a team tradition, and one the players supported wholeheartedly.

Crossing the infield, she was proud of her guys. They'd checked their egos at the clubhouse door and had come together as a team to support the cause. Each of them, even Dave Rizzo, was making the rounds with the kids and parents. Out of the corner of her eye, she saw Matt posing with a dark-haired girl who looked to be about nine or ten. The little girl's complexion was wan but her smile was wide and joyful.

Kelly had been observing Matt ever since the players had taken the field to mingle with the kids. She was curious to see if he'd blow them off like he did the interviews. At first he'd hung back, as if hesitant to approach the children. It made sense. After all, he'd only been with the team for a couple of weeks, and was a former Dodger, San Francisco's most hated rivals. She couldn't blame him for being a little leery. But as it turned out, he needn't have worried, the kids had flocked to him. Now he appeared relaxed and too damn sexy for his own good in faded jeans and a blue button-down cotton shirt. She'd been aware of him watching her during the game and had been worried it might affect her performance. Thank God it hadn't. Striking out in front of him would have been embarrassing.

Threading her way through the crowd, she headed toward Katherine and her assistant, who was holding the ceremonial cardboard check that would be presented to the charity. As she approached, Katherine's enigmatic blue eyes skimmed over her before she smiled. "Nice game," she said.

"Thanks." Kelly glanced down at her dirt-covered uniform and then at her boss who, as always, looked casually elegant in a pair of tailored black pants and a sleeveless tie-neck animal-print blouse. Next to Katherine, who was much shorter, Kelly felt positively Amazonian. "I didn't have time to shower and change."

Katherine waved a well-manicured hand at her. "Don't worry about it. You won the game…and in exciting fashion to boot. Thanks again for stepping in for Jill."

"It was fun. Are you ready to present the check?"

"Yes." Katherine nodded and then said, "But before I do, I need a favor."

"Name it," Kelly said quickly. She was used to Katherine's hectic schedule and tried to help her out whenever possible.

"I've had an important meeting come up unexpectedly. I won't be able to make the lunch with the winner of the drawing. Would you be willing to stand in for me?"

"Of course. I'd love to."

"Wonderful." Katherine put her hand on Kelly's forearm and squeezed. "You're a life saver." She glanced at her assistant. "All right, Liz, let's present that check."

Kelly's smile faded as she watched Katherine and her assistant head off toward the podium that had been set up near home plate. Her work clothes were hanging in her office. She'd planned on using the shower in the women's executive restroom and changing back into them. But now that she was representing Katherine at the lunch, the serviceable navy blue pants and matching blazer seemed inadequate, and more than a little drab. Luckily, since she lived two blocks from the ballpark, going home to shower and change wouldn't take much time at all.

And she wasn't doing it because Matt might be the player attending the lunch.

Or was she?

Hell, no. She didn't care what Matt Scanlon thought of her. They were adversaries, not friends. She'd probably just imagined that hot look they'd exchanged after she'd won the game.

Hadn't she?

Of course she had. Matt's taste in women was public knowledge. He had a certain type, and she wasn't it.

That was fine. He wasn't her type either.

No one had been more surprised than Matt when one of the young girls he'd spoken to, and had posed for a picture with, won the drawing and chose him as her fa-vorite player. Well, maybe Dave Rizzo had been more surprised. His slack-jawed expression when Lily Lovett had declared Matt her favorite player was a picture-perfect moment for sure.

Stepping out of the elevator on the second floor of the stadium where the Blaze front office staff was housed, he nodded to the receptionist sitting behind the gleam-ing chrome and glass desk and strode down the hallway toward Katherine Whitton's office. She was the senior vice president of communications and media relations, and would be accompanying him on his lunch with Lily and her mother. He wasn't sure why she was tagging along but he wasn't going to question it. He was trying to clean up his act, not make things worse by arguing with the suits.

He'd met with Katherine once and didn't have an opinion about her one way or the other. She'd given him the standard welcome to the club speech and made it more than clear what she expected of the players in regard to the press. And while she hadn't brought up his behavior for the past year, her message was clear—*don't fuck up here in San Francisco like you did in L.A., Scanlon.*

After that meeting he'd glimpsed her once or twice, usually when she came down to the clubhouse to talk to the Blaze skipper, Tom Morgan. From what Matt had observed, the two seemed to have a contentious rela-tionship. If the rumors in the clubhouse were to be be-lieved, they had some sort of history prior to working for the Blaze.

As he passed Kelly's office he glanced inside but the room was dark. He'd seen her leave the field about forty minutes ago and assumed she'd returned to her office to change her clothes and go back to work. Maybe she'd gone home instead. Slightly disappointed by this, he made his way to the office not far from Kelly's. Katherine's assistant wasn't at her desk but he heard voices so he moved to the doorway and halted at the threshold. Lily Lovett and her mother sat together on a low floral-covered bench placed by a large picture window that overlooked the field.

Lily's dark eyes lit up when she saw him. Her face was slender but she had a big smile on her face. Just like the one she had when she told him that God had answered her prayers and brought him to San Francisco to play for the Blaze. Lily was probably the only person in the Bay Area happy about the trade.

"Hi, Matt." Her voice was strong and clear despite her fragile appearance.

"Hey, Lily." He moved into the office. "Are you ready for lunch?"

Lily nodded so vigorously her wire-rimmed glasses slipped down the bridge of her nose. "My mom's coming too," she said, pushing the glasses back into place. She seemed like a sweet girl. He'd been worried about being around the kids, especially because they were ill, but so far he'd handled it better than he'd thought.

"I know." He glanced at Dorie Lovett, who had her arm around Lily's too-thin shoulders. "Where would you ladies like to go? I heard the choice was up to you."

"Lily wants to go to Kamu's." Dorie gazed down at her daughter with undisguised warmth. "She says all the players hang out there."

"Some of us do. And there's a lot of Blaze memorabilia to look at." He smiled at Lily. "Good choice. I think you'll like it." Glancing at the vacant chair behind the tidy dark walnut desk, he frowned. "Where's Katherine?"

"Katherine won't be able to make it today. I'm filling in."

Matt recognized Kelly's husky voice immediately. Turning toward the door, he took one look at her poised at the threshold and his breath jammed in his throat. *Holy fucking shit.* She was wearing a dress.

It wasn't just any dress. It was a sundress. He'd always been a sucker for a woman in a sundress, and Kelly Maxwell in a sundress was a sight to behold. The black dress itself was modest. It wasn't even that short, but the soft fabric clung to her body and showed off her toned arms and her amazingly long legs to perfection. She wore low-heeled sandals and her toenails were painted a deep shade of red. He felt a tug of arousal in his groin and swallowed. Hard.

Unable to resist, he let his gaze travel leisurely up her shapely body and was further stunned when he noticed she'd forgone her usual ponytail. Her light brown hair cascaded around her shoulders like silk. He wanted to touch it. *Jesus*, he wanted to touch her.

What the hell?

"Matt?"

"What?" he said and then caught the quizzical look in her eyes. "Did you say something?"

"I asked if you're ready to go."

"Yeah." He forced his gaze from her and discovered both Lily and Dorie had risen from the bench and were looking at him expectantly. "Let's go. I'm hungry."

"Me too." Lily beamed at him. Despite her pallor, her eyes sparkled with happiness. "This is so cool." She giggled and moved forward to grab his hand. She looked up at him with adoration and despite his best intentions to remain unmoved, the wall he'd built around his heart during the past year crumbled just a tiny bit. It caught him by surprise. He glanced at Kelly. She was looking at Lily with a tender expression, a slight smile curving her lips. She looked both maternal and sexy at the same time.

Damn. A lot of things had caught him by surprise today.

As LILY AND Dorie checked out a memorabilia display case on their way back from the restroom, Kelly's heart constricted when she thought of what lie ahead for Lily. There were a lot of things in life that weren't fair, but what was happening to Lily made them all seem pretty damn insignificant.

"What's wrong with her?" Concern was etched on Matt's face. "It's not good, is it?"

"No. It's not," she said sadly. "Cardiomyopathy."

"That's a heart disease, right?"

"Yes." She reached for her iced tea. "I don't know a lot about it, but from what Dorie told me, Lily's heart muscle is too thick. She was diagnosed a few years ago."

Matt leaned back in his chair and ran a hand over his jaw. "Shit."

"My sentiments exactly." She took a sip of her tea and then set her glass down. "I can't imagine what Dorie's going through. To watch your child suffer and not be able to do a damn thing about it. It's heartbreaking."

"Yes, it is." The bleakness in his eyes and the sadness in his voice caught her off guard. Even before she'd met him and had it confirmed, she'd thought him to be a cocky, arrogant jerk. But his interaction with Lily during lunch proved he had a heart. It was obvious Lily was star struck, and a little nervous. But Matt soon put her at ease, and before their entrée had arrived he and Lily were practically best friends. Kelly searched his face trying to find a trace of the man who could piss her off like none other, but at this moment, that man was gone.

"She worships you, you know," she said softly. "She was hanging on your every word all through lunch."

Matt's lips curved into a half smile, erasing his desolate expression. "I think she was pretty impressed with you too." He leaned forward to pick up his water glass. His light blue shirt contrasted against his deeply tanned skin. His tousled dark hair curled over the collar; she had a sudden urge to touch it, to run her fingers through it and then press her lips to—

"You kicked ass today."

"What?" Her cheeks burned as she met his amused gaze. Thank God he couldn't read her mind. And what the hell was she doing thinking those kinds of thoughts about him anyway? This just proved she'd been without a man for far too long. They might be getting along at the moment but it wouldn't last. She still had to do her job. Yes, he'd done the interview with Trevor Jackson earlier today but she doubted he was going to start going into the media room after games, or sit down with any more reporters.

"You kicked ass today," he repeated.

"I did. Didn't I?" she said, not bothering to deny it. For some idiotic reason it pleased her that Matt was impressed.

"And modest too, I see," he said before sipping his water.

"What can I say?" Kelly couldn't help but smile. "I love to win."

"There's nothing wrong with that." He set his glass down. "I love to win too." His eyes roamed over her. For some reason, he reminded her of the swashbuckling heroes on the covers of the historical romance books her mom loved—dangerous and sexy at the same time. It was a potent combination. Her skin prickled with excitement under his bold perusal. "I think this is the first time I've ever seen you in a dress."

"I wore a dress that night in L.A."

"You did?" His eyes widened a fraction. "I didn't notice."

She cocked her head and gave him a wry smile. "That's because you were too busy checking out my sister."

One of his dark brows lifted. "Was I?"

"I don't blame you. Kayla's gorgeous. I'm used to it."

He regarded her intently for several seconds, his eyes enigmatic. "About that night..." he began.

"We're back," Lily interrupted as she and Dorie returned to the table. She slid onto her chair and grabbed her napkin. After she spread it over her lap, she looked at Matt. "Matt, can I ask you a question?"

"Sure, kiddo. What do you want to know?" he asked, looking at her with affection. Kelly was amazed at the rapport that had developed between him and Lily so quickly. He seemed to be a natural with kids. Another thing about him that surprised her.

Squirming on her chair, Lily glanced at her mom and then said, "Will you come to my birthday party next month?"

"Lily," Dorie exclaimed with alarm. "We talked about this in the restroom."

Lily bit her lip and lowered her gaze to her plate. "I know," she said in a soft voice. "I'm sorry, Mom."

"It's okay, Dorie," Matt said and then turned to Lily. "When is it? If I'm not on road that day I might be able to make it."

Lily's head shot up, her wide eyes hopeful. "August third."

"I think I'll be in town." He looked at Kelly. "We play the D-Backs the beginning of August, right?"

"That sounds right." She shifted so she could reach into her purse hanging off the back of the chair. "Let me check." She pulled out her cell phone and went to her calendar. She'd entered all the Blaze games and their start times at the beginning of the season. "You're right. We play Arizona. It's a day game and the start time is twelve forty-five."

"What time's your party?"

"It's at six," Dorie answered for Lily. Her face was flushed with embarrassment. "But please, don't feel obligated. We know you're busy during the season."

"It wouldn't be an obligation," he said to Dorie and then turned to Lily. "How old will you be?"

"Ten."

"Wow. Ten is an important milestone. I'd be honored to come to your party."

"OMG," Lily squealed with excitement. Her pale cheeks turned rosy. "I can't wait to tell my friend Bobby. Next to me, he's your biggest fan."

He frowned. "OMG?"

"It means 'Oh my God,'" Kelly supplied for him. "Don't you text?"

"Rarely."

She turned to Lily. "LOL," she said and Lily giggled.

Matt shook his head. "I'm not even going to ask."

"WILL YOU BE at the game tonight?" Matt asked Kelly as they walked toward the employee entrance to Blaze Field. He was enjoying this sudden truce between them and wondered how long it would last. Until she started badgering him about those damn interviews again, that's how long. The interview with Trevor Jackson had gone well but he didn't want to make a habit of them. The media was a distraction he didn't need right now.

"Yes. But I'll be leaving right afterward. I have a soft-ball game that starts at eight."

"Where do you play?" He glanced at her, his gaze lingering on the swell of her breasts. She wasn't overly endowed but what she had was more than enough. He appreciated a nice rack as much as the next guy, but he'd always been a leg man, and hers were sexier than hell. The glimpse he'd gotten that night in the kitchen proved that.

"At a park over near 6th and Folsom."

"I think I know that park. I run there sometimes."

"Kelly," a feminine voice called from behind them. Both he and Kelly turned to see Stacia heading toward them with a wide smile on her face.

Shit. Stacia was the last person he wanted to see.

"I thought that was you," Stacia said to Kelly and then shifted her attention to him. "Hi, Matt."

"Hey." He nodded at her. A few nights ago he'd been ready and willing to take her to bed but now that he knew she was Kelly's roommate there was no way he was hitting that. A month ago he wouldn't have cared.

But then, a month ago he hadn't cared about anything except numbing the pain he was in.

"I thought you were flying to Tokyo," Kelly said to Stacia.

"That's next week." Stacia looked pointedly at him. "I'll be around until then," she said with a suggestive smile.

Great. Now he was going to have to have "the conversation." Ironically, that particular conversation usually came after he'd scored with a woman, not before.

Kelly glanced at the slim watch on her wrist. "I've got to get back to my office. My email inbox is overflowing and I've got some press releases to write. I'll see you at home, Stacia." She turned and put her hand on his forearm. Her fingers were warm and soft against his skin. A spike of heat caught him low in his gut, taking him by surprise. She squeezed his arm gently and continued, "Thanks for being so kind to Lily."

"It wasn't hard," he said, very aware of the faint citrusy scent of her perfume. "She's a good kid."

"And brave too." Withdrawing her hand, she reached up to brush her hair back. The next time he saw her it would be back in a ponytail. A pity—her hair was beautiful. "I'll see you at the airport tomorrow morning."

"You're going on the road with us?"

"Yep." Her eyes gleamed with bemusement. "Usually, either Katherine or I go. Someone's got to keep an eye on you guys," she said with a wry grin and then turned and headed for the stadium. As she walked away he couldn't help but watch and enjoy the gentle sway of her hips and the long sexy stride of her legs. Kelly Maxwell could rock a sundress that was for damn sure.

"Kelly has a game tonight." Stacia put her hand on

his arm. "She'll probably be home late. Why don't you come by?"

He tore his gaze from Kelly's athletic body and met Stacia's hopeful eyes. "I have a game too."

Her smile faltered. "Oh, I forgot. Maybe another night then."

"I've got a long road trip coming up." His profession really did come in handy sometimes. "And honestly, I need to concentrate on baseball right now." It wasn't a lie, and truth be told, it wouldn't have stopped him if he really wanted to have sex with her. But he didn't. Not anymore. She looked like every other woman he'd been with the past year. He couldn't remember any of their names, or why the hell he'd thought sleeping with them was the answer to his problems.

"You didn't feel that way the other night." As she let go of his arm, her eyes narrowed. "It's because of Kelly, isn't it?"

"What do you mean?"

"She told me how you guys are always fighting. You probably don't want to be around her any more than you have to."

"It's not that. She's…she's not half bad." He shoved his hands in his pockets. Behind Stacia, a couple of guys in Blaze T-shirts were taking his picture with their cell phones. One of them gave him a thumbs-up sign accompanied by a lascivious grin and then they headed for the Blaze souvenir and apparel store adjacent to the stadium. "The truth is I'm starting over here in San Francisco. Baseball has to be my top priority right now." He paused and used the old standby. "It's not you. It's me."

Stacia let out an incredulous laugh. "That's usually my line," she said and shrugged. "It's your loss."

"I'm sure it is," he said. "I've got to go warm up with the team. The game is starting soon."

Her eyes flickered with annoyance. "Sure. Whatever. I'll see you around."

"See you." He didn't bother watching her walk away. Instead he headed for the ballpark.

All of a sudden, that six-day road trip he'd been dreading didn't seem so bad.

SEVEN

PLAYING PROFESSIONAL BASEBALL and traveling around the country had seemed exciting when Matt was twelve years old. Actually doing it, not so much. It was grueling, especially near the end of a 162-game season. Road trips to the Midwest and the East Coast were the worst. The long flights, different time zones and hotel rooms that looked exactly alike no matter what city they were in took its toll. Even on a player who was in excellent physical condition.

Still, he wouldn't trade his profession for another. Baseball was in his blood. It was a fact of his life. Just like the color of his eyes, or his blood type.

The road trip was half over. An hour or so ago, the Blaze had won their third and final game in Philadelphia. Tomorrow morning they would board their chartered plane and head for Cincinnati to play the Reds in a three-game series. If they could sweep that series, the Blaze just might return to San Francisco leading the Western division. That, of course, depended on how the Dodgers and the Padres fared in their respective games.

It was after eleven but he wasn't tired. Instead he was wired—a usual occurrence after a night game. He was also hungry. As soon as he got off the bus transporting the team from Citizens Bank Park to their hotel he was going to take advantage of the hotel's 24-hour room service and get some grub.

"The Dodgers and Padres both lost," J.T., who was sitting next to him checking game scores on his cell phone, said.

"That's good news for us," Matt replied. It was the first time since he'd been traded that he didn't feel like a traitor because he was happy the Dodgers had lost a game. He cocked his head and focused his gaze two rows in front of him where Kelly was sitting next to the skipper. The light in the bus was dim, but he could see they had their heads together. Tom Morgan had made it a point to sit next to Kelly when they all got on the bus. He couldn't help but wonder what they were talking about. He'd assumed it was media business but he'd heard her husky laugh several times so now he wasn't sure.

Not that he cared. Yeah, he and Kelly had enjoyed a nice lunch with Lily and her mother, but since then she'd reverted back to her old ways. Hounding him to make nice with the reporters and beat writers in the clubhouse. The tentative truce they'd forged had disappeared the minute he'd adamantly told her the interview with Trevor Jackson was a onetime thing and that his stance on the media hadn't changed.

"Morgan said I'll probably get a start against the Reds," J.T. was saying.

"That's a wise move." Matt turned to look at him. "The next two months are going to be brutal. You need more playing time and I'll need the rest. It's a win-win for both of us."

J.T. rested his phone on his thigh. "I really think we can take the division. We've got the pitching, and our bats are starting to come alive. Lopes has been on fire the last four games."

"He's getting hot at the right time," Matt said. "And

the rest of the lineup is starting to produce. If we can keep the momentum going we'll get to the postseason. There's no doubt in my mind about that."

J.T. regarded him thoughtfully. "This has to be hard on you. I mean, the Dodgers drafted you in college. You've spent your whole career with them."

Matt shrugged. "It is what it is. It's not like I didn't make it easy for them to trade me."

"Some of us were worried when we heard you were joining the team."

"I figured that."

"I can't speak for Rizzo and his buddies, but the rest of us aren't worried anymore. Mark my words, you'll be bleeding orange and black by the time the season is over."

"I just want to get to the World Series," he said. "And I'll do whatever I have to do to get there. Including rolling over the Dodgers."

J.T. grinned. "Can I quote you on that?"

"You can tattoo it on your ass," Matt shot back and then turned his attention up front where Morgan and Kelly still had their heads together.

What the hell were they talking about?

LESS THAN AN hour later, Matt opened his hotel room door expecting room service and instead was surprised to find a stunning blonde on the other side. Since she wasn't wearing much, and there was no service cart nearby, it was safe to assume she wasn't on staff at the hotel. Her smile was suggestive. She wasn't at his door for just an autograph.

"Hi, Matt." Her eyes bore into his in silent expectation. "You said to look you up the next time you were in Philly."

Christ. Did he know her? He searched his brain for some sort of recollection. She resembled a young Pamela Anderson, circa *Baywatch*, but he didn't recognize her at all. That didn't mean squat, though—in the past year he'd been with a number of women. She could be—*hell*, she probably was—one of them.

"Aren't you going to invite me in?"

No. He wasn't. But he didn't want to be rude. Keeping one hand on the door he struggled in vain to remember her name but was coming up blank.

"It's late," he said, glancing at his watch.

"It's not that late." Undeterred, she cast him a sly smile. "Besides, after I get through with you, you'll sleep like a baby," she added, gazing at him with sexual confidence. She took a step forward; the floral scent of her perfume was so overpowering he had to fight the urge to step back. "Remember how relaxed you were the last time?"

Again, that would be a no. He didn't remember her, or having sex with her. But she obviously did, and now he was relatively certain he'd given her some sort of cock and bull line about seeing her again when his team rolled into Philly on the next road trip. He'd used that line a lot and never once meant it. The women he'd been with over the past year had been nothing more than a way for him to forget the hell that was his life. Not one of them had meant a damn thing. It wasn't something he was proud of, but it was the truth.

"I don't think it's a good idea." At the far end of the brightly lit hallway the elevator chimed its arrival. It was probably room service with his late supper.

"Why not?"

"Because..." He paused as he noticed she was wearing one of those necklaces that spelled out her name. Why would anyone wear their name around their neck? He didn't get it, but it saved him from admitting he didn't know who the hell she was. "Tiffany, I—" He broke off when he heard muffled footsteps on the carpeted hallway.

He looked to his left just in time to see Kelly rounding the corner. She wore her standard work attire of pants and a blazer—today's color was navy blue. Her hair was pulled back in a ponytail that swished from side to side as she walked. In one hand she clutched a tan leather tote bag, and in the other she held the key card for her room. The moment she saw Tiffany, in her micro mini skirt and halter top standing in front of his door, her mouth pressed into a grim line and a frown marred her forehead.

Of course, she was thinking the worst. Not that he blamed her; his less than stellar behavior had been well documented. While some of the more salacious details had been exaggerated, the majority of them had been true and were the major reason he'd recently had a full physical and lab tests. He always wore a condom but, for his own peace of mind, he needed to know if his exploits over the past year had resulted in an STD. To his relief, they hadn't.

Somehow he had to get rid of Tiffany *and* let Kelly know he wasn't carrying on like he had in L.A. He wasn't sure why he cared what she thought, but he did.

"Hey, baby," he said, thinking fast as she approached. He brushed past a surprised Tiffany and moved toward Kelly. "I've been waiting for you."

Kelly stopped short, one dark brow arching as she cast him an incredulous look. He stood in front of her, blocking her view of Tiffany. "What did you call me?" she asked in a low voice. "Because I *think* I just heard you call me baby."

"Can you play along, please?" he whispered. "I need to get rid of her."

"What's the matter? Already have another groupie in your room?" Her eyes flickered with amusement. "What? You don't want to make it a threesome?"

Matt scowled. "I don't do threesomes."

"Too bad. They're fun," she said and grinned when he was rendered speechless. *She was kidding, right?* She tilted her head to peer over his shoulder at Tiffany and gave her a quick once-over. "She looks like your type. Blonde and easy." Looking back at him, she continued with a smirk, "I have washcloths larger than that skirt she's wearing."

"Are you going to help me, or not?" he asked through clenched teeth.

"What's in it for me?"

"What do you want?"

"You know what I want." Her husky voice sounded suggestive, but that couldn't be. He knew her well enough to know that what she wanted wasn't him. "I'll help you out with your little problem if you help me out with mine." She held his gaze unflinchingly, just as she had that night in L.A.

Damn it. She had him over a barrel. Unless he wanted to deal with Tiffany on his own. He didn't—the last thing he needed was some scantily clad woman making a scene outside his hotel room. The press would have a field day with that.

"What are your terms?"

Triumph sparkled in her eyes. "I want you to start going to the media room after the games to answer questions from the press."

Son of a bitch. She was blackmailing him. He had to hand it to her, she was clever.

"How about one interview?"

"How about you get rid of what's-her-name without my help?" Kelly replied sweetly.

"Fine," he gritted out. "But you'd better make this good."

"Kayla isn't the only actress in the family." She reached up and patted his cheek with her key card. "I've dabbled in the performing arts myself. I played Kate in *Taming of the Shrew* when I was in college."

"I can't think of a better part for you," he snapped. "Let's get this over with."

THE DISMISSIVE LOOK in the blonde's eyes wasn't anything Kelly hadn't seen before. Only nowadays she didn't care too much what anyone else thought about her appearance. Still, it rankled that this…this…Pamela Anderson wannabe had sized her up with one glance and immediately concluded she was no threat, and no competition.

We'll see about that.

"Hello," Kelly said as she and Matt halted in front of the blonde. She made note of the nameplate necklace. Somehow, the name fit. "I'm Kelly, and you must be Tiffany."

Tiffany's perfectly made-up face turned suspicious. "How did you know that?"

Was she serious? She was wearing that stupid necklace, or had she forgotten?

"Matt told me all about you." She felt him watching her but didn't spare him a glance. Contrary to what she'd just told him, she couldn't act her way out of a paper bag. Kayla was the one with all the talent, not her. Her performance in *Taming of the Shrew* hadn't been well received. But hell, Shakespeare was hard.

Tiffany's eyes widened. "Really?"

"Yes. Now that we're together, Matt's been totally honest about his past."

"Together? *You're* with Matt?" Tiffany's dumbfounded expression might have been funny if it wasn't so insulting. Was it that much of a stretch that Matt could find her attractive? "Since when?"

"A few months ago." Turning her head, Kelly met Matt's enigmatic eyes. He seemed content to let her do the talking. How typical. "We met in L.A. It was fireworks from the very beginning." She looked back to find Tiffany's disbelieving baby blues had zeroed in on Matt.

"Is this true?"

He nodded. "It was fireworks, all right. *Major* fireworks."

"And we've been together ever since." Kelly suppressed a grin when Tiffany's mouth gaped open.

"I haven't read anything about the two of you." Tiffany's skeptical gaze moved from Kelly to Matt.

"We're keeping a low profile," he said quickly.

"I can see why." Tiffany's sneer matched the tone of her voice.

Kelly's good humor evaporated. "Excuse me?"

"You're not his type," Tiffany said. "He's not a chubby chaser."

Kelly's blood started to boil. She gripped the handle

of her tote and fought the urge to swing it at the bimbo's smug and overly Botoxed face.

"She's exactly my type," Matt said, surprising Kelly by sliding his arm around her waist and pulling her to his hard body. Her pulse kicked, an instant reaction to the masculine power he exuded so effortlessly. "I knew it the moment we met."

Tiffany let out an unladylike snort and crossed her arms over her well-endowed chest. Her gaze raked disdainfully down Kelly's body. "Do you always dress like that?"

Oh, she was going there, was she?

Kelly returned the blonde's rude stare with one of her own. "Yes. Do you always dress like *that?*"

"Like what?" Tiffany's tone was defensive.

"Like you just got off your shift working the pole."

"How dare you." Tiffany's eyes bulged with outrage. "I'm not a stripper."

"Could have fooled me."

Tiffany put her hands on her hips. Her nostrils flared as her cheeks turned bright pink. "I don't have to stand here and take this. I'm out of here," she said with a theatrical flounce of her head and brushed past them to stalk down the hallway.

After Tiffany rounded the corner, Kelly tried to keep a straight face, but couldn't quite manage the feat. "Was it something I said?"

Matt's lips twitched in amusement. "I think the pole comment hit a little too close to home."

"I can't believe you were with her."

"Me either." His smile faded and his expression turned solemn. "Thanks for your help."

Meeting his gaze, she realized his arm was still

around her. The heat from his body seemed to burn through the fabric of her blazer and she was so close to him that she could see the faint stubble on his jaw. Primal desire bombarded her senses. This couldn't be happening. Not now and not with him. Needing to put some distance between them, she moved to her left which forced Matt to relinquish his hold on her waist.

"Why didn't you just tell her to get lost?" she asked as Matt leaned against the door frame and shoved his hands into the pockets of his faded jeans. Try as she might, she hadn't been able to forget that brief glimpse she'd gotten of his naked body in the locker room. Hot tingles erupted low in her belly and inched downward. *Damn it.* The man was too appealing for his own good.

"I didn't want to be rude."

"Are you kidding? You've been rude to me since the minute we met."

"Jesus." He scowled. "You're never going to let that go, are you?"

"I might if you apologized."

"I tried to apologize when I got to San Francisco."

"When?" Kelly demanded. "I don't remember any apology."

"Maybe that's because you were too busy rubbing in the fact that you were right about me being traded. It's hard to apologize when someone's gloating, you know."

"I wasn't gloating." She paused, trying to remember their first encounter after that night in L.A. Her defenses had been up, she knew that much. She'd been nervous as hell, and right now she couldn't remember what she'd said. "Was I?"

"Yes. You were."

"I was still angry with you."

"I know. And I don't blame you for that." She stared at him, the pounding of her heart filling the taut silence that stretched between them. His eyes searched her face; the intimate gaze caused a quiver to surge through her veins. "Is it too late for me to apologize for that night?" he asked.

"No."

"I'm sorry, Kelly. You didn't deserve the things I said to you."

"Then why'd you say them?" she whispered. His hurtful words had nearly caused her to relapse.

"Because my life was pretty fucked up and I was taking it out on just about everyone who crossed my path."

Stunned by his admission and by the vulnerable expression on his face, she wasn't sure what to say. She'd glimpsed this side of him at lunch with Lily and Dorie. She hadn't expected to see it again. Not with her.

"Will you accept my apology?" he asked before she could speak.

"Yes."

A flicker of relief flashed in his eyes and his mouth tipped in a roguish smile that had, no doubt, charmed the panties off many a woman. "Any chance you might let me slide on that little deal we made a few minutes ago?"

Shaking her head, she grinned. "Hell, no. I fulfilled my end of the bargain and got rid of Tiffany for you. Now you have to fulfill your end."

"Shit," he grumbled.

"I told you I was tenacious." Still smiling, she checked her watch. "It's late and we've got an early flight. I'll see you in the morning."

"G'night, Kelly," he called after her as she headed for her room. At her door, she glanced over her shoulder to find him watching her. Unnerved by his dark eyes, she whipped her head around and with trembling fingers, unlocked the door.

LYING ON THE king-size bed and propped up against the rustic oak headboard, Matt stared at the day's sports headlines on the television screen, his empty plate next to him on the bed. He'd wolfed down the Philly cheesesteak sandwich and fries like he hadn't eaten in a week. Which wasn't true. His last meal had been an early lunch. Like the majority of his teammates, he was convinced he played better on an empty stomach.

Eating this late wasn't good, but it couldn't be helped. A cheesesteak sandwich wasn't the best choice either, but he was in Philly and couldn't pass it up. Just like he couldn't pass up barbecue in Kansas City, or pizza in Chicago. There was little time for sightseeing on the road, but he sure as hell knew the culinary treats in each city.

In the past year he'd also sampled the available women each city had to offer. Or he had right up until the moment the Dodgers had traded him. Tonight he could have indulged in a night of no-strings sex but as hot as Tiffany definitely was, he wasn't even tempted.

Instead he was thinking about the one woman on the planet who couldn't stand him, and with good reason. Kelly had accepted his apology but it still didn't erase the insults he'd hurled at her that night. Looking back, it was easy to see he was out of control and she had borne the brunt of it. It wasn't her fault he was a mess, but she'd been the perfect punching bag because she hadn't fawned all over him like every other woman who crossed his path.

Thankfully, the ringing of his cell phone distracted him from the woman who'd been invading his thoughts more and more as each day passed. Reaching for it on the nightstand, he picked it up and grinned when he saw his best friend's name on the caller ID.

"I figured you'd still be up," Sean Barrett said when Matt answered the phone. "Good game tonight."

"You caught it?"

"It was on the MLB channel." Sean paused. "By the way, the Dodgers lost."

"I heard." Matt reached for the remote and turned off the television. The screen faded to black. "It's getting easier for me to be okay with that."

"Speak for yourself. You may be playing for San Francisco now, but there's no way I'm rooting for the Blaze."

Matt chuckled. "I totally understand. Hey, how's Kayla?"

"She's good. In fact, she's leaving for Hawaii tomorrow to shoot some exteriors for the miniseries."

"What about that psycho who was stalking her?"

"Locked up. The trial won't start for several months."

"I'll bet she's breathing easier."

"We both are."

"So things are good between you two?"

"Couldn't be better." Sean hesitated and then continued, "I'm going to ask her to marry me."

"What?" Surprised, Matt sat up. "Marry you? Isn't it a bit soon for that?"

"No. I want to spend the rest of my life with her."

"But…"

"I know what I'm doing. Trust me, when it's right, you know."

"When are you going to ask her?"

"I have a few days off from the show so we made plans for me to join her in Hawaii. I'm going to pop the question there."

"You don't waste any time."

"I almost lost her in Savannah. I'm not taking any chances."

"Then I'm happy for you."

"Thanks," Sean said and after a lengthy pause asked, "So, how are you doing? Really?"

"Better." Swinging his legs over the side of the bed, he ran a hand through his hair. "I haven't been tossed out of a game since I got here. I'm keeping my nose clean and staying out of trouble. I even turned down some primo pussy tonight."

Sean laughed. "What about Kelly Maxwell?"

"What about her?"

"Did you apologize to her?"

"As a matter of fact, I did." Okay, so the apology had come a little late, but he'd done it. That had to count for something.

"Does that mean you two are getting along?"

Rising from the bed, Matt walked to the window and pushed back the heavy drapes. "Sort of." He stared out at the dark night sky sprinkled with bright white stars. "At least we're not at each other's throats."

"I'm glad to hear it," Sean said. "Well, I'll let you get some shut-eye."

Matt let the curtain fall. "Good luck in Hawaii," he said and hung up.

Moving to the dresser, he put the phone down and picked up the baseball he took with him whenever he went on the road. Gripping it tightly, he stared at the crayon scribbles on it. Tears pricked the backs of his eyes. He'd just told Sean he was getting better and there were days when he really believed it. Then, during a game, he'd catch a glimpse of some little boy sitting with his dad and the pain would hit him all over again.

Until last year he had no idea of the depths of despair he could sink to. Even with parents as dysfunctional as his, he'd led a fairly comfortable life in the upscale beach community of Pacific Palisades. Behind the veneer of a perfect marriage, his parents were cold and unfeeling. They weren't normal, he'd figured that out pretty early on. He'd spent a lot of time at Sean's house before Sean's mom had died. Laura Barrett had treated him like a son, and she had doted on Sean and Sean's father.

That was the kind of parent he wanted to be. Kind, loving, involved. Only it hadn't worked out that way. That's when he discovered what real agony was. It was sharp, brutal and cut into his soul like a knife. He'd tried to escape it, but no matter how much he partied, no matter how many women he slept with, and no matter how many fights he got into on the field, he couldn't outrun it. It was always one step behind him, its breath hot on his neck.

Not long after that night in L.A. when he'd insulted Kelly, it finally caught up to him. He'd hit rock bottom and when he'd pulled his head out of his ass, he found his entire life was in shambles.

There wasn't a chance in hell of getting back what he'd lost, but maybe, just maybe, he could salvage his career. Right now, it was the only thing he had to hold on to.

EIGHT

Two days after the Blaze had returned to San Francisco, Kelly was at her desk going through her emails when a soft knock sounded on her office door. Turning her head, she found Katherine poised at the threshold with a warm smile on her face. "May I come in?"

"Of course." Kelly swiveled her chair around as her boss moved forward to take a seat on the chair opposite the desk. As always, Kelly admired Katherine's chic style. Today she had paired a slim gray pencil skirt with a pale pink cashmere sweater and her auburn hair was pulled back in a sleek chignon.

Katherine crossed a slim bare leg over her knee and leaned back in the chair. "How was the road trip?"

"It went well. I met with a local reporter in Philadelphia. He requested an interview with Trey Gentry. Trey's from the area and there's a lot of interest in his career there. You know, local boy makes good. I approved it and it turned out to be a really nice piece. Surprisingly, there are a number of Blaze fans in Philly."

"Were there any PR issues I need to be concerned about?"

"No." Kelly pushed aside the stack of pink message slips she still needed to get to and folded her arms on the desk. "Everyone behaved themselves."

"Scanlon has started going into the media room after

the games. He's been pretty adamant about not doing any press. How did you manage to convince him?"

Not wanting to divulge she'd resorted to blackmail, Kelly shrugged. "I didn't do anything special. I think he's getting more comfortable with the team."

"Why do I think there's more to it than that?" Katherine asked with a speculative gleam in her eyes and then waved her hand. "Never mind. I'm not going to question it. I'm just thankful he's finally talking. I was starting to get some heat from the GM." She sighed. "Not that I blame Doug. The press has been pressuring him pretty hard. The longer Scanlon kept mum, the worse it got."

"Tell me about it," Kelly said. "Trevor Jackson was going to go over both of our heads."

Katherine rose from the chair, smoothing out her skirt with her hands. "Whatever you did, I'm glad it worked."

After Katherine had left her office, Kelly got back to work. While on the road, she'd prepared several letters in response to public-appearance requests for several of the players, and the team as a whole. Quickly attaching them to an email, she sent them to Alexis who would format them for signature.

By noon, she'd written several press releases, spoken to three local media editors and updated the injury report. The team was healthy. Only Rick Taylor was on the disabled list. She hoped it would stay that way. The Blaze were locked in a three-way tie for first place in the Western division. They would need every single player they had if they were going to make it to the postseason.

Her stomach rumbled, reminding her it had been a long time since her morning bowl of shredded wheat. Instead of leaving the ballpark, she decided to grab a salad at the team's cafeteria adjacent to the clubhouse and bring it back to her office for a working lunch.

An hour later, she'd finished her Chinese chicken salad and was in the middle of preparing a new post detailing the Blaze wives' online auction for the team's website when a knock on her door startled her. Looking up, the sight of Matt standing in the doorway sucked the air right out of her lungs.

It really was criminal for a man to be that hot. He wore loose gray sweats that didn't do much to disguise his rock-hard thighs, and a Blaze T-shirt that clung like a second skin to his well-defined torso. She'd spent a good deal of time in the Blaze clubhouse around players either buck naked or close to it, but not one of them had ever affected her like Matt was affecting her right now. The intensity of her attraction to him was damn unsettling.

"May I come in?" he asked.

"Sure." She swung around as he moved into the office and lowered himself onto her visitor chair.

"Nice office," he commented, surveying the room with interest. As offices on the floor went, it was one of the smaller ones, and one of the few with no view. In fact, there wasn't even a window. It didn't bother her, but several of her coworkers, including Angie, said it made them claustrophobic.

"Thanks," she said as he checked out the framed pictures of her family on the pale yellow wall behind her. "Are you here to tell me you want to do more interviews?"

"Hell, no." Since his hair was damp, she surmised he'd recently showered. It curled at the ends as it dried and he smelled of shampoo and soap—a clean scent that drifted into her senses and sent a shiver of awareness over her skin. "It's bad enough I have to go to the media room after the games."

She leaned back in her chair. "C'mon, it's not that painful, is it? I've sat in on most of those sessions and I think the press is going pretty easy on you. It could be worse."

"They're just waiting for me to fuck up." Matt scowled. "They're going to have a long wait."

"Then you don't have anything to worry about." Kelly grinned. "Unless you fuck up, of course."

A smile quirked his lips before he sobered. "Do you think I will?"

Kelly hesitated before answering. She wanted to believe his current good behavior would continue, but his track record spoke for itself. "To be honest, I'm not sure. Ask me again in a few weeks."

"That's fair." He leaned forward to rest his elbows on his knees. The move drew her attention to his powerful arms. How would those arms of his feel wrapped around her? The mere thought of it caused a flutter low in her belly. "I'm here because I have an invitation to extend to you," he said.

"Invitation?" She shifted in her chair, grateful he couldn't read her mind.

"From Lily. She wants me to bring you to her birthday party tomorrow night. Can you make it?"

"Really? She wants me to come?"

"Yes. I think she's in awe of your softball prowess."

"As well she should be," Kelly said with a grin. "I'm damn good."

Matt rolled his eyes and chuckled.

"Hey, I just know what I excel at, and softball is one of those things."

A half smile curved his lips and the intensity of his dark gaze caused her stomach to do a full somersault. "I'll bet you excel at a lot of things."

Hold up. Put the car in park. Was he flirting?

Flustered, she picked up her pen and began doodling hearts on a notepad in front of her. "To answer your question, I can go to Lily's party with you. I have a softball game tonight but tomorrow night is wide-open."

"Great. Lily will be thrilled." He rose from the chair and stood before her desk. "So, you have a game tonight? Is it at the park you were telling me about?"

"Yes." She nodded. "It's our last game of the season. If we win we're the fast-pitch champions."

"Sweet." Matt smiled, his eyes crinkling at the corners. "I hope you kick their ass."

"That's the plan."

"I should go." His lingering gaze made her tingle in places that shouldn't be tingling while she was at work. "Morgan doesn't like it if we're late for our pregame meeting."

"So I've heard." She tried to keep her gaze from traveling down his impressive body. "I'll see you in the media room after the game."

"You're pretty pleased with yourself about that, aren't you?" he asked, noting her amusement. He didn't look angry; in fact, his expression was quite the opposite. For the first time since they'd met he seemed completely relaxed.

"Maybe a little," she admitted with a wry grin. "And I owe it all to Tiffany. I may send her a thank-you card and a gift certificate to Macy's so she can buy a skirt that covers her ass."

Matt let out a short laugh and shook his head. "I don't think she shops there."

"Oh, right. She's more the Frederick's of Hollywood type, isn't she?" She set her pen down and covered the hearts she'd drawn with her hand. "I prefer Victoria's Secret myself."

"Really?" A wicked gleam lighted his eyes. "Interesting."

Kelly's mouth went dry. Why the hell had she said that? "They have excellent sales," she said quickly, feeling her cheeks start to burn.

"I'm sure they do." Matt grinned, his strong features softening with boyish charm. "So we'll talk later about Lily's party?"

"Yes. Have a good game," she called after him as he left her office.

For a long while Kelly stared at her computer screen without seeing a thing on it. She was going to Lily's party with Matt. It wasn't a date, was it? No. No way. Matt had just been relaying Lily's invitation and since he was going to the party anyway it made sense to go together. Besides, she was the last woman on earth Matt would date. He was into skinny blondes with big breasts like Tiffany or Stacia.

Besides, I'm fat. No man wants a fat chick, remember?

"Stop it," she whispered to her subconscious.

Closing her eyes, she took a deep breath and replaced the negative words with positive ones.

I'm the right weight for my height. I'm fit and healthy. Any man would be lucky to have me.

It took several minutes but she was able to push the negative thoughts away. At first, the whole positive thoughts thing had been difficult. For years, even before the worst of her eating disorder, her thoughts about herself had been brutal. As a kid she'd always been taller than her peers, and the sometimes cruel comments they made to her had cut like a knife and made her even more self-conscious. Then later, when she was older and had become interested in boys, none of them were interested in her. They all seemed to prefer the more petite and less athletic girls.

Every day, she'd wished she was like the other girls, and that's when she'd started obsessing about her body. Then in her senior year of high school it got worse. She'd overheard a guy she liked talking about her with his friends. Unaware she was listening, he told them he'd never go out with a fat-ass like her, and how it was too bad she didn't have a hot body like her sister. She'd been crushed, but instead of realizing that the guy was an immature and insensitive jerk, she became convinced that losing weight was the answer to all of her problems.

Rising from her desk, Kelly left her office and headed for the elevator. She needed to clear her head and the best way to do that was to take a walk. The ballpark was situated right on the edge of the bay and there was a promenade with a spectacular view of the Bay Bridge. A brisk walk would do wonders for her state of mind and since she'd eaten lunch at her desk while working, she still had her lunch hour to spare.

It was a beautiful August day. The morning fog was long gone and the warm sun kissed her face. The air smelled of salt, and the seagulls squawked as they hovered over the area looking for scraps of food. She watched, amused, as two of the gulls fought over a discarded French fry.

She strolled past Java Joe's, a small white shack that was—as usual—packed and headed toward the promenade. As she walked, she made it a point to really look at the people around her. It was something her therapist had recommended when she was going through recovery and as odd as it had seemed at first, it really helped. People came in all different shapes and sizes. Only a few could attain the perfect image worshipped by the media and Hollywood. Those individuals were a very small percentage of the population and many of them had developed eating disorders striving to maintain that illusion of perfection.

An illusion was just what it was. At least for her. During the worst years of her eating disorder—right after college—she had lost a great deal of weight and yet it had never been enough. There wasn't one single day when she'd felt happy. She had shunned her friends and ignored her family. She'd stopped playing softball and spent long lonely hours at the gym trying to burn as many calories as possible.

It was a nightmare she wasn't sure she'd ever wake up from. Then one day she'd come across a program on television that had changed her life. It was a talk show devoted solely to eating disorders. It scared her. The young women on the show were emaciated yet still believed they were fat.

Talk about a wake-up call. Horrified, she'd watched knowing she was going down that same destructive path. She had called Kayla that evening and, after a shaky start, told her sister everything. The next day, at Kayla's urging, she'd started an outpatient treatment program.

That program had saved her life. And while she now considered herself recovered, sometimes those negative thoughts would pop into her head—just like they had today. Or something would upset her that made her want to ignore what she was feeling by bingeing. The trick was in knowing how to deal with those thoughts and her feelings so she didn't fall back into those old patterns.

Maybe Matt wouldn't date a woman who looked like her. She could accept that. After all, everyone had their preferences. It didn't mean she was unworthy of love. It meant that despite the attraction she felt for him, he wasn't the man for her.

Her mom's favorite saying was "there's a lid for every pot." She was a pot that hadn't yet found its lid. But she would.

SITTING ON A bar stool at Kamu's gleaming oak bar, Matt took a long pull of his beer and watched the highlights of the game the Blaze had just fought hard to win. A walk-off home run by Marquis Lopes in the bottom of the ninth inning had capped a come-from-behind rally that had sealed the Diamondbacks' fate and, combined with a Padres loss, had put the Blaze and the Dodgers in a dead heat for first place in the division.

Next to him, J.T. was also engrossed in the highlights. They both watched and listened as an annoying sports channel reporter speculated on whether the Blaze could keep up their winning ways.

"This dickhead is pissing me off," J.T. said irritably after polishing off the last of his beer.

"Why's that?" Matt asked, still staring at the flat screen.

J.T. set his bottle on the bar and waved off the bartender. "No thanks, man. One's my limit after a game." The bartender nodded and then moved to the other end of the bar. "When we were on that losing streak they wrote off our whole season. And now that we're winning, they're saying it's a fluke. We can't catch a break from those assholes."

"Don't listen to them. Trust me, letting them get inside your head isn't worth it." He took another sip of his beer.

"Is that what happened to you last year? Is that why you…"

"Why I fucked up?" Matt finished for him. "No. I can't blame the media for my behavior. That's all on me. But I did let what they were saying about me fuel my anger."

J.T. cast him a sidelong glance. He was dying to know more, but because J.T. was a stand-up guy he wouldn't ask. Matt appreciated that about him. J.T. was becoming a good friend. The same couldn't be said for Dave Rizzo. After their little confrontation in the clubhouse lounge, the pitcher had stopped questioning Matt's pitch calls but his surly attitude hadn't changed. In fact, Rizzo's animosity seemed even stronger.

Forgetting Rizzo, Matt glanced at his watch. It was still fairly early and he wasn't at all tired. Nor did he relish the thought of going home to his empty condo. It didn't feel like a home. All the furnishings were rented, including the dishes. It was like living in a hotel. Hell, Kelly's office was more inviting than his place. It was small, but she'd hung several photos of her family on the walls and several potted plants sat atop the credenza near her desk. Plants that weren't dead. He'd never had much luck with houseplants. Along with her stellar softball skills, Kelly also had a green thumb.

Softball. That's right. Kelly had a game tonight. The

championship, she'd said. At the park on 6th and Folsom—an easy walk from Kamu's.

Matt turned to J.T. "Got any plans?"

"Nope." J.T. cocked his head and regarded him with curiosity. "Why?"

"Kelly's softball team has their final game tonight. I was thinking of taking a walk over there and checking it out. You in?"

J.T. flashed a wide grin. "Beats going home and watching reruns."

KELLY SPRUNG UP from her crouched position behind home plate and trotted toward Angie, who had stepped off the pitcher's mound and motioned for her to come out for a little pitcher-catcher convo. Slipping off her catcher's mask, she wondered what had Angie so distracted. It was the top of the third inning and until just moments ago her friend's concentration had been razor sharp. Angie had struck out every single batter until walking the opposing team's overconfident shortstop.

"Don't let that guy rattle you," Kelly said, glancing at the trash-talking jerk who'd just informed her he was going to steal second base and there wasn't a thing she could do to stop him. Yeah, right. If he thought he could steal a base off of her, let him try. She didn't have the most picks in the coed league for nothing. "We beat these guys before, remember?" Wiping her moist brow, she frowned as Angie looked over her shoulder, her usually smiling face dead sober. "*Hello?* What's going on with you?"

Angie bit her lip as she swung her gaze back to Kelly. "Matt and J.T. are here," she whispered. "Don't look. They're watching our game."

"So what?" Kelly said, even as her heart started to pound. Despite the evening chill, her body was suddenly hot. *Matt was here?* She itched to turn around but forced herself not to. She knew why *she* was suddenly flustered. It was that damn attraction she felt for Matt. But why was Angie affected? Angie didn't give ball-players the time of day and dated a guy who worked for the city. Scott. An accountant. Kelly had met him once and found him boring as hell, but if Angie was happy, who was she to judge? Angie couldn't care less about the guys on the team. It didn't make sense that Matt and J.T. showing up would send her into a tizzy.

Angie glanced down at the ball in her hand. "None of the players have ever come to our games. It's weird. It threw me, that's all."

"Then let's show them how it's done." She playfully tagged Angie's arm with her catcher's mask. "C'mon, let's kick some ass."

A wry grin split the somberness of Angie's face. "You're a cocky bitch, you know that?"

Kelly laughed, not at all offended. "Damn straight. It's my best *and* worst quality." She paused as the idiot on first base yelled for them to hurry it up. "Ten to one, that douche bag tries to steal on the first pitch. Make it a fastball, would you? I want to nail his ass."

Two hours later, after the final out, Kelly was on the field alongside her teammates just after they'd participated in the traditional after-game handshake with the other team. The ritual was a lot more fun when her team won. Which they had. The Panthers were the new coed league fast-pitch champions.

It felt good.

What was even better was that the trash-talking shortstop had to shake her hand. He'd done it, but grudgingly. Getting thrown out on an attempted steal had pretty much shut him up for the rest of the game. The next time he'd come up to bat he didn't even look at her.

"Are you joining us at Kamu's?" the Panthers left fielder, Richie, asked her as they crossed the infield together.

"Not tonight." She glanced at the row of stands on the side of the field. Matt and J.T. were still there, both talking to Angie, who'd already changed out of her cleats and had her gym bag looped over her shoulder.

"Are you sure?" Richie put his hand on her arm, pulling her to a stop. "One beer won't hurt."

Kelly laughed. "There's no such thing as one beer at a Panthers celebration bash."

"True," Richie said.

"You're signing up for next season, right?"

"Of course. And just so you know, I'm predicting another championship."

"Those are bold words," she said as they stopped outside of the caged area that served as a dugout. Most of the team had grabbed their stuff and were heading off in the direction of Kamu's. "But I think we can do it if we have the same group of players."

Richie grinned and then enveloped her in a hug. "Good game tonight, Maxwell," he said when he pulled back. "I'm glad we're on the same team. I'd sure as hell hate to play against you." He looked over her shoulder and squinted. "Isn't that Matt Scanlon?"

"Yeah."

"I didn't peg him for a guy who'd come out to watch a coed game." Richie released her. Kelly followed him into the dugout and sank down on the metal bench. As she set her mask and glove on the bench next to her, Richie picked up his gym bag and slung it over his shoulder. "I'll down a few for you at Kamu's," he said and then patted her on the arm. "Catch ya later."

"See you," she called after Richie and then bent over to untie the laces of her cleats. She'd slid them both off and had pulled on her sneakers when footsteps crunched on the gravel in the dugout. Looking up, she met Matt's eyes and couldn't help the way her breath caught in her throat at the sight of him.

"Good game," he said and then motioned with his hand. "Can I sit?"

"Sure," she said, leaning forward to tie her shoelaces. The move bought her a little time to get her reeling emotions under control. She'd been able to block out his presence during the game, but now there was nothing to distract her. He was inches from her. So close that she could smell his clean soapy scent, close enough that if she moved her thigh to the right just a bit she could touch him.

And *damn it all*, she really wanted to touch him.

"Are you going to Kamu's?"

"No." She grabbed her gym bag from under the bench. "I've got a status meeting with Katherine early tomorrow morning." Forcing herself not to yearn for what she could never have, she reached for her glove and mask and shoved them inside her bag. What was happening to her? Ten days ago she couldn't stand Matt Scanlon and now she couldn't seem to stop wondering what it would be like to kiss those firm lips of his.

It had to be lack of sex. That was it. Lack of nookie was the underlying cause of her overwhelming urge to drag Matt back to her place, strip off his jeans and Blaze sweatshirt, and have her way with him. There could be no other reason. It wasn't like they had anything in common. Well, except maybe baseball. But that didn't count. In every other way they were polar opposites.

"Where did J.T. go?" she asked after noticing that, besides a few of the opposing team's players, the Panthers were pretty much gone.

"I think he went with Angie to Kamu's." He leaned back against the chain-link fence and stared out at the field. "You love it, don't you?"

"Love what?" Turning, she studied his profile. She could see the faint dark stubble on his chin, and his lashes were amazingly thick for a guy. Most women would kill for eyelashes like that. Her included.

"Playing ball."

Tearing her gaze from him, she looked at the now empty diamond. The park's groundskeeper would soon pull up the bases and rake the infield. By tomorrow it would be in pristine condition. But now it looked a bit used and roughed up. Two teams had battled on that field tonight and during those nine innings every single one of them had given it everything they had. Some would say it was only a game, but it was so much more than that.

"After my first T-ball game I told my dad I was going to play for the Blaze. I was too young to realize that girls couldn't play in the majors." Pulling off her cap, she slapped it against her knee and watched the dust particles float into the air. She leaned back, her arm touching Matt's as the chain link pressed into her back. "When I found out, I was pretty ticked off."

"You're really good. When I watch you, it reminds me of why I started playing. For the love of the game." His tone was wistful.

"Don't you love it anymore?"

Matt turned to look at her, his expression enigmatic. "If you'd asked me that a month ago, I would have said no."

"And now?"

"I don't know. Ask me again in a few weeks." He pinned her with his unreadable eyes for several long seconds before he put his hands on his knees and pushed up from the bench. "It's getting late, I'll walk you home."

"You don't have to..."

"No arguments." A grin split his face. "Peanut."

Kelly slapped her cap against his knee. Hard. "Damn it, Scanlon. Don't call me that."

NINE

"I NEED YOUR ADVICE," Matt said as he and Kelly stopped near the curb at the intersection of 3rd and Townsend to wait for the light to change. Despite the late hour, there was a steady stream of traffic whizzing by, leaving exhaust fumes in their wake. From what J.T. had told him, the whole area had been revitalized when Blaze Field was built and the Blaze moved from their former stadium in South San Francisco.

"On what?" Kelly pressed the pedestrian button on the streetlight pole. She had her baseball cap on backward, the brim resting on the elastic band where she'd gathered her hair at the nape of her neck. The golden glow of the streetlights illuminated the faint smudges of dirt that dusted her cheeks and reminded him of that night at Kamu's a few weeks ago. Another night when he had gone out of his way to insult her. Not his finest moment.

"On a gift for Lily."

"That's easy." Kelly hit the button again, and then once more.

"Punching that thing won't make the light change any faster," he said, amused by her impatience.

"I know. Force of habit." She gave him a sheepish smile as she adjusted the strap of the black gym bag she'd slipped over her shoulder and across her chest when they'd left the softball field. "Lily wants an official Blaze warm-up jacket."

"How do you know that?"

"I can read minds. It's a gift I have." She tilted her head, her suddenly serious gaze roaming over his face as if she could indeed read his mind. "In fact, I bet I know what you're thinking right now."

"What's that?"

"Kelly Maxwell is full of shit."

"You're good." Matt chuckled as she let out a husky laugh. "That's exactly what I was thinking." In reality, what he was really thinking was that there was a lot more to Kelly than he'd ever suspected. And that he liked her. A lot more than he ever imagined he would.

The light changed. They stepped off the curb and as they crossed the street she continued, "I called Dorie and asked her what Lily wanted for her birthday. Number one on her list is the jacket, and number two is a baseball autographed by all the players. I'm taking care of the ball, so feel free to get her the jacket. They sell them in the Blaze souvenir store at the ballpark."

"I'll stop by there tomorrow before the game." They reached the other side of the street and continued walking.

"Be prepared to get mobbed. The fans will go crazy when you walk in."

"I doubt it," he said as they skirted an elderly couple walking their dog. The tiny white toy poodle gave a shrill bark and then went about its business of sniffing the ground. "They still see me as the enemy."

"Are you serious?" Kelly shot him a surprised look. "The fans adore you."

Matt snorted. "They adore Rick Taylor. Me, they just tolerate."

"Your jersey is selling like hotcakes—Angie's words, not mine. And we've sold out every home game since you joined the team."

"Whatever." He shoved his hands into the front pockets of his Blaze sweatshirt. It was damn cold, yet Kelly didn't seem affected by it at all. Maybe it was growing up in Southern California, he was used to much warmer weather in the summer. "Don't attribute it to me. The team's been on a hot streak and the fans are dying to see the Blaze win the division."

"You're helping them get there. Don't discount your contribution, Matt." The sincerity in her voice rattled him. Or maybe it was the thick beat of awareness that had threatened to consume him ever since he'd sat next to her at the softball field. Her face was covered in dirt, her uniform was filthy, but watching her play tonight, he couldn't help but wonder if she was as passionate in the bedroom as she was on the field. If anyone had told him he would be thinking about what Kelly Maxwell was like in bed the first night they'd met, he would have said they were out of their mind. But now, here he was, thinking about it. It wasn't the first time either. That night at the hotel in Philly when he'd put his arm around her and pulled her body against his, he'd wondered then.

"Is it always this cold in August?" he asked, trying to ignore the feelings Kelly stirred in him. It wasn't working. His mind went right to the image of her standing in her kitchen wearing almost nothing, her body athletic and sexy as hell.

She shot him a cursory glance. "You're changing the subject."

"Am I?" Matt grinned. "But honestly, it's August."

"It warms up a bit in late September and early October," she said as they rounded the corner on 2nd Street. He moved closer to Kelly to let a couple holding hands pass by. That it was two men didn't faze him—this was San Francisco, after all.

"Who was it that said that thing about the coldest winter they ever spent was a summer in San Francisco?" he asked, thinking of the famous quote.

"I believe it was Mark Twain," she said as they stopped in front of her building. "You'll get used to it. Next season you won't even notice it."

"I probably won't be here next year."

Kelly's smiled faded, and was that a stricken look on her face? No. Couldn't be. She was probably counting the days until Rick Taylor returned to the Blaze, and he was shipped off to God knows where.

"Why do you say that?"

Matt shrugged. "Taylor will be back in time for spring training. The Blaze only brought me here because they lost him for the year. You know how it works, Kelly. He's good, and he's young."

"You're not old."

"I'm thirty-one. That's getting up there for a ball-player. Especially a catcher."

"You're in excellent shape and you've never had any major injuries."

She was playing devil's advocate, but why? "You sound like you want me to stay. I'm surprised. I know for a fact you were livid when the Blaze picked up my contract."

One dark brow arched. "How'd you know that?"

"Kayla told Sean and he told me."

"Oh." She bit her full bottom lip. "Well, that was when I hated you."

"And now you don't?"

Averting her eyes, she shrugged. "You're not so bad."

"You're not so bad yourself."

"We got off on the wrong foot." She reached into the side pocket of her gym bag to pull out her keys, still avoiding his gaze. "Thanks for walking me home," she said as she reached for the door handle.

"Wait." He touched her arm, not wanting her to disappear just yet. "What time should we leave for the party tomorrow?" he asked as she pivoted to give him a questioning look.

"About five. Dorie gave me the address. She and Lily live in the Richmond district. Parking can be a bitch so we want to make sure we give ourselves plenty of time."

"Where is the Richmond district?" Although San Francisco was fairly small geographically, he hadn't done much sightseeing. In fact, other than an occasional run down to Fisherman's Wharf and back, he'd done none at all.

"How about I drive?" she offered. "I know my way around the city."

"Works for me."

"Meet me in my lobby at five tomorrow and we'll go down to the garage to get my car."

"Hey," he said as she pulled the glass door open. Bracing her hand on the door frame, she turned to look at him. "That pick in the top of the third inning was dead on. You have a great arm."

Color suffused her cheeks. "Thanks. The jerk basically dared me to throw him out."

"I noticed he shut his trap after you did."

"I have that effect on men," she said dryly. "You're the only one who ever gave me any real lip."

"I'm not like most guys."

Her soft laugh was as husky and sexy as her voice. It sent a lick of heat up his spine. "You're certainly not." She glanced at her sports watch. "I should go up, it's late."

Matt stood at the door and watched her as she crossed the lobby and stood in front of the elevator. After she pressed the call button, Kelly turned to meet his gaze and smiled. The way it lit up her heart-shaped face was breathtaking. *Damn.* He could get used to being on the receiving end of that smile. Giving her a final wave, he headed toward King Street, feeling lighter than he had in more than a year. The gnawing ache in his heart, while not completely gone, had eased just a bit. Maybe being traded to San Francisco had been a blessing in disguise.

"WELL, DON'T YOU look lovely?" Kelly grumbled as she pulled the elastic band out of her hair and observed her dirt-covered face in the mirror. Tossing the band next to her baseball cap on the vanity, she moved to the shower enclosure just as her cell phone rang. Since it was understood she was on call 24/7, she glanced longingly at the shower before leaving the bathroom and crossing the bedroom to pick up her phone from the dresser. If, for some reason, one of the guys had gotten himself arrested, or accidentally put a bullet in some part of his anatomy with a concealed weapon he wasn't licensed to carry, she was going to be royally pissed. The only thing she wanted right now was a hot shower.

Her annoyance disappeared the moment she saw her

sister's name on the caller ID. Eagerly, she answered the phone. "How's paradise?"

"Amazing," Kayla replied happily. "It's not too late to call, is it?"

"No. I just got home from my softball game."

"Did you win?"

"We're the champs."

"Congrats. How come you're not out celebrating?"

"Early meeting with Katherine tomorrow morning." Kelly moved to the end of the bed and sank down on the homemade quilt her mother had given to her for Christmas. Her mother hadn't sewn it—Patricia Maxwell wasn't domestic—but she swore it was handmade because she'd bought it in a quilt store in the Danish-themed town of Solvang on a road trip to L.A. to visit Kayla.

"How's it going on the set?" Kayla was taking a break from her role on *A New Dawn* to film an HBO mini-series about Pearl Harbor. She was on the island of Oahu filming exterior scenes.

"It's wonderful." Kayla's sigh sounded particularly blissful. "Everything is wonderful. Sean's here." Her voice lowered. "He's in the shower right now."

Kelly grinned. "Why are you whispering?"

"Because he'll be done in a minute and then we're going out to celebrate. I wanted to tell you the good news before we left."

"What good news?"

"Sean asked me to marry him."

"*What!* Oh my God." Kelly squealed in delight and almost slipped off the bed in her excitement. "Are you kidding me?"

"No. It was on the beach at sunset. It was so romantic, like one of those chick flicks you love."

"I don't love chick flicks," she protested. Just like her childhood nickname, she didn't want word getting out that she *occasionally* watched romantic comedies. That was classified information and if it got out, it would *not* be good for her hard-as-nails reputation.

"Yes, you do." Kayla laughed. "*Pretty Woman* is your favorite movie."

"Actually, my favorite movie is the one where your head got chopped off. It's a classic. I particularly liked the way your head rolled several feet after that psycho chopped it off with the meat cleaver. How'd they do that? Trick photography?"

"They took an impression of my face and made a fake head, you doofus."

"But it was so real." Kelly shifted on the bed. "I assume you said yes. To Sean's proposal, I mean."

"Of course I said yes. I'm totally in love with him."

"When's the wedding?"

"We haven't set a date, but we talked about having an engagement party soon and you, Mom and Dad have to be there."

"I wouldn't miss it." Kelly sniffed and began to trace the quilt pattern with her index finger. "My baby sister is getting married."

"I know. Can you believe it?"

"It was obvious when I was there in July that you and Sean were crazy about each other."

"Speaking of which. How are you and Matt getting along?"

"Better. He finally apologized to me for that night in the restaurant."

Kayla let out a soft snort. "It's about time."

Kelly bit her lip. Now that Matt had apologized, she couldn't ignore her own behavior any longer. "If we're being completely honest, I wasn't exactly 'Miss Manners' that night myself."

"Hmm. I sense a certain softening toward the man with the obsidian eyes."

"Obsidian eyes?" Her finger stilled on the quilt. "Where'd that come from?"

"From you." Kayla sounded surprised. "Don't you remember? You told me he had obsidian eyes."

"I did not."

"Yes. You did."

Kelly scowled. "I don't use words like that."

"I know. That's why it stuck with me. Usually you're swearing up a storm."

"I've cut back," she said defensively. "I don't swear nearly as much as I used to."

"Mom will be happy to hear that." Kayla paused. "Hey, if you happen to talk to Mom or Dad, don't let on about the engagement. I'm going to call them tomorrow to tell them the news. Oh, Kel, I'm so happy." The joy in her sister's voice caused her eyes to well up again. If anyone deserved to be happy, it was Kayla, who was, like, the nicest person in the universe. "I've gotta go." Kayla's voice lowered. "I'll call you this weekend when we can talk longer."

"I can't wait to hear all the details." She rose from the bed to move to the dresser. "Oh wait, how did Sean do with the ring selection?"

"It's absolutely gorgeous," Kayla whispered. "I'll take a picture with my cell phone and text it to you."

"I can't wait to see it." She smiled at the hushed excitement in her sister's voice. "Enjoy your celebration. I love you."

"Love you too."

Kelly returned the phone to the nightstand and headed for the bathroom, unbuttoning her uniform as she crossed the room. Kayla had sounded over the moon about Sean's proposal. As she stripped off her clothes in the bathroom, she couldn't help but imagine how it would feel to have a man she was madly in love with propose to her on a romantic tropical island. Moving to the shower, she turned on the water, closed her eyes and imagined fine white sand between her toes and a warm sea breeze tickling her skin as a man with obsidian eyes slipped a diamond on her finger just before he leaned forward and—

She opened her eyes and groaned. *Good God.* Was she insane? Yes, she had to be to be daydreaming about a marriage proposal from a man who looked a lot like Matt Scanlon. Stepping into the shower, she gasped as the cold water pelted her skin. It was a good thing. A cold shower was exactly what she needed.

EARLY THE NEXT MORNING, Kelly stared at the picture of Kayla's engagement ring, impressed as hell. The round diamond solitaire with side stones was breathtaking—at least four carats, if she had to guess. Which she would, since she wasn't a connoisseur of fine diamonds. "That is some rock," she murmured as she rose from her chair and slipped her phone into her pocket.

After rifling through the in-box on her desk, she cast an irritated glance at her watch. She was due to meet with Katherine in fifteen minutes and Alexis still hadn't submitted the statistical data she'd asked for on the team's website. When she left her office, she saw Angie at the end of the hall in deep conversation with another accounting employee. Seeing her friend reminded her of how J.T. had supposedly tagged along with Angie to Kamu's after last night's game. What was up with that? Was J.T. interested? She'd definitely have to follow up with Angie about that.

Kelly detoured to her left and moved down a row of identical gray cubicles. At the end of the row was the one occupied by Alexis, but unfortunately, her intern wasn't at her desk. She wasn't one to intrude into another person's workspace but she really needed that website information.

Moving into the cubicle, she scanned the papers sitting on top of the desk but as far as she could see the data she was looking for wasn't there. To her left, there was a step file with several colored folders arranged in precise order next to a shallow bowl filled with assorted paperclips in the shape of stars. One of the folders had a label that read *Website*. Moving to reach for it, her foot came into sharp contact with Alexis's small garbage can.

"Damn it," she muttered as the can toppled over and several pieces of trash spilled out onto the carpeted floor. Bending over, she picked up the crumpled papers and an empty coffee cup before righting the overturned trashcan. As she went to throw the cup and papers into the can, she noticed an empty large-size bag of chocolate chip cookies as well as two flattened hot apple pie containers from McDonald's.

"What are you doing?" Alexis's accusatory tone startled her. She straightened to find the girl standing at the entrance of the cubicle glaring at her. "Are you going through my trash?"

"No." Kelly held up the folder. "I was looking for the information I needed for my meeting with Katherine. You were supposed to have it for me by eight. It's almost nine."

Alexis's affronted expression changed immediately to one of contrition. "I'm sorry," she whispered, pushing a lock of blond hair behind her ear and then smoothing her hands down her plaid skirt. "It… It was ready. I just forgot to put it on your desk." Alexis's guilty gaze darted to the trash can. "I'm really sorry."

"Are you all right?" Kelly clutched the file folder to her chest, her gut telling her that her suspicions about Alexis were on the money. She was almost certain the girl had an eating disorder.

"I'm fine." Alexis gnawed on her fingernail. "I didn't mean to snap at you. I've had a bad morning."

Bad enough to stuff herself full of chocolate chip cookies and two hot apple pies? Kelly was no stranger to that routine, or to where it led—straight to the bathroom to purge, or to the gym to exercise. Since Alexis hadn't come from the gym, it wasn't a stretch to assume she'd just come from the ladies' room.

"We all have those kinds of mornings," she said softly, not quite sure how to handle the situation, or even if she should intervene. If there was one thing she knew from her own experience, it was that if Alexis did have a problem she had to first admit it to herself. Most women with eating disorders were in denial for years, no matter how many people tried to help them. Some would seek treatment, but a good percentage never did.

Kelly stepped around Alexis and moved into the hallway. "I'll be with Katherine for about an hour. I've emailed you several letters to format." Turning, she noted that Alexis had moved the garbage can out of sight under her desk. "Have them ready for my signature when I return."

Without waiting for Alexis to reply, she strode quickly down cubicle row. As she entered her office, she went over her options. There were only two—talk to Alexis, or keep quiet. Keeping quiet went against her nature. She'd once been in Alexis's shoes. How could she, in good conscience, not try to help her?

TEN

MATT STARED AT KELLY, mouth agape, over the roof of her car. "*This* is yours?"

Kelly let her gaze wander over the car. Its white paint with blue racing trim gleamed under the bright lights in the underground garage. She inserted her key into the lock and turned it. "Yes. Is there a problem?"

"You drive a '69 Trans Am?"

"Apparently so." She opened the door, amused by the dumbstruck expression on his face. "Are you okay? You're a little pale."

"Where did you get this?" he asked, ignoring her question.

"My dad. He restored it and gave it to me for my high school graduation."

"But...but you don't even like cars."

"I like cars. I'm just not all gaga over them like *some* people," she said, giving him a pointed look. For the life of her, she'd never understand the fascination with cars. They were a mode of transportation. A way to get from point A to point B. No more, no less.

"This is a classic." Matt skimmed his palm over the roof as if he were caressing a lover. Gently. Reverently. "Do you know how hard it is to get one of these babies?"

"I'm vaguely aware of the difficulty." She tossed her purse behind the blue leather bucket seat and then climbed inside. Leaning to her right, she unlocked the passenger door. Matt slid inside, holding his wrapped gift for Lily, and pulled the door closed. His large body took up a lot of space, but that didn't stop him from shifting in his seat to check out the back.

"This is sweet," he said with a hint of awe in his voice. "Your dad does good work. It's pristine."

"Hey, give me a little credit. I may not be as nuts about cars as Dad and Kayla are, but I take care of it." After sliding the key into the ignition, she closed her door. "Do you want to know the best thing about this car?" she asked him with a sly smile.

"What?"

"It goes really fast."

His eyes widened with wariness. "Don't tell me you've got a lead foot?"

"Let's just say I know my way around traffic court." Kelly turned the key and as the powerful engine roared to life, she grinned. "Fasten your seat belt."

THE RICHMOND DISTRICT was closer to the ocean and therefore was cooler and, frequently, much foggier than the SoMa district. This evening there was no fog, just a slight chill in the air that made Kelly grateful she'd chosen to wear her favorite brown suede knee-high boots and a short trench coat over her skirt and blouse. She and Matt had just walked three blocks. Street parking was difficult to find in San Francisco, which meant she'd had to circle the area four times before she'd found an open space.

"Have you considered a career in racing?" Matt asked as they climbed the brick steps to Dorie and Lily's house near the corner of California and 21st Ave. "You're like Speed Racer, or something."

"Who's Speed Racer?" she asked, unfamiliar with the odd name. "Is he a professional driver?"

Matt chuckled. "No. He's a character from a cartoon I watched when I was a kid. He drove a cool car, had a girlfriend named Trixie and a chimp for a pet."

"I was a Scooby Doo fan, myself," she said as they reached the porch. "I didn't scare you, did I? My driving sometimes has that effect on people."

"Oh, no." He shook his head. "I've always enjoyed that chase scene in *Bullet*. You gave Steve McQueen a run for his money."

Kelly smiled, tucked a stray lock of hair behind her ear and tried not to notice his spicy cologne. Earlier, in the close confines of her car, awareness of him had filled every pore in her body. And it didn't help her equilibrium any that he looked absolutely delicious in his dark-wash jeans, gray pullover and black sport coat.

As Matt shifted Lily's gift to his other hand and reached for the doorbell, Kelly admired the oval stained-glass inlay in the door as the bell chimed inside the house. She glanced at Matt and noted his somber expression.

"Everything okay?" Just seconds ago he was laughing, now he seemed apprehensive.

"I hope Lily likes the jacket."

"She'll love it. I think what matters most is that you're—" She broke off as the door opened. An elderly woman with beautiful silver hair and blue eyes that were moist and red-rimmed stared at them with a somber expression on her lined face.

Were they at the right house? There didn't seem to be a birthday party going on at this address.

"Are you Kelly?" the woman asked in a low raspy voice.

"Yes." She looked past the woman into the large living room. Save for an orange tabby cat sitting regally on a floral love seat, the room was empty. The hairs on her arms stood up—something was terribly wrong. "This is Dorie and Lily's house, isn't it?"

The woman nodded and swung her gaze to Matt. "You're Matt Scanlon. Lily was so excited…" Her voice choked as tears filled her eyes.

"What happened to Lily?" Dread closed around Kelly's heart like a vise. She forced herself to remain calm as she cast a glance at Matt. He stood stiffly beside her, his mouth pressed into a taut line. "Is she okay?"

"The ambulance took her to the hospital about fifteen minutes ago." The woman put a gnarled hand to her mouth and shook her head. A tear spilled down her cheek, followed by another. Her shoulders shook and then she bowed her head and let out a subdued sob.

Kelly stepped forward and put her hand gently on the woman's thin arm. "Ma'am, can you tell us what happened?"

After several seconds, the woman lifted her head. She wiped her eyes and then reached into the pocket of her black cardigan and pulled out a crumpled tissue. After dabbing at her nose, she nodded. "Lily had an episode."

"Was it a heart attack?" Matt asked in a bleak voice from behind her.

"I'm not sure. It all happened so fast." The woman paused. "This isn't the first time. Lily was in the hospital a few months ago."

"Are you Lily's grandmother?" Kelly squeezed the woman's arm gently.

"No. I'm Frances Limer, a neighbor. I've known Lily her whole life." Frances's smile was tremulous. "She's a fighter, that one."

"What hospital did they take her to?"

"UCSF Medical Center." Frances stuffed the tissue back into her pocket. "Dorie asked me to stay here and let you know what happened. She said she'll call you and give you an update as soon as she can."

"Are you going to be all right?" Kelly asked, concerned that Frances was too upset to be alone. "Would you like us to stay with you for a while?"

Frances shook her head. "I'll be fine." She patted Kelly's hand. "But thank you for the offer. It's very kind of you." She looked at Matt, her lips, feathered with fine lines, curved in a tremulous smile. "You're all she's talked about since that charity game. She was beside herself with joy when you agreed to come to her party. Lily's your biggest fan."

"I know." Matt's voice was strained. "And I'm hers. She's a special little girl."

"That she is." Frances's voice cracked and she reached for the tissue again. "I hope she's got a little more fight left in her."

AFTER PULLING THE Trans Am into her designated parking space, Kelly turned off the ignition. "You haven't said a word since we left Lily's house. Are you okay?"

Matt stared straight ahead. His view was a gray concrete wall with a Reserved for Tenant sign posted prominently. "I'm fine."

Shifting in her seat, she studied his tense profile, noticing a slight tick in his jaw. He wasn't fine—not even close. "Do you want to talk about it?"

"About what?"

"About Lily. I know you're worried. So am I."

"Talking about it won't change anything."

"It might make you feel better." Or would it make her feel better? She hadn't been able to get Lily out of her mind since they'd left Dorie's house.

After an imperceptible shake of his head, he said, "I doubt it."

"Why don't you give it a try," Kelly suggested.

"No. Talking only makes it worse. Trust me. I know that from firsthand experience." He turned to look at her then, the lights of the garage spilled into the car, illuminating his face. His narrow gaze sharpened on her. She shivered. Again, he reminded her of a pirate—dark, brooding and dangerous. "The best you can do is to find something to make you forget."

Call it a hunch, or maybe a gut feeling, but what had happened with Lily had triggered something painful for Matt. On the drive back from the Richmond district tension had emanated off of him in waves.

"Is that what you've been doing for the past year?"

His brows lowered and his eyes turned to granite. "What are you talking about?"

"You were the poster boy for good behavior until just over a year ago. And then, all of a sudden, you started getting into fights on the field, partying it up with strippers and porn stars and—"

"I've never partied or done anything else with porn stars," Matt said, a scowl darkening his face.

"Sorry, my bad. Just strippers, right?" She lifted her chin and met his angry gaze. "And let's not forget groupies like Tiffany. I bet she knew all the right moves to

take your mind off of whatever the hell you've been trying to forget."

"Are you jealous?" His mouth twisted into a smirk.

Outraged, Kelly was left speechless. For about five
seconds. "*Jealous? Are you kidding me?*" She pulled
the key out of the ignition and opened her door. "Like
I would ever be jealous of a...a bimbo like her." With
quick movements, she unlatched her seat belt, grabbed
her purse and climbed out of the car. After slamming
the door, she stalked toward the elevator, fuming. The
nerve of the man. Jealous? Of a cleat chaser who'd un-
doubtedly screwed dozens of ballplayers? Not likely.

When she reached the elevator, she jabbed at the call
button furiously. She heard footsteps, but didn't turn
around. Matt Scanlon could go to hell for all she cared.

"Punching that thing won't make the elevator come
any faster." The amusement in his voice only fueled
her anger.

"Shut up." She hit the button again, for good measure
and as if in answer to her silent prayer, the doors slid
open. Not sparing him a glance, she stepped inside and
automatically hit the button for her floor. Matt slipped
in as the doors began to close. With casual grace, he
leaned against the stainless-steel panel opposite her as
the elevator ascended. The elevator was roomier than
the interior of her car, but still, his larger-than-life presence filled it.

As upset as she was, she was affected by his powerful body, his scent and those dark bedroom eyes of his.
Damn it all. She really hated that he could get to her
like no man ever had. Kelly hit the lobby button but it
was too late, they'd bypassed the lobby and were heading to the sixth floor.

Crossing her arms over her chest, she leveled her gaze at Matt. "You can take the elevator back down once we get to my floor." She paused. "And for the record, I'm not jealous of your little plaything."

"Could have fooled me." His cocky grin ticked her off even more. She opened her mouth to fling a doozy of a curse word at him and then it dawned on her what he was doing. Oh, he was good. He was *real* good. But she was better.

"Don't think I don't know what this is about. I'm on to you, Matt."

His brows rose. "On to me?"

"That's right. I was getting a little too close for comfort and it scared you."

"I'm not scared of anything."

"Yes, you are. You're afraid Lily's going to die." She tilted her head and, seeing his suddenly stricken face, softened. Why was she picking a fight with Matt when Lily was fighting for her life? "I'm scared too," she admitted.

Matt averted his eyes, concentrating on the elevator's safety certificate above the red emergency button. The chime sounded, indicating they'd reached the sixth floor. The doors opened but neither of them moved.

"I'm afraid I'll go to bed tonight and wake up in the morning and hear that Lily…" she whispered as unexpected tears welled in her eyes. Mortified at losing her composure in front of him, she fled the elevator and practically ran down the softly lit hallway. When she reached her door, her keys slipped from her shaky fingers and hit the carpeted floor with a dull thud. "Damn it," she muttered and bent to pick them up. When she straightened she found Matt standing next to her.

For one insane second she longed for him to take her in his strong arms and comfort her. She wasn't a woman who needed comforting often, but Lily Lovett had touched her too, and the thought that Lily could be dying right now had shaken her more than she'd realized.

"Are you all right?" Matt's gentle tone was almost her undoing.

"No." With a trembling hand, Kelly unlocked the door, stepped inside and hit the wall switch. Light flooded the living room, illuminating the sleek furniture that had come with the sublet. It wasn't her style. Too stark and modern. "I could use a beer," she said, turning toward Matt, who was still standing at the threshold. "Do you want one?"

"Sounds good," he said, then entered the apartment and closed the door behind him.

She motioned toward the couch. "Have a seat, I'll be right back."

When she returned from the kitchen, Matt had taken off his sport coat and draped it over a side chair. He sat on the couch, his large frame almost dwarfing it. Kelly couldn't help but notice the gray pullover sweater emphasized his broad shoulders and powerful arms. Rounding the couch, she handed him a beer and then moved to the gas fireplace opposite where he was sitting and turned the silver key next to the mantel. Flames spurted and danced merrily behind fake logs. Staring at the fire, she sipped her beer and then turned to find Matt's eyes on her.

"I didn't mean to fall apart like that in the elevator." Moving toward the coffee table, she set her beer down and unbelted her trench coat. After shrugging out of it, she tossed it on the black leather chair next to the couch.

"It happens." He shrugged, lifted his bottle to his lips and took a long pull of his beer. He searched her face and then his gaze traveled quickly down her body before he turned his attention to the fire.

"Not to me." Moving past the chair she sank down on the couch next to him. "Being too soft in this business is a weakness." With a mirthless laugh, she quoted the famous movie phrase, "There's no crying in baseball."

"This isn't baseball. This is life…and death." His words had been quietly spoken, but the dark pain in his eyes pierced her soul and at the same time triggered something else. Something she'd been wondering about even before she'd met him—the reason for his yearlong meltdown.

"That's it, isn't it? Someone you loved died." The words slipped out before she could stop them and by the tightening of his jaw, it was evident she'd struck a nerve.

Maybe she was way off base, but it would explain his sudden change of behavior on and off the baseball field. The loss of a loved one could send anyone over the deep end—even someone as strong as Matt. The only thing was she hadn't heard of any tragedy surrounding him. If someone close to him had died, it would have been all over the media—he was that big of a sports star. But there had been nothing. Not one word.

"I don't want to talk about it." He averted his eyes, staring at the fireplace as he took another long draw on his beer.

"You don't have to." She plucked at the hem of her skirt. "Lord knows I've been through a few things in my life that I don't care to share with anyone."

"Then I guess we have that in common." He leaned forward to set his bottle on the glass coffee table. He

looked around the room, and not with a lot of appreciation. "Did you pick out this furniture?"

"Hell, no." She smiled, sharing his distaste for the
modern decor. "We're subletting the place from Stacia's
godfather. He furnished it."

"Where is Stacia?"

"On her way back from Tokyo. I think the flight she's
working gets in sometime this evening." Kelly froze
at the sound of her cell phone ringing in the kitchen.
"That could be Dorie," she said, and quickly rose from
the couch. She rushed into the kitchen and reached for
her purse sitting atop the counter. Frantically, she rummaged through it and finally found her phone in the inside pocket. "Hello," she said, breathless with worry.

"Kelly, it's me, Dorie."

Turning, Kelly nodded at Matt, who had followed her
into the kitchen. "Dorie, what's going on? How's Lily?"

"She's stable."

Kelly let out a relieved breath. "That's good news.
What happened?"

"Lily had some chest pain and dizziness. This has
happened before so I called an ambulance. She fainted
right before they arrived."

"Was it a heart attack?" She lifted her hand and
rubbed her temple as Matt moved to stand next to her.

"Part of Lily's heart is enlarged. They've been treating it with medication but her doctor is recommending
surgery to remove the enlargement."

"Surgery?" she whispered, lowering her hand to
Matt's forearm and squeezing tightly. The thought of
Lily having heart surgery was frightening. "When?"

"In about a month." Dorie paused and then continued

in a steady voice, "This has always been a possibility. Is it okay if I call you tomorrow? I need to get back to Lily."

"Yes…call me tomorrow. Lily is your most important concern right now."

"Thanks, Kelly. Tell Matt he was the first person Lily asked about when she woke up."

"I will."

"How is she?" Matt asked as she put the phone on the counter.

"Dorie said she's stable, and awake." She let go of his arm and turned toward the counter, bracing her palms on the rounded edge to try to gather her roiling emotions. "Lily asked for you when she woke up."

"You said surgery," he said from behind her. "Is it a heart transplant?"

"No. A part of her heart is enlarged. They're going to remove that part."

"That sounds serious."

Kelly nodded and imagined a fragile Lily on the operating table. She squeezed her eyes shut as if that could block out the awful image. It didn't work. Soon that sweet little girl would have her chest cut open and a part of her heart would be removed. People died every day from even the simplest of surgeries. This wasn't even close to simple.

"I'm scared," she whispered as a tear slid down her cheek. "I'm afraid for Lily, and for Dorie. But she was so calm on the phone just now." She lifted her hand to wipe the wetness from her cheek. "How can that be? I barely know Lily and I'm a damn basket case right now."

"Dorie has to be calm. For Lily." Matt rested his hand on her shoulder. It was warm, comforting. "Inside, she's just as frightened as we are. Probably more."

"So you admit it," she said and turned from the counter. Matt lowered his hand from her shoulder. "You're scared."

"Yes." He searched her face with haunted eyes. "I admit it, but it doesn't make me feel any better."

"I wish I had some ice cream," she said, longing for something to take her mind off of Lily and what she was going through.

His lips quirked in a smile. "Is that your weakness? Ice cream?"

"It used to be."

"What's your weakness now?" Matt lifted his hand and brushed her hair back from her face with gentle fingers. She shivered, suddenly aware of how close he was. A warning voice inside her head implored her to step back, but she couldn't move. His mesmerizing eyes held her captive.

"I don't have one." Well, that wasn't quite true. Her knees felt a little weak. Almost like rubber. Did that count? "What's yours?" she asked as his fingers slid slowly, reverently, down the length of her hair.

"Do you really want to know?" His gaze lowered to her lips and his husky voice sent a shiver of anticipation down her spine. For a long moment she couldn't speak, her senses were filled with the scent of warm spice, and the smoldering heat in his eyes sent a jolt of sexual energy through her body that rocked her to her core.

"Yes." Her breath caught in her throat when he moved his hand behind her head and threaded his fingers in the long strands of her hair. He lifted his gaze from her lips to stare deeply into her eyes. Time stood still. Her heart, not so much. It was pounding like crazy.

"Right now. You are," Matt whispered, then fisted his

hand in her hair, leaned forward and captured her mouth in a kiss that made her head reel. With a low moan, she pressed the softness of her body into the hardness of his, reveling in the forceful demand of his mouth.

Sliding her arms around his waist, she arched against him and opened her mouth, eager for the taste and the feel of his tongue stroking hers. A lick of desire, hot and sizzling, ignited inside of her; she was burning up from the inside out. No longer able to deny the delicious heat of carnal attraction, she slid her hands under his sweater and touched his bare skin. It was warm and supple. He groaned against her mouth, splayed his other hand on her lower back and kissed her even more voraciously.

Lost in a vortex of passion, she didn't hear the sound of the front door opening, but Stacia's voice managed to penetrate her consciousness.

"Kelly?"

Kelly froze and pulled her lips from Matt's. He opened his eyes. They were dark and aroused.

"Are you here?" Stacia called out and then Kelly heard the front door close.

The sensual expression on Matt's face turned to annoyance. Immediately, she dropped her arms from around his waist. He released her and moved to the other side of the kitchen, running a hand through his disheveled hair.

"In here." Kelly smoothed her palms down her skirt and took a deep breath. It didn't help one bit—she was still feeling the effects of Matt's blazing kiss. She didn't look at him. She couldn't if she was going to regain some semblance of normalcy. How the hell did he do it? She'd never been this turned on, this quickly.

"My flight got in earlier than expected," Stacia was

saying as she entered the kitchen, still in her flight attendant uniform. As soon as Stacia saw Matt, she stopped in her tracks and stared at him, taken aback by his presence. "What are you doing here?" she asked and looked at Kelly. "What's going on?"

"Nothing," Kelly said in the most nonchalant voice she could muster. She didn't want to discuss Lily with Stacia. "Matt has an interview tomorrow and we were going over some potential questions."

It was lame and she knew it. Even Stacia knew it. Her eyes narrowed with suspicion but she didn't say a word. Instead she crossed the kitchen to open the refrigerator. "I'm hungry," Stacia said, peering inside.

"I was just leaving." Matt moved past Stacia and headed for the living room. "Thanks for your help, Kelly."

"I'll see you out," Kelly said, trailing behind him and leaving Stacia in the kitchen. Watching him grab his sport coat, all she could think about was the kiss, and how pissed off she was that Stacia's ill-timed arrival had interrupted it.

Stepping around Stacia's travel bag, she opened the door for Matt. Once he was in the hallway, she followed him out and closed the door behind her.

"You're a good liar." His eyes flickered with amusement.

"Thanks. I think." She smiled, leaned against the door and let her gaze roam over his handsome face. Unable to resist, she focused on his lips and unconsciously licked hers.

"Don't do that," Matt said in a low thick voice filled with frustration. Kelly knew the feeling. She was frustrated as hell right now.

"Sorry."

"Your lips were already driving me crazy."

They were?

"Will you let me know if you hear from Dorie tomorrow?" he asked as he pulled on his sport coat. The coat fit him like a glove and he looked devastatingly handsome in it, but at the moment what she really wanted was an up-close-and-personal look at what she'd glimpsed in the locker room a few weeks ago.

"Of course," she said and tamped down the erotic images running through her head. "Thank you for...for being here when I lost it."

"You're welcome." Matt lifted his hand to her cheek and caressed her skin. Kelly shivered. *Good God.* If the man could do that with a mere touch of his fingers, what could he accomplish with a full arsenal?

ELEVEN

MATT HATED HOSPITALS—with good reason. He was certain the children's hospital at UCSF Medical Center was a top-notch facility but as he walked toward Lily's room, the cloying antiseptic smell that all hospitals seemed to have, invaded his senses and triggered memories so vivid that the only reason he didn't turn around and walk out was because it would hurt Lily's feelings.

When he'd returned from his morning run along the wharf, he'd discovered two voice mails on his cell phone. One was from Sean. It was short and to the point. Sean had proposed to Kayla and she'd accepted. There would be an engagement party next month and Sean and Kayla were trying to schedule it on one of the Blaze's off days so Matt could attend. The other message was from Kelly. Even before he'd heard her husky voice, he'd been thinking about her. Kissing her last night hadn't been planned, but he wasn't one damn bit sorry it happened.

Kelly's voice mail was brief and also to the point. Dorie had called her again this morning and informed her that while Lily was improving, she would be staying in the hospital for a few more days for observation. She'd left him Lily's room number and the visiting hours in case Matt wanted to pay her a visit.

Clutching Lily's birthday present, which he'd had the presence of mind to retrieve from Kelly's car after he'd left her condo last night, he nodded at a nurse coming out of a patient's room and then sidestepped a wheel-chair being pushed by another nurse. In the chair was a young boy with a smooth bald head and an all-too-familiar pallor. Matt's heart clenched and he dug his fingers into the gift-wrapped box.

Engrossed in their conversation, neither the boy, nor the nurse, gave him a second glance. The boy was smil-ing at the nurse, who was gazing affectionately at her young charge. He'd witnessed, firsthand, the bond that could develop between seriously ill children and those who cared for them. He'd also witnessed the pain those nurses felt when their patients didn't survive. More often than not, they were as devastated as the parents.

Pushing away memories still too difficult to think about, he focused on room numbers and as he reached Lily's room, Kelly walked out. Surprised to see her, he stopped short, the soles of his shoes making a squeaky sound on the shiny linoleum.

"You got my message," she said and halted in front of him. She was dressed in her work clothes but that didn't stop him from remembering how sexy she'd looked in the short skirt and knee-high boots she'd worn last night, or how perfectly her body had fit against his. As usual, her hair was pulled back into a ponytail; now that he knew how soft it was, he itched to pull the band from her hair and let it flow over her shoulders.

"Lily will be thrilled to see you," Kelly continued as she slipped the strap of her purse over her shoulder. Her demeanor was totally professional. There was no indica-tion she was at all affected by the kiss they'd shared last night. It irritated him. He wanted her as hot and bothered by that kiss as he was. "She's already antsy to go home."

"I don't blame her." Matt couldn't help but grimace.

He'd just gotten here and, despite his affection for Lily, he couldn't wait to get the hell out.

"I see you brought her birthday present," she said with a smile. Unable to resist, he focused on her full lips and felt the thick beat of lust in his blood. *What the hell was happening?* He'd kissed at least a dozen women in the past year but none of them had left him like this—aching for more. Furthermore, none of them had ever tempted him to talk about the most devastating thing that had ever happened to him. But last night he'd almost spilled his guts. He wasn't sure if it was because she'd come close to figuring it out, or if it was the genuine compassion he'd seen in her eyes. For one crazy moment he'd believed that maybe, just maybe, confiding in Kelly would set him free.

"Matt?"

"Sorry. What did you say?" he asked, meeting her puzzled gaze.

"I asked if you wanted me to wait and drive you back to the ballpark. Did you take a taxi here?"

"No. I drove. The SUV I'm renting has GPS."

"Well, then, I'll see you later." She pulled her keys from the side pocket of her purse. "I've got a meeting with Rizzo in an hour."

"Why?"

The change in Kelly's expression reminded him of a stormy day—dark and foreboding. "Just a discussion about media policy."

Her vague answer meant that Rizzo was probably doing something he shouldn't—par for the course for the arrogant bastard. He didn't envy her having to deal with the guy, but if anyone could put Rizzo in his place, it was her. Funny how the one thing that used to piss

him off about her now garnered his admiration. Kelly
Maxwell was tough, but inside there was a softness not
many people got the opportunity to see.

"Good luck with that," he said with a grin.

"Thanks. I'll need it."

Matt watched her walk down the corridor and admired the gentle sway of her hips that even the pants
and blazer couldn't conceal. Tearing his gaze from her,
he turned and stepped inside Lily's room. It was eerily
similar to the last hospital room he'd been in. Right
down to the sterile white walls and vertical blinds in
the windows.

"Matt." Lily looked up from the baseball she was
holding, a happy grin wreathing her face. "You came."

"Was there ever any doubt?" He moved into the room
and managed a grin even as it broke his heart to see Lily
hooked up to a monitor that continuously flashed her
vital signs and beeped ominously. He swallowed hard
and managed to keep a smile on his face. "Where's your
mom?" he asked, looking around the room. There was
another bed, but it was empty.

"She went home to shower and change. She's bringing me some books to read." Lily pushed her glasses up
to the bridge of her nose and held up the baseball. The
bed was in an upright position and despite the paleness of
her face she seemed in good spirits. "Look, Matt. Kelly
gave me this ball. It's signed by all the Blaze players."

"Sweet. Trade you," Matt said and took the ball from
Lily's outstretched hand while he handed her the gift
he'd planned to give to her last night.

"What you'd get me?" Lily asked as she eyed the rectangular box wrapped with baseball-themed gift wrap
he'd found at the drugstore not far from his building.

"Open it and find out." Instead of tearing off the paper, Lily painstakingly slid her index finger under each flap to loosen the tape. Then she turned the box over and did the same with the tape along the long seam down the middle. "Are you saving the paper or something?" he asked with amusement as he moved to the visitor chair next to the bed and sat down.

Lily giggled and gave him a shy smile. "I like to open presents super slow. It lasts longer that way."

Matt eased back in the chair. "I never thought about it like that."

While Lily carefully removed the gift wrap he took the opportunity to observe her. She was extremely frail. Kelly said Lily was supposed to have heart surgery in a few weeks. Was she strong enough to survive it? Surely they wouldn't operate until she'd regained some strength, would they? Maybe they didn't have the luxury of more time. That was something he'd learned the hard way.

Gazing at Lily's downturned face, his heart constricted and a lump formed in his throat. In the past year, he'd frequently questioned the existence of God. For if there was a God, how could He let innocent children suffer? It didn't make sense, and it never would.

Lily set the gift wrap beside her on the bed and then lifted the lid off the box. She pushed away the orange-and-black tissue paper decorated with the Blaze insignia and let out a squeal of delight. "OMG," she said as she lifted the warm-up jacket out of the box and clutched it to her chest. "I love it," she said, staring at him, her eyes filled with wonder. "How did you know I wanted this?"

Matt shrugged. "Just a hunch."

Her smile faltered as she lowered the jacket. "I'd put it on but I've got all these wires…" She looked down at the wires attached to her chest and coming out of the arm of her hospital gown. When she looked up, the fear in her eyes hit him hard, like a sucker punch.

"Lily." He leaned forward, set the autographed baseball on the bed and reached for her hand. "Are you okay?"

"I have to have surgery," she whispered, blinking rapidly behind her wire-rimmed glasses to keep her unshed tears at bay.

"I know."

"I'm scared."

"I would be too." Matt kept his voice calm even though his stomach was churning. He had no clue how to comfort her. It reminded him of how helpless he'd felt last year. How despite his money and his fame, he wasn't able to do a damn thing to save the most important person in his life. "That's normal for anyone having surgery."

A tear trickled slowly down Lily's cheek. "I want to see the Blaze win the World Series before I die."

"You're not going to die," he said, unable to prevent his eyes from becoming moist.

"Everyone dies." Lily's tone was matter-of-fact and much too serious for a ten-year-old girl. Life wasn't fair. Nothing illustrated that more than the brave little girl in front of him.

"That's true." Matt blinked as he nodded. "No one gets a pass on that."

"I asked God to send you to the Blaze because I knew you could help them win the World Series." Lily sniffed and wiped her nose with the back of her hand. "If you win tonight, you'll be in first place. And if you keep winning I know you can get to the World Series. But

Mommy said my surgery is going to be sometime next month."

"So it'll be over in time for you to watch the Series in October." Matt pasted a smile on his face. "Perfect timing." Lifting his hand, he brushed the tears from Lily's cheeks with his fingers. "How about we make a deal?"

Lily tilted her head and frowned. "What kind of deal?"

"From now until the day of your surgery, I want you to do everything your doctor and your mom tell you to do." He paused to move several wispy dark strands of hair out of her eyes. "If you do that, I promise to win the World Series for you."

Lily regarded him with nothing short of skepticism. "Even you can't do that all by yourself."

"Sure I can," he assured her. "I've got two MVP awards, six Gold Gloves, a few batting titles *and* I've got one of the best pitching rotations in Major League Baseball."

Lily bit her lower lip and nodded. "Okay. I promise to do everything Mommy and Doctor Mike tell me to do."

"Good girl," he said softly. "Now tell me about the food in this place. Does it suck?"

"DAMN HIM," KELLY muttered as she glanced at her watch. Rizzo was a no-show. Why wasn't she surprised? Mainly because the jerk thought he was God's gift to baseball, and that he was allowed to do whatever he damn well pleased just because he'd won two Cy Young awards.

We'll see about that. She would talk to Dave Rizzo today even if she had to go out on the damn field to do it.

"Kelly?"

Kelly turned from her desk to see Angie leaning

against the door frame with a pensive expression on her face. "Got a minute?"

"I've got more than a minute. My appointment didn't show so I'm free for the next half hour."

Angie ventured into the office and took a seat in the chair opposite the desk. She wore a navy blue wrap dress with an adorable red cardigan over it. Somehow Angie was able to wear just about anything and look fabulous. That was the advantage of not being six feet tall.

"Was it one of the players?" Angie asked.

"Yes." Kelly picked up her pen and began doodling stars on the notepad in front of her. "I haven't talked to you since the game the other night." She stopped doodling and looked up. "I heard J.T. went to Kamu's with you."

Angie frowned, leaned back in the chair and linked her hands across her stomach. "Where'd you hear that?"

"Matt mentioned it." She pointed her pen at Angie and chuckled. "You're turning an interesting shade of pink."

"I am not." Angie shifted on the chair. "I just don't like being the subject of gossip."

"Relax. There's no gossip." Kelly lowered her pen. "Wait. Is there something to gossip about?"

"No," Angie snapped. "I made it clear to J.T. that I'm very happy with Scott."

Kelly couldn't let that go by without comment. She'd held her tongue far too long about the dour accountant who didn't treat Angie the way she deserved to be treated. "You're happy spending every Saturday night eating the same Chinese take-out food and watching Scott's favorite movies? Because that's all the two of you ever do."

"We pick movies I like too," Angie said, going on the defensive.

"When was the last time you guys watched a movie you picked out?" Angie's brows drew together and several seconds passed. Kelly rolled her eyes. "Good God, woman. If you have to think that long then I'm guessing it's been a while." She dropped her pen on the desk, hardly able to believe Angie put up with her boyfriend's peculiarities.

"I'm not here to talk about my relationship with J.T.—" Angie broke off, her cheeks turning an even deeper shade of pink. "I mean...with Scott."

"Whatever." Kelly grinned. "What did you want to talk about?"

"I'm worried about Alexis," Angie said in low voice. "I've heard her throwing up in the restroom a couple of times, and whenever I eat lunch with her she heads straight for the bathroom right afterward."

"Do you think she has an eating disorder?" Kelly wasn't happy her suspicions had been confirmed, but she was relieved that someone else had heard Alexis purging.

Angie hesitated a moment. "I'm not sure what to think. But it happened again this morning and I can't sit idly by and not say anything. I didn't know whether to approach her directly or come to you."

"It's best not to confront her," Kelly reassured her. "You did the right thing coming to me."

"What are you going to do?"

She sighed. "I'm not sure. But I have to do something."

Several hours later, Kelly sat at her desk staring at her computer screen while she massaged her temples with her fingers. She had press releases to write, the injury list to update, autograph signings to schedule and a boatload of press credentials to approve, but all she could think about was how to approach Alexis without alienating her. Just because she'd gone through recovery didn't mean she was qualified to counsel Alexis, or anyone else. What if she made things worse? When her cell phone rang she was thankful for the interruption.

"Hi, Dad," she greeted her father after a quick glance at the caller ID.

"Hey, Peanut."

"Are you coming to the game tonight?"

"That's why I'm calling. I can't make it tonight. Pharmacy business. I won't be there Sunday either. I gave my tickets to our new neighbors. But I had a great idea. Since it's an early game, I was thinking you could bring Matt over afterward. He seemed real interested in taking a look at the Chevelle."

Bring Matt to her parents' house? After that kiss last night she wasn't sure where things stood with them. Did it mean something, or nothing? And did she want it to mean anything when it was clear by his past behavior that Matt wasn't a guy who was big on commitment?

"I can ask him." Kelly heard a light tap on the door and turned to find Alexis poised at the threshold. She motioned for her to enter. "I'll miss you at the game tonight, but I'll call you tomorrow and let you know about Sunday."

"I'm barbecuing."

"Then I'm coming for sure," Kelly said with a smile. "I'll see you Sunday, Dad." She put her phone on the desk and gave Alexis a quick once-over. Angie was right, her intern had lost a lot of weight very quickly. Her round face had thinned, there were dark circles under her eyes that hadn't been there before and her skin was sallow. Alexis didn't look healthy, however the tight skirt and figure-hugging knit top she was wearing emphasized her slimmed-down body. She supposed a lot of young girls would envy Alexis's new svelte shape. That was the problem. Like Alexis, they would do anything, including jeopardizing their health, to attain the lowest weight possible.

"The Twitter hashtag battle has begun." Alexis rested her palms on the back of the chair and smiled. "The Phillies claim their fans are more passionate. Our fans didn't take that lying down. I predict the tweets will be hot and heavy all night long."

"That's good. The more the fans are involved the better it is for the team." Kelly folded her arms on her desk. "How are you?"

"I'm fine."

"You've lost a lot of weight." She kept her tone neutral lest Alexis think she was praising her.

"Almost twenty-five pounds now."

Kelly didn't miss the pride in Alexis's tone. "Just a few weeks ago you'd lost eight and now it's up to twenty-five? That's a lot to drop in such a short time period."

A sour look crossed Alexis's face as she lifted her arms to cross them over her chest. "I've been doing really well on my diet."

"Is it a healthy diet? Are you eating plenty of fruits and veggies?"

"Of course." Alexis was too quick with her reply. "And I drink lots of water. It helps me lose faster."

"You do know that extreme dieting can ruin your metabolism, and your health, right?"

Irritation flickered in her intern's eyes. "Yes. But there's nothing to worry about. My diet is healthy. In fact, I had a salad for lunch."

Deciding to back off, Kelly nodded and pushed her chair back. "I'm going down to the clubhouse. Rizzo and I need to have a little chat."

STANDING IN FRONT of his locker, Matt pulled his uniform pants over his compression shorts and zipped them up. Next to him, J.T. sat on the slatted bench staring glumly into his locker. The guy had been grumpy as hell for the past two days. Which was odd—J.T. was one of the most amiable guys on the team.

Before he could say anything to J.T., Kelly came around the corner and, judging by her expression, she wasn't happy. Her ponytail swung back and forth like a pendulum as she marched over to Rizzo and tapped him on his shoulder.

"You missed our meeting," she said, and just like that, the noise level in the clubhouse lowered noticeably. Several of the players stopped what they were doing and watched with blatant curiosity.

Rizzo turned from his locker, lifted his foot and rested it on the bench. "I forgot," he said with a smirk that made Matt want to punch his lights out. "Sorry."

"Not a problem." Kelly kept her tone professional. "We can talk right now in the lounge. It won't take long."

Rizzo's smirk was still intact as he glanced around the clubhouse. He had an attentive audience and was enjoying it. "Whatever you have to say to me, you can say it here."

"Fine. It's been brought to my attention that you've

been giving interviews without informing me or Katherine."

"I don't need your permission to talk to reporters."

"Actually, you do. Read your contract."

"I have."

"I don't think so," Kelly replied quickly. "Because if you had, you'd have read that as long as you're a member of this team, all interviews must be cleared by the office of media relations. You see, the image of the team is more important than you are. We've never denied any interviews. However, we reserve the right to do so if we believe the interview could tarnish the Blaze brand." Kelly pulled out a folded piece of paper from her jacket pocket and shoved it at Rizzo. "This is a copy of the page in your contract I'm referring to."

Rizzo scowled as he took the paper and unfolded it. Matt caught J.T.'s eye; they exchanged a grin.

"I've highlighted the paragraph regarding media interaction," she continued with cool confidence. "You'll also note that there are potential fines for not complying. So, in the future, please have your agent call my office before agreeing to any interviews. Is that clear?"

Rizzo looked up and with both hands crumpled the sheet of paper into a ball. Without saying a word, he dropped the paper on the bench and lowered his foot to the floor. A hush fell over the clubhouse as Rizzo and Kelly stared at each other. Having been in a staring contest with her the first night they'd met, Matt already knew who would win this battle. And it wasn't Rizzo. Several tense seconds elapsed before Rizzo turned his back on Kelly and rummaged for something in his locker.

Kelly let out an almost imperceptible breath. As if

remembering where she was, she turned and surveyed the locker room. No one spoke. It was as if each and every player had been struck dumb by what they'd just witnessed—the Blaze's star pitcher being schooled by a woman. When her gaze landed on him, her lips twitched but she didn't smile. She'd bested Rizzo, but she wasn't going to rub his nose in it. Matt was pretty sure if the situation was reversed, Rizzo wouldn't exhibit the same class.

"Have a good game, you guys," she said and left the still-hushed clubhouse.

"Cunt," Rizzo muttered under his breath.

"What did you say?" Matt demanded, stepping over the bench. Anger rode him as he approached Rizzo.

"You heard me." Rizzo turned, his eyes narrowed slits and his face mottled with fury. "She's a cunt."

Seeing red, he reached for Rizzo's T-shirt, fisted his hand in it and jerked him forward. Rizzo's eyes widened and flickered briefly with fear. "Don't you *ever* call her that again."

"Or what?" Rizzo sneered. "Are you fucking her, Scanlon? If so, I'm sure you can do better than a lard-ass like her."

Without hesitating, Matt clenched his other fist and took a swing at Rizzo's smirking face. His knuckles connected with the asshole's jaw and he felt a great deal of satisfaction in the grunt of pain Rizzo emitted. Blood pumped at warp speed through his veins as he drew back to try to land another blow. Before he could follow through, a large strong hand wrapped around his upper arm, preventing him from throwing another punch.

"Don't do it," J.T. said tersely.

"Yeah, man," Marquis Lopes, who'd come up behind

Matt and rested a hand on his shoulder, said in his lightly accented voice. "He's not worth it."

Tension permeated the room. Matt could feel the eyes of every single player in the clubhouse on him. They'd been waiting for him to do just this. To lose control and start a fight; that's exactly what he'd been doing for the past year.

Immediately, he released his grip on Rizzo's shirt and stepped back. He pulled his arm from J.T.'s grasp and took a deep breath. Putting his hands on his hips, he returned Rizzo's contemptuous glare. Rizzo rubbed his jaw and winced.

The motherfucker was in pain. *Good.* He deserved it.

"If I ever hear you call her that again, I'll put you in the hospital," he warned Rizzo in a low controlled voice. "Do we have an understanding?"

As HE HEADED OUT of the media room after the game, Matt was curious as to why Kelly hadn't attended the press conference. At first, he thought her continued presence was to check up on him to make sure he followed through on their little arrangement, but now he realized it was an integral part of her job. When she wasn't in the room tonight, it didn't feel right.

The thought of going straight to his condo wasn't appealing, so after spending about fifteen minutes signing autographs outside the ballpark he walked in the direction of Kamu's. A beer and a cheeseburger would hit the spot. The moment he entered the tavern he knew he'd made the right decision. Several of the servers greeted him with waves and welcoming smiles. What a difference from the first night he'd walked into the place. After a few short weeks in San Francisco he was beginning to feel like he fit in. No one was more surprised about that than him.

He was about to slide onto an empty stool when he spotted Kelly sitting alone at the far end of the bar. There was a bottle of beer sitting in front of her and she was gazing at one of the flat-panel televisions replaying highlights from the various games around the league. So this was where she'd come instead of the media room. This wasn't like her, which told him that the confrontation with Rizzo had rattled her more than she'd let on.

Kelly didn't notice him until he sat on the stool next to her. "Drinking alone?" he asked when she turned her head and their eyes locked.

"Not anymore." The smile she gave him was seductive. *Or was it?* Maybe he was just seeing what he wanted to see.

He nodded his thanks to the bartender as he brought him his favorite beer. "You weren't in the media room."

She lifted her beer. "I didn't feel like it tonight," she said, then put the bottle to her lips and took a sip. He wrapped his fingers around his icy bottle, unable to look away from her mouth. A tug of arousal pulled at his groin. *Jesus.* He was getting turned on just watching her drink a damn beer.

"Because of Rizzo?"

"Not entirely." She lowered her bottle to the bar, then pushed it aside, leaving a wet trail on the shiny surface. "That was quite the scene in the clubhouse, wasn't it?"

She didn't know the half of it. "Rizzo's a punk," Matt muttered, then took a pull from his bottle.

"That's what you said that night in L.A." Kelly's beautiful eyes sparkled with genuine amusement. "And you know what? You were right."

"You called *me* a punk that night," he reminded her. "Well, not in so many words, but you implied it."

"You deserved it." She shifted on her stool, causing her thigh to brush against his. The contact sent an arrow of liquid heat through his body. She leaned forward, her lips curving slightly as she searched his face. Suddenly, the bar chatter ceased to exist and all he heard was the sound of his heartbeat echoing in his ears. Kelly's clean citrusy scent surrounded him, reminding him of last night when he'd held her in his arms and kissed her. Their eyes locked and the sexual heat between them intensified. "You were such a prick that night."

Her words were hardly a compliment, so why was he getting turned on? Maybe it was that husky voice of hers. Even her insults sounded sexy.

"Forget about *that* night. Let's talk about what happened *last* night." Matt grinned as he met Kelly's puzzled eyes. "You know, when you kissed me."

TWELVE

"*I* KISSED YOU?" Kelly couldn't believe what she was hearing. "Oh, hell, no." She pointed her finger at Matt's handsome, yet smug, face. "*You* kissed me."

"That's not how I remember it."

"Then you have faulty memory, mister."

"I don't think so." He wrapped his fingers around his bottle of beer. Instantly, she remembered those long tapered fingers of his entangled in her hair during that amazing kiss. Butterflies danced madly in her stomach. "You practically attacked me in your kitchen," he added with an impudent grin.

Her jaw dropped. "Of all the…" she began hotly, then saw the mischievous gleam in his eyes and poked his hard bicep with her finger. He feigned a pained look before the corner of his mouth lifted in a self-satisfied smirk. "Ha, ha. Very funny." She tried not to smile. It was difficult, though; she liked this lighter side of him.

Matt shrugged. "It was mutual. How about that?"

Pursing her lips, Kelly thought about it. She couldn't deny she'd avidly participated in their searing kiss. In fact, if there was an award for participation, she'd win hands down. "I can agree to that," she said, unable look away from his heated gaze.

"Do you want to talk about it?"

Put the car in park. What man ever wanted to talk? Had she just landed in *The Twilight Zone*?

"There's nothing to talk about. It was just a kiss." Flustered, she reached for her purse on the bar. "We were upset about Lily…it was a moment. That's all."

His dark brows rose. "A moment?"

Kelly slid off her stool, trying her best to appear cool and unruffled. Like Matt seemed to be. Were they going to analyze the kiss like it was a box score or something? "Yes. A moment."

"A hot moment." His gaze lowered to her lips and lingered, reminding her of last night. A little ball of need burst to life low in her belly.

"I should go." She had to get out of the bar right now. It was extremely warm, or maybe she was, but in any event, talking about the kiss was not what she wanted to do. Talking about it could lead…well, it could lead to almost anything and if he kissed her again she'd probably go up in flames. No, make that definitely, she would *definitely* go up in flames.

"I'll walk you home." Matt eased off of his stool and reached for his wallet in his back pocket.

"I'm a big girl. I can get home by myself." She clutched her purse tightly; a mixture of both anticipation and nervousness flooded her. Here, inside Kamu's, with a crowd around them, she felt safe and totally in control. But alone, with Matt, that control was in serious danger of being shattered.

"So you've said before." He slapped a twenty on the bar. "But I'm an old-fashioned guy, so humor me and let me walk you home."

"Fine." She gave him a perfunctory nod and headed toward the exit. Matt followed after calling out a farewell to the bartender.

When Kelly stepped outside Kamu's, the cool bay

breeze whispered across the heated flush of her body. She waited as he held the door for an older couple and took a moment to study him unobserved. Even wearing faded jeans and a black-and-orange Blaze V-neck sweat-shirt layered over a polo shirt, he looked exactly like a cover model. Come to think of it, he had graced quite a number of magazine covers in the past seven years. She'd seen those covers, and while each one of them had effectively captured his dark sensual good looks, they couldn't compare to Matt Scanlon in the flesh. In person, he oozed power, authority and raw animal sexuality.

"So I imagine you've heard the good news," Matt said as they walked side by side up the block toward her building. "About Sean and Kayla."

Kelly nodded, relieved the topic had switched to something safer. "Kayla called me the other night. Sean had just proposed. She was thrilled."

"I got a text from Sean today. They've scheduled the engagement party to coincide with the team's travel day to San Diego next month. I talked to the skipper and he gave me the okay to attend the party that night. But I have to be at the Padres ballpark the next day in time for warm-ups."

"As I recall, all of our games with San Diego next month are night games. That should give you plenty of time to get to the ballpark."

"Have your parents met Sean?" he asked as they approached her building. As usual, the street was jam-packed with cars parked along the curb. Thank God she had garage parking. Finding a parking spot in this neighborhood was like trying to find a single straight man in the city. Nearly impossible. "It seems to me that this is all happening pretty quickly."

Kelly halted in front of the double glass doors. "My parents met Sean when they went down to L.A. after Kayla got back from Savannah. They wanted to make sure she was okay after what that asshole did to her."

"Sean told me what happened. That guy is seriously disturbed."

"He's a sick freak," she said as Matt opened the door for her. "I hope the judge locks him up for a long time." She crossed the threshold and turned. "Thanks for walking me home."

"Nice try, but I'm seeing you to your door." The determination in Matt's eyes meant he wasn't taking no for an answer. "Just to be on the safe side."

Kelly opened her mouth to protest, but then snapped it shut. Somehow she didn't think he would acquiesce.

As they waited for the elevator, those pesky butterflies made a return visit to the pit of her stomach. She couldn't get that damn kiss out of her mind. It almost made her long for the days when all she and Matt ever did was fight. At least when they bickered she could concentrate on the next stinging barb or insult she wanted to fling at him. Now all she could concentrate on were those sexy lips of his, and how much she wanted to feel them on hers again.

When the elevator doors opened, Matt motioned for her to precede him inside and like last night, she was struck by how completely he filled the space. It wasn't just his muscular frame; it was the aura of masculinity he exuded even as he leaned casually against the wall and pressed the button for her floor. As the doors closed, he turned, his penetrating gaze sinfully wicked.

Kelly's throat went dry and she moved to the opposite corner, clutching the strap of her purse like a lifeline. He was much too close for comfort. His clean and bracing scent surrounded her. He smelled good. Really good. Betraying heat flooded the area between her legs and a hot blush crept over her face. She was getting turned on in an elevator, for heaven's sake.

"My dad called today." She said the first thing that came into her head. "He's gung-ho about showing you the Chevelle. He's barbecuing on Sunday after the game and asked me to invite you over."

"Sweet." Immediately, Matt's expression transformed into one of eager enthusiasm that was both endearing and boyish at the same time. "I've been dying to see that car."

"Then I'll tell him you'll be there. You can ride over with me if you'd like." She smiled. "Unless you've decided that my driving could be hazardous to your health."

"I do have a clause in my contract about not taking any unnecessary risks." Amusement flickered in his eyes. "But what's life without risk?"

"Boring as hell."

"Exactly," Matt said as the elevator chimed its arrival at her floor. He held the open door button. "Any news on Lily?" he asked after joining her in the hallway.

"Dorie called me with an update late this afternoon. Lily will be released from the hospital on Sunday morning. Her surgery is tentatively scheduled for the last week of September."

Matt didn't respond and was quiet as they moved down the carpeted hallway. Sterling silver sconces hung on the pale lilac walls every few feet and bathed the hallway in a subdued glow. Although there were four residences on her floor, Kelly rarely saw her neighbors, nor did she ever hear them. The walls were soundproof and there were times when she came home from work that the floor was so eerily silent that it was downright creepy. Living in the upscale building was a far cry from the East Bay bedroom community of Pleasanton where she'd grown up. On the block where she'd lived, the Maxwells were close with all of their neighbors. There was a sense of camaraderie and caring there she hadn't found since she'd left home and gone off to college.

When they got to the black lacquer door, Kelly reached into the side pocket of her purse for her keys. "Lily is crazy about the warm-up jacket you gave her."

"I promised her the Blaze would win the World Series." He scrubbed a hand over his jaw and sighed. "I shouldn't have, but I couldn't help myself. I think Lily wants the team in the Series more than I do."

She turned toward him. "You gave her something to look forward to. There's nothing wrong with that."

"I guess so." He searched her face; as their eyes locked there was a moment of sizzling awareness. "It wasn't just because of Lily, you know." His voice was low and husky. "That kiss," he reminded her as if she didn't have a clue as to what he meant. But she did.

"Matt, we shouldn't…"

"Shouldn't what? Talk about the kiss, or do it again?"

Kelly pressed her hand over her heart, hoping that might stop its frantic pounding. No such luck. "Both."

"Why? We're way past disliking each other, aren't we?" His mouth tipped in a lazy smile. "And I'm pretty sure you enjoyed it. I know I did."

"I'm not one of your groupies."

"I've known that since the night we met." Matt lifted his hand and traced the ball of his thumb across her cheek. She tried to ignore the thrill that fluttered in her body. "But I can tell you this much, even though we were at each other's throats, from the moment I sat down at that table, I felt more alive that night than I had for months."

So had she. That's what scared her. Matt's reputation with women was well documented. There was no way in hell she was going to be another notch on his bedpost.

"Matt…" she said as he slid his hand to the nape of her neck.

"Your voice is so sexy," he murmured, gently caressing the skin of her nape. His thumb brushed over a sensitive spot near the back of her ear. Her keys slid from her fingers and jingled as they landed on the carpet. "Your eyes are the color of fine whiskey." He lowered his gaze to her lips. "And your mouth…" He leaned closer—so close their bodies almost touched. So close, the clean male scent of him invaded her senses. She tried to throttle the dizzying current running through her, but couldn't. "I want it."

"Then take it," she whispered and let out a low gasp of surprise as she realized she had said the words aloud. Before she could recant, his fingers tightened on her neck, his dark eyes flared with sexual heat and he pulled her tightly against the solid wall of his chest.

His mouth covered hers and it was as if time stopped. There was nothing…nothing but this moment, and Matt, ravishing her lips with his. Unable to resist, she melted against the hard length of him and parted her mouth to his seeking tongue. Seconds later, she felt his other hand on the small of her back, anchoring her to him, pressing her to his groin. The ache between her legs intensified as they kissed openmouthed, wet and deep.

Barely aware of her actions, she slid her hands up his powerful shoulders to his neck and threaded her fingers through his hair, reveling in its softness as he kissed her as if he wanted to devour her. She let out a soft sigh when, much too soon, he pulled his mouth from hers, touched his lips to her jaw and then moved to lightly nip at her earlobe, causing her to shudder.

When his lips found the sensitive spot at the base of her neck, she moaned and tilted her head, giving him better access. His mouth opened on her neck, placing soft yet insistent love bites along her sensitive skin. Her body quivered. She was drowning in this man. In the taste of him, the scent of him, the feel of him.

Warning bells went off in her head. This was Matt Scanlon—the man who, for the past year, had bedded more women than she could count on two hands. She couldn't be—wouldn't be—one of them. No matter how hot he was, and no matter how hot she was for him.

"Matt..." she murmured and lowered her hands to his shoulders. "Stop."

He lifted his head and pinned her with his dark gaze. Kelly's breath caught in her throat at the hot desire burning in his eyes. He made no move to loosen his hold on her, making her acutely aware of how intimately their bodies were pressed together. She could feel almost every inch of him; it did nothing to lessen her arousal.

"We can't do this," she whispered, trying to gather her composure. She'd never experienced such a primitive attraction to a man before. It would be so easy to give in to it but she'd never been any good at one-night stands. To her friends in college it had been no big deal, but the one time she'd done it she'd felt empty and somewhat cheap.

"Why not? We both want to." His voice was husky. "Are you going to deny it?"

"No. But I'm not some cleat chaser looking to score with a professional athlete."

"I never said you were." Matt scowled, dropped his arms from her and stepped back. "I'm not the same man I was a year—hell—even a month ago, but you think I'm still that guy in the tabloids, don't you?"

"Are you saying those stories weren't true?" Kelly lifted her chin. "How many women were you with anyway?"

"I have no clue, but not as many as you seem to think," he snapped and ran a frustrated hand through his hair. "Look, I'm not proud of my behavior last year, but I'm sure as hell not going to apologize to you for it."

"I didn't ask you to." She crouched to retrieve her keys. "In fact," she continued icily when she straightened. "I don't care what you do. There are hundreds of women in this city who would love to fuck you. Why don't you go find one who doesn't mind being another one of your many conquests?"

"Fine." Matt's tone was dark, his expression darker. "Maybe I'll do that," he said and then turned and strode down the hall.

"Damn it," Kelly whispered as she turned and unlocked the door. Once inside, she headed straight for the kitchen and set her purse and keys on the counter. As if on autopilot, she opened the freezer and reached for the pint of Stacia's cookie dough ice cream. Moving to the utensil drawer, she pulled it open and grabbed a spoon.

Leaning against the center island, she pulled off the lid, tossed it on the counter and then shoved the spoon into the ice cream. The first spoonful soothed her, but when the entire pint of cookie dough was gone within minutes all she felt was sick. Sick that even after all this time she could still use food like a drug, and sick that her first thought was to go to the bathroom and force herself to throw up.

I won't do it. I won't go back there.

With trembling hands, she put the container and spoon in the sink and then rummaged through her purse until she found her cell phone. Scrolling through her contact list, she came upon the entry for someone she hadn't had to call on very often in the past few years—her recovery sponsor. She hit the speed dial button and waited. Her sponsor answered on the second ring.

"I need to talk."

THE LAST THING Matt wanted to do was go back to his empty condo. Instead he shoved his hands into the pockets of his sweatshirt and took a left when he got to King Street. Because the evening was chilly, and it was late, there weren't many people out and about. He walked along the Embarcadero and didn't bother to stop to admire the brightly lit Bay Bridge, its length spanning from San Francisco to Oakland and the East Bay. While maybe not as iconic as the Golden Gate, it was still an impressive sight. But tonight, that marvel of engineering was lost on him.

As long as he lived he'd never understand women. Maybe it was him. He'd had it pretty easy in that department for a while now. Women had been throwing themselves at him for years. Even before last year, he'd taken advantage of that fact. Only back then, he'd been discreet about it. When the women got too clingy, or too demanding, he'd move on with no regrets. The one serious relationship he'd had in college had ended badly and he'd never wanted to repeat it.

Now there was Kelly. The last woman on earth he ever thought he'd be attracted to. But he was. Even now, when she'd pretty much told him to go pound sand, he still wanted her with an intensity that surprised him. He wasn't sure when it happened, but Kelly Maxwell and her smart mouth had gotten to him.

He stopped in front of the Fog City Diner and would have gone in for some coffee but it was closed so he resumed walking down the Embarcadero, lost in thought. A few people passed him by but no one recognized him, or if they did, they didn't care. It was odd after the overwhelming adoration in L.A., but he liked the fact that he could go out here in San Francisco and not be constantly besieged by fans and the paparazzi. The San Francisco fans were a different breed. It was as if they were too cool and sophisticated to fawn all over some guy who played a game for a living. He liked that about them.

Kelly had never fawned over him either, and obviously believed he was still living the womanizing lifestyle he'd been living in L.A. She couldn't be more wrong. Somehow, he was going to prove it to her.

By THE TIME Sunday morning rolled around, Kelly couldn't remember ever being in a darker mood. Two full days had passed since she and Matt had their encounter at her front door. It wasn't like her not to go down to the clubhouse and talk to the guys before each game, but other than sitting in her usual spot in the media room after the last two games, she'd given the clubhouse a wide berth.

How could she face him after what she'd said? She'd picked that fight with him because of her own stupid fears and for no other reason. It was childish, like avoiding him now was childish.

She couldn't avoid him forever. Tomorrow Matt and the team would be leaving on a two-week road trip—the longest one of the season. Kelly wished like hell she didn't have to join them but she couldn't very well tell Katherine she couldn't make the trip. It was part of her job, after all. Fourteen days cooped up on charter planes and buses with him would be uncomfortable. It would be much easier to stay in San Francisco and not have to deal with him, or her insane attraction to him.

Coward.

Pushing up from her chair, she rounded her desk and left her office. By the time she reached the women's restroom, she'd managed to silence the pesky little voice inside her head and pushed open the bathroom door. The sound that greeted her was agonizingly familiar and sent a chill up her spine. Someone was vomiting, and there was no doubt in her mind that it was Alexis.

Evidently, the sound of her own retching had masked the noise of the door opening so Alexis continued to purge. With a heavy heart, Kelly leaned against the double sink counter and waited. Finally, the toilet flushed; she steeled herself for the moment when Alexis discovered she wasn't alone in the bathroom.

As expected, Alexis's expression was one of shock when she stepped out of the stall. Her eyes grew round and wide as their gazes locked across the small space between them.

"Kelly...uh, hi. I'm not feeling well. I think I should go home."

Nice save. But it wasn't good enough.

"I'm fine with that. But before you leave, I need to tell you something."

Alexis clasped her hands together in front of her. "What?"

"I have an eating disorder." Kelly paused. "I'm in recovery and have been for several years. I'm past the worst of it but it's a lifetime struggle."

Unease flickered in Alexis's eyes. "What's that got to do with me?"

"Because I recognize the signs. I've binged and purged too. Sometimes the purging was hours spent in the gym after I'd binged, and sometimes I threw up, just like you were doing."

"I don't have an eating disorder, if that's what you think." Alexis crossed her arms over her chest. "I'm coming down with the flu. My whole family has been sick with it."

"I don't believe you. You'd say anything right now not to have your secret exposed."

"There is no secret," Alexis shot back in a defensive tone.

"It's getting worse, isn't it?" Kelly moved to stand in front of the girl. "You used to do it in the privacy of your home, but now you're doing it at work. It's escalating, and that isn't good."

"You're just jealous because I'm losing weight." Alexis's assessing gaze traveled down Kelly's body and then back up. "You could stand to lose a few pounds."

"I'm happy with my weight, but it took me a long time to get to this point," Kelly replied, not offended. Alexis was deflecting, a common response when confronted. She lifted her hand to Alexis's shoulder. "I'm concerned about your health. I don't want to see you go down the same path I did. I can help you." She squeezed Alexis's shoulder gently. "If you'll let me."

Alexis jerked her shoulder away and treated her to a scathing look. "I don't need your help because I don't have a problem. I'm coming down with the flu and that's all." Alexis stepped around her and moved to the door. Kelly turned to watch her. Had she just blown her one chance to help her intern? "I'll get my things and go. I don't want to spread my germs around the office."

"Fine. But think about what I said. I can help you."

IT WAS CLOSE to six when Kelly pulled the Trans Am in front of her parents' modest ranch-style home in Pleasanton. Its pale green paint with white shutters was a welcome sight after a rough couple of days. She and Kayla had grown up in this house and it held a lot of wonderful memories.

The game had ended at four with another Blaze victory, and after doing her stint in the media room she'd gone straight to the condo, changed clothes and hit the road for the East Bay. Since Matt seemed to be avoiding her as well—it was pretty clear he wasn't interested in the barbecue at her parents' house, or seeing the Chevelle. Still, she had extended the invitation and felt a tad bit guilty that she hadn't followed up with him.

But he could have followed up with her, right? If she was being childish, then he was doubly so.

As she climbed out of her car, she noticed a shiny black SUV parked on the other side of the street in front of the Andrews' house. The Andrews had lived on the block as long as the Maxwells had and Mr. Andrews was famous for leasing a new vehicle every two or three years. This was his first SUV, though. He usually preferred sedate four-door sedans.

The aromatic smell of barbecue wafted in the air. Kelly's stomach rumbled happily. It had been a while since she'd had her dad's famous barbecued ribs. Her talk with her sponsor had helped her put the ice cream incident into perspective. However, the lapse did reinforce the fact that she would never be completely cured. But that didn't mean she couldn't enjoy food and tonight she intended to do just that. As she approached the side gate and opened it, she heard voices in the back so she bypassed the side door into the garage and headed straight for the backyard.

Rounding the corner, the first thing she saw was her father in his usual spot, manning the grill. The second thing she saw made her stop short and let out a soft gasp of surprise.

What the hell was he doing here?

"Hi, Kelly." Standing next to John Maxwell, holding a beer and looking extremely satisfied with himself, Matt grinned. "It's about time you got here."

THIRTEEN

IT WAS DIFFICULT, but Kelly managed to keep her jaw from hitting the patio. "Hi, Dad," she said, totally blown away by the fact that Matt was standing in her parents' backyard, looking quite at home, and extremely attractive, in faded jeans and a light blue polo shirt that accentuated his deeply tanned skin. "Matt." She gave him a curt nod as she moved to the redwood picnic table covered with a colorful red-gingham tablecloth. She set her purse on the bench as her mother opened the screen door and stepped outside.

"Kelly, we didn't expect you so soon." Patricia Maxwell's eyes lit up. "Matt said you were running late."

"Did he?" Kelly looked from her mother to Matt and manufactured a wide smile. "Well, I'm here now," she said as she gave her mother a hug. Over her mom's shoulder, she gave Matt a hard stare. Oh, how she wished she could wipe the smug expression clean off his face. He was totally enjoying her discomfiture and it was annoying as hell. "And it seems *you* were able to get here without any trouble at all," she said with a frosty tone to Matt.

"GPS is an amazing thing," he replied with a self-satisfied twist of his lips and lifted his beer to his mouth.

Patricia stepped back and beamed at Kelly as only a mother could. "You look beautiful, as always." Before she could say a word, her mother grabbed her hand. "Come inside, I need to check on the beans."

"Check on the beans?" Kelly asked with suspicion. "Don't you usually open a can and nuke them? What's there to check?"

"I made them myself."

"You what?" Kelly whipped her head around and met her father's gaze. He gave her a sheepish shrug and then focused his attention on the grill. *The traitor.* How could he let her mother make something from scratch? Nothing good ever came of that.

"The recipe was easy," Patricia commented and chuckled softly. "Don't worry. There won't be a repeat of the great chili disaster of 2010."

Kelly clutched her stomach. "God, I hope not. I was sick for a week."

"I didn't know there was a recall on that ground beef." Her mother's tone was defensive. "This time I think you'll be pleasantly surprised."

Yes, they'd be surprised all right, but not pleasantly. Patricia Maxwell wasn't exactly a wizard in the kitchen. Unfortunately, both she and Kayla had inherited their mother's lack of skill in the cooking department. On the plus side, though, they both could work a microwave and order takeout like nobody's business.

"I'm sure the beans will be great, Mrs. Maxwell."

Kelly rolled her eyes. *What a suck-up.*

"Why, thank you, Matt." Patricia's cheeks turned pink. "Didn't I ask you to call me Patricia?"

Oh good God. Her mother was just as smitten with Matt as she was with Sean Barrett. The man couldn't have been here more than thirty minutes and already he'd charmed her mother as easily as he'd charmed her father. Whatever voodoo he'd used on both of them had worked.

"Sorry. I forgot." He flashed her mother that same disarming smile that had won over every Blaze fan in the Bay Area and, of course, her mother was eating it up. It was disgusting. "Patricia," he added in a smooth tone and took another draw of his beer.

"Come with me, honey." Her mother pulled her toward the screen door. "We won't be long," Patricia called over her shoulder as she opened the door and led Kelly into the house.

Once inside, she followed her mother's trim figure through the family room and into the kitchen. "How long has Matt been here?" she asked and moved to the stove where a pot was simmering over a low gas flame. She lifted the lid and stared at the sorry-looking concoction her mother was trying to pass off as baked beans. Bile rose in her throat as the pungent aroma of God-knows-what strange spices her mother had used invaded her nostrils. Following a recipe to the letter wasn't Patricia's strong suit—she liked to experiment. Sadly, those experiments usually resulted in the ingestion of large dosages of antacids by those unlucky enough to sample her culinary creations. Kelly replaced the lid. Matt would get an extra-big helping…she'd make sure of it.

"About forty-five minutes." Her mother opened the refrigerator door and pulled out a bowl containing a tossed green salad and set it on the square wooden chopping block in the middle of the room before reaching back inside for a couple of bottles of dressing. The kitchen wasn't large, but it was warm and inviting with its pale melon-colored walls and white lace curtains. An antique oak table was placed in a nook near the window that overlooked the street. There was a formal dining room in the house, but when she was growing up her family had always dined in the kitchen unless they'd had guests over for dinner.

"He's such a charming and personable young man. And awfully handsome, don't you think?"

Still annoyed, Kelly brushed an errant lock of hair from her face. "I hadn't noticed."

Patricia closed the refrigerator door, put her hand on her hip and pinned her with a perceptive gaze.

"What?" she asked when a sly smile played over her mother's lips.

"He's single. That means he's available."

Kelly suppressed a snort. "Mom, don't even go there. Matt and I are complete opposites."

Patricia's eyes twinkled mischievously. "And you know what they say about that, right?" She paused for dramatic effect. "Opposites attract."

Kelly moved forward and picked up the salad bowl. "Matt Scanlon and I barely tolerate each other. It was hate at first sight and not much has changed." Except for maybe those extremely hot kisses they'd shared. But there was no way she was mentioning that to her mother. That would only fuel her not so subtle attempt at match-making.

"There's a thin line between love and hate," her mother continued on undeterred. "Why else would he be here if he wasn't interested in you? I saw the way he was looking at you."

"Stop with the clichés," Kelly grumbled. "He wasn't looking at me in any special way. He's only here to see the Chevelle, remember? Just concentrate on Kayla and Sean and their wedding, would you?"

Patricia's mouth formed a perfect O. "A double wedding," she whispered reverently. "Wouldn't that be some-thing?"

"What the hell is wrong with you?" She stared at her mother in disbelief. "Have you been watching that stupid wedding show again?"

"Don't swear," her mother admonished and then continued, "Yes. I love that show. And one day—" Patricia picked up the salad dressing bottles "—you'll thank me."

SITTING ACROSS THE picnic table from Matt, Kelly could barely contain her glee as he choked down his fourth spoonful of her mother's beans. She had volunteered to serve and, as planned, made sure he got a supersize portion. After taking a bite of potato salad she watched with satisfaction as his shoulders heaved and his eyes began to water. He reached for his beer and took a long drink. It was hard not to laugh, but she managed to keep a straight face as he set the bottle down and gave her a pitiful look.

Kelly hadn't planned on sharing her tried and true method for saving his ass but she was wavering. How could she not help him out when it appeared he was trying to spare her mother's feelings by eating every spoonful of those horrible beans? Not many people would do that.

Next to her, her father had already bitten the bullet and eaten his small portion. Across from him, sitting beside Matt, her mother was digging into her beans with gusto. This proved her mother's taste buds were completely trashed, or maybe she had none. *Was that it?* Patricia Maxwell ate anything and everything and never complained. Could it be she had no sense of taste? Did such a thing exist? An internet search on the topic was in order as soon as she got home.

As Matt stared glumly at his plate. Kelly had to give him credit, his fortitude was amazing. By the look of it, he was going to finish the beans even if it killed him. That was when she decided he'd had enough. His good manners should be rewarded.

"I'd love some more of those ribs," she said and reached for the platter sitting next to the pitcher of iced tea that sat in front of her. As she went to grab the platter, she shifted her hand ever so slightly and, in a move borne of practice, discreetly knocked over the pitcher. It clattered to the table, the tea spilling onto Matt's plate, flooding it. "Oh no." She feigned shocked surprise and quickly righted the pitcher. "I'm *so* sorry. Did that get on your jeans?"

"No." Matt moved quickly to blot the tablecloth with his napkin so the liquid wouldn't spill over the edge of the picnic table.

"Here's another napkin." Patricia quickly grabbed one from a basket at the end of the table and handed it to Matt, who used it to dry the plastic tablecloth.

Kelly rose from the bench and picked up his plate. "Let me get you a clean plate."

He gazed at her with something that looked a lot like gratitude.

"I should have known better than to put that pitcher out," her mother grumbled and shook her head. "It seems every time we have a family dinner, the iced tea always ends up on the table."

"You know me, Mom. I'm clumsy." Kelly avoided her father's all-knowing gaze and headed for the screen door. Just before she pulled it open to step inside, she glanced over her shoulder and winked at Matt. His eyes widened a fraction and a slow smile tipped one corner of his mouth. "I'll be right back," she said, and stepped into the house before she blew the whole thing by laughing.

AFTER SHE'D FINISHED the last of her ribs, Kelly wiped her fingers on her napkin and blew out a happy sigh. "Dad, you haven't lost your touch, the ribs were excellent."

"Thank you, Peanut," her father replied as he reached for the green salad.

Kelly didn't bother with her usual mock outrage. After all, Matt already knew her childhood nickname so why bother? She set her napkin on the table next to her plate and slid off the redwood bench. "I'll be right back."

Her mother's head shot up, her face shadowed with a mixture of suspicion and worry. It was a look Kelly had seen before. "Where are you going?"

"In the house." Her heart sank as she looked from her mother's anxious face to her father, who wore the same troubled expression on his. Was it always going to be like this? She was way past the worst of her eating disorder, but it was evident that her parents were afraid she was going into the house so she could run to the bathroom to purge. "I'm going to the kitchen to get the cherry pie you ordered from Fiorio's. Would you like to help me slice it?" she asked in a sharp tone.

"No, honey," her mother said with a weak smile. "I'm sure you can handle it."

Kelly glanced at Matt who was regarding the entire exchange with puzzlement. The sudden tension had to be odd to him, but he didn't say a word.

"I'll only be a few minutes," she said with false cheeriness and went inside the house.

In the kitchen, she sliced the pie with jerky movements. She'd just snapped at her mother for being concerned about her. What kind of person was she anyway? How could she blame her parents for worrying about a relapse, when she'd almost done that very thing two nights ago? Her whole family had been affected by her eating disorder, and obviously, they still were.

Would there ever be a time when it wasn't a part of who she was? Dumb question. It was the same as being a recovered drug addict or alcoholic. Just like they did, she had to take it one day at a time.

AFTER SPENDING AN hour with John in his garage checking out the Chevelle, Matt returned to the backyard to find Kelly stretched out on a cushioned chaise on the redwood deck next to the Maxwells' modest swimming pool. Beneath its calm surface, a light was on, giving the water a tropical blue-green hue.

The weather was much different in the East Bay than in San Francisco. Of course, Kelly knew that and had arrived wearing a short denim skirt that showed off her toned athletic legs, and a turquoise tank top that hugged her body like a second skin. Even now, with the sun just beginning to set, it was at least 85 degrees. Now *this* was summer.

Next to the picnic table, Matt halted at the small cooler that held iced bottles of beer and water. He reached for a bottle of water and looked over at Kelly, who hadn't noticed him and was staring straight ahead, seemingly lost in thought. She'd been quiet ever since that odd exchange between her and Patricia.

Before that tense moment the evening had been enjoyable. Kelly had been surprised to see him and after the initial shock, had been subdued but cordial. She'd even taken pity on him and finagled a way for him to avoid finishing those god-awful beans. He needed to thank her for that. If he'd had to eat one more bite, he would have puked for sure. Patricia Maxwell was a very nice woman, but her cooking skills left a lot to be desired.

John and Patricia did the majority of the talking during the meal, mostly asking him questions about his baseball career and his long-standing friendship with Sean. The Maxwells were thrilled Sean was marrying Kayla, and it was evident they doted on both of their daughters. He envied Kelly her close-knit family, so different from his own. He couldn't remember the last time he'd talked to his parents.

"Do you want some water, or a beer?"

When Kelly turned toward him, the few remaining rays of sunlight glinted off of her hair, picking up the golden highlights to create a halo-like effect. She looked almost ethereal, and so damn beautiful his breath caught in his throat. "No. Thanks," she said and turned her attention back to the pool.

He crossed the patio to the deck and motioned to the chaise next to her. "May I join you?"

"Be my guest." She crossed one ankle over the other, a graceful move that drew his attention to her smooth lightly tanned legs. "How did you get my parents' address?"

"Simple," he said as he lowered himself to the chaise and got comfortable. "I called directory assistance. Your father mentioned Pleasanton the night we had dinner, and I knew his name. Turns out their number is listed. I called and got the address."

"You're smarter than you look."

"Ouch." Matt grinned as he removed the cap from his bottle.

"I should have spoken to you about tonight but…"

"But we're clearly both very stubborn people," he finished for her.

"Clearly."

He took a long pull of water and then cradled the bottle between his thighs. "By the way, thanks for the save."

"Kayla and I perfected that move years ago." Her husky laugh washed over him with the effect of a hot, hard kiss.

Matt let his gaze wander over the endless length of her legs. All day, even during the game, he'd thought about the kiss they'd shared two nights ago. No matter how hard he tried, he couldn't stop thinking about taking those kisses further. For the first time in over a year he felt fully alive. Was his grief finally easing, or was it Kelly? He wasn't sure. What he did know was he couldn't get her out of his head.

During the national anthem he'd checked the section where she and her father usually sat, but today there had been two people he didn't recognize sitting in the seats. The disappointment had been acute, so acute that he'd resorted to calling John to get directions to the Maxwells' house. He'd wanted to see her that badly. He couldn't remember the last time a woman had gotten under his skin the way Kelly had. It was slightly disturbing, but that still hadn't stopped him.

"You seem quiet tonight. Is it because I'm here?" he asked after a long, but not uncomfortable silence.

"No," she said softly. "It's…it's just…well, I've got a problem at work."

That wasn't surprising, considering what he'd witnessed in the clubhouse the other day. "Is it Rizzo?" His pulse started to pound. If Rizzo was hassling her, the prick was going to regret the day he was born.

"It's not one of the players. But every time I see Rizzo, he gives me the evil eye. He hates me."

Matt took another sip of water. "He's an asshole," he said a second later.

"No argument there."

"If it's not one of the players, then what's this problem you're dealing with?"

"It's complicated. I have an intern this season—"

"The young blonde?" he interrupted her. "Alexis, right? I've seen her around the clubhouse. In fact, I saw her yesterday for the first time in a couple of weeks. She's dropped a lot of weight."

Kelly shifted to her hip, her expressive face pensive. "I'm worried about her, and today I think I blew my chance to help her."

"What happened?"

She bit her bottom lip and hesitated before continuing. "Between us, I think she has an eating disorder. All the signs are there."

"That can be serious."

"Don't I know it?" She sighed. "And, as usual, I opened my big mouth and pushed her even further into denial."

"Have you thought about contacting her parents? She can't be more than twenty. She probably still lives at home."

"That might make it worse." She paused. "If only I'd been more prepared. I knew I was going to have to talk to her but I hadn't worked it all out yet. When I walked into the restroom this morning and heard her purging I went with the first thing that came into my head."

"Which was?"

Instead of answering him, she sat up and tucked her knees to her chest. She wrapped her arms around her shins and stared at the smooth flat surface of the swimming pool. For several seconds all Matt could hear was the soft whirring sound of the pool motor, and the occasional chirping of a few blackbirds.

"I thought she might relate to someone who'd been through it," she finally spoke.

"So you asked her to talk to someone you know?"

"Sort of." He sensed she wanted to elaborate but he didn't press her. Her concern for Alexis seemed more than just that of a supervisor concerned about an employee—it felt deeper, more personal than that. "I told her I could help her because I knew what she was going through."

"How would you know…?" he began and then paused. "Hold on. Are you saying…?"

"Yes." She turned to look at him, her expression solemn. "I had an eating disorder. Bulimia. It was a nightmare…even after I sought help."

Matt was speechless. Nothing could have surprised him more. The thought of a woman as strong and as confident as Kelly caught up in the throes of any kind of addiction was impossible to comprehend.

"I can't believe I told you that." She flipped her hair over her shoulder in a gesture he might have perceived as nonchalant if he hadn't just seen the haunted look in her eyes. "I never talk about it with anyone."

"I won't say a word." Kelly had entrusted him with something deeply personal. And because she didn't appear to be one of those women who shared every bit of their life with anyone who would listen, this meant something.

"I know. Despite everything, I trust you." Her lips curved in a wry smile. "That's odd, isn't it? I never thought I'd say those words to *you*."

"Stranger things have happened." And nothing was stranger than how this woman, a woman he'd once loathed, had become someone he wanted to spend time with. What else didn't he know about her? Damn if he didn't want to find out. "Are you in recovery?" He didn't know all that much about eating disorders, but he did know there could be serious health risks if it wasn't treated.

"For about four years now. I consider myself recovered, but it's still something I deal with." Her eyes grew moist. "My parents still worry about me."

The tense moment at dinner now made sense. He'd read that bulimics usually threw up after eating. Patricia had probably been worried Kelly was going into the house to purge.

"What are you going to do about Alexis?"

"I don't know." Her brows knitted. "Her desire to be thin is very strong right now. She doesn't realize how she's affecting her health. I do know one thing. Until she can admit she's got a problem, there's not a damn thing anyone can do to help her."

KELLY WASN'T SURE exactly what had prompted her to tell Matt about her eating disorder. Maybe it was because she was still unsettled by her encounter with Alexis, or maybe it was because it had killed her to see her parents so worried she was going to relapse. Whatever the reason, it was done now and she had no regrets.

There had been surprise in his eyes, but no censure or condemnation. He hadn't pressured her for details, and had seemed genuinely concerned for Alexis. This wasn't the surly ballplayer she'd first locked horns with in L.A. This was a good and decent human being.

A good and decent human being who also happened to be the most attractive man she'd ever met. A fact she was fully aware of as he walked her to the Trans Am after they'd said their goodbyes to her parents. Although his body was large and powerful, he moved with athletic grace and supreme confidence. The combination was exciting, and left her wanting more than just those two kisses they'd shared. A lot more.

The sun had long since set, but the street was lit by the glow of a nearby streetlamp. Although the evening air was warm, a late-summer breeze had kicked up, causing the leaves of the old walnut tree across the street to rustle gently in its wake.

"I'm not looking forward to getting up at the crack of dawn," Matt said as they halted by the car door.

"Early morning flights can be brutal." She smiled. "Oh, and Katherine made it clear that she expects the team to be on their best behavior. I've been charged with making sure that happens."

"Son of a bitch." He frowned. "That means you'll be watching us like a hawk."

"Damn straight. You'd better make curfew or you'll be in deep shit…I mean…big trouble. You'll be in big, big trouble."

Matt laughed. The low rich sound heightened the beat

of her pulse. "What is this? Are you seriously trying not to swear?"

Kelly leaned against the Trans Am, trying to ignore the effect Matt had on her. And it wasn't only when she was in his presence. It was unsettling how much she thought about him when he wasn't even around. "I've been told it's not attractive," she said as he moved to stand in front of her.

She couldn't help but notice the smattering of dark hair at the V-neck of his polo shirt. She'd seen his sculpted chest on display in the clubhouse a few times. He wasn't a hairy beast, but neither did he wax his chest like a few of his teammates did. A practice she found odd, but then that was probably because she liked a man with a bit of chest hair. It was sexy.

"Who said that?"

She tilted her head and smiled. "You did."

"Did I? Well, I hope you don't give it up completely. Your penchant for swearing has grown on me." He moved a fraction of an inch closer; she caught a whiff of his clean male scent. The combination of the soap and shampoo he used after every game. That scent, along with the penetrating look in his eyes, caused her heart to skip and then start beating rapidly. "A lot of things about you have grown on me."

"Does that line work on all your women?"

"It's not a line, and there are no other women." He hesitated a moment, and then continued, "There hasn't been since that night in L.A."

"What about that hostess you flirted with?" she asked, remembering the beautiful blonde Matt had chatted up after their heated encounter.

"I slept alone that evening."

She grinned. "You really shouldn't let that get out. It might ruin your reputation."

A wry smile quirked his mouth. "Would you care if I'd slept with her?"

"Me? Hell, no. I didn't even like you. You were rude, arrogant and…"

He put a finger to her lips. The gentle touch effectively silenced her. "What about now?" he asked in a husky voice that sent goose bumps over her entire body. "Do you like me now?"

She stared at him, her heart pounding so loudly she thought the whole block might hear it.

"It's okay," he said softly when she didn't reply. "The way you kissed me the other night told me everything I need to know."

"Did I mention conceited," she said, as he traced her lips with the tip of his finger. "It was one kiss, Matt. Don't get cocky." She hoped he couldn't see how much he affected her. He was already way too sure of himself.

"Two." His finger stilled on her bottom lip, then traced a path across her jaw. "Two kisses." He leaned in close, his breath warm on her lips. "Why don't we make it three?" he said, and in one swift motion covered her lips with his and kissed her with such unrestrained passion she almost couldn't breathe.

When she did draw breath, it was to part her lips to accept the forceful demand of his mouth. She felt one of his hands in her hair, fisting it, and the other was on her back, holding her steady as their mouths fused hotly. Did he know she was burning up inside? Because she was. And not only that, his kisses had awakened an aching hunger deep inside of her body. All she wanted, no, all she needed, was for that hunger to be sated.

When their lips parted, her eyelids fluttered open and, dazed, she stared into the ebony pools of his eyes. The air shifted and seconds passed, seconds filled with sexual yearning. It throbbed between them, impossible to ignore—impossible to forget.

A car turned onto the street from the main road, illuminating them briefly with its headlights. As it passed, Matt released her and slid his hands slowly down her bare arms. She shivered at his light touch and, unbidden, the thought of him caressing every inch of her body flashed in her mind. Her breath caught at the potent image.

"I'm glad you're coming on the road trip." Matt took a step back, putting space between them.

"Why?"

He searched her face, his gaze lingering briefly on her lips. "Because now I don't have to wait two weeks to kiss you again."

His words, along with the raw heat in his eyes, ignited a sudden, fierce longing inside of her that almost knocked her off of her feet. Stunned by its onslaught, she pressed her palms to the car for support and took a deep breath to regain her equilibrium.

"You're presuming I want you to kiss me again," she said in her haughtiest tone.

A smile teased the corner of his mouth. "I think you want me to do a lot more than that."

"You're wrong." Actually, he was right, but there was no way in hell she was going to admit that to him. No way in hell.

"Am I?" Matt fished his keys from his front pocket and flashed a cocky grin. "I guess we'll find out."

FOURTEEN

LIKE A NUMBER of ball clubs in the league, the Blaze had a strict curfew when the team was on the road. In the past year Matt had blatantly ignored that policy, but since being traded to San Francisco he'd made it a point to behave himself.

Which was why, instead of enjoying an ice-cold one downstairs in the bar, he was alone in his hotel room watching ESPN's rundown of the divisional standings. With tonight's come-from-behind victory, the Blaze were in sole possession of first place. They'd bested the Marlins in three out of four games while the Dodgers had lost two of their four-game series with the Colorado Rockies.

It was good to be in first place, but with six weeks left in the regular season anything could happen.

As ESPN went to game highlights, he turned off the television and glanced at his watch. It was just after eleven but he was nowhere close to being tired. Maybe it was time to start that mystery novel he'd purchased in the hotel's gift shop. He had to do something to keep his mind occupied. If not, he'd start thinking about Kelly and then he'd never get any sleep.

Five days into the road trip Kelly was doing her best to keep her distance. She made sure not to sit near him on the team's charter planes and buses, she spoke to him only in the presence of his teammates, and she steered clear of him in the media room. He wasn't buying her disinterested act one bit. She wanted him as much as he wanted her even if she wouldn't admit it.

He knew this not only because of the way she'd kissed him, but because there had been a few times during the trip when he'd looked up and found her staring at him, heat smoldering in those whiskey eyes of hers. This past year he'd easily found women to satisfy his physical urges. Now he couldn't fathom it. The only woman he wanted was Kelly.

The ringing of his cell phone prevented him from wondering just what that meant. He rose from the foot of the bed, moved to the dresser and grabbed the phone.

"Dude. You gotta come down here," J.T. replied to his greeting, and judging by the excitement in his voice, his mood was much improved from earlier in the day.

"Where is here?"

"The bar. Whoever said Miami women were hot wasn't lying."

"You know you're out past curfew, right?"

"Fuck curfew." J.T.'s voice rose over the loud salsa music. "I'm tired of the women in San Francisco. Miami women know how to *par-tay*."

Matt was fairly certain J.T. wasn't referring to *all* women in San Francisco. Just one. Angie DeMarco. Ever since the night of the softball game when J.T. had accompanied Angie to Kamu's J.T. had been prickly as hell. But whenever Matt asked him about it, J.T. brushed him off.

"C'mon, man. I need a…a…whaddaya call it?" He paused. "A winger. No wait, that's not right. A wing man. Yeah, that's it. I need a wing man."

"A wing man? Are you drunk?" J.T. had a strict policy of only one beer after a game but by the sound of it, he'd had a lot more than that.

"Gettin' there."

"Great." Matt shook his head and sighed. "You know if the skipper or Kelly find out about this you're fucked, right? You could be fined."

"I don't give a…" J.T. began and then a loud wolf whistle pierced Matt's eardrum. "Damn, she's hot."

"Don't move." He picked up his key card and shoved it into the pocket of his jeans. He had a gut feeling this wasn't going to end well. "I'm coming down."

KELLY LET OUT an annoyed groan as the insistent ringing of her cell phone jerked her into consciousness. She brushed her hair out of her eyes, rolled to her side and reached for the phone. As she picked it up she noted the time on the clock radio. Twelve-ten. Not good. Calls at this hour could mean only one thing. One or more of her players had been doing something they shouldn't have been doing and got caught doing it.

"Speak," she said groggily, not looking at the caller ID. Bottom line—it didn't matter who delivered the bad news, just that they did it quickly so she could handle the fallout with the least amount of media coverage. Whoever had coined the phrase "any publicity is good publicity" was an idiot of the highest order.

"You need to come to the hotel bar right now." It was Matt and his tone was serious. "Before this gets out of hand."

Kelly pushed herself up, fully alert. She reached for the button on the base of the lamp and pressed it. Bright light filled the room, causing her to squint. "Before what gets out of hand? And what the hell are you doing at the bar after curfew?"

"I'll tell you later. Just get down here."

Less than ten minutes later, Kelly pulled open the door to the hotel's bar, aptly named Trouble. She stepped inside, let the ornate glass door close behind her and took root at the entrance to get her bearings. Most of the hotel bars she'd been in were on the sedate side, but not Trouble. Up-tempo Latin music filled the air, along with the animated chatter of its clientele, which seemed to consist mainly of young women showing off their ample assets in the skimpiest outfits she'd ever seen. Since it was widely known that the hotel was utilized by most of the teams in the league when they traveled to Miami, it was obvious why all the women were here—to score with a ballplayer.

The room was oblong, with a horseshoe-shaped bar in the middle of it. There was a parquet dance floor to the left of the bar, and to the right was a section with strategically placed tables, chairs and small plush couches for customers to talk and mingle. The lights were low, and the women plentiful. It was the ideal place for a Blaze player to hook up with a cleat chaser—if he were so inclined.

Advancing into the bar, she threaded her way through the crowd. Several of the overly tanned and heavily made-up women gave her pitying looks. She ignored them. In her rush, she'd hastily pulled on jeans, a T-shirt and a pair of flip-flops. She'd dressed for speed, not style. Her only goal to diffuse whatever situation Matt had gotten himself into.

The sound of raised voices caught her attention. Following the sound, she saw Matt standing between J.T.

and another man, who were glaring angrily at each other. Matt had his hand on J.T.'s chest as if restraining him. Kelly quickly headed toward them and noted that a group of onlookers had gathered around the trio.

"What's the problem?" She met Matt's exasperated gaze as she stepped between two gawkers.

"I'll tell you what the problem is," the stocky man standing next to Matt said before Matt could answer. "This guy," he pointed toward J.T. with a short pudgy finger, "punched me in the face."

Kelly peered at him. His face was doughy and he had a bushy mustache with eyebrows to match, but there was no evidence he'd been struck. There wasn't a mark on him.

"That's a lie," J.T. protested hotly. "You came at me and I pushed you." J.T. turned toward her, worry clouding his expression. "I swear I didn't punch him."

"The hell you did." The man's voice rose. "Someone call the cops. I'm pressing charges."

"Wait a minute." Kelly held up her hand and directed her attention back to Matt. "What did you see?"

"Not a damn thing. I went to the bar to get a beer. When I came back they were shoving each other."

"Take J.T. to his room. I'll talk to…" She swung her gaze to the man. "I'm sorry, what's your name, sir?"

"Chuck. And I don't take kindly to anyone talking shit about my team."

"I don't wanna go back to my room." J.T.'s tone was belligerent.

"And I'm not leaving you here with…" Matt glared at Chuck, "…this clown."

"Who are you calling a clown, Scanlon?" Chuck demanded, but quickly shut his mouth when Matt gave him his trademark stink eye.

"I can handle this," Kelly said sternly and looked from Matt to J.T. "It's past curfew. If you don't want me to report this infraction then you'd better get your asses back to your rooms and let me talk to Chuck." She glared at Matt and pressed her lips together into a grim line. As far as she was concerned he was just as guilty as J.T. Maybe even more so since he was older than J.T. and should be setting an example.

Matt put his hand on J.T.'s shoulder. "Let's go." His tone was stern. J.T. seemed to know when to cut his losses and gave Chuck a stony glare before Matt nudged him toward the door.

"So you're a Marlins fan?" She turned to Chuck as Matt and J.T. headed for the exit. The lookie-loos dispersed, leaving her alone with the man who could get J.T. in a lot of trouble if she didn't handle him properly.

"Since their first season in '93." He frowned, which made his two bushy eyebrows come together in such a way that he appeared to have a caterpillar across his forehead. "That idiot was talking trash about my team. I couldn't let that go."

"I understand," she said with a sympathetic nod. "I'm sorry this happened and I totally get why you feel the need to press charges." She put her hand on his arm and squeezed lightly. "But I'm sure we can settle this without any police involvement."

Chuck's caterpillar brow lifted. "Are you trying to bribe me?"

"That depends." She smiled. Chuck's expression was one of interest, not outrage. This was going to be easier than she thought. "Can you be bribed?"

Chuck tilted his head and regarded her with a calculated expression before replying, "Maybe."

"Then let's get a beer and have a little chat." Kelly slipped her arm through his and led him toward the bar. "I think you'll be very happy with what I have to offer."

AFTER KISSING CHUCK'S ass for almost an hour, Kelly let herself into her room and made a beeline for the bathroom where she stripped off her clothes, pinned her hair up and took a hot shower. Once she'd washed the stench of Trouble off of her body, she dried herself and slathered scented lotion over her skin. Grabbing her robe off of the hook on the door, she slipped it on, gathered her clothes and returned to her room.

The Blaze were leaving for Washington, D.C., tomorrow morning so she shoved her clothes into a plastic bag with the others she'd worn this week and set it next to her suitcase on the floor. The hotel they'd been booked into had a laundry service and she planned to use it. She wasn't one to pack a lot of clothes and counted on either a laundry service or coin-op washing machines to get her through long road trips.

A quick glance at the clock on the nightstand caused her to wince. It was nearly two, and not only was she wired, the beat of Latin music still throbbed in her head. How many times could they play the extended version of "Conga" in an hour? Three times, that's how many. Evidently Gloria Estefan was big in Miami.

Damn Matt and J.T. They were the reason she'd be one of the walking dead tomorrow. Their charter flight was leaving at nine-thirty, which meant she'd have to be up no later than seven. That meant virtually no sleep since she wasn't going to be nodding off into dreamland anytime soon.

The sharp knock on her door didn't surprise her. It had to be J.T. come to find out about his fate. She squared her shoulders, moved to the door and pulled it open.

"You're damn lucky..." she began her rant and then went silent. It wasn't J.T. at her door, it was Matt. "What do *you* want?" Kelly demanded, taken aback by his unexpected presence. And it didn't help that despite his well-worn jeans and faded UCLA T-shirt, he looked just as sexy as he had in the sport coat and dress pants he'd worn to and from the ballpark.

"To find out what happened after J.T. and I left the bar." His gaze slid downward, reminding her she was wearing just her robe. It was short, and the coral-colored fabric brushed against her skin like satin. Feeling practically naked, she reached for the belt and tightened the knot.

"You could have asked me tomorrow."

"I want to know now." Matt lifted his gaze. His eyes were unreadable, but by the stubborn set of his jaw it was clear she wasn't going to get rid of him easily. "Can I come in for a few minutes? I don't want to talk about this in the hall."

Even as her common sense screamed *don't let him in* she motioned for him to enter. "Fine. It shouldn't take long."

As he brushed past her she caught a whiff of his scent and steeled herself against the memories it evoked. It didn't work. She was transported back to their last kiss; she could almost feel his mouth on hers, devouring her. Her body reacted just as it had that night—her nipples pebbled against her silky robe and frissons of heat raced up her spine. Flustered by her response, she closed the door and took a deep breath before she turned to face him.

"Is J.T. in trouble?" he asked. He stood at the foot of her rumpled bed. The sight conjured up erotic images she couldn't shake and deep in the center of her being was a sweet ache that didn't want to be denied. *Jesus.* What was wrong with her? She'd been avoiding Matt since they'd left San Francisco and within the space of two minutes she was turned on. It had to stop. She had to *make* it stop before she did something really stupid. Like have sex with a man who'd left a long trail of women in his wake.

"No." Kelly averted her eyes from the bed and cleared her throat. "I saved his sorry ass and yours too. Chucky isn't going to press charges and I'm not going to report you for being out past curfew."

"How'd you get him to back off?"

"I called a friend from college who works for the Marlins. He wasn't too pleased about being woken up at one in the morning but he owes me so I cashed in the favor. Chuck will be getting field-level Marlins seats for the rest of the season."

"Sweet. You saved the day," Matt said with a hint of admiration in his voice.

"I wouldn't have had to 'save the day,' as you put it, if you and J.T. had been in your rooms where you were supposed to be." Irritated, she put her hands on her hips and glowered at him. She wouldn't let his approval sway her. "So much for changing your ways."

His expression darkened. "For your information, I was in my room at curfew until J.T. called. He was well on his way to getting hammered, so I went downstairs to get him."

"Yet you ordered a beer. That doesn't sound like you planned on leaving anytime soon."

"So sue me." Matt dragged a hand through his hair. "I was thirsty."

"Oh, I'm sure you wanted to sample more than just a beer."

"What the hell does that mean? Do you think I went down there to pick up a woman?"

"Wouldn't be the first time."

Matt took two steps, halted in front of her and pinned her with a stare so intense she had to force herself not to take a step back. He looked like a pirate—dark, dangerous and forceful. "Do you know what I think?"

She rolled her eyes. "Do I look like a mind reader?"

"I think you *want* to think the worst of me. Because as long as you let yourself believe I'm the same guy I was a year ago you don't have to deal with what you're feeling."

"What am I feeling?" She met his gaze head-on despite the thundering of her heart and the slight quivering of her knees. "Come on, Mr. Know-It-All. Tell me what I feel."

"You want me." The hunger in his eyes stole her breath. "Just as much as I want you."

"Could your ego be any bigger?"

"Could you be in any more denial?" he shot back.

"Denial?" She almost snorted. "*You*—you're the one in denial. You can't seem to get it through that thick skull of yours that I'm not interested."

"Wanna bet?" he said, just before his hand snaked around her waist to pull her roughly to him. Her outraged protest was smothered when he took possession of her mouth, his kiss so voracious her mind went completely blank and her insides melted like butter on a hot griddle. His fingers burned through the fabric of her robe and his lips tasted like everything she'd been dreaming about since the first time he'd kissed her.

When he pulled his mouth from hers she was breathless. Their eyes locked and the air around them crackled with sexual energy.

"Do you want me to leave?" Matt asked in a low voice, not loosening his hold on her.

Her heart pounded in double time as she considered his question. She should tell him to go. To get the hell out and never touch her again. But the words wouldn't come. As much as she hated to admit it, he was right; she couldn't deny it any longer. Her body ached from wanting him. She was going to have him right here— right now—even if she regretted it tomorrow.

"No," she whispered and slid her hands up his biceps to his shoulders to plunge her hands into his hair. She pulled him to her and kissed him; there was no mistaking the hungry, sensual growl low in his throat as she opened her mouth, eager for the feel of his tongue stroking hers.

Now that her decision was made, Kelly's pulse spiked when he reached between them and fumbled with the knot of her belt. Reluctantly, she tore her lips from his, lowered her arms and took a step back. Matt scrubbed his jaw, puzzlement evident in his dark eyes.

"You first."

A slow sinful smile transformed his face. "Not a problem."

Obviously it wasn't. In less than a minute he'd divested himself of his clothes and stood before her as naked as the day he was born. And, *holy shit*, he had the most perfect body she'd ever seen in her life.

"Satisfied?"

Not yet. Kelly couldn't help but let her gaze steal down his wide shoulders to his sculpted chest where, hidden beneath dark hair, she saw small brown nipples. Glancing lower, her gaze rested on his rippling abs and then she followed the trail of dark hair that started at his navel and ended at his groin. Her breath caught in her throat when she saw proof that she wasn't the only one turned on. Anticipation surged through her veins and turned her knees to gelatin.

"Wait," Matt ordered as she began to loosen the knot on her belt with trembling fingers. She paused as he bent over, grabbed his jeans off the floor and pulled his wallet out of his pocket. He dropped the jeans, opened his wallet and, with a roguish grin, pulled out a condom.

She couldn't suppress her smile as he held up the foil packet and let the wallet fall to the floor. "You carry a condom around with you?"

"Better to have one than none." He tossed the packet on the bed behind her and met her gaze with an amused glint in his eyes. "You're overdressed," he said and moved to stand in front of her. He covered her hand with his. "I'd like to do the honors, if you don't mind." He nudged her hand away and began to untie the knot.

When the belt was undone, Matt slipped his thumbs under the lapels of her robe and slid it off of her shoulders. It fell to the floor and pooled around her ankles. His gaze raked boldly over her. Kelly's heart pounded. Before her stood a man with the perfect body, and hers, well, hers wasn't. Just as those old fears began to take hold Matt looked up; the sexual heat in his eyes chased them away.

Without saying a word, he reached behind her and removed the pins from her hair. As it cascaded to her shoulders, he pulled her against the hard wall of his chest and covered her mouth with a blistering kiss that was hotter than any one of the four that had come before it—not that she was counting, or anything.

Like before, everything faded away and the only things that registered were his warm moist mouth, and the exquisite feel of his bare skin against hers. Every part of her body seemed fused to his. Her breasts crushed against his chest, his erection nudged between her legs and his thighs felt like granite against hers. Slipping her arms around his muscled back, she didn't resist as he urged her toward the bed and broke their kiss to gently ease her to the mattress.

A mixture of anticipation and desire throbbed through her veins as he settled beside her. "I'll bet you never thought we'd end up here." His mouth quirked with amusement as he gazed down at her.

"Never." She reached up to brush a lock of hair from his forehead and then lightly caressed his temple. "It's funny how quickly things can change."

"Yeah. It is." His gaze roamed over her face, then he lowered his head to reclaim her mouth. His kiss was scorching; every nerve ending in her body started to sizzle. She sifted her fingers through his hair as he expertly seduced her with his firm lips and hot tongue.

Dear Lord, the man could kiss, and more than that, he didn't seem to be one of those guys who kissed a woman once and then proceeded directly to the main event. No,

Matt was thorough, and in a matter of minutes his kisses alone had reduced her into a mindless puddle of desire.

As he trailed his lips to her jaw, he moved his hand to her breast. Her breath hitched as he lightly brushed his thumb over her taut nipple and then leaned down to draw it into his mouth. The sensation was incredible, the throbbing ache between her legs intensified. Again, he was patient, content to tease her by tonguing and sucking her nipples as if he had all the time in the world. By the time he slid his hand to her abdomen, her body was practically screaming for him to touch her where she was wet and oh-so-ready for him.

He was ready for her too. Kelly could feel his cock pressing insistently into her hip. The thought of him hot and hard inside of her was almost too much. She loved everything he was doing, but if she didn't have him soon she was pretty sure she'd lose her damn mind. She was a woman with needs—damn it—and right now she needed him to make her come.

"Matt," she managed to whisper. He lifted his head; a wicked gleam sparkled in his eyes. "You're driving me crazy."

"Good." He slid his hand even lower. Her body pulsed with anticipation. "That was my intention."

"Then you've achieved your objective." She slid her palm down his shoulder to smooth her fingers over the light coating of dark hair on his forearm. "And I'm really close to achieving mine so..."

"Cut to the chase, right?" The corners of his sensual mouth tilted in a sexy half smile. "No problem," he said and in one quick movement slipped his finger into her wet heat. She gasped in surprise and couldn't contain a soft moan as he stroked her expertly, brushing her clit with each movement of his finger. She met his hot gaze, unable to look away.

Over and over, he teased her. Bringing her to the brink with his languid and swirling strokes and then backing off, leaving her breathless and almost begging him to make her come.

Grasping at the bed, she fisted the sheet with her fingers, closed her eyes and lifted her hips, seeking relief. He still didn't give it to her. Her body was on fire and it wasn't until a low moan slipped past her lips, a helpless sound of want, that he zeroed in on her clit and set her off. Her orgasm was so intense she couldn't contain another moan—this one much louder as wave after wave of pleasure rocked her body and left her breathless. He stayed with her, gently stroking her as she calmed from his sensual onslaught.

Her body was still radiating with pleasurable aftershocks when she felt Matt move. She opened her eyes and found him kneeling beside her and reaching for the foil packet he'd tossed on the bed earlier. She watched, enjoying the play of his muscles as he made quick work of slipping the condom over his rock-hard erection.

He turned and their eyes locked. No words were spoken; none were needed. The pure unadulterated hunger in his eyes said it all. This moment was inevitable and had been since the first time his lips had touched hers.

When he lowered himself over her and entered her with one smooth thrust, a ragged murmur of satisfaction slipped from his throat. Sliding her hands to his shoulders, she arched up to meet his next thrust and then dug her nails into his skin as he fucked her with excruciatingly slow strokes that stimulated her already sensitive clit. Could she possibly come again? For her, it wasn't always a sure thing when it came to intercourse.

"You feel so good." He lowered his head to plant a searing kiss on her lips. "Wrap your legs around me, baby," he whispered against her mouth.

Kelly did as he asked and let out a soft gasp as he drove into her even more deeply. She clung to him as each stroke became a little bit harder, went a little bit deeper and brought her a little bit closer to another orgasm. Stunned by the unlikely occurrence, she found herself grinding her hips against his at each thrust. Within seconds she was over the edge again, the pleasure just as explosive as the first time. As it crashed over her body, she couldn't stop the passionate moan that slipped past her lips. It was probably loud enough to wake the dead, but she didn't care. Not when it felt this good.

"Jesus," he whispered huskily and began to move faster. A few strokes later, he drove into her one final time and let out a masculine groan of pleasure as he collapsed on top of her.

With her legs still wrapped around his hips, Kelly trailed her fingers down his back. His skin was moist with perspiration, as was hers. The room was quiet except for the sound of their slightly labored breathing. She savored the moment, unsure of what was next. Was this a one-night stand, or something more? God help her, she wanted it to be something more.

Matt lifted his head and grinned. "I'm crushing you."

"I'm fine," she assured him, and relaxed her legs to cradle him between her thighs.

"You won't be in a minute." He pushed himself up and eased off of her. "Besides, I need to use the bathroom."

After he'd shut the bathroom door behind him, Kelly was at a loss as to what was going to happen next. Would Matt leave or would he stay? Should she get up and put her robe on or stay put? She was still mulling her options when he left the bathroom sans condom and crawled into bed beside her.

He was staying. Her heart did a happy dance and then resumed its normal beating.

"It's after three," he said as he stretched out beside her and rolled to his side. "I guess we'll have to get some sleep on the plane tomorrow."

"I can't sleep on planes. Or any type of public transportation. The thought of people watching me sleep freaks me out."

"Then I promise not to stare at you when you fall asleep." His brow furrowed. "That is if you want me to stay. I want to, but we are on a road trip and there's a chance someone might see me leave your room."

"I'll take that chance."

Matt touched the faded scar on her abdomen. "What's this from?"

"Appendectomy." Goose bumps rose on her skin as he traced the scar with his finger. "When I was sixteen. It hurt like hell."

"And this one?" He moved his finger to her other scar—the one just below her left breast.

"I had a run-in with a barbed-wire fence when I was a kid." She smiled when he glanced up at her. "In case you haven't figured it out, Kayla was the girly girl, and I was the tomboy."

"You may have been a tomboy back then," a wicked smile curved his lips, "but, baby, you're all woman now."

FIFTEEN

A LOUD AND irritating chirping noise roused Matt out of a sound sleep. "What the hell?" he muttered as, next to him, Kelly groaned and reached blindly for her cell phone on the nightstand. She fumbled with it and then finally—blessed silence.

"It's time to get up, isn't it?" he asked as he slipped his arm around her waist and pulled her to him. Against his flesh, her body was warm and soft; his dick, already at half-mast just because it was morning, pressed into the crevice of her ass.

"Mmm...unfortunately, yes." Her voice was even sexier in the morning. "It's six-thirty. We have to be on the bus for the airport by seven forty-five," she added, but made no move to get out of bed.

Fine with him. It had been a long time since he'd woken up next to a woman he actually liked. It was different—in a good way—and he wanted to prolong the experience for as long as he could.

Content, he pressed his lips to her satiny shoulder and inhaled her sweet fragrance. Then he slid his hand across her rib cage to cup her breast and with his thumb made slow lazy brushes over her nipple. Last night he'd discovered her breasts were very sensitive, and so he'd paid them a lot of attention. Her breathy moans excited him, but he'd taken his time. It wasn't until he'd touched her between her legs and found her soft and wet that he felt like he was going to lose his mind if he didn't fuck her soon. And when he did, it was pretty damn hot. So hot he wanted to do it again right now.

Right now was out of the question. First, he'd only had the one condom in his wallet, and second, he had to get back to his room without any of his teammates, or the skipper, seeing him. If word got out that he and Kelly had slept together, the news would spread like wildfire throughout the Blaze organization and could adversely affect her reputation, and maybe even her job if the team had a no-fraternization policy between the front office staff and the players. He couldn't let that happen. Kelly loved her job. There was no way he would let her become the subject of gossip or possibly be fired because of him.

With great reluctance, he slipped his hand from her breast, shoved the sheet aside and got out of bed. He stepped over his clothes and went into the bathroom to take care of business. When he returned to the room, Kelly was sitting up, clutching the sheet to her chest, covering her statuesque body. Her golden-brown hair was in tangled disarray around her shoulders, her lips were still swollen from last night's kisses, and her amber eyes were sultry as her gaze skated over his chest, then lower.

She looked sexier than hell, making it awfully hard for him to leave. Again, something he wasn't used to. Leaving was his specialty.

Trying to ignore the arousal that tugged at his groin, he made quick work of picking his clothes up from the floor and getting dressed. Kelly was silent but he could feel her watching him. Did she regret last night? He hoped not. He didn't regret it and wanted a repeat—as soon as possible.

When he finished tying his shoes, he looked up. "For the record, I really don't want to leave right now," he said and noted the slight widening of her eyes.

"I don't want you to leave either," she said almost shyly. Funny, shyness was one trait he'd never associated with her.

"Finally." Matt grinned broadly. "We agree on something."

"Who says miracles can't happen." She laughed softly. "For weeks we've hated each other's guts and now…" She twisted the hem of the sheet with her fingers.

"And now we don't. Don't worry. I know you're still going to ride my ass about those interviews."

Kelly lifted her chin and gave him the same indomitable glare he'd seen ever since the night they'd met. Only now it didn't piss him off. "Damn straight, I am."

"I go to the media room after every game." Matt moved to the bed and looked down at her. "That's more than enough."

"Tell that to the dozens of reporters and sports anchors I've been putting off ever since you were traded." She let out a long sigh. "It's not easy placating them."

"Yet you make it seem effortless." He bent down intending to give her a quick kiss, but the moment his lips met hers it turned into much more than that. She parted her mouth and he couldn't resist deepening the kiss. He reached behind her head and fisted her hair in hand, his primal instincts kicking in just from the warm moist feel of her mouth against his. Her unrestrained response sent a shot of liquid heat straight to his dick; it was all he could do not to get back into bed and kiss every inch of her amazing body.

He was about five seconds from doing that when

common sense reared its annoying head. With a low groan, he pulled back. "Rain check?" His gut kicked as he met her luminous gaze and erotic images from the night before played in his head. How the hell was he supposed to function when all he could think about was making her come in every way imaginable?

Kelly's lips tilted in a suggestive smile. "Rain check." The husky sound of her voice didn't help to cool the lust in his veins or between his legs. He could listen to her read the box scores and get turned on.

He let go of her hair and lightly brushed her soft cheek with his fingers. "See you later," he said and then headed for the door. After opening it, he checked the hallway and slipped out, closing it behind him. As he strode toward his room, he made a mental note to buy condoms. Maybe it was presumptuous, but he had a strong feeling he was going to need them.

AFTER FINISHING HER latest press release, Kelly saved the file and powered down her laptop. As soon as she checked in to the hotel in D.C., she'd email it to her media contacts and check in with her Washington Nationals counterpart. A number of local reporters and broadcasters had requested interviews, and since most of them wanted to be the one to score an interview with the elusive Matt Scanlon, she was going to have to siphon them off to other players. That task should be easy to accomplish. Rizzo had never met a reporter he didn't like, Marquis Lopes was currently on a highly touted hitting streak and rookie pitcher Trey Gentry had come within one inning of throwing a no-hitter during the Marlins series. All of them were in demand for interviews. She could—and would—use that to her advantage.

She sipped the Frappuccino she'd picked up at the coffee shop in the airport before takeoff, vaguely aware of the muted chatter of the players and coaches sitting around her. The chartered airplane was spacious. Some of the players congregated in groups and talked baseball, others preferred to sit by themselves and listen to music on their MP3 players. Matt and J.T. usually sat together and this morning was no different—except for one thing: they were both sound asleep, dead to the world.

When J.T. had boarded the plane, it was obvious by his wan complexion and bloodshot eyes that he was hungover. Kelly didn't feel one bit sorry for him. He'd brought it on himself by drinking way more than he was used to. He was damn lucky Tom Morgan had changed up the roster and had him starting tomorrow's game in Matt's place instead of tonight's as planned. He'd fallen asleep with his head against the window before the plane had left Miami.

As for Matt, well, when he boarded the plane he didn't resemble a man who'd only gotten a few hours of sleep. Instead he looked refreshed and stunningly handsome, if not a bit preppy, in his brown corduroy sport coat, light blue button-up shirt and khaki pants. He and J.T. had chosen a row two up from hers and when their eyes met, the scorching heat in his almost melted her panties. It was one of those *remember what we did last night?* looks followed up with a *and we're going to do it again* smile that made her quiver with anticipation. After that, it was hard to concentrate on that press release.

Or anything else, for that matter.

Two hours later, Kelly sat on an extremely comfortable tweed-covered chair in the dramatic lobby of the Liaison Capitol Hill hotel. In no hurry to check in, she snorted derisively as she read Angie's latest text. If there was an award for the worst boyfriend ever, Scott would win by a landslide. It was bad enough that he rarely took Angie out, or socialized with her friends or family, but now the tightwad had really crossed the line. Angie's birthday was approaching and she had her heart set on a weekend trip to the Napa Valley. But stick-up-his-ass Scott had canceled the trip because gas prices were too high. According to Angie, his exact words were "there's no way I'm paying that much money just to watch grapes grow."

"Loser," she muttered, shoved her phone into the side pocket of her purse and gazed up at the large portrait of Martin Luther King, Jr. on the wall opposite her. She studied it for a moment, imagining what it might have been like to live through those turbulent times. Here she was, so close to the Lincoln Memorial where Dr. King gave his "I Have a Dream" speech but she had no time to visit the memorial, or any other of the historic sites she'd always wanted to see. Unfortunately, traveling with the team left little time for sightseeing.

Shifting her gaze from the portrait, her pulse spiked when Matt moved toward her, key card in hand. She tried not to devour him with her eyes—a losing battle because the man was just too damn gorgeous not to ogle. He'd forgone his morning shave. A dark shadow stubbled his sculpted jaw. *Could he be any sexier?* She thought not and despite her best effort not to be, she was affected. Looking at him reminded her of last night and how he'd taken her to a place she'd never been before. A place where her usual inhibitions had slipped away; where, for the first time in her life, she'd existed wholly in the moment. No uncertainties—just pleasure.

"What are you doing after the game?" he asked after he'd halted in front of her.

"The usual. I'll either get something to eat at the ballpark or order something when I get back to my room."

"Have dinner with me."

Kelly glanced past him to where Gentry and Rizzo stood near the front desk speaking with the concierge. As much as she wanted to say yes, it wouldn't be wise for her and Matt to be seen alone together. It wasn't as if she hadn't shared a meal with the players before, but it was usually in a group, never alone. Was she being paranoid? Maybe, but her job was important to her; she had to remain professional at all times. Or, at the very least, in public.

"We can't," she said with a decisive shake of her head. "Anyone on the team could see us."

"They won't if we order room service." When she hesitated he continued in a low voice, "Look, I want to spend time with you, and since we can't do it the normal way right now, we have to improvise."

Right now? Did that mean things would be different when they got back to San Francisco?

"It's just dinner," Matt said when she didn't respond.

It wasn't just dinner and they both knew it. The attraction between them was too strong for that. They would start with dinner and end up in bed. The thought of making love with him again was exciting—all the more because it was clandestine. The Blaze didn't have a formal policy prohibiting front office personnel from dating the players, but because of the possible professional ramifications she had never once considered getting involved with any member of the team.

Until now. Now that she'd gotten a taste of him, she wanted more. One night with Matt wasn't enough.

Rising from the chair, Kelly slung her purse over her shoulder. "My room. After the game." The wicked gleam in his eyes made her body hum with anticipation. "I'll call room service." She gave him a naughty smile. "You bring the condoms."

MATT SAT AT the oblong table in the Nationals' visiting team's media room facing a myriad of reporters who, from his perspective, resembled a bunch of hungry vultures waiting to pounce and pick his carcass clean. After each question, a few of the older vultures wrote furiously on their notepads, while the younger ones used laptops and recording devices. It was insane how many reporters had squeezed into the small room. They were packed in like sardines but none of them seemed to care as long as they got a good sound bite.

"Okay, folks," Kelly said from the back of the room where she'd been standing since the grand inquisition had begun. "One more question and we're done."

Thank God. He wanted to kiss her for finally bringing this circus to an end. That wasn't the only reason. She looked seriously hot and he wasn't the only one who'd noticed. Several of his teammates had done a double take when she'd strolled into the locker room before the game. For some reason she'd worn a dress tonight. Not that he was complaining, but it was unusual. He didn't know much about women's clothing but he'd undressed enough women in his day to know she was wearing a wrap dress. He hoped to unwrap that dress very soon.

"Matt, what do you have to say about that play at home plate in the bottom of the ninth?" a reporter from a prestigious baseball magazine asked. "It's clear on the replay you tagged Zimmerman before he touched the bag. That call cost you guys the game."

The reporter was right. Not only did that call cost them the game, the loss had dropped them down in the standings and into a tie with the Dodgers, who had won their game earlier in the evening.

Matt shot a sideways glance at Marquis Lopes and Trey Gentry who sat next to him at the table. Their somber expressions spoke volumes. They were worried. It was coming down to the wire. The division was up for grabs and any mistake could potentially cost them the title. But what was worse than a bad call was if his teammates let this loss get into their heads and fuck up their thinking. Mental mistakes at this time of the year could be devastating.

"There's not much to say." He leaned forward to rest his arms on the table. "Zimmerman was out. The ump couldn't see the tag from his vantage point. It happens." He scanned the room, his gaze resting on Kelly's solemn face for a few seconds before moving on. "There's still a lot of baseball left to play. I have no doubt the Blaze are going to the postseason."

"Is that a prediction?" another reported called out.

Matt shrugged. "Call it whatever you want," he said and looked at Lopes and Gentry before staring directly into the camera recording the press conference. "This team has the most talented group of guys I've ever played with. I'm not worried," he said confidently, and with that took the first step to putting his past with the Dodgers behind him. Even if it was only for the rest of the season, he was a member of the San Francisco Blaze and he'd do everything in his power to get them to the

World Series, and then win the whole fucking thing. It wasn't about him. It was about Kelly, J.T., Lopes, Gentry and the rest of the team—even that jerk-off Rizzo who he disliked intensely. But more importantly, he had to do it for Lily. He'd made her a promise, and unlike the last promise he'd made, he was going to keep this one.

After the longest bus ride in history, and then making a pit stop in his room to change into jeans and a polo shirt, Matt finally knocked on Kelly's door. Feeling a bit shady, he glanced to his left and then his right. The hallway was clear. As he waited he hoped no one from the team would happen by and question why he was standing outside of Kelly's room after curfew.

When she opened the door, she was smiling, radiant, and still wearing the print dress she'd worn during the game. The only difference was her hair was no longer in a ponytail, and she'd taken off her shoes. She looked so damn gorgeous his breath jammed in his throat, and then his brain faltered as her sweet citrusy scent enveloped him. He didn't know what the fuck was going on with him, but he wasn't going to question it. He was, however, going to enjoy the hell out of it.

"I have good news and bad news," she said as she pulled the door open so he could enter. "Which do you want first?"

"The bad news," he said as he moved past her. The room was a carbon copy of his. The walls and furniture were dark, and the bed had a high chocolate-brown leather-covered headboard. The cream-colored bedspread, off-white ceiling and silver light fixtures contrasted with the dark colors and saved the room from looking like a dungeon.

"The bad news is the restaurant that provides in-room

dining is closed for the evening." She closed the door and turned toward him. "The good news is that the front desk clerk recommended a place across the street that's open until three in the morning. She sent a bellman over to pick up the order. I hope you like cheeseburgers." Kelly lowered her eyes to the small brown bag he held in his hand. Her lips curved in a sly smile as she pointed to it. "Is that what I think it is?"

"You said bring condoms." He grinned. "So I brought condoms."

Less than an hour later, Matt was sitting on the only available seating option other than the bed—the dark brown couch placed against the wall parallel to the bed and just under the large picture window that afforded a view of the rooftops of the buildings across the street. Not that he cared about the view outside, he was more interested in the view inside the room.

He'd finished his cheeseburger, which wasn't half bad considering it came from a place inexplicably called the Billy Goat Tavern and Grill. Kelly had eaten half of hers and had excused herself to go to the bathroom. He used the prepackaged wet napkin that had come in the bag to wipe his hands and then got up and disposed of the paper bag in the trash can next to the dresser. He heard the toilet flush and then the sound of running water. When Kelly came out of the bathroom, she stopped short and her cheeks turned a faint shade of pink.

"Were you listening?" Her tone was accusatory, her face tight with tension.

Surprised at her reaction, he shook his head. "I was throwing the bag in the trash."

"Oh." She tugged at her bottom lip with her teeth and then gave him an apologetic smile. "Sorry, it's just when

I saw you it reminded me of…" She shrugged a shoulder. "My parents used to stand outside the bathroom door whenever I came over for dinner. They wanted to make sure I wasn't purging."

"Was it hard to stop?" He'd been curious about her eating disorder ever since she'd shared it with him, but it didn't feel right to come at her with a million questions so he'd decided not to say anything unless she brought it up.

"It was the hardest thing I've ever done in my life."

He shoved his hands into the front pockets of his jeans. "I thought that was dealing with me."

The tension eased from her face as she laughed. "You were the second hardest thing." She brushed her hair back over her shoulder. "That reminds me. Nice job in the media room tonight. The team really needed to hear what you said."

"I meant every word. I honestly believe we have what it takes to get to the Series."

"You're making them believe it too. After we lost Rick, the team's morale tanked big-time." She moved to stand in front of him and put her hand on his biceps. Her touch was electric. A current of heat shot straight to his groin. "You've changed that. You're becoming their leader."

"I don't think Rizzo would agree." He slipped his hands from his pockets and slid them around her waist, drawing her closer. She stepped into his embrace, a perfect fit.

Kelly wrinkled her nose. "Let's not waste time talking about him."

"Works for me," Matt said, very much aware of the length of her body pressing into his. He dipped his hands to the sweet curve of her ass and nudged her hips forward. The ridge of his cock pressed into her softness. A knowing smile curved her lips—she was fully aware he was quickly becoming turned on. "So, what do you want to talk about?" he asked as he gently kneaded her pliant flesh.

"I don't want to talk." The sudden intensity in her eyes mesmerized him. He could barely think, or breathe. All day, even during the game, he'd thought about this moment—the moment when he would have her again.

"What do you want?" he asked, surprised by the need that threatened to consume him.

"I want you." Her voice was low, hypnotic and unbearably sexy. "Can I have you?"

SIXTEEN

COULD SHE HAVE HIM? Matt didn't have to think twice
before answering *that* question. But instead of words,
he gave Kelly his answer by capturing her mouth with
his. The taste of her, silky and warm, was all it took. He
parted her lips and groaned when their tongues met in a
slow sensual duel that rocked him to the bone.

Completely immersed in her, he was only marginally
aware of her hands sliding up his shoulders. But then,
when she caressed his nape with her fingertips, a tingling sensation ran up his spine and made him shiver.
What the hell was that? Whatever it was, he damn well
wanted to feel it again. And he did when she massaged
the back of his neck with soft gentle strokes. Growling
soft and low in his throat, he pulled his lips from hers,
surprised by his body's reaction to the mere touch of her
fingers on his skin.

Kelly's lids fluttered open, revealing eyes smoky with
desire. "I guess that answers my question." She rested
her hands on his shoulders and continued with a suggestive tilt of her lips, "I have a confession to make."

"After last night, I know you're not a guy. So what's
the big confession?" he asked and chuckled when she
let out a short burst of laughter. He kept one hand on her
firm ass and slid the other along the curve of her back.
He could feel the band of her bra under her dress. Both
would be coming off very soon.

"I've been thinking about this all day."

"Join the club," he said and kissed her again. He couldn't believe how sweet she tasted, how good she smelled and how right it felt to hold her in his arms. As their lips fused together passionately, his only thought was he wanted to bury himself inside of her and not come out until he'd gotten his fill.

With that goal in mind, he broke their kiss and took a step back. She stared at him mutely as he reached for the bow tied at her waist. Before he could get it undone, she put her hand on his. He looked up and saw a flicker of apprehension in her eyes.

"What's wrong?"

"Maybe we should turn the lights out."

"Why?"

"It's kind of bright in here," she said, averting her gaze.

He cocked his head. "You can't be nervous about me seeing you naked. Not after last night."

"Maybe a little." She looked back at him, her expression pensive. "Last night, well, it just happened so fast and the light in the room was pretty dim."

"It wasn't that dim." He lifted his hand and gently stroked her cheek. "Baby, you're beautiful. Every inch of you."

"And there *are* a lot of inches, aren't there?" Her tone was flippant, but it was evident this was no joke.

Lowering his hand, he quickly figured out what was going on. This insecurity had to be a part of her eating disorder. Almost every woman he'd ever been with had some sort of complaint about her body, but for someone like Kelly, every perceived flaw was most likely magnified a hundred times, or more.

"If you want the lights off, that's fine. But I'm telling you right now, your body looks pretty damn amazing to me." He grinned. "Speaking of confessions, I have one of my own to make."

She regarded him warily. "What?"

"That time in the kitchen—you know—the night Stacia brought me back to your condo."

Kelly's eyes narrowed. "I remember you had a handful of Stacia's ass. That's what I remember."

"Yeah, well." He cleared his throat. "That was before you walked in. After I saw you in those skimpy shorts and tank top, I sure as hell wasn't thinking about Stacia, or her ass. You hide your body under those baggy clothes at work, but you don't have to, Kelly. You're tall, strong and athletic. That's nothing to be ashamed of."

"It doesn't bother you that I'm as tall as you are?"

"Not at all."

"And it doesn't bother you that I weigh over 150 pounds?"

"No. You're almost six-one and you play ball. My guess is you have a pretty low percentage of body fat."

She regarded him thoughtfully for several seconds. "Maybe we could turn off one light." A rueful smile curved her full lips. "Unless I've totally killed the mood."

"You haven't," he said and meant it. He was beginning to realize just how hard she had fought to overcome her illness. And he knew from being with her last night that when she wasn't thinking so much she was able to let go and fully enjoy the moment. "Which light do you want off?" he asked.

She pointed to the floor lamp next to the couch. "That one."

Matt moved to the steel-based lamp and switched it off. That left only the small table lamp atop the nightstand on. The room was considerably less bright, but not so dark that you couldn't see anything. "Is this okay?"

"Yes. Thank you for…for understanding." The luminous smile she gave him took his breath away. How had he not seen how beautiful she was that night in L.A.? Dumb question. He was too busy ogling her sister. But now he couldn't even conjure up an image of Kayla Maxwell. All he saw was Kelly.

Their eyes locked and a deep sexual hunger stirred to life in his midsection. He didn't break eye contact until Kelly reached for the tie of her dress. With deft fingers, she unraveled the bow and tugged at the dress until it was partially open, revealing a glimpse of her black bra and what appeared to be a matching half-slip. She paused and inclined her head. "Take off your shirt."

Matt obeyed her husky command and when his shirt was in a heap on the floor, she stared at his chest. Her bold perusal sent a prickle of anticipation over his skin. "Take off your dress," he said, enjoying this little thing they had going on right now.

Without a word, she slipped the dress from her shoulders and let it fall to the carpet. As he suspected, she was wearing a sexy and sheer black bra and a black slip with a lace hem short enough to reveal a tantalizing glimpse of her creamy thighs. Although she was athletically built, her defined waist and curved hips were enticingly feminine. His grin faded and the blood in his veins burned hot as he took in the magnificence of her body.

"I know the drill," he said before she could speak. Using his feet, he kicked off one shoe and then the other, glad he'd forgone socks. He sensed her eyes on him as he unbuttoned his jeans and tugged at the zipper. He slid both the jeans and his briefs down over his hips, stepped out of them and straightened.

Kelly's gaze, dark and smoldering, slowly slid downward. Whether it was unconscious or not, she licked her lips. It was his undoing. A primal reaction kicked in and, unable to wait any longer, he crossed the short distance between them, and pulled her to his body. He smothered her soft sound of surprise with his mouth. It was no gentle kiss. He sucked at her mouth, groaning as their tongues scraped together. Like a starving man, he dove deeper; she reciprocated, kissing him ravenously, devouring him just as he was devouring her. Completely immersed in her, he couldn't remember ever wanting a woman so badly. His heart thundered in his chest, his body was on fire and his dick was getting harder by the second.

Sliding his hand up her supple back, he unhooked her bra and then, still kissing her, he backed her toward the bed. It must have been closer than he realized because they toppled to the mattress together and Kelly let out a grunt as he landed on top of her.

"Are you okay?" He rolled off of her and, leveraging himself on his elbow, he stared down at her flushed face.

"I'm fine. Help me with this damn thing." As she tugged at the straps of her bra, he eased it off of her and flung it across the room. "Be careful with that," she said indignantly. "It's from Victoria's Secret."

"Duly noted. Do the panties match or are you wearing a thong?"

"No. I hate thongs." She wrinkled her nose and hooked her finger into the waistband of her slip. "When I wear one it feels like I've got a constant wedgie."

Matt laughed as she extricated her legs from her slip and panties and tossed them on the floor beside the bed. She didn't seem to be self-conscious about her body anymore and she was definitely more relaxed. He hoped it was because she felt comfortable with him.

She lifted her arm and gently touched his cheek with her fingers. "You didn't shave today."

"I got lazy. I'll shave tomorrow." He stared at her breasts and then lowered his head and drew a rose-colored nipple into his mouth. Her breath hitched and she twined her fingers in his hair. Just because he knew it drove her crazy, he took his time, moving from one nipple to the other, lavishing both with his tongue until they were taut and glistening from his mouth.

"Matt," she whispered and tugged at his hair. He lifted his head, desire twisting in his gut at the arousal glittering in her eyes. "I want you."

He wanted her too. Badly. But before he had her there was something he had to do. Something he'd been thinking about all day.

"The condoms," she said after he'd moved over her and was between the thighs she'd spread readily for him. "They're on the nightstand."

"Don't worry. I know where they are."

"But..." she began just before he lowered his head and cut off her words with a kiss. She sighed against his mouth and then her hands were on his shoulders, her fingers teasing his skin with featherlight strokes. Although supporting his weight with his palms braced on the bed so he wouldn't crush her, his cock was in direct contact with the softness between her thighs. With memories of last night still fresh in his mind, it took all of the will-power he possessed not to slide into her and fuck her until they were both sweaty and satisfied.

He couldn't do that. At least not yet.

For the past year he'd sought out women to assuage his pain, to help him forget what he'd lost. He was fairly certain that if those women had been polled about his performance in the sack, *selfish* would be right there at the top of the list. It was true. He'd cared more about his own needs than he had about theirs. But now, everything had changed.

Consumed with the need to please, he kissed his way to the pulsing hollow of Kelly's neck and then moved lower. His cock got harder as he suckled her taut nipples and she made those same breathy sounds of pleasure that had turned him on last night. He dipped lower and pressed his lips to her smooth flat stomach, tracing the outline of her belly button with his tongue. She quivered beneath his mouth, but he was the one affected when he caught a whiff of her womanly scent. His body reacted immediately, the need for release strong. It would have to wait. Right now, Kelly came first.

When he reached his final destination, the wetness shimmering on her feminine folds mesmerized him. Her soft pink flesh, swollen with excitement, was both erotic and beautiful. Unable to resist, he lowered his head and tasted her for the first time. It was everything he'd imagined, and more. Soft, silky and wet. Wet for him. It was intoxicating.

"Matt." Her husky voice invoking his name spurred him on, reminding him of his quest. He grasped her hips, lifted her to his mouth and licked her thoroughly before he zeroed in on her clit and circled it with his tongue. "Oh God, that feels so good," she whispered.

Withdrawing, he did it again. He felt her shudder and her low moans of pleasure filled him not only with satisfaction, but with the desire to make her come so hard and so good she would never forget it.

He teased her. First circling her sensitive bud and then flicking it gently until she was whimpering with need and spreading her legs even wider, offering herself to him with no inhibitions or insecurities whatsoever. Before long, the only sounds in the room were her soft pants of pleasure. The quivering of her body told him everything he needed to know. She was on the brink and it was time to send her over the edge. Covering her clit with his mouth, he sucked on it until her body shook, and those soft pants turned into one long moan of pleasure that filled the room and echoed off the walls.

Fully aroused, Matt couldn't wait one more second to be inside of her. He tore his mouth from between her legs, crawled over her and reached for the box of condoms on the nightstand. After making quick work of putting one on, he moved back between her luscious thighs and entered her with one smooth thrust.

After that, there was no thinking. It was all about how she looked up at him with passion-glazed eyes, and how her hips quickly matched his rhythm as they rocked together on the bed. It was about how warm, wet and tight she felt around his cock, how soft her skin was and how her fingers, caressing the back of his neck, were driving him fucking crazy. With his orgasm closing in, he shifted his weight to one side, lifted Kelly's knee over his shoulder and went deeper. She gasped but matched him stroke for sensuous stroke until the heady rush of pleasure exploded in his groin. He rode it out and with a satisfied moan, he collapsed on top of her, content and completely relaxed.

"If I don't move I'm going to fall asleep on top of you." He lifted his head from the crook of her neck. She was smiling. "So, I *am* that good," he said and grinned. "I mean, why else would you look so happy?"

"That's not why I'm smiling," she said but recovered quickly when he gave her a pained look. "Not that you aren't *that* good. Because you are. You're very good. Spectacular even."

Matt rolled his eyes. "Yeah, whatever."

"I was thinking about the night we met," she said as she skimmed her fingers languidly down his back. Her touch was soft and soothing. He didn't want to move a muscle.

"How could that put a smile on your face? Didn't I tell you to fuck off? Or was it you who said that?"

Kelly's eyes sparkled mischievously. "*You* said, 'Fuck you.' And then *I* said, 'Fuck me? You should be so lucky.'"

"And your point is?" He stared at her, not quite getting it.

"My point is you got lucky."

He thought about it for a second and then gave her a cocky grin. "Actually, if you count last night, I got lucky twice."

SEVEN DAYS LATER, Kelly sat in a window seat on the plane taking her and the team back to San Francisco. It was late and the plane, quiet. The interior lights were off and almost all of the guys were asleep. Their final game with the Cardinals had gone into extra innings and in order to secure the win, nearly every player on the team had been utilized. There hadn't been time to celebrate the much-needed victory, or even send the clutch players to the media room to take questions. The team showered immediately, then everyone got onto the bus and they were whisked away to the airport.

She had mixed feelings about returning to the Bay Area. Yes, she was tired of living out of a suitcase, sleeping in hotel rooms and ordering room service every night but, undeniably, this had been the best road trip she'd been on all season. Could anyone blame her for not wanting it to end?

Every night while they were in Washington, D.C., Matt had spent the night in her room, but due to a screwup by the Blaze travel department, the players had to share rooms at the hotel in St. Louis. Of course, Matt and J.T. had buddied up, but after J.T.'s curfew snafu in Miami, neither she nor Matt thought it appropriate for J.T. to see Matt ignoring the same rule they expected him to abide by.

Staying in their respective rooms had to happen at some point. They even joked about finally getting a good night's sleep. But what she hadn't counted on was the way she missed him lying next to her, his body warm and protective as he held her in his arms. Or the way he tenderly kissed her goodbye each morning before he slipped out of her room and went back to his.

Now, because of the feelings he stirred in her, she couldn't help but worry about how things would be between them when they got back home.

Would their relationship continue? Did they even have a relationship, or was it just sex? Matt's past told her that whatever they had would be casual and short-lived, but her heart was having a hard time believing what her mind knew to be true. Matt didn't do commitment, and she just might be nearing her expiration date.

At the front of the plane, Tom Morgan's overhead light was on. As usual, he was preparing for the next game. The man worked hard, she'd give him that. He was one of the younger managers in the league, and although she spoke to him nearly every day she knew as little about him now as she did on the first day she was introduced to him. He was one of those strong silent types who rarely got ruffled. Come to think of it, the only time she'd ever seen him lose his cool was when he and her boss got into it. Katherine seemed to be the only person on the planet who could make the skipper see red.

Just as she was contemplating why there was so much animosity between her boss and Tom Morgan, she felt the row shift. Turning from the window, her heart skipped a beat as Matt settled his large frame on the seat next to her. He smelled of soap and shampoo, reminding her of the steamy nights they'd spent together in D.C. The memories stirred her in a way she definitely shouldn't be stirred right now.

"Not much to see out there." He pointed at the window. "It's pitch-black."

"I thought you were sleeping."

"Can't. I'm too wired." He grinned. "That was some game."

That was an understatement. The game had been tied at one-all until the top of the thirteenth inning. Then with two outs, Matt hit a solo home run to center field and put the Blaze up by a run. In the bottom of the inning, the Cardinals got their first two men on base and were threatening to score when Morgan made the decision to pull their closer and put in Trey Gentry. Trey was able to strike out the next three batters and the Blaze moved one game ahead of the Dodgers in the standings.

"I have a feeling the rest of the season is going to be one helluva roller-coaster ride," Matt said, with an underlying edge of excitement in his voice.

Kelly shifted in her seat, and because she'd raised the armrest, her thigh brushed against his and heightened the beat of her pulse. He looked rakishly handsome in his black slacks and pale blue dress shirt unbuttoned at the collar. "It may come down to the last series of the season," she said, trying to tamp down the urge to run her fingers through his thick wavy hair.

He nodded. "The Dodgers."

Even in the dim light of the cabin she could see Matt's upbeat expression had turned somber. It was unusual for him to talk about his former team. "How do you feel about that?"

"It's surreal."

"I can imagine."

"They were my team for…since always." He hesitated before going on. "When I was a kid I used to imagine playing for them. And when I actually became a Dodger it was like a dream come true."

Kelly smiled. "That's the way I felt when the Blaze hired me."

"I threw it all away." Matt shook his head. "Even while it was happening I knew I was making it easy for them to get rid of me, but that didn't stop me. I wasn't surprised when they traded me, just pissed off at myself for letting it happen."

Her heart constricted. "I know this is the biggest cliché in the world, but sometimes things really do happen for a reason."

A wry smile tugged at his mouth. "Is this where you tell me that the Blaze and I needed each other or some psychobabble like that?"

"We *do* need you," she said adamantly. "Rick Taylor may have been a rookie, but he quickly became the heart and soul of this team. The day we learned he was out for the season we hit rock bottom."

"That's where I was at when I got to San Francisco. Rock bottom."

"But you're not anymore, and neither is the team. We've got a real shot at the postseason because of you."

Matt tilted his head, his eyes quizzical. "How do you know I'm not at rock bottom anymore?"

"Simple," she said with a smile. "I watch you play every day. You're having fun again, aren't you?"

"Yeah." He searched her face and as seconds passed the intense attraction they could no longer deny throbbed between them. "I want to kiss you right now," he said, lowering his voice.

Kelly wanted that too. So much. But they were on the team charter, for heaven's sake. Anyone could walk by and see them making out. *So* not professional.

"You'll have to wait until we get back to the city."

Matt took her hand and with his thumb, made slow lazy circles on her palm. Her skin prickled pleasurably at his light touch. He wasn't making it easy to resist him. "I want to keep seeing you when we get back."

"Seeing me, or sleeping with me?" she asked softly. Might as well see where things stood sooner rather than later. If she was just a booty call then it was *hasta la vista, baby*, no matter how much she wanted him.

"Both," he replied and gave her a slow, sexy grin.

"We'd be dating, then?"

"Yes." He paused. "Am I assuming too much?"

"No." Happiness bloomed inside of her. "I want to keep seeing you too."

"Seeing me, or sleeping with me?" Matt asked with a smart-ass smirk on his face.

"Both."

He leaned forward, his lips mere inches from hers. "Now I *really* want to kiss you."

Lowering her gaze to his mouth, Kelly was sorely tempted to bridge the short distance between them. She knew exactly what he could do with that mouth. Just thinking about it sent a surge of yearning through her body so powerful it was hard to breathe.

"Matt," she whispered, aching to kiss him even as common sense told her it was insane. "We shouldn't."

"One kiss," he said huskily, then his lips covered hers and every coherent thought was stripped from her mind. Passion overrode caution as his mouth coaxed hers open. She surrendered to the demanding urgency of his kiss, welcoming the hot licks of desire coursing through her body.

She wasn't sure when it happened, but he wasn't holding her hand anymore. In fact, his hand was on her thigh. Her *bare* thigh, thanks to her trusty wrap dress—the dress she always brought with her on road trips in case of emergencies like an impromptu dinner with the opposing team's VIPs or—more importantly—when she didn't have access to a washer and dryer in a hotel and wasn't able to wash her regular clothes.

"Matt…" she whispered against his mouth. "What are you doing?"

He trailed his lips to her ear. "I want to touch you," he murmured in a low gravelly voice that sent a hot gush of need between her legs. His hand inched up her thigh, and while a part of her knew she should put an end to this right now, the other part of her—the part that was turned on as hell—won the battle.

Angling her head, she scanned the cabin. Tom Morgan's light was still on. As always, she'd chosen a row in the back of the plane. The guys usually congregated in the front and it was easier to concentrate if she needed to get some work done. There was no one in her general vicinity, but that didn't mean one of the players wouldn't walk to the back to use the restroom.

Did she want to take that chance? As soon as Matt nuzzled her neck, the matter was no longer up for debate.

"Do you want me to stop?" His voice was so low she could barely hear him. Turning her head, she gave him his answer by leaning forward to press her mouth to his. He reacted immediately, seducing her with a long, slow kiss that clouded her mind and set her body aflame.

After that, she didn't know what came over her. All she knew was when his hand reached the top of her thighs, she spread her legs and had to hold back a moan of pleasure when he rubbed her over her panties. And, *holy shit*, did it feel good. Pulling her mouth from his, she sucked in a breath and leaned her head against the seat. Between her legs, Matt stilled his hand. She met his heated gaze. "Don't stop," she whispered, shocked yet totally aroused by what they were doing.

Matt took direction well. He didn't stop. And thankfully, he smothered her lips with another kiss or she would have cried out the second he slipped his hand into her panties and found her hot and wet for him with a stroke of his finger.

That was when the exquisite torture began. Exquisite, because with each gentle movement of his finger against her delicate flesh, he was bringing her closer and closer to fulfillment; torture because she couldn't make a sound for fear of them being discovered.

It was sweet agony.

Soon the tension became almost unbearable. As their kiss deepened, Matt teased her by brushing his thumb over her clit. A tremor of desire shot through her body. This was madness, but she didn't care. She arched her hips, demanding release. And finally, he gave it to her. A rush of pleasure flooded her body; she moaned against his mouth and then froze.

Oh shit.

Matt relinquished her lips. "You weren't that loud," he assured her as he slipped his hand from her panties and scanned the cabin. "All clear," he whispered.

"Are you sure?"

"Yes." He turned to her with a wicked smile on his face. "That was hot."

"We could have been caught," she murmured as she pulled the hem of her dress over her thighs and then pressed her fingers to her cheeks. Her skin felt flushed, *hell*, her whole body felt flushed—and very satisfied. "You should probably go back to your seat."

"Give me a few minutes, okay?"

"Why?"

Matt looked down at his lap, then at her and grinned. "Take a wild guess."

SEVENTEEN

ON MONDAY MORNING, the day after the team had returned to San Francisco, Kelly stepped off the elevator, waved to the receptionist and headed to her office. Today the players were enjoying a much-needed day off, but she wasn't allowing herself that same luxury. Although Katherine had encouraged her to take some time off after the lengthy road trip, the thought of all the emails and media requests awaiting her had been enough for her to resist the temptation to do so.

After she'd watered her plants and turned on her computer, there was a light knock on the office door. She looked up to find Angie at the threshold with a welcoming smile on her face. Her dark hair was tied back and she wore a blue-and-black-print dress that accentuated her slender waist and made her blue eyes seem even brighter. "Hey." Kelly motioned for her to come in.

"How was the trip?" Angie moved to the chair opposite the desk and plopped down. "Did the guys behave themselves?"

"Other than J.T. staying out past curfew one night, they didn't give me any trouble." Kelly opened the desk drawer and dropped her purse inside.

The pleasant expression on Angie's face vanished. "Was he with a cleat chaser?"

"Not that I know of. When I got to him, he'd had more than a few beers at the hotel bar." Kelly closed the drawer and leaned back in her chair. "He got into a fight with a Marlins fan. The guy was going to call the cops but I was able to talk him down."

"That doesn't sound like J.T."

No. It didn't. Matt had mentioned that J.T. had been out of sorts ever since the night he and Angie had gone to Kamu's together. And since Angie's cleat-chaser remark had been tinged with more than just a little jealousy, it didn't take a genius to put two and two together. Something had happened between J.T. and Angie that night. But what? That was the million-dollar question.

"J.T. promised it would never happen again. He was pretty hungover the next morning." She paused. "That reminds me. How's Alexis?"

"She's been keeping to herself. I think she's using the bathroom down by the cafeteria now."

"Damn it." Kelly rubbed her temples. "That's probably my fault. Right before I left on the road trip, I caught her throwing up in the bathroom and confronted her. She denied it, of course."

"Maybe she needs some sort of intervention," Angie suggested. "Have you thought about talking to her parents?"

"Yes." She met Angie's concerned gaze. "I've been going back and forth about it for over a week now."

"If she was my daughter I'd want to know."

Kelly sighed. "Me too."

AT NOON, MATT was standing in front of the mirror in the Blaze gym doing biceps curls when Rizzo entered through the double doors behind him. *Shit.* Just when he'd been enjoying the solitude, the one guy on the team he couldn't stand decided to work out too.

Rizzo caught his glance in the mirror but ignored him and got on one of the treadmills in the back of the room. As much as he disliked the guy, he did admire Rizzo's work ethic. Rizzo wasn't a Cy Young award winner for nothing. He trained hard and was in excellent shape.

Matt finished the curls and replaced the dumbbells on the rack in front of him. He'd been working out for almost two hours and was ready to call it a day. He picked up the towel on the bench next to him, wiped his sweaty brow and headed to the locker room without giving Rizzo another thought.

After he'd showered and dressed, Rizzo strode in and went straight to his locker. Matt was stuffing his work-out clothes into his gym bag when Rizzo walked up to him and stuck a magazine a few inches from his face.

"I thought you weren't giving interviews." Rizzo's tone was accusatory.

Matt recognized the popular weekly baseball magazine and was surprised to see he was on the cover. It was a shot of him with his fist in the air after he'd hit a home run in one of the games they'd played in Miami. The caption read: MATT'S BACK!

"I'm not." Matt shoved the magazine away and glared at Rizzo, whose shaved head glistened with beads of sweat. "What's your problem?"

"My problem is you." Rizzo pointed at him, the contempt in his eyes hard to miss. "I don't like you coming here acting all high and mighty, like your shit doesn't stink."

"I'm just doing my job," Matt said, trying to keep his temper in check. The asshole was always talking smack about him and he was getting damn tired of turning the other cheek. This trying-to-be-a-better-man thing definitely had its drawbacks. "I didn't ask them to put me on the cover, but they did. So get the fuck over it."

Rizzo flung the magazine to the floor. "Enjoy it while it lasts," he snarled. "Because it won't last long." And with that final parting shot, Rizzo stalked to his locker.

Matt glanced at the magazine lying on the floor and couldn't help but feel an odd sense of satisfaction that he'd made the cover. Mostly because the last time he'd been on it, he'd been photographed coming out of a Hollywood nightclub with a well-known supermodel on his arm. Neither the caption nor the article inside had been flattering. As he recalled, the words *out of control* as well as *contentious* had been used on numerous occasions. At the time, he'd been more than a little ticked off at the sports writer who'd written it and had even called him out publicly. It was an ugly tirade, but back then it was one more stop on the trashing-his-life tour.

Just then, his cell phone rang. He turned to his locker to grab it off the top shelf. "Hey, Lily," he said after glancing at the caller ID. "What's up?"

"Matt's back!" she exclaimed with a girlish squeal. "Did you see the cover, Matt? Did you?"

"I sure did." He pulled his wallet from the shelf and stuck it in the back pocket of his jeans. "How are you feeling?"

"Pretty good. I'm doing everything Dr. Mike says I should do," Lily said. "How was the plane ride?"

Matt thought of Kelly and their sexy interlude. They were damn lucky they hadn't gotten caught. But the threat of discovery had made it even hotter. "It was the best flight ever," he said with a grin.

"That's because you were coming home."

"Yep. That's it," he said as he turned and zipped his gym bag.

"We're gonna watch *Major League* tonight."

"That's a great movie." Matt nodded at one of the assistant equipment managers who walked through the locker room clutching a basket of clean towels.

"You should come over and watch it with us. My mom makes the best popcorn in the whole world. It's way better than microwave. Kelly could come too. It would be fun."

"Well, I…"

"Please, please come," Lily pleaded in a voice that would melt the hardest of hearts.

"All right, you talked me into it."

"Yay!" Lily cheered. "Call Kelly and tell her to come too, okay? Tell her it's the funniest baseball movie ever."

"I'll call her right after I hang up with you," he promised.

"Tell her about the popcorn," Lily added in an eager voice. Obviously, in Lily's book, homemade popcorn was enough to seal the deal.

"Will do. Now let me talk to your mom just to make sure she's okay with this."

"You wanted to see me?"

Kelly looked from her computer screen to find Alexis standing in the doorway. The poor girl looked like she was about to face a firing squad. Her hands were clasped together tightly and her expression bordered on fearful. A pang of remorse shot through Kelly. The last thing she wanted was for Alexis to be intimidated. But she was. Confronting her intern in the bathroom hadn't accomplished a damn thing. It was time to try a different tactic.

"Yes." She swiveled her chair around. "Come in."

"How was your trip?" Alexis asked politely and stood stiffly behind the visitor chair.

"We won more games than we lost, that's always good," Kelly said. "How are you? Did you get over that bout with the flu?"

Alexis's face colored. She reached up to tuck a lock of hair behind her ear. "I went to the doctor. She gave me some antibiotics. I was fine after a few days."

"I'm sorry if I came off a bit harsh before I left," she said, hoping it would ease Alexis's discomfort. "I was worried about you."

"There's nothing to worry about. I'm fine."

Kelly studied her intern. The red dress she was wearing had been snug the last time she'd worn it but now it was loose. Alexis had dropped several more pounds, and Kelly was positive she'd lied about the doctor visit. It was obvious Alexis wasn't ready to admit she had a problem but, if and when she did, Kelly wanted her to be able to come to her if she needed to talk.

"I'm glad you're doing well. Please know that you can talk to me about anything." She held Alexis's gaze for several seconds. "I mean it. There are no judgments here."

"Okay." Alexis shrugged and averted her eyes. "But I don't really have anything to talk about." She pointed to the desk. "There are some letters in that folder that need your signature. Just let me know when you've signed them and I'll send them out."

Kelly gave a cursory glance to the folder. "I'll do that." Alexis stared at her mutely. "You can go." She smiled to ease the tension. "I'm glad you're feeling better," she called after Alexis as she left the office.

Not ten seconds later, Angie rushed in. "How did it go?"

Kelly stared at her in surprise. "That was fast. Do you have a hidden camera in here, or what?"

Angie chuckled. "I was going to the break room to get a soda and saw her come out of your office." Her humor faded and was replaced with concern. "Did she say anything?"

"No. I didn't press her. I let her know that I'm here if she wants to talk. Speaking of which, talk to me. What's going on with Scott? Did he change his mind about Napa?"

Angie's eyes clouded. "We're doing something else."

"I'm afraid to ask," Kelly said and then snapped her fingers. "No. Wait. Let me guess. You're separating the two-ply toilet paper." She snapped her fingers again and grinned. "Oh no, I've got it. You're spending the day cutting napkins in half, and then in the evening you'll go online and read *Tightwad Central* together."

"I should never have told you about any of that." Angie gave her a mutinous look.

"Ah, but you did. And you can't expect me not to bring it up when the guy can't even take you to Napa for your birthday. It's not that far, and besides, that old car he drives takes regular gas not premium."

Angie lifted her chin. "If you must know, he's taking me out for a very nice dinner."

"McDonald's?"

"No." Angie scowled.

"Taco Bell?"

"No," Angie snapped and gave her an annoyed look. "We're going to his mother's place."

"Are you fucking kidding me?" Kelly exclaimed in

disbelief. The son of a bitch was really pissing her off now, and what's more, he'd made her swear. Something she was trying to cut back on. After taking a deep breath, she forced herself to speak calmly, "Scott's mother lives in a senior facility, Angie."

"I know." Angie blinked as moisture filled her eyes. "But it's a nice one. The food isn't bad."

"Why do you stay with him?" she asked, noting Angie's death grip on the back of the chair. "You deserve better," Kelly added gently even as she wanted to take Angie by the shoulders and shake some sense into her. Why in the world was she settling for a miser like Scott?

"Perhaps." Angie shrugged. "But at least I know what I get with Scott. He's loyal and trustworthy. And he'll never cheat on me."

"Do you love him?" Kelly asked. "When you see him does your heart pound? Do your knees go weak?"

"That's not important." The lack of emotion in Angie's eyes broke Kelly's heart. "I want security and Scott can give me that."

"And J.T. can't?"

Angie's mouth fell open. "Why are you bringing him up? He's nothing to me."

Kelly tilted her head and observed Angie shrewdly. "Then why are you getting so upset?"

Angie raised a hand in protest. "I'm not upset."

"What happened between you and J.T. the night of our softball game?"

"Nothing," she said quickly, but her pink-stained cheeks told a different story. "Nothing at all."

Kelly let out a soft sigh. "I just want you to be happy, Angie."

"I am." Her response was curt. "I care about Scott and

I accept his…his limitations. And in the future, I'd appreciate it if you kept your opinions to yourself," Angie
said, then turned and stalked out of the office.

"Good one, Maxwell," Kelly muttered as her cell
phone rang. Reaching for it, her mood lightened when
Matt's name appeared on the screen. "Hi," she said, unable to control the rapid beating of her heart. She'd bet
all the money in her bank account that Angie didn't feel
this way when Scott called.

"Did I catch you at a bad time?"

"No." Kelly stared at the empty doorway. *Damn it.*
She really needed to be less blunt. It was either that or
tape her mouth shut.

"I just talked to Lily. She invited us to come over
and watch *Major League* with her and Dorie tonight."

"I love that movie." She perked up. A comedy was
exactly what she needed to make her forget her worries
about Alexis and Angie. "And I'd really like to see Lily
and Dorie."

"Great. I'll come by around six to pick you up."

Kelly turned to her computer and clicked on a new
email from Katherine. "How about I drive since I know
the area?"

"Only if you promise to get me there in one piece."
Matt's voice was tinged with amusement.

"My driving isn't *that* bad," she said with a smile.

"You think? Tell that to the guy who flipped you off
the first time we went to Lily's house."

MATT FOLLOWED KELLY into the elevator and automatically pressed the button for her floor. As the doors
closed, he leaned against the stainless-steel panel thankful he'd survived another wild ride on the streets of San

Francisco. To be fair, though, if he owned a bad-ass car like the Trans Am, he'd be just as much a speed demon as she was.

"I'm looking forward to Kayla and Sean's engagement party this weekend," she said as the elevator ascended. "My parents and I are flying down to L.A. together on Friday evening. When's your flight?"

"Saturday morning." It would be his first trip home since he'd been traded. Unfortunately, it was for one night only. On Sunday he'd join the team in San Diego for the three-day series with the Padres.

"Lily was in good spirits tonight. She doesn't seem to be worried about the surgery at all."

"She's worried." He thought of Lily's confession in the hospital. "She just hides it well," he said and let Kelly precede him into the hallway after the elevator eased to a stop and the doors slid open. He joined her, then together they walked down the hallway to her condo.

"This must be so hard on Dorie. I didn't ask because it's really none of my business, but I wonder where Lily's father is. Neither Dorie or Lily ever mention him."

"I've wondered the same thing."

Kelly's compassionate eyes met his when they reached her front door. "I can't imagine a father not being there for his child."

Matt's heart constricted. Most people would think the same thing, but he'd learned a long time ago that there were two sides to every story. "Maybe he doesn't know he has a child."

"How could he not know?" she asked and inserted her key into the lock.

"Believe me. It happens."

"I'm lucky. I have a wonderful father." She pushed the door open. "Would you like to come in?"

He shook off the past and flashed a grin. "I thought you'd never ask."

Once inside, Matt followed Kelly into the dimly lit living room and couldn't help but admire the sway of her hips and the curve of her ass in the snug jeans she wore. Although he had enjoyed spending time with Lily and Dorie tonight, he'd be a damn liar if he said he hadn't been thinking about getting Kelly alone the entire evening.

He'd taken a seat next to her on Dorie's couch. *Big mistake.* The tantalizing scent of her perfume had played havoc with his concentration, and her bare arm occasionally brushing his reminded him of how soft and satiny her skin was. It had been torture being so close to her and not being able to touch her. Never had he been more aware of a woman than he was of Kelly tonight.

If she was feeling the same way, she hid it well. Not that he expected her to act in a suggestive manner in front of Dorie and Lily, but other than offering him some popcorn she'd barely acknowledged his existence.

Was it wrong that he wanted her to feel the same level of sexual frustration he was feeling? Probably. But women weren't like guys in that respect. Guys thought about sex on average every seven seconds. Or at least that's what he'd heard.

The weird thing was it wasn't just about the sex— which was off-the-chart hot—it was how he'd unexpectedly discovered that he liked waking up with her curled against him, soft and warm in his arms. And there was something about her face, so serene and unguarded when she slept, that fascinated him. Not that he'd ever tell her he watched her sleep. Not after she'd told him it freaked her out. That would be his little secret.

"Come and sit," she said as she sank down on the couch and slipped out of her heels. Matt settled next to her and stretched his arm out along the back of the black leather cushions. Kelly's hair was loose around her shoulders, tempting him to touch it, so he did. It was as soft and silky as he remembered.

"It's a good thing I've seen *Major League* about ten times," he said.

Kelly turned to him with one brow arched inquisitively. "Why is that a good thing?"

"Because tonight I couldn't concentrate on the movie to save my life."

"I know the feeling." Her lips curved in a suggestive smile, his pulse kicked and his body hardened at the thought of making love to her again.

"What caused your lack of concentration?"

"A certain catcher sitting next to me."

"Would you care to elaborate?" he asked as she shifted her body toward him and put her hand on his thigh. Her light touch reawakened the aching hunger he'd been suppressing all night.

"Do I really need to tell you about the birds and the bees?" Amusement lit her eyes. "Okay, here's the deal. When a man and a woman like each other they may have certain urges—"

"So you like me?" he interrupted her with a triumphant grin. "Finally. You admit it."

"*Hello.* I slept with you. Of course I like you."

"How could you not?" He grinned. "So go on about those urges you were talking about. Or better yet, maybe you can show me."

"I think that can be arranged," she whispered and leaned forward to kiss him. Her mouth was warm and moist, and her tongue stroking against his was better than anything he'd imagined. With a moan, he cupped her nape and kissed her with all the pent-up desire he'd been feeling since he'd touched her so intimately on the plane. As their mouths fused hotly, the only sound he heard was the hammering of his heart. Nothing else registered until...

"Isn't this a surprise?" Stacia's voice was like stepping into an ice-cold shower. Startled, Matt jerked back and both he and Kelly looked to the foyer where Stacia stood with her keys in one hand and her purse in the other. "Sorry I interrupted," Stacia said in a tone more sarcastic than apologetic.

"I thought you were at Mission Rock," Kelly said as she eased away from him and put some distance between them. Not that he needed cooling off. Stacia's surprise entrance had pretty much killed the mood.

"I was. It was dead so I left." Stacia smiled, or maybe it was a sneer. Matt couldn't tell, but it was directed toward him. "So much for concentrating on baseball, right?" she added, drilling him with her arctic blue eyes. Okay, that confirmed it. It *was* a sneer.

What the hell was he supposed to say to that? It wasn't like he could deny he'd blown her off with that very line because he had. Only when he'd said it he never dreamed it would come back to haunt him. He should have known that one of his lies would end up biting him in the ass. An uncomfortable tension filled the room as the silence stretched on. How would Stacia take the whole "I'm just not that into you" speech right about now? His guess... not well.

After what seemed like an eternity, Stacia turned her sights on Kelly. "I'll let you have some privacy," she said in a terse voice, and without another word walked past them to the hallway. He braced himself for the slamming of her bedroom door, but no sound came. Was she eavesdropping? He wouldn't put it past her.

"That was uncomfortable," Kelly said with a wry twist of her mouth. "I think she's upset."

Matt snorted. "What was your first clue?"

EIGHTEEN

A LATE-AFTERNOON breeze carrying a subtle hint of roses ruffled Kelly's hair and softly caressed her skin. Reportedly, there was a rose garden on James Barrett's estate but, as of yet, she hadn't seen it. Perhaps before the evening was over, she would get a glimpse of what Kayla called the secret garden. Like in their favorite childhood book, the garden was enclosed, and only recently had Sean's father allowed anyone to enter his late wife's sanctuary.

"She looks absolutely radiant, doesn't she?"

Holding a class of expensive champagne, Kelly observed her sister standing with her fiancé, his father, James Barrett, and her parents on the far side of the tiled terrace. Radiant was the right word, for that's exactly how Kayla looked, radiant and blissfully happy.

"Yes." She turned to her companion and smiled. "Did you do her hair?"

Lance Del Rey, Kayla's friend and frequent hairstylist, nodded. "Great hair runs in your family, darling," he said, giving her a thorough once-over. "Are you still seeing William for your highlights?"

"Religiously." Kelly took a sip of her champagne. "Thank you for recommending him."

"How could I not?" Lance put a well-manicured hand to his chest. "I hate to see bad things happen to good hair. Whoever was doing your highlights before William should have their license revoked. Thank God he moved up to San Francisco when he did." Lance made a face of mock horror. "I shudder to think of what those glorious locks of yours would look like now."

Amused, she scanned the assembled guests and waved when she caught the eye of Kayla's longtime publicist and friend, Lisa Harrison, who was chatting with Sandy, the makeup artist on *A New Dawn*. Lisa was a tall willowy blonde with the lithe figure of a fashion model. There was a time when Kelly would have given anything for a body like that, but now there was no envy, or jealousy. Thankfully, she'd moved past that.

"Did you see the Oscar?" Lance leaned toward her and whispered. "It's in the living room. Near the baby grand piano."

"I didn't notice it."

Lance stared past her and gasped softly. "Girlfriend, don't look now, but tall, dark and damn hot just arrived."

Curious to see who had Lance's undivided attention, Kelly turned to see Matt heading directly for Sean and Kayla. And yes, he did look tall, dark and damn hot in a tan suit, light blue button-up shirt and a multicolor blue tie. The suit had to be custom made, it fit him like a glove, emphasizing his broad shoulders and strong arms. Just looking at him ignited a frisson of heat low in her belly. She couldn't take her eyes off of him as he shook James Barrett's hand, and then her father's. As if he could feel her watching him, he turned his head and their eyes locked for several heart-stopping seconds.

"Who is that?" Lance asked, forcing her attention from Matt.

"Matt Scanlon," she said, hoping Lance hadn't no-

ticed her visceral reaction. "I'm surprised you don't recognize him. He played for the Dodgers for years."

"I don't follow sports." Lance continued to devour
Matt with his eyes. And seriously, who could blame
him? "But if they all look like him I might have to start."

Kelly couldn't help but smile. She liked Lance, and
all of Kayla's friends. When her sister had decided to
move to Hollywood at the age of twenty, she'd been worried to death about the kind of people Kayla might meet,
and about what could happen to her in such a cutthroat
business. As it turned out, Kayla could take care of herself. She'd surrounded herself with good, solid people
and had never changed from the sweet, caring person
she'd always been. And now she was getting married to
a man she adored. No one deserved it more.

A gentle touch on her arm startled her. It was Kayla,
breathtaking in her white Grecian-style dress with an
embellished scoop neckline. Her hair was swept up in
an artfully tousled top knot, and a pair of chandelier ear-
rings sparkled against her skin, lightly tanned from her
recent location shoot in Hawaii.

"Come with me," Kayla said and shot a conspiratorial
smile toward Lance. "Do you mind if I steal my sister
for a few minutes?"

"Not at all." Lance lifted his champagne glass to his
lips and winked. "I'll stay here and enjoy the scenery."

Kayla laughed. "You do that. But remember, Sean
is mine."

"Where are we going?" Kelly asked as Kayla grabbed
her hand and led her down a stone path that began at the
edge of the terrace and meandered toward a small cottage at the far end of the expansive grounds.

"You'll see," Kayla said with an impish grin. "But I can tell you this, you're gonna love it."

MATT WATCHED AS Kayla whisked Kelly away from the party and knew exactly where they were going. The view from the deck outside the guest cottage was amazing and, right now, with the sun about to set, very romantic. It should be him with Kelly on that deck, not Kayla. If he hadn't gotten stuck in traffic on the PCH, he'd be the one showing her the magnificent view—not her sister.

"Earth to Matt."

Matt turned and found Sean's amused gaze on him. "Did you say something?" he asked.

Sean chuckled. "Yeah, I asked if you might find time to get some surfing in."

"No. I'm flying to San Diego tomorrow morning." He unbuttoned his suit jacket and slipped a finger under his collar. He hated suits, but for his best friend's engagement party he couldn't very well turn up in jeans and a T-shirt. "I was lucky to get today off."

"I'm glad you could make it. It wouldn't be the same without my best man."

"Best man?" Matt echoed, then it dawned on him and he grinned. "I hope the wedding is during the off season. With Taylor coming back, who knows where I'll be next year."

"It will be," Sean assured him. "We're thinking about a Christmas or New Year's Eve wedding."

"That's only four months away. Is that enough time?" Matt had no idea what went into planning a wedding, but maybe Sean and Kayla were going for a small no-frills type of deal.

"Kayla's very organized, and Patricia has offered to

help. Between the two of them, I think we can pull it off."

Matt studied the man he'd known since the first grade. A lot of people thought Sean Barrett had it all and, truthfully, he did until the day his mother died. After that, Sean changed, and so had James Barrett. Both of them had shut each other out of their lives until, finally, after years of emotional distance, they repaired their fractured relationship. The Sean standing before him now was free of the baggage that had weighed him down for so many years, and he looked happier than Matt could ever remember seeing him. It was a safe bet that Kayla Maxwell had a lot to do with that.

"John and Patricia seem to have taken a liking to you," Sean said, glancing at the Maxwells, who were chatting with James Barrett near the gated entrance to the rose garden. "What's that about?"

"John's restoring a '69 Chevelle. He asked me to come over and take a look at it. I had dinner with them. They're nice people."

"Kelly was there, I assume." Sean's grin was sly. "Are you two getting along now?"

"You could say that," he said carefully. Sean was his best friend, but this was neither the time nor the place to talk about what was going on with Kelly. He wasn't even sure what was going on, to be honest. He liked being with her, and he wanted her. But until he figured out what the hell he was feeling he was keeping his damn mouth shut.

"How long have you been sleeping with Matt?"

Stunned, Kelly looked from the amazing view and met Kayla's all-knowing gaze. "How did you know?"

she asked, not bothering to deny it. "Did Matt say something to Sean?"

"No." Kayla turned and rested her arm on the rail near Kelly's champagne glass. "But from the moment he joined us on the terrace he couldn't take his eyes off of you. And that look you gave him was a scorcher." Kayla's eyes softened. "This might sound corny, but you have a glow about you I've never seen before."

"It's this So-Cal sun. My skin isn't used to it," Kelly joked, and found her gaze drawn back to the ocean. It was majestic—dark and mysterious in the waning hours of daylight. Wavy ribbons of orange and pink colored the sky as the sun dipped out of sight on the horizon. It was one of the most beautiful sunsets she had ever seen.

She wished Matt was here to watch it with her. *Great. Now I'm behaving like a heroine in a romantic melodrama.* All sugary and sappy. That was *so* not her. Or at least it never had been before.

"Is it serious?" Kayla asked.

"I don't know." Kelly braced her hands on the rail and sighed. "Matt doesn't have the best track record with women."

"I think it's because of something that happened to him last year. I don't know the details. Sean promised Matt he'd never breathe a word of it to anyone unless Matt gave him the okay. He's kept that promise."

"Sean's a good man."

"He is, isn't he," Kayla said dreamily. "We've been talking about a Christmas wedding."

"Christmas Day?" she asked, shifting toward Kayla. "But that's your birthday."

"Oh, it won't be on the twenty-fifth, just around there,

or maybe even on New Year's Eve." Kayla paused. "I'd like you to be my maid of honor."

Kelly's mouth fell open. "What about Lisa?"

Kayla reached for Kelly's hands and squeezed them gently. "I can't imagine anyone else other than my big sister standing beside me on my wedding day. Please say yes."

"Are you kidding?" she exclaimed happily as her eyes filled with moisture. "Of course I'll do it."

"Don't cry." Kayla's lips curved. "You'll ruin your makeup. By the way, you look stunning. Where did you get that dress?"

"I found it on sale at that cute boutique on Union Street you love." Kelly glanced down at the lilac satin dress that hugged her figure in a way her usual dresses didn't. It had a low-cut neckline, a pleated bodice and a deep V-back. With her long legs it was difficult to find the right hem length, but this one showed just the right amount of leg, *and* it was comfortable. "I got the shoes there too."

Kayla gave her a quick once-over. "All I have to say is this is much better than those pants and blazers you wear to work."

"They're not that bad," she said, defending her reliable work clothes.

Kayla let out an unladylike snort. "The hell they are."

Twenty minutes later, Kelly had to answer the call of nature and headed inside James Barrett's Tudor-style home to use the guest bathroom. When she finished, she detoured to the formal living room and was admiring James Barrett's Oscar in its lighted cabinet when she sensed a presence behind her. Turning, she found Matt standing beside the beautiful mahogany baby grand piano. Her breath caught as his magnetic force struck her anew, but it was his eyes, so dark and smoldering, that caused every nerve in her body to go on high alert.

"Hi." She smiled and brushed her hair back from her shoulders. "I wanted to see the Oscar," she said and gestured behind her.

"It's impressive." His eyes raked boldly over her. "But I'd rather stare at you. You look absolutely incredible."

It was rare for her to be at a loss for words, but she was now. The sensual heat in Matt's gaze burned into hers, reminding her of those steamy nights on the road trip. As cliché as it was, he'd evoked a passion in her she never knew she possessed. But what was even more unexpected was his kindness. He'd never shown any indication that she was weak because of her eating disorder. For years, she'd hid it because of fear of what others would think, but it turned out that admitting it aloud had set her free. How ironic was that? That this man, the one who used to piss her off on a daily basis, had helped her clear the last hurdle on her path to recovery.

"Thank you," she whispered as he moved deliberately toward her.

"Isn't there some rule about not upstaging the bride-to-be?" Matt asked when he halted in front of her and searched her face. His cologne, a dark rich fragrance, invaded her senses and left her a bit light-headed. "You're the most beautiful woman here." He lifted his hand and gently stroked her bare arm. Her skin tingled with excitement. "Come home with me tonight," he said in a low husky voice.

"Home?" she said and then remembered. "Oh, that's right. You live near here, don't you?"

"Santa Monica. It's not far."

"But I came with my parents. We're staying at Kayla's."

"I'll make sure you get back there safely. Tomorrow."

"I can't do that. Just stroll into Kayla's house in the same dress I wore the night before? That's the walk of shame." She shook her head vehemently. "No. No way. It would be one thing if it was just Kayla, but my *parents* are there."

"How is it the walk of shame?" he asked. "Doesn't that only apply if it's a one-night stand? Tonight wouldn't be the first time we've made love, and it sure as hell won't be the last."

Kelly opened her mouth to speak and then closed it. He *did* have a point.

"We still have a couple of hours before the party breaks up." He gave her arm one final caress and stepped back. "Think about it," he said softly, then turned and walked out of the room.

And think about it she did. For the rest of the evening it was *all* she thought about. Even as she listened to several toasts to the happy couple, and even as she mingled with Sean and Kayla's friends and coworkers. To make matters even more complicated, whatever resolve she did have was sorely tested every time she found Matt watching her with those sexy bedroom eyes of his. *Damn him.* That was *so* not fair.

Around ten, she observed her father shaking hands with James Barrett. Her parents were ready to leave. It was time to make up her mind. Would she go back to Kayla's and sleep on the sofa bed, or share a bed with Matt? Hell, when she put it that way, there was really only one right choice.

Several minutes later, her parents were walking into

the house and she was on the steps not far behind them when strong fingers closed around her arm. She turned and met Matt's questioning gaze.

"Are you leaving?"

"Yes." She smiled and gave him her final answer. "With you."

As Matt closed the front door behind them, the first thing that grabbed Kelly's attention was the huge picture window just beyond the rust-colored sectional couch in his living room. Right now, there was nothing to see. It was a dark night with only half a moon, but she'd heard the sound of the waves crashing on the beach as soon as they'd gotten out of the SUV. The ocean was on the other side of that window.

"I saw several surfboards hanging on racks out front." She moved to the couch and set her purse on the square glass-topped coffee table. Pivoting, she admired the celery-green walls set off by white trim around the window and matching crown molding at the ceiling. Across from the couch was a big-screen television set placed inside what had to be a custom-made built-in cabinet. There were shelves on either side of the cabinet. One held DVDs and CDs, and the other housed a collection of hard-backed books. The room was warm and inviting. So very different from the condo she shared with Stacia. The black and chrome was cold and impersonal. This room had personality.

"I've been surfing since I was a kid," Matt said as he draped his coat and tie over the arm of the couch. "Back then Sean and I hit the beach just about every day."

"Even in the winter?"

Kelly noticed a framed photograph on one of the

bookshelves. Curious, she moved to the cabinet and sucked in a breath when she got a good look at the photo. It was of a young boy, and he was the spitting image of Matt. It took only a matter of seconds for her to put it all together and when she did, her heart began to ache. She'd suspected several weeks ago that someone close to Matt had died and, in her mind, this all but confirmed it. Now, his reckless behavior for the past year made sense.

"The best waves are in the—" Matt stopped talking and there was dead silence in the room.

She turned to find him watching her with wary eyes. "You had a son, didn't you?" she whispered.

For long seconds he stared at her, his face now a mask of misery. She wanted to run to him, to put her arms around him and make his pain go away, but she didn't move a muscle. Whatever happened now was up to Matt.

Without a word, he moved to the French doors next to the window, opened them and disappeared outside.

For almost a full minute she stayed rooted to the spot. Of all the things she thought would happen when she got to Matt's house, this was the last thing she had expected. She was pretty sure it was the last thing he'd expected as well. He probably hadn't planned on bringing her back here or the photo would have been put away. For quite some time he'd gone to great lengths to hide the fact that he had a son and now, in the space of five minutes, someone other than Sean knew his secret.

Taking a deep breath, she crossed the room and stepped outside. The air was salty, and a bit chilly due to the close proximity to the ocean. Goose bumps formed on her arms as she let her eyes get accustomed to the darkness. She was on a deck, but it wasn't a large one. It ran the length of the back of the house and jutted out about six feet. There appeared to be steps that led to the beach, but when she looked to her left she realized Matt hadn't used them. He was standing at the rail at the far end of the deck, staring out at the vast darkness that was the ocean.

Her heels made a clicking noise as she walked toward him, but he didn't look at her. Even when she halted next to him, he didn't move. Copying his stance, she braced her hands on the top rail and listened to the waves as they hit the shore. The sound was hypnotic. She didn't speak, just stood beside him and waited. For what, she didn't know. But she would stay until he asked her to leave.

"His name was Joey," Matt finally spoke, still staring straight ahead. It was hard not to touch him, to comfort him. She resisted the urge. Her intuition told her he wasn't ready for solace. Not yet. "He was seven when I met him and nine when he died. Leslie was my girlfriend all through college. In our senior year I was preoccupied with baseball and pretty much ignored her. That's when she fell in love with some guy in her English Lit class. When she broke up with me I had no idea she was pregnant." He paused for a few seconds before continuing, "She didn't tell me about Joey until after he got sick. By that time she was desperate to find a bone marrow donor for him."

"So you got tested," Kelly whispered.

"Yes, but I wasn't a match. Usually siblings are the best donors."

"What was he like?"

"He loved baseball, and just like Lily, he worshipped me. I was his favorite Dodger. Posters and pictures of me covered the walls of his bedroom."

"Did he ever find out you were his father?"

"We told him after I got tested. Joey never really had a father figure. The English Lit guy was long gone so he was thrilled when he found out I was his dad." Matt turned to look at her. He was shadowed in darkness, but she could make out the faint smile on his lips. "You should have seen his face. It was like Christmas and his birthday all rolled into one."

"I can imagine." She smiled despite the tears welling in her eyes.

"He was a smart kid," Matt said proudly. "He was just starting to read when I met him but he took to it like a duck to water. Every time I saw him he wanted to read a book to me. I always thought kids liked their parents to read to them, but for us, it was the opposite."

"Did you ever take him to one of your games?"

"I arranged for him and Leslie to sit in the skybox at a number of games. No one had any idea he was my son. I knew if I told anyone, the press would have a field day with it. It's the kind of story those vultures thrive on. A star athlete with a terminally ill child. There was no way I was letting any of them come near Joey. Luckily, Leslie agreed. I was pissed as hell at what she'd done, but I didn't have the heart to rip into her. She'd already been through so much. I couldn't add to her pain."

So it festered deep inside of him, and when Joey died, that rage, along with his grief, exploded like a ticking time bomb. Tears spilled down Kelly's cheeks as she imagined the unbearable pain he must have been in.

"I had two years with my son. I spent all of my free time with him until he—" Matt's voice cracked "—until he died." He squeezed his eyes shut, as if it would take away the pain, and then, with a strangled sound of anguish, he pulled her against him and buried his face into her neck. She felt his hot tears on her skin and slipped her arms around him, holding him tightly as silent sobs shook his body.

Several minutes passed before he lifted his head and stared into her eyes. "It wasn't fair," he said in a ragged voice. "He was a little boy with his whole life ahead of him."

Kelly gently stroked his back. "You're right. It's not fair. But think of the joy you brought to him. He adored you, and before he left this earth he found out *you* were his father. I know it doesn't ease the pain, but think of what that meant to him."

"I know what it meant to me," Matt whispered. "That's why I went fucking nuts when he died."

"You were in pain. Pain you didn't know how to deal with."

"That's no excuse, Kelly. You, of all people, know how out of control I was. I've never insulted a woman the way I insulted you the night we met. It was inexcusable."

"That wasn't you."

"Yes, it was. It was what I'd let myself become."

"You need to forgive yourself."

"For what?" His eyes widened. "For treating you like dirt, or everything else I did since the day Joey died?"

"No. You need to forgive yourself for not being able to save him."

"I told him everything was going to be okay." His voice rose, echoing into the dark night. "I lied to my son. I promised him he would live and then I couldn't deliver. I let him down."

"Don't say that," Kelly said sharply. "You didn't let him down. You made the last two years of his life special. That means something. No one else could have done that for him except you."

Matt stared at her. "Do you really believe that?"

"Yes." She shivered as a soft breeze whisked against her skin.

"We should go inside." He loosened his arms from around her and took a step back. "It's chilly out here."

Once they had entered the house, Matt closed and locked the door before turning to face her. His dark eyes were inscrutable; it made her think he might want to be alone, or that he regretted confiding in her.

"I should probably get back to Kayla's," she said and moved to the coffee table to retrieve her purse. "You don't have to drive me. I'll take a cab."

"Kayla's house is miles from here. The cab fare would be astronomical."

"Oh." She clutched her purse tightly. "That's right. I forgot."

"If you want to leave, I'll drive you." His eyes softened. "But I'd really wish you'd stay. Here. With me." When she didn't answer, he moved toward her and when he stood in front of her he lifted his hand and tenderly brushed her cheek with his fingers. "You've got mascara all over your cheeks."

Kelly's face warmed. "I guess I should have bought the waterproof kind. I must look a mess."

"You've never been more beautiful than you are right now," he said huskily. "Please stay." It was then that she saw it, the slight flicker of desolation in his eyes. It sealed the deal. There was no way she could leave him now.

"Okay," she whispered. "I'll stay."

NINETEEN

THE RHYTHMIC RISE and fall of the waves as they spilled onto the shore was music to Matt's ears. Although he ran along the wharf in San Francisco almost daily, he'd missed this beach. His beach, or so he liked to imagine. In reality, this stretch was open to the public, but this early in the morning he was completely alone and could indulge in a bit of grandiose thinking.

The sand, wet and packed, was firm beneath his feet. He'd covered about three miles, but at an easy pace. He wasn't concerned about getting his cardio in. Today, for the first time in over a year, he was running for the sheer enjoyment of it.

As he neared his house, he slowed to a walk, put his hands on his hips and breathed in the salty air, damp from the fog that had rolled in overnight and still loomed like a heavy blanket over the entire coast. The ocean was gray and restless—perfect for surfing. If he had time, he'd put on a wetsuit, grab his favorite board and ride a few waves. But he was due to join the team in San Diego by noon so surfing was out of the question.

A swell of seawater rushed up the shore. He moved to avoid it and when it washed back out a sand dollar had been left in its frothy wake. He picked it up and studied it. There were no chips or cracks marring its smooth surface. That was a rare occurrence. He rubbed it gingerly on his sweats to remove the clinging sand and then headed inland.

About halfway between the shore and his house he noticed Kelly on the deck staring intently at the ocean, not yet aware of his presence. She wore one of his UCLA T-shirts and looked just as beautiful as she had in that hotter-than-hell dress she'd worn to Sean and Kayla's party. He'd never met a woman so unaware of how stunning she was. Or one who downplayed it as much as Kelly did.

From the moment they'd first locked eyes at the party all he'd thought about was getting her naked. But the night hadn't turned out quite like he'd planned.

First, he'd totally forgotten about the picture of Joey on the bookshelf. Then, when Kelly saw it and astutely put two and two together, he couldn't help himself. He'd spilled his guts, then completely lost it.

Not very manly of him, he supposed, but after it was all said and done he suspected that subconsciously he'd wanted to talk about Joey. Not with just anybody, but with Kelly. He wasn't sure why, exactly. Maybe it was because she'd had the courage tell him about her eating disorder. She'd trusted him with something she never spoke about to anyone. No one knew better than he did how big of a deal that was.

Later, as Kelly slept tranquilly in his arms it dawned on him that revealing his heavily guarded secret had brought him something that vaguely resembled peace. It was an odd, but welcome state of being, and one he hadn't felt in an extremely long time.

"Good morning," Kelly said cheerfully as he approached the steps that led to the deck. "I made coffee."

She offered him a wide smile. "I was going to make us some eggs but your refrigerator is bare."

"I threw out everything before I went up to San Francisco. I wasn't sure when I'd be back." He joined her near the railing and noted that she'd found a pair of his sweatpants to go along with the T-shirt. That particular attire had never struck him as sexy before, but on her statuesque body it was that, and more.

"It's just as well," she said with a shrug of her shoulder. "I'm not a good cook."

"I guess it runs in the family."

Kelly laughed. "I can't argue with that." She searched his face, no doubt looking for some sort of sign that he was sorry for confiding in her about Joey. She wouldn't find it. He wasn't the least bit sorry. "How was your run?"

"Good." He held out his hand. "I have something for you."

"What?" She pushed back her sleep-tousled hair, glanced down and gasped softly. "A sand dollar." When she looked up her expression was wistful. "Kayla and I used to comb the beach for these whenever our parents took us to Santa Cruz."

Matt rested his hip against the wood railing. "When I was younger I believed a perfect sand dollar was a good omen. It seemed like every time I found one something amazing happened."

She tilted her head and regarded him curiously. "Like what?"

"When I was seventeen, I found one and the next day I got a letter informing me that I'd been accepted into UCLA on a full baseball scholarship."

"I think that had more to do with your hard work than finding a sand dollar on the beach."

"Maybe so, but a few years later I found another one and the next week I was drafted by the Dodgers."

"Again." She gave him an indulgent smile. "I think it was your talent, not the shell, that made you a top draft pick."

"Perhaps." He reached for her hand and pressed the sand dollar to her palm. "I want you to have it."

"Are you sure?" she asked with a devilish twinkle in her eyes. "I'd hate for you to miss out on some *amazing* future opportunity." Not waiting for his reply, she snatched the shell from his hand and clutched it to her chest. "Too late." Her laugh was low and husky. "It's mine now. I think I'll buy a lottery ticket, maybe it will bring me good luck."

"Don't mock the sand dollar." He slipped his hand around her waist and pulled her to his body, still amazed at how perfectly she fit against him. The soft citrusy fragrance she wore invaded his senses, making him supremely aware of her in every pore of his body. "It has strange and mysterious powers."

She rolled her eyes. "You are *so* full of shit."

Matt chuckled. "Now that's the Kelly I know and—" He stopped cold. *What the hell?* Was he going to just say *love*? His heart started to pound and he stared at her in shock as it hit him just how much she'd come to mean to him.

But that wasn't love. *Was it?*

"I'm doing much better with the not swearing thing. Sometimes I can go for hours without cussing," she said with a grin, unaware he was in a state of near panic over what had almost come out of his mouth. "Mom would be so proud." She leaned forward, her tempting lips just inches from his. "How soon do we have to leave?"

"We still have a couple of hours." He paused, still reeling in confusion. "Why?"

"I was thinking. I can't do the walk of shame when all we did last night was sleep."

"Are you suggesting what I think you are?"

Her full lips curved in a wicked smile; he felt an involuntary tightening low in his gut. *Damn*, a mouth like hers ought to be illegal. "I *did* just receive the lucky sand dollar. I think something amazing is in order, don't you?"

"But…what about the lottery?"

"To hell with the lottery," she said and pressed her lips to his.

EARLY WEDNESDAY AFTERNOON, Kelly walked out of Katherine's office and saw Angie heading for the break room. Squaring her shoulders, she stepped up her pace and followed her friend into the small sterile room that contained two vending machines and a small rectangular table with two chairs.

"How long are you going to keep avoiding me?" She let the door close behind her and watched as Angie fed the soda machine several coins and then made her selection. The can made a clanking sound that echoed in the room as it dropped to the dispenser tray. Angie retrieved her soda and turned to look at her.

"I'm not avoiding you, I'm busy," Angie said, her tone frosty as she popped the top and took a sip.

"You're never too busy to come by my office and say hello." Kelly clutched her notepad to her chest. She'd hurt Angie's feelings and that was the last thing she wanted to do. "I'm sorry for what I said about Scott."

"No, you're not." Angie's eyes narrowed. "You don't like him and you're not shy about saying so."

"I know." She sighed. "But I've been thinking about it, and since you're my best friend, I should support whatever decision you make."

Even if I don't agree with it.

"Are you saying you'll stop lecturing me about Scott?"

"Yes. That's what I'm saying."

"You promise?"

"I swear." Kelly smiled and then noticed the small diamond ring on Angie's left hand. Her heart plummeted to her stomach. That ring hadn't been there on Friday. "Did Scott propose?" she asked, forcing her expression to remain neutral.

Angie nodded solemnly. "On my birthday."

"Oh." She paused as Angie regarded her with wariness. This was it, the moment when she had to walk the talk. "Congratulations, or is it best wishes?" She was able to smile, but it was an effort. "I can never remember which one you say to the bride."

"I believe it's best wishes."

"Then, best wishes," she said, and moved to give Angie what turned out to be an awkward hug. She wished she could be happy about the news, but honestly, a Brazilian bikini wax sounded more enjoyable than attending Angie and Scott's nuptials. "When's the wedding? Did you set a date yet?" she asked as she stepped back.

Angie's expression brightened. "We're thinking about May, or maybe June."

"Good months," she said lamely to fill the silence and fought the urge to slap Angie across the face and yell "snap out it." Instead she gritted out another faux smile. "I'm happy for you. You'll be a beautiful bride."

Sadly, the latter was the only thing she could say with absolute truthfulness.

For the remainder of the day, Kelly couldn't stop thinking about Angie's engagement. Her gut instinct told her that Angie was making a huge mistake but if she said something it would only cause a rift between them, and Angie—as stubborn as she was—would dig her heels in even more.

No. It was better to go along with it for now and hope that Angie came to her senses before the wedding day. If she didn't, there was always that part of the ceremony where someone could speak now or forever hold their peace. That might work as a last resort.

It was after five when Kelly slung her purse over her shoulder, closed her office door and strode down the corridor toward the elevator. Heading to the restroom, she pushed open the door and gasped in horror. Alexis was sprawled unconscious on the tile floor.

"Oh my God," she whispered as panic knotted in her stomach.

Dropping her purse, she sank down next to Alexis and put her fingers against her intern's neck. Relieved when she found a pulse, she gently eased Alexis to her back and checked her mouth. Her airway was clear, and she was breathing, but her face was still and waxy.

With shaky hands, she reached for her purse and pulled out her cell phone. As she called 911, all she could do was pray she'd found Alexis in time.

Two AND A half hours later, Kelly let herself into the condo, surprised to find it dark. She was almost positive that Stacia had said she'd be back from her New York route tonight, but maybe she'd misunderstood, or maybe Stacia's schedule had changed. It wasn't like they always informed each other of their whereabouts, and Stacia *had* been on the cool side after the night she'd come home to find Kelly and Matt kissing on the couch.

Well, boo-fucking-hoo. It wasn't her fault Matt wasn't interested in pursuing something with Stacia. Stacia was used to men falling at her feet and now, the one time when a man didn't look twice at her, she was acting like a sore loser.

After turning on the lamp in the living room, she went to her bedroom, changed into a green knit tank dress and then padded barefoot to the kitchen. Her stomach rumbled, reminding her she hadn't eaten since lunch. Pulling the refrigerator door open, she surveyed the meager contents and sighed. So much for dinner. She'd forgotten to do her grocery shopping before going to L.A. for the engagement party.

She heard her cell phone ringing and, thinking it might be an update on Alexis's condition, she rushed to her bedroom.

"Hey," she said after seeing Matt's name on the caller ID. "Are you back?"

"We got in an hour ago and I'm starving. Do you want to meet me at Kamu's for dinner?"

"Thanks for the invite, but I'm not in the mood to go out." Kelly sank to the bed and traced the quilt pattern with her finger. "I've had a rough day."

"How about I pick up something and come over?" he suggested. "That is…if you feel like some company."

"I'd like that. I'm hungry too. Can you get me my usual?"

286 THE WINNING SEASON

"You got it. I'll see you in about fifteen minutes."

It was more like thirty minutes before he arrived, but that had given her time to set the table in the kitchen's small nook. The kitchen was as stark and sterile as the living room. Black quartz countertops, stainless-steel appliances and gray walls didn't make for a calming dining experience.

Matt sat across from her looking relaxed and ruggedly handsome in jeans and a white polo shirt—a vivid contrast against his deeply tanned skin. That's what had taken the extra fifteen minutes. He'd stopped by his place and changed out of his travel clothes before picking up the food.

"Spill it. What made this day so rough?" Matt picked up his beer and took a sip.

"For starters, I found out Angie got engaged."

"Angie's engaged?" His brow furrowed. "To whom?"

"A jerk who works for the city." Kelly took a taste of her tomato basil soup and shook her head in disgust. Not because of the soup—it was delicious—but because the thought of Angie marrying Scott still left a sour taste in her mouth. "And I have to keep my big mouth shut and go along with this crap because Angie is my friend and I have to support her."

"I really thought there might be something going on between Angie and J.T." Matt set his bottle on the table. "I guess the engagement blows that theory right out of the water."

"I'm not so sure about that. Something went down between them, but Angie isn't about to admit to it."

"Neither is J.T." He picked up a French fry. "I hope I'm not around when he finds out about the engagement."

"I hope you are." She set her spoon in the soup bowl then pushed it aside. "He might need someone to talk to."

"I'll do what I can to help him, but he's been extremely tight-lipped when it comes to Angie." Matt popped the fry in his mouth and chewed. "Can I ask you a personal question?" he asked after he'd finished the last of his fries.

"Sure."

He studied her thoughtfully for several seconds, almost as if he was hesitant to continue. "What caused your eating disorder?"

Kelly leaned forward and folded her arms on the table. She wasn't surprised by the question, just at how long it had taken him to ask it.

"I think the seeds were planted when I was about twelve. I had a growth spurt over the summer between seventh and eighth grades. That September when I went back to school I was about five-ten. A lot of the kids called me the Jolly Green Giant and asked me stupid questions like 'how's the weather up there?'"

Matt's dark eyes filled with compassion. "That had to be rough."

"It was, but I pretended like it didn't matter. I even laughed along with them so they wouldn't see how much it bothered me. Between then and my sophomore year in high school I grew another two inches. When I was a senior, Kayla was a freshman. Of course, the kids compared the two of us, and the comparisons didn't favor me."

"Were you bingeing and purging back then?"

"No. That started during my senior year at St. Mary's. Every day I looked in the mirror and saw a girl that none of the guys wanted to date. I couldn't do anything about my height, but I thought if I lost weight they would be attracted to me. I stopped eating regular meals and whenever I got hungry I'd binge on whatever I could get my hands on. Afterwards I'd feel guilty about all the calories and either go throw up or spend hours in the gym." She reached for her beer. "It's such skewed and dangerous thinking, I know that now, and that's the main reason I've been concerned about Alexis." She pointed her bottle at him. "Oh, that's the other awful thing that happened today. I found Alexis in the bathroom. Unconscious."

Matt's eyes widened with alarm. "Is she all right?"

"I think so." She took a quick sip of beer and then continued, "I called her parents and met them at the hospital. I told them about my suspicions. They were shocked, just like my parents were. They had no idea what's been going on with her."

"Maybe now she'll get some help."

"Maybe." She shrugged. "But she has to want to get well because it's extremely hard to change those thought processes. It's still a struggle for me," she set the bottle on the table, "as you know."

"What I know is you're the strongest woman I've ever met," he said with a hint of admiration in his voice. "I wish I would have had half that strength when Joey died."

"You can't compare our situations, Matt. You found out you had a son seven years after he was born, and on the same day you were told he was terminally ill. It's not the same at all."

"Still, I'm not proud of how I handled it.

"Everyone handles grief differently."

"I suppose so. The funny thing is I never thought

much about having kids. I figured if I did have them, it would be after I stopped playing ball—you know—when I had the time to really be there for them. I only had a short time with Joey, but I'm grateful for every second of it." He leaned back and managed a weak smile. "He hated hospital gowns so I brought him one of my jerseys. He wore it all the time—never even let Leslie take it home to wash it." Matt bowed his head and after several silent seconds looked up at her, his moist eyes filled with sadness. "We buried him in it."

Unable to bear witness to his pain without comforting him, Kelly pushed out of her chair and rounded the table. When she put her hand on his shoulder he turned, slipped his arms around her waist and buried his face into her midriff. He didn't cry. He just held her tightly as she gently stroked his hair.

A minute or so later, he pulled back and gazed up at her. "I didn't realize how much I needed to talk about him."

"You've kept it inside for a long time." She lifted her fingers to his temple and brushed back his hair. "Talking about him will help you heal."

"Are you sure?" Sorrow darkened his expression. "Because it still hurts."

Her heart constricted. "It will always hurt. But that hurt will lessen in time."

"God, I hope you're right." He stared at her with something akin to relief in his eyes. "I'm glad I told you about him."

"So am I," she said softly and then stiffened. "Did you hear that?"

Matt shook his head and lowered his arms from

around her waist. "I didn't hear a thing. Stacia's not home, right?"

"I didn't think so." She turned and crossed the kitchen. When she got to the foyer, it was empty—as was the living room. She stood there for a moment hearing nothing but silence. "It's probably the refrigerator. It's always making weird noises. Especially when the ice maker is running," she said as she returned to the kitchen to find Matt standing at the counter shoving their take-out plates into the Kamu's sack. "Hey, you don't have to do that. You brought dinner, I'll clean up."

He shot her a quizzical glance. "Are you sure?"

"Positive."

"Do you mind if I watch ESPN before I leave? I'd like to check the scores."

"Be my guest." She put her hands on his back and pushed him toward the foyer. "The remote is on the coffee table."

After she'd tidied the kitchen, she joined him in the living room. "How'd the Dodgers game end?" she asked as she sat next to him on the couch. He put his arm around her shoulders and pulled her close to his body. He smelled wonderful—that clean Matt scent that lingered in her senses even when she wasn't with him.

"They won."

Kelly swore softly under her breath and rested her head on his chest. "That means we didn't gain any ground at all in San Diego."

"The Dodgers are heating up again. But their next series is in Atlanta, and luckily for us, the Braves are on a tear right now so there's a good chance we can pull ahead if the Braves win the series and we win ours with Colorado."

"Piece of cake. The Rockies have been decimated with injuries this year." Kelly snuggled against his solid body. "And their pitching staff has the highest ERA in the National League as well as the most walks."

"Don't get cocky." His voice was tinged with amusement. "It's not always about the stats. The Rockies have some damn good hitters. On any given day they're a threat."

"I'm not cocky." She grinned. "Just confident."

Matt chuckled and then they watched the remainder of the baseball highlights. When the commercial came on, he gave her shoulder a gentle squeeze. "I should head out. I still need to look over my notes for the game tomorrow."

Lifting her head, she met his gaze and smiled. "Thanks for bringing food."

"You're welcome." He lowered his head and gave her a kiss that was far too brief. She considered asking him to stay, but he had notes to study so when he rose from the couch she followed him to the door, pretty much unable to keep her eyes from devouring his broad shoulders and muscular arms. Men didn't have the monopoly on ogling a fine body. In fact, women ogled just as much as men, only more discreetly.

When they reached the door, Matt opened it and stepped into the hallway and then turned.

Oh shit. Busted.

Kelly jerked her gaze up to meet his. Hot blood rushed to her cheeks when he gave her a grin of pure masculine satisfaction. "Were you checking out my ass?" He braced his palm on the door frame and flashed a sexy smile.

She shrugged and moved closer. "Maybe. You got a problem with that?"

"Not at all." He lifted his hand and ran his fingers through her hair. "Turnabout is fair play. I check yours out quite frequently."

"Then you won't mind if I watch you walk down the hall when you leave, will you?"

"Tell you what." He grinned cheekily. "I'll put a little strut into it, just for you."

Her laugh was smothered when Matt leaned forward and kissed her. Not the gentle kiss of a minute ago, but a hot ravishing kiss that washed her with heat and desire. With a soft moan, she melted against him and slipped her arms around his waist. Needing to touch him even more intimately, she slid her hands under his shirt and stroked his smooth warm skin. He reacted with a low guttural growl, reached behind her to grab a fistful of her hair and all but consumed her with the forceful demand of his mouth.

The man didn't play fair. Kissing her like this, getting her all hot and bothered just before leaving her to—

Wait. Wait just a damn minute. She wasn't the only one hot and bothered. The hard ridge of Matt's erection pressing into her was proof of that. Lowering her hands, she cupped his ass and pulled him against her. With a low groan, he pulled back. Their eyes locked, the sexual heat between them palpable.

"Stay," she whispered over the pounding of her heart.

A wicked smile tugged at Matt's lips. "Baby, I thought you'd never ask."

TWENTY

FOUR DAYS LATER, Matt stood next to Marquis Lopes waiting to take his turn at batting practice. BP was a game-day ritual he'd always enjoyed, mainly because he'd never felt any pressure to do anything other than connect with the ball and send it flying. At the moment Trey Gentry was in the cage and, for a rookie *and* a pitcher, he had a decent swing. The kid was going to be a star. He had talent, brains, looks and a helluva hanging curve ball. He was a general manager's wet dream.

Turning from the batting cage, Matt surveyed the ballpark. The seats were empty, but there were several reporters camped out near the visitors' dugout waiting for batting practice to end so they could conduct on-field interviews. Since it was common knowledge he only did press after the game, most of them had given up hounding him. Maybe someday he'd grant more interviews, but truth be told, after a year of being weekly tabloid fodder he liked keeping a low profile.

As he was about to turn his attention back to the cage, he spied a lone figure sitting in the Blaze dugout. It was J.T.

Ever since learning of Angie's engagement from Kelly he'd been wrestling with whether or not to tell J.T. the news. Bottom line, the guy was going to find out sooner or later, and if he was hung up on Angie, maybe it would be easier coming from someone he knew.

"I'll be right back," he said to Lopes and resting his bat on his shoulder, headed for the dugout. The cameras began clicking furiously—the press might not be able to talk to him but they were still able to take his picture. Three months ago he would have flipped them off; today he couldn't care less.

Taking the steps into the dugout, Matt shoved his bat into one of the bat cubbies and then sat next to J.T. on the long metal bench that ran the length of the dugout. "No BP today?" he asked as he slipped off his baseball cap and tossed it on the bench.

J.T. didn't spare him a glance. "Nope."

"Lopes suggested we hit Kamu's after the game. You up for it?"

"Don't think so."

"Do you want to talk about it?" Matt leaned back, stretched his legs out in front of him and got comfortable. This might take a while.

"Talk about what?"

"Whatever the hell has been eating at you for the last month."

J.T. turned to look at him, his expression stony. "Maybe I'm tired of being backup."

Matt's jaw dropped. *This was about baseball, not Angie?*

"I'm good enough to be a starter," J.T. continued tersely. "But as long as you or Taylor are around I'll always be second string."

"You *are* good," Matt assured him. He had to handle this one with care. A ballplayer's ego could be a fragile thing. "The problem is there are a lot of guys who are just that—good. To be a starter you have to be more than that. You have to be the best."

J.T. scowled at him. "So what you're saying is I'll never be in your league, or Taylor's?"

"You can be. You're not that much older than Taylor. This league is like a gossip mill, you know. We all talk. When I was with the Dodgers the word in the clubhouse was Taylor trained like a fucking maniac."

"I train," J.T. said defensively.

"Train harder. Spend every spare minute you have studying hitters. Watch film until your eyes cross. You've got a lot of natural talent, but in my opinion you haven't reached your full potential."

"Why the hell didn't you tell me this before?"

"Because you didn't ask, and also because I didn't want to antagonize the one guy on the team who bothered to give me the time of day when I got here. That meant a lot to me."

"It did?"

"Yeah. Everyone else thought I was a fuckup."

A slow grin split J.T.'s face. "You *were* a fuckup."

Matt laughed. "That's true."

"Notice I used the past tense."

"I noticed." Matt scrubbed a hand over his jaw. "Man, I'm glad this was about baseball. I could have sworn it was about Angie."

"Angie?" J.T. narrowed his eyes and sat up, ramrod-straight. "Why?"

"I thought maybe you found out she got engaged and you were upset."

"Angie's engaged?"

Fuck. By the stunned expression on J.T.'s face this was the first he was hearing of it.

"Yeah."

J.T.'s shoulders slumped as he turned to stare at the

field. "I didn't know," he said quietly after several seconds. "Good for her." J.T. shot to his feet and slipped on his baseball cap. "Come on," he said with a grin that might have fooled someone who didn't know him better. "Suddenly I'm in the mood to hit the shit out of those balls."

ENGROSSED IN READING her latest batch of public-appearance requests, Kelly almost jumped out of her chair when the ring of her desk phone shattered the silence. With a racing heart, she picked up the receiver.

"Kelly Maxwell."

"Hey, Kelly. How's life in the big city?"

She let out a short laugh and leaned back in her chair. She'd recognize that voice anywhere. "Rick. Hi. How's the rehab going?"

"Couldn't be better," Rick Taylor replied in a voice that held just the slightest trace of Texas. "I finally got that damn cast off of my leg and I start physical therapy tomorrow. I'm sure my doctor will be calling you to give you the official version, but you've been so good about checking in with me I thought I'd fill you in myself."

"I'm glad you did," she said warmly. "Sounds like you're right on schedule."

"I don't see any problem making it to spring training."

"We're looking forward to having you back." Her smile faded as she realized exactly what that meant. As much as she liked Rick, his return to the Blaze meant Matt would no longer be needed. "I hear congratulations are in order. The last time I talked to Jill she told me she's pregnant."

"Yes, ma'am. She's three months along. We announced it to the family yesterday. This'll be the first grandchild for both of our parents."

Kelly smiled. She'd forgotten Rick's propensity to call all women "ma'am." It was probably a Texas thing. "I'm sure everyone is thrilled. You've got a lot to look forward to."

"That I do," Rick said. "Hey, I've been talking to a few guys on the team and they're telling me Scanlon's a decent guy. Do you think he'll be on the team next year?"

"I'm not sure." She reached for the baseball magazine that had been delivered with the morning mail. On the cover was a picture of Matt, Rizzo, Lopes and Gentry. The magazine had dubbed them The Fab Four. It wasn't a posed shot, just separate images spliced together. Matt's picture showed him raising his glove in the air after making a tag at home plate. The determination on his face was evident and a far cry from the man who had first arrived in San Francisco. "Matt was only picked up because of what happened to you. From what I've heard, the GM and Morgan are committed to you being our starting catcher for the long term."

"That depends on how well I bounce back from this injury."

"True, but from what your doctors are reporting to us, we're not worried." She tossed the magazine on the desk. "You were extremely lucky the leg break wasn't as bad as originally thought."

"It still hurt like hell."

"I hope this has taught you to stay off that motorcycle," she said, unable to stop herself from chiding him. It was a foolish thing he'd done, especially when there was a clause in his contract about refraining from engaging in any activities that might cause him extreme bodily injury. Granted, the accident could have occurred if he was in a car, but his injuries probably wouldn't have been as severe.

"It wasn't the bike." Rick's voice was edged with annoyance. "It was the jerk on the bridge. He decided to change lanes and didn't bother to look to see if anyone was in the lane next to him."

Kelly rubbed her temple. If Rick came roaring into spring training on a motorcycle she would lose her damn mind. "You won't be riding that thing when you come back, right?"

"Right," Rick said after a lengthy pause. "I sold it to my brother. Jill insisted."

"Smart woman. You're lucky she married you."

"I tell myself that every day, ma'am."

"You're making me feel old with that ma'am stuff." She smiled. "A word to the wise, it's best not to call any woman under the age of sixty ma'am."

"I'll try. Oh, I forgot to tell you, Jill says thanks for subbing for her in that charity game."

"It was my pleasure. We kicked their asses."

Rick let out a bark of laughter. "Winning is good, isn't it?"

"You bet it is." She checked her watch. "Hey, I'm sorry, but I have to cut this short. I'm meeting my mom for lunch."

After she and Rick had said their goodbyes, Kelly stared at Matt's picture on the magazine cover. Talking to Rick had just made it real. The odds were highly in favor of Matt not being on the team next year, and she doubted Matt would want to be a backup to anyone. He was still more than good enough to start for any Major League team. But what she'd told Rick was true, upper management believed he was a phenomenon, just as Matt had been eight years ago. As long as Rick came back as healthy as he was before the injury there was no way in hell they'd let him go. And even if Matt would consider staying, the Blaze couldn't afford both him and Rick. They would let Matt go, keep J.T. as Rick's backup and pick up someone on the cheap to be third string. It was good business and that's what Major League Baseball was—a business.

On the short walk to the Fog City Diner where she was meeting her mother, Kelly's stomach was tied up in knots. From the first moment she'd learned Matt was joining the Blaze she couldn't wait for him to leave. Now, the thought of him leaving San Francisco and going—God knows where—was like a hammer blow to her heart.

Her mother was sitting in a booth next to the window when she walked into the diner. Patricia had been watching for her and waved.

"Hi, honey," her mother said with a warm smile as she sat across from her. "I'm glad you could meet me."

Kelly set her purse beside her on the leather seat and thanked the waitress who quickly brought her a glass of ice water. From the amount of shopping bags piled on the seat next to her mother, it appeared her morning had been a success. In her early fifties, Patricia Maxwell appeared at least ten years younger and could probably still fit into her wedding dress. She didn't shop for clothes often, but when she did, she came to the city and made a day of it.

"Did you drive in, or take BART?" Kelly asked as she picked up her water and took a sip.

"I took BART. It's much more relaxing than fighting the traffic and trying to find a place to park."

Kelly set her glass on the table and gazed out the window. Across the street was the wharf and it bustled with people—tourists and city dwellers alike. Matt usually ran along the wharf. She occasionally did too but only in the early morning when it was quiet and all she could hear was the sound of her feet hitting the pavement. Matt had suggested they run together but they hadn't managed it yet. Now that he was most likely leaving San Francisco after the season, it might never happen. The thought was depressing.

"Kelly."

Her mother's voice startled her. "What?" She turned from the window and met Patricia's puzzled gaze. "I'm sorry, did you say something?"

"You were a million miles away. What were you thinking about?"

"Nothing." She grabbed her menu. "Let's order. I'm hungry."

As they ate lunch, Kelly told her mother about Alexis, and how although her intern was now out of the hospital, she wasn't coming back to work. Alexis's parents had talked her into entering an eating disorder treatment facility in Arizona. It was for the best, but she hoped Alexis was doing it because she truly wanted to get well, and not because her parents had talked her into it.

"Have I ever told you how proud I am of you?" Patricia asked her after the waitress had taken away their plates.

"For what?"

"For admitting you had a problem and overcoming it." Her mother's eyes grew misty. "I can't imagine how hard that was."

"It wasn't a piece of cake." She grinned. "Pardon the pun."

Patricia chuckled and shook her head. "We don't talk much about it, mostly because I know it's not something you like to discuss. But I wanted you to know how much I admire you."

Kelly blinked back the moisture the unexpected praise had brought to her eyes. "Mom, stop or I'll start crying."

"Okay, okay. I'll drop it." Patricia leaned forward and rested her arms on the table. "How's Matt?"

"He's fine." Her mother's probing gaze had her shifting uncomfortably in her seat. "Is there something you want to say?"

"It didn't go unnoticed that you didn't come home the night of Sean and Kayla's party. Are you and Matt together now?"

Damn that walk of shame.

Kelly reached for the small rectangular container that held packets of sweeteners and sugar and began arranging them in a uniform manner. "Sort of." She concentrated on making sure the sugar was on one side and the artificial sweetener was on the other.

"Sort of?" She looked up to find her mother's delicate brows arched. "Either you are or you aren't."

Kelly shrugged and slid the container back to its place by the salt and pepper shakers. "It's complicated."

"Why?"

"Because when Rick Taylor comes back the Blaze will cut Matt loose."

"So that's why you look so melancholy."

"I don't look melancholy," she protested. "Matt and I are…are just sleeping together, okay? It's nothing more than that. I doubt I'll ever see him again after he leaves San Francisco."

"I think it's more than that, Kelly. I know you. You don't indulge in casual affairs. Neither you nor Kayla are built like that."

"That's because we have you and Dad as role models. Both of us want what you have." She sighed. "And it looks like Kayla has found it."

"Maybe you have too." Patricia paused to give the waitress dropping off their check a friendly smile and waited until the young woman left before continuing. "I saw the way Matt was looking at you at the party."

Kelly resisted the urge to roll her eyes. "How was he looking at me, Mom?"

"Like a man in love." Her mother smiled wistfully. "And you were looking at him the same way."

"I think you need to have your vision checked." She picked up the check and then reached into her purse for her wallet. "There is no love involved. None at all." Kelly opened her wallet. "Lunch is on me."

"Why are you so flustered?"

"I'm not...flustered. I just have to get back to work," she said as she laid two twenties on the table.

"Maybe you should tell Matt how you feel."

Bracing her palms on the edge of the table, she met her mother's concerned gaze head-on. "Mom, I can't talk about this right now. I can't tell Matt anything when I don't even know what the hell it is *I'm* feeling."

Her mother treated her to the disapproving look Kelly knew only too well. She should, she'd seen it enough times in her life. "Don't swear," Patricia reprimanded her curtly.

"Oh my God. Mom. All I said was hell."

"You know how I feel about swearing. It's unlady-like."

She sighed. Even at thirty, her mom could still make her feel like she was thirteen years old.

Five minutes later, Kelly stood next to her mother outside the diner. "Do you want me to walk with you to the BART station?" she asked as she stepped to the side to avoid blocking the sidewalk.

"No. It's not far." Patricia smiled. "I wore my comfy shoes." Her smile morphed into a look of contrition. "Kelly, I didn't mean to badger you in there. About Matt. It's just that I want you to have what I've found with your father."

"How did you…" She hesitated and then forged ahead, "How did you know you were in love with Dad?"

A wistful smile tugged at her mother's lips. "I knew I was in love with him when I couldn't imagine my life without him in it. It made me physically ill to even think about it."

"Maybe you just ate some bad sushi."

Patricia's smile was wry. "Dear Lord, you *are* your father's daughter."

"I love you, Mom," Kelly said softly and leaned forward to kiss her cheek. "I'll see you soon."

Instead of going directly back to Blaze Field, Kelly took a walk to the cove. Although the game was still several hours away, the cove was starting to fill up with the kayakers who hoped to catch one of the home-run balls that made it out of the ballpark. They were quite a colorful army as they paddled around, laughing and joking with each other. The laughter and jokes would cease the second a ball made it into the water. When that happened it was every man and woman for themselves as they fought over one of the coveted home-run balls.

The incessant cawing of the ever-present seagulls

filled the air. Like vultures, they circled the kayakers waiting for someone to toss them some food. Turning from the view of the cove and of the East Bay beyond, Kelly stared at the beautiful brick ballpark. The gem by the bay as it was sometimes called. Matt was inside there now, most likely taking batting practice or warming up with the team. He'd been in San Francisco only a little over two months, but now it seemed like he'd been here forever.

Soon he would leave.

Another knot formed in her stomach. Only it wasn't bad sushi, or even bad fish tacos, which was what she'd had for lunch. It was the thought of never seeing Matt again, of never touching him, or feeling his lips upon hers. They'd shared things with each other—personal things they never spoke of to anyone. That meant something, or at least it did to her. It was more than just sex, it was—

Kelly clutched her stomach as the knot inside tightened.

Oh shit. She was in love with Matt Scanlon.

MATT LET HIMSELF into his condo and locked the door behind him. After hitting the light switch, he moved to the kitchen where he dropped his keys and gym bag on the breakfast bar and opened the refrigerator. He grabbed a bottle of water, kicked the door closed with his foot and walked to the large picture window in the living room.

Across the street, Blaze Field was still bathed in light and dozens of people were milling around the grounds outside—no doubt checking out the Blaze store and the statues of former Blaze players that surrounded the park. It wasn't Dodger Stadium, but it had a unique charm all its own. He couldn't imagine playing anywhere else. *When the hell had that happened?*

The Blaze had shut down the Rockies tonight and Atlanta had trounced the Dodgers. It was, once again, all tied up at the top of the Western division, and it was looking more and more like it might come down to the final week of the season before the title was clinched.

Never in a million years had he imagined this scenario. Going up against his beloved Dodgers as a member of the team he'd always hated. Just a few months ago the thought would have been inconceivable.

He wanted to win badly, even at the expense of his former team. He wasn't angry anymore, largely because he'd come to terms with the fact that he'd given them no other choice but to get rid of him. Winning wasn't about payback, it was about finding something he'd lost after Joey died. His self-respect.

Interestingly enough, his agent had informed him that should the Blaze let him go, there were a number of teams who would gladly pay him for his services. It was welcome news because he was nowhere near ready to retire, but on the other hand the thought of going to another team and starting all over again wasn't at all appealing.

Damn it all. He liked San Francisco, and with the exception of Rizzo, he liked his teammates. But most of all he didn't want to leave Kelly.

As he twisted off the cap and took a long swig of water, he found a certain irony in that fact. That this woman, the one he'd insulted and bickered with for weeks, had become so important to him that he couldn't fathom leaving her behind.

Matt finished off the water and returned to the kitchen to put the bottle in the recycle bin. He thought about turning on the big screen in the living room and catching the highlights, but it was getting late and tomorrow's game started at one. He needed rest, especially since the next two weeks were the most crucial of the season. It was do-or-die time and everyone on the team was feeling the pressure.

He'd just turned off the kitchen light when his cell phone rang. Moving toward the bedroom, he pulled it out of his back pocket and checked the caller ID before answering it.

"What's up?"

"Are you watching ESPN?" Sean asked.

"No." He hit the switch on the wall; the bedroom flooded with light. "I just got home."

"Turn it on." Sean's voice was strained.

"What's going on?" He moved to the cherrywood armoire in the corner of the room and opened it. "Did someone die?" he asked as he grabbed the remote and hit the power button.

The channel was already tuned to ESPN and when the screen lit up Matt's heart plummeted to his stomach the second he saw a picture of himself on the screen and next to it, a picture of Joey. "What the hell?" he muttered and read the caption underneath the photos.

BREAKING NEWS: MLB All-Star's Personal Tragedy

Neither he nor Sean spoke as they listened to the sports announcer report that an unknown source had contacted a tabloid and informed them that Matt Scanlon had a secret son. A son he never knew he had until two years before the boy tragically died from chronic leukemia. That tabloid would be on sale tomorrow, but the sports channel had gotten a tip from someone who worked for the rag and was reporting the story first.

"Son of a bitch," Matt whispered, trying to hold back the wave of nausea that threatened to overtake him. This was it—his worst nightmare coming to life right before his eyes. "Do you think it was Leslie?"

"No." Sean was adamant. "She called me a few minutes ago, extremely upset. Evidently, the press are calling her and pressing her to speak with them. She's refusing to talk."

Matt hit the mute button and turned away from the television. "Not one reporter asked me about this after the game. This must be the first broadcast of it."

"Who do you think did it?" Sean asked. "One of the nurses at the hospital?"

"After all this time?" He shook his head. "No. Besides, Leslie and I were careful. We never told them I was Joey's father. They all thought he was a Make-A-Wish kid and I'd taken a liking to him."

"Someone had to talk," Sean insisted. "Have you told anyone else about Joey besides me?"

Matt's blood turned cold. "Yes," he said through clenched teeth.

"Who?"

"Kelly."

"I don't think she'd—"

"It had to be her." His fingers tightened on the phone as a wave of pulsing fury shot through him. "This is no coincidence."

"Don't jump to conclusions," Sean began calmly.

"It was her, damn it!" He hurled the remote with all of his might. It hit the wall, broke into several pieces and clattered to the hardwood floor. He stared at it as the sting of Kelly's betrayal twisted like a knife in his gut. "I'll talk to you later," he said grimly and didn't bother waiting for Sean's reply.

In less than one minute he'd left the condo and was on his way to Kelly's.

WHEN KELLY HEARD the knock at the door, she assumed it was Stacia. Her roommate, on more than one occasion, had come home after a night of clubbing too wasted to even put her key in the lock. It wasn't like Stacia to come home early on a Friday night, though—not before eleven anyway.

"Did you forget…" she began as she opened the door. Her heart skipped a beat when she found Matt there instead of Stacia. "Hi." She smiled and then noticed the dark glitter of his eyes. Something was wrong—very wrong. His expression was as hard as stone and his fists were tightly clenched at his side.

"Why'd you do it?" Matt asked harshly as he brushed past her and into the foyer.

Not sure what was going on, she closed the door and turned to find him watching her with a hostile expression. "Why did I do what?" she asked carefully and wrapped her arms around her midriff. She'd never seen him like this, not even during the time when they couldn't stand each other. He looked like the devil incarnate. It frightened her.

Matt's expression was hard and unyielding. "Oh, so you haven't seen your handiwork on ESPN yet?"

"What are you talking about?"

"Don't play dumb, Kelly." He put his hands on his hips and glared at her. "It doesn't suit you. Just admit it. You told them about Joey."

"What?" Kelly felt the blood drain from her face.

"It's all over the news." He pointed at her. "Because of you." Just then, her cell phone rang from the bedroom. "You might want to get that," he said with a sneer. "I'm sure you'll be fielding a lot of calls now that you've spilled my personal business to the whole *fucking* world."

"Matt." She put up her hands. "I swear, I didn't tell anyone about Joey. I'd never do that to you."

"I don't believe you."

"It's the truth."

"I trusted you." He advanced toward her but she held her ground. "God, I really was a sucker, wasn't I?" He halted before her, the anger emanating off of him in waves. "I know Sean didn't do it. And neither did Leslie." His mouth twisted into an ugly grimace. "That leaves you." He grabbed her by her arms, his fingers digging into her skin. "I'll never forgive you for this."

Kelly opened her mouth to protest, but quickly changed her mind. At this moment he was so furious he wouldn't believe anything she said.

"I think we should talk about this tomorrow," she said calmly even though her heart was racing a mile a minute. "I'll do some investigating and find out who's behind this."

"Don't bother. I already know who's behind it." His fingers tightened on her arms causing her to wince.

"You're hurting me," she whispered.

Immediately he let her go, stepped back and ran a hand through his hair. His dark, furious eyes bore into hers. "Don't worry. I won't *ever* touch you again," he said in an icy voice and then stepped around her and moved to the door. By the time she turned around, he'd slammed it behind him and was gone.

TWENTY-ONE

"No. He's not giving interviews. Not to *Good Morning America*, not to the *Today* show and most definitely not to your piece of trash rag," Kelly said, not bothering to hide her disgust that the editor of the tabloid that had printed Matt's story had the nerve to call her and ask if they could get a one-on-one interview with him. "By the way, who was your source?" she asked, but all she got was silence. The editor had hung up.

"Damn it." She slammed the receiver down so hard her desk shook. Putting her fingers to her temples, she rubbed hard. The headache she'd woken up with was showing no signs of easing.

"That bad?"

Kelly looked up to find her boss standing in the doorway. As usual, Katherine was dressed in a beautifully tailored suit that fit her slender figure like a glove. "Sorry." She lowered her hands and rested her arms on the desk. "I've been fielding calls all morning."

Katherine moved forward and gave her a sympathetic smile. "If it's any consolation, I've been getting them too. Everyone is clamoring to be the first to get Matt on the record about his son."

"I got a call from his agent as soon as I got into the office. He informed me that for the foreseeable future Matt won't be taking questions in the media room after the game." Kelly sighed. "I don't blame him one bit."

Katherine glanced at her watch. "The game is due to start in about an hour. Before then I'd like you to write up a press release stating that the organization is deeply sorry for Matt's loss and we're supporting his decision not to speak to the media regarding the death of his son."

"I've already started it." Kelly glanced at her computer screen. "I'll have a draft ready for your review in about fifteen minutes."

"I'll be in my office." Katherine turned to leave, then stopped and looked back, her gaze curious. "Have you been able to find out who spoke to the tabloid?"

"No," she said with a grimace. "But I'm sure whoever it was received a huge check."

After Katherine had left, Kelly opened her drawer and retrieved the small bottle of aspirin she kept inside. She took two with a huge gulp of water and wished they would ease the pain in her heart as well as the ache in her head.

How could he? How could Matt believe the worst of her? Without any hesitation whatsoever he'd tried and convicted her of betraying him without even letting her speak.

And, to make matters worse, he wasn't taking her calls. She'd left three messages but all she'd received in return was silence. Obviously he didn't want to talk to her. A dry sob burned in her throat. How could this be happening? Matt hated her. And what was worse— despite everything—she was still in love with the jerk.

WITH QUICK EFFICIENT movements Matt buttoned his shirt. Although he faced his locker, he could feel the tension in the room. It was that palpable. This morning when he'd walked into the clubhouse every single one of his teammates had looked at him with varying degrees of pity. He sensed many of them wanted to say something—to offer their sympathies, but unsure of his reaction they'd kept quiet.

As much as he didn't want to address the situation, it had to be dealt with. And now was the perfect time. Today all media had been restricted from entering the clubhouse. It was just him and his teammates.

Taking a deep breath, he turned from his locker. "I'd like to say something," he said, raising his voice as he did a quick scan of the room. Next to him, Lopes and J.T. stopped talking and turned their attention toward him. The rest of the guys, including Rizzo, quieted down and watched him with somber expressions.

"I'm sure you all saw the report on ESPN last night or this morning." He paused to gather his thoughts. "Everything they said is true. I…lost my son a year ago in July. The reason I never went public was because I didn't want the media hounding my son's mother, or me. What we went through, and the circumstances surrounding it, were private, and I wanted to keep it that way.

"Unfortunately, someone," he took a breath as the pain of Kelly's betrayal knifed through him, "found out about Joey and decided to make it public." He let his gaze move around the room, resting briefly on each of his teammates. "So that means on top of all the media scrutiny we're under because of the division race, the press will not only be hounding me, but you guys as well. And that's the last thing we need right now."

Matt cleared his throat and continued, "I know a few of you have questioned my loyalty, but I'm telling you right now that you don't have to. I'm not going to let this affect my focus and I don't want it to affect yours. We've got two weeks left to win the division and, with all due respect to my former team, on the last day of the season, the Blaze *will* be the last team standing."

"Damn straight," J.T. said and pumped his fist, which caused several of the guys to do the same thing.

That seemed to lighten the mood, and not feeling the need to say anything further, he turned back to his locker and reached for his watch. As he was putting it on, he felt a tap on his shoulder. He pivoted to find Rizzo standing behind him.

"I'm sorry for your loss," Rizzo said in a low voice.

"Thank you." He looked over Rizzo's shoulder to the pitcher's locker where a framed photo of Rizzo's young son was displayed. They didn't like each other and probably never would, but as one father to another, they understood each other perfectly.

"Good game tonight," Matt said and grinned. "Thanks for not shaking off all my pitch calls."

Rizzo smirked. "Just trying to make you look good out there, Scanlon."

"No. That was me making *you* look good."

"Whatever," Rizzo said with a shake of his head, then returned to his locker.

Before leaving the clubhouse, Matt checked his phone. Other than Sean and his agent, he hadn't taken any calls or returned any messages. There had been three messages from Kelly but he'd deleted each one without listening to them.

Last night, after he'd left her place, he'd gone back to his condo feeling like he'd been punched in the gut and had the wind knocked out of him. As he sat in the dark and watched the ESPN report over and over as it played each half hour like clockwork, he'd cursed himself for being such a fool—for trusting Kelly and confiding in her about Joey.

Why did it hurt so damn much? This wasn't the same kind of pain he'd experienced when Joey died, it was different. Kelly had made a conscious decision to stab him in the back—maybe that was the difference.

"Matt." Kelly's husky voice came from behind him. He turned to face her and for one moment he felt guilty for the shadows under her eyes. "May I speak with you for a few minutes?" she asked politely. "Alone."

"Fine," he said and followed her to the empty players' lounge. He watched her ponytail swing back and forth and tried not to remember how soft her hair was and how he'd never tired of running his fingers through it. Pushing the memory away, he folded his arms across his chest when she came to a stop in front of the vending machines.

Kelly was all business as she turned around. "A press release just went out regarding the…the situation. The organization supports your decision not to speak with the press. Also, for the duration of the regular season we'll make the clubhouse off-limits to all reporters." She lifted her hand and rubbed her temple with her index finger. "We can't ban them completely so they will be on the field before games and, of course, in the media room afterward."

When he didn't reply, she lowered her hand and continued, "I've declined all interview requests on your behalf. If you change your mind let me know."

"I won't change my mind," he snapped, searching her face for some trace of guilt. But there was nothing—no remorse at all. "How could you do this to me?" He put his hands on his hips and glared at her.

"I could ask you the same question," she shot back, her eyes blazing with anger.

"What are you talking about?"

"I'm talking about the fact that you immediately assumed I was the one who went to that sleazy tabloid. That you would think that of me made me realize you don't know me at all." She paused and gave him a disdainful look. "And you're certainly not the man I thought you were."

She was acting like the injured party. *What the hell?*

"What else am I supposed to think?" he demanded. "Joey died over a year ago and not one word has been mentioned in the media. Then I tell you and less than a week later I'm watching it on ESPN."

"And that makes it all right for you to storm over to my house, accuse me of betraying you and leaving bruises on my arms?"

"Bruises?" A wave of nausea hit him. He remembered grabbing her arms, but he didn't think he'd been that rough.

"Yes. If I didn't have this blazer on you'd see the marks you left."

"It won't happen again."

"You're damn right it won't." Her frigid gaze held his with mesmerizing force. "Because you and me... we're done."

Stunned, he turned and watched her after she pushed past him and stalked away. And with each step she took the more alone he felt. When she slammed the clubhouse door behind her it finally hit him. Now he knew why it hurt so fucking much.

Son of a bitch. He was in love with Kelly Maxwell.

TEN LONG MISERABLE days after she'd talked to Matt in the clubhouse, Kelly sat in Kamu's with Angie. Sitting next to her was their softball teammate, Richie, who had called the meeting to discuss the Fall/Winter coed league. She half listened as Richie and Angie discussed practice times and recruiting. A few of their teammates had opted not to participate, which had Richie all fired up and ready to poach a few players from the other teams.

"How about that guy who plays shortstop for the Lions?" Richie asked, looking from Angie to her. "I'll bet he's dying to get on a team that actually has a chance at the championship."

Kelly nodded. "Can't hurt to approach him."

"I agree," Angie said from across the table. The smile on her face faded as she looked past Kelly and toward the entrance. Kelly turned her head, curious to see who or what had caused Angie's very noticeable reaction. When she saw Matt and J.T. heading for the bar, her heart stopped and then started beating again with a thudding that pounded in her ears. Neither Matt nor J.T. glanced in their direction, and since they were still dressed in their travel clothes it was safe to assume the team's charter had just returned from their four-day road trip to Chicago. A road trip that, thankfully, she'd been spared from. Katherine had gone in her place.

Kelly let her gaze linger on Matt's handsome profile for several seconds and then forced herself to look away. She missed him—so much so that the past week and a half had been the longest of her life. The media spotlight had faded from Matt and Joey, and the press had, for the most part, moved on. She still received interview requests, but not as many as before. Matt's continued silence on the subject had effectively shut down the story and the focus was back on the Blaze and their quest to win the division.

Turning back to the table, Kelly noted Angie's attention continue to stray toward the bar and in her eyes, there was something Kelly had never seen when Angie talked about Scott. Something that looked a lot like lust.

After more discussion of potential players, Kelly left Angie and Richie at the table and made her way to the restroom. When she was finished and had washed and dried her hands, she walked out of the restroom and stiffened in surprise as Matt sauntered toward the men's room.

Damn, he was sexy. He was wearing the same sport coat and charcoal-gray sweater he'd worn the night of Lily's birthday party that never happened. His hair was longer, the ends curling around his collar, and there was dark stubble on his jaw. Tall, dark and damn hot— Lance's description fit Matt to a tee.

He halted in front of her, and for a second she thought she saw longing in his eyes, but if it *was* longing it was gone quickly and replaced with an enigmatic look she couldn't read.

His gaze traveled over her body and then lifted. She'd worn a dress today—only because she hadn't gotten around to doing laundry.

"Who's the guy you're with? Angie's fiancé?"

So he had seen her.

"No," she said, not bothering to elaborate. It was none of his damn business who she was with. Not after the way he'd treated her.

"Funny, I didn't peg you for the type to go right from

one man to another," Matt's eyes narrowed, "but then I guess I never really knew you, did I?"

"Obviously not," she said and was forced to move closer to him as a man rounded the corner and passed them on his way to the restroom. "Otherwise you would have known that I would never tell a soul about Joey."

"Who's the guy?" he asked again.

"Why do you care?" Kelly asked, hating the fact that despite how angry she was with him he still had the power to excite her. The warm spicy scent of his cologne coupled with the memory of the hot nights they'd spent together was almost too much to take. Instinctively, her body reacted. Her nipples grew taut against her bra and desire ignited low in her belly.

Their eyes locked, the electricity between them just as intense as ever.

"Looks like we're right back where we started," Matt said, breaking the taut silence.

"Yes. It does." She should walk away but she couldn't bring herself to do it. Being this close to him would probably never happen again—the thought of it filled her with sadness.

"Then it's a good thing I'll be gone after the season." He lifted his hand as if to touch her hair but then quickly lowered it.

"Best for both of us," she whispered and fought the urge to lean into him and feel his lips upon hers one last time. With a start, she realized that's exactly what she was doing and jerked back and collected herself. "The media restrictions are still in place," she said, getting back to business. "However, when you win the division they'll be lifted for postseason play."

"You sound pretty confident we're going to win." Matt cocked his head. "Why is that?"

"Because you promised Lily you'd win the World Series. You can't do that without winning the division." She paused. "And for what it's worth, I hope you win it all. After what they've been through, both Lily and the team deserve a winning season."

Without waiting for him to reply, she turned and returned to the restaurant. As she passed through the bar, she waved at J.T. but he didn't notice her. He was staring at the table where Richie and Angie were still sitting. He didn't look happy.

It seemed that more than one person in Kamu's tonight was in a bad mood—she was in good company.

MATT FORCED HIMSELF not to groan aloud when Stacia slid onto the bar stool next to him.

Shit. She always seemed to show up at the most inopportune times.

"Do you mind if I join you?" she asked, giving him a wide smile.

"Suit yourself." He lifted his bottle and took a long swig as Stacia ordered some fancy drink from the bartender. He silently cursed J.T. for leaving him alone to finish his beer and wished he'd left at the same time. Making small talk with Stacia wasn't his idea of fun.

"I'm glad I ran into you." Stacia set her small purse on the bar.

"Why is that?"

"I saw the story about your son and I wanted to tell you how sorry I am for your loss."

"Thank you." He set his beer on the bar and reached for his wallet. It was time to leave.

Stacia thanked the bartender for her drink and wrapped her fingers around the slender stem of her glass. "I can't imagine how difficult it's been for you. I mean, finding out you had a son and learning of his illness on the same day." Her sigh was dramatic. "So tragic."

Matt opened his wallet, pulled out a twenty and couldn't help but think Stacia wasn't as genuine as she'd like him to believe.

"Has the media attention died down?" she asked.

"Pretty much."

"That's good." Stacia sipped her drink. "I'm sure it was devastating to have all the details broadcast to the entire world." She turned to him with moisture-filled eyes. "And how sad was it that you buried him in your Dodgers jersey?"

Done with the conversation, Matt slapped the twenty on the bar. This was one night when her low-cut top and push-up bra weren't going to yield any results—at least not with him.

"I'm sorry but I've gotta go. Early day tomorrow," he said and slid off the bar stool. "See you around."

Stacia's smile was suggestive. "If you're lucky."

Matt choked back a laugh. He was absolutely sure most guys got lucky with Stacia. Hell, he'd almost been one of them. Thank God that had never happened.

As he walked back to his condo, he couldn't stop thinking about Kelly. The second he'd walked into Kamu's he'd seen her. A woman like her was hard to miss. But what really got his attention was the guy who'd been sitting with her and Angie. It wasn't Angie's fiancé, Kelly had confirmed that.

Who was it?

The thought of Kelly with another man made him

want to smash something—like the mystery man's face. It wasn't how he should be feeling about the woman who had betrayed him, but he couldn't help it. He hated what she'd done, but he couldn't turn his feelings off just like that.

Damn the woman. Even now he still loved her.

LATER, AS HE lay in bed, he reached for the picture of Joey on his nightstand. He was surprised when it didn't evoke the same sharp pain it had a few months ago. In the picture, taken about three months before his death, Joey was wearing his Dodgers jersey and was holding the puppy Leslie had given him for his birthday. Besides baseball, Joey loved dogs with a passion, and had been hounding Leslie for one for months. Leslie wasn't an animal lover but had finally given in. Matt was convinced it was because, by that time, barring a miracle, it was clear Joey wasn't going to make it.

After he'd returned the picture to the nightstand and turned off the light, he stared up at the ceiling and replayed the brief conversation he'd had with Stacia in his head. Something about it was off, but he wasn't quite sure what it was. Maybe it would come to him later but he wasn't too concerned about it right now. He had more important things on his mind.

Tomorrow, the Dodgers were in town for the final series of the regular season. Three games in three days and whoever won two out of the three would be the division champs.

So it had come to this. Strangely enough, he was looking forward to it.

THE NEXT DAY, Kelly sat next to her father in his seats just behind the Blaze dugout and, like everyone else in the ballpark, was caught up in the excitement of the game. The Dodgers and the Blaze had been rivals for years so anytime the Dodgers came to town the fans got rowdy. And, with a postseason berth on the line, the atmosphere was downright intense.

"Gentry's in the zone," her father said as they watched Trey deliver a hanging curveball that completely fooled the hitter who swung and missed. "That kid's got something special."

Kelly agreed. Trey Gentry had the potential to be better than Rizzo. She fully expected him to have a tremendous career. Today he was on fire. It was the top of the eighth inning and he'd struck out ten batters. She was confident of a victory. The Blaze were ahead thanks to Marquis Lopes, who'd belted a grand slam in the bottom of the sixth.

"How's Matt doing?" John Maxwell turned in his seat as the crowd cheered wildly when the Dodgers' main threat struck out and slammed his bat into the dirt. "Did you know about his son?"

"Yes." Kelly looked at her dad. He didn't know she and Matt were on the outs and that she didn't know how Matt was feeling—other than being pissed at her, that is. This wasn't the time to share that with her father, though. Maybe after the season and Matt was gone. Perhaps then it wouldn't hurt so much. "He told me a few weeks ago."

"It explains a lot, doesn't it?"

She nodded. "He was in a lot of pain."

"He seems to be past the worst of it," her father commented and turned his attention back to the field where Matt stood behind home plate waiting for the next batter to take his stance. "Two hits so far and a hell of a pick at second. If anyone was concerned he was going to tank against the Dodgers, they were dead wrong."

As she shifted her knees to allow the fan to the left of her father to pass in front of her and get to the aisle, her phone vibrated in her jacket pocket. She pulled it out and read the text highlighted on the small screen.

"Dad, I'll be right back. Katherine needs me in her office right now." She shoved the phone back into her pocket and rose to her feet. "I shouldn't be too long."

After navigating her way through the fans milling around the food and drink stands, Kelly made her way to the front office and hurried down the carpeted hallway to find Katherine's door open and her boss sitting at her desk with her head cradled in her hands.

"What's wrong?" she asked as she stepped inside the office. "Is everything okay?"

"No." Katherine lifted her head; it was plain to see she'd been crying. Her eyes were red and her cheeks wet. A feeling of dread tiptoed up Kelly's spine. Her boss rarely showed emotion; for her to do so now meant something serious had occurred. "Sit down." Katherine motioned to the floral-covered chair opposite her desk. "I just received a call from Rick Taylor's agent."

Kelly sank to the plump cushion and clutched the padded arms with her fingers. "What happened? Is Rick okay?"

"It's not Rick." Katherine reached for a tissue from the box on her desk. "It's Jill. She's dead."

Caught off guard, Kelly sucked in a shocked breath. "Oh my God," she whispered. "When? How?"

Katherine dabbed at her cheeks with the tissue and then tossed it on her desk. "Late last night. Jill's car was hit by another vehicle in the middle of an intersection. She died instantly."

Kelly put a hand to her mouth and blinked back tears. Katherine grabbed another tissue. They sat in silence, both too stunned to speak.

"She was pregnant," Kelly finally said, lowering her hand to her lap. "I talked to Rick two weeks ago. They had just announced it to their families."

"I know." Sadness shadowed Katherine's eyes. "As expected, Rick's taking it pretty hard." Katherine pushed the tissue box forward. Kelly plucked one out of the box and wiped away the moisture from around her eyes. "We need to handle this with the utmost sensitivity. Rick is a member of the Blaze family. Doug has made it clear that we'll respect any decisions he makes regarding his return to the ball club."

Kelly sagged against the chair. Jill was dead. She still couldn't believe it. "I'll get to work on a press release. Do we know about funeral arrangements yet? I'm sure several of the players will be asking."

"Those details will be forthcoming. Rick's agent wasn't sure if Rick and Jill's family want a public service. It may be for family members only."

"I can't wrap my head around this." Kelly crumpled the tissue and shifted to push it into her pocket. "When I talked to Rick he was so happy. He couldn't wait to get to spring training." She paused and sat up straight. "What does it mean for us if he doesn't come back?"

"That remains to be seen," Katherine said. "He may show up. February is still five months away. If he doesn't, then we'll have to adjust, just like we did when he was injured in July. I do know that Doug and Tom Morgan plan to contact Matt's agent about the possibility of him staying with us for another year. He's in the last year of his contract and with his resurgence, he's a hot commodity right now."

It was too much to digest. Jill and her unborn baby were dead. *How could that be?* How could someone so young and full of life be taken from her husband and family? And Rick. Oh dear Lord, it was obvious from the first moment she'd met him that he was head over heels in love with his wife. They'd grown up in the same small town and had been high school sweethearts. She couldn't even imagine the pain he was going through.

And in addition to that, Matt might be staying in San Francisco. While one part of her—the part of her that was still in love with him—was thrilled at the prospect, the other part of her dreaded it. How could she work with him for another season when he hated the sight of her?

Kelly shook herself out of her reverie. Now wasn't the time to be thinking about her issues. A man had just lost his wife and baby. Her problems with Matt were minuscule in comparison.

"I'll go get started on the press release," she said as she rose from the chair. "Let me know if you need anything else."

Katherine gave her a wan smile. "Thank you, Kelly. I don't know what I did without you. Hiring you was the best decision I've ever made."

TWENTY-TWO

"I'M REALLY SORRY about Joey."

After two weeks Matt was getting used to hearing that, or variations on it, wherever he went. But when it came from Lily, who was going under the knife tomorrow at noon, it scared him to death to think she might suffer the same fate as his son.

It wasn't logical—the circumstances were totally different—but still, in the back of his mind, it was there. Another child could die. Another parent could go through the same hell he and Leslie had endured. He wouldn't wish that on anybody.

"You know, you're a lot like Joey." He put his video game controller next to him on Dorie's floral couch. They'd just played Lily's favorite baseball video game and she'd kicked his ass. A rematch was definitely in order. Now that he was used to the controller he hoped to vindicate himself in the next round.

"But I'm a girl," Lily protested so vehemently he had to smile.

"I know, but Joey loved baseball and so do you. He also loved animals and you love that big orange cat that seems to disappear whenever I come over."

A smile wreathed Lily's thin face. "Tabitha's just shy. In a few months, she'll get used to you and come out to say hi."

Matt chuckled. "I can hardly wait."

"I wish my surgery wasn't tomorrow." Lily leaned forward and set her controller on the coffee table. From the kitchen, he could hear Dorie's low and melodic humming as she washed the dinner dishes. She and Lily had invited him over for dinner.

"Are you scared?"

"A little." Lily flopped back and began twisting a lock of her hair with her finger. "I'm mad I'm gonna miss the game. I wish I could see you guys win the division."

Matt shifted and stretched his arm out over the top of the couch, getting comfortable. "I'm sorry we couldn't do that today," he said. The Blaze had won game one, but this afternoon the Dodgers had beaten them with a two-run homer in the top of the ninth. "But Rizzo's pitching tomorrow so we've got our best guy out there on the mound."

Lily looked at him pensively. "Matt, can I ask you a favor?"

"Sure, kiddo."

"Do…do you think I could meet Trey Gentry sometime?"

Matt's jaw dropped. He wasn't expecting that. "So, I've been replaced." He grinned. "Is that it?"

Lily's face turned pink. "No, you're still my favorite player of all time. But…" Shyly, she averted her eyes.

"I get it." He reached down and ruffled her hair. "And I think I can arrange for you to meet Trey."

Lily squealed, turned and threw her arms around him, burying her face in his chest. "I love you, Matt," she mumbled and then angled her head to gaze up at him. "Joey was really lucky to have you for a dad."

"I was the lucky one." Tears swam in his eyes as he gave Lily a hug. "And you know what else?" Lily shook her head, her glasses askew. He straightened them on the bridge of her nose. "I love you too."

An hour later, after Lily had once again annihilated him at video baseball, Matt was driving down California Street and trying not to think about tomorrow. While Lily was having heart surgery he'd be playing in the most important game of the season. It wasn't lost on him that to some people the outcome of the game meant a whole lot more than what would be going on in that operating room, or that Rick Taylor was mourning the loss of his wife and unborn child.

Losing Joey had changed him. He loved baseball and always would. He wanted to win the World Series more than anything, but if given a choice between winning a game and Lily's life, he'd gladly lose the game if it meant Lily could live. He didn't want to bury another child wearing his jersey.

Son of a bitch. The jersey.

He almost swerved into the other lane as what was bothering him about his conversation with Stacia became crystal clear. With an apologetic wave to the driver who had honked at him, his fingers tightened on the wheel and he hit the gas hard.

It took him twenty-five minutes to get back to his building, park the SUV in the underground garage and then walk to Kelly's building. He took the elevator to her floor, all the while feeling like the biggest idiot on the planet. He hoped and prayed Kelly would forgive him. But if she didn't, how could he blame her?

After sprinting to her door, he knocked and waited. But it wasn't Kelly who opened the door. It was Stacia.

"Matt," she said with obvious surprise. "What are you doing here?"

"Is Kelly home?"

"No. She texted me a while ago and said she was driving her dad back to Pleasanton. She might stay the night, she does that sometimes."

He ran a frustrated hand through his hair. "May I come in?" Actually, it was probably best Kelly wasn't here for this. It could get ugly.

"Of course." Stacia's eyes took on a predatory gleam as she opened the door wider so he could enter. "Can I get you anything? A beer? Wine? Water?" She closed the door and turned to face him with a smile curving her lips.

"I don't want anything except the truth," he said, not wasting time with pleasantries. "I know you were the one who leaked the story about my son. Now I want you to tell me why you did it."

As her smile faltered, Stacia put a hand to her chest and had the nerve to look affronted. She was a damn good actress, he'd give her that.

"I don't know what you're talking about. I had nothing to do with that."

"Save the innocent routine. I'm not buying it." He pinned her with a hard stare. "A few nights ago when I left Kamu's, I had this feeling that there was something very odd about our conversation. It's been nagging at me ever since and tonight I finally figured it out."

Stacia's eyes flickered with unease. "Figured what out?"

"I've watched all the news reports and read every article written about Joey. And you know what? Not one of them mentioned that Joey was buried in my Dodgers jersey." Matt pointed at her. "But you knew. And the only way you *could* know is if you were home the night

I was here and were eavesdropping on the conversation Kelly and I had in the kitchen."

"You're crazy," she exclaimed. "Why would I do such a thing?"

He shrugged. "I don't know. Maybe it was for the money. Or maybe you're a jealous vindictive bitch who's pissed off because she didn't get what she wanted."

"And what did I want?" Stacia crossed her arms over her chest and glared at him.

"Me," he snapped. "And I bet it irritated the hell out of you that I preferred Kelly to you."

Stacia's snort was derisive. "Like I'd ever be jealous of that cow."

"You should be," Matt retorted and wondered if Kelly knew how much Stacia despised her. Probably not, or she wouldn't be living with her.

"You can't prove it was me." Stacia's tone was cool—it appeared she was just smart enough not to admit to anything.

"Are you sure about that?" He cocked his head and gave her a mirthless smile. "I could call that tabloid editor right now and offer him an interview in exchange for the name of the person who tipped them off about Joey." Stacia pressed her lips together in a thin line as he continued, "These people have no scruples, Stacia. They'd sell you down the river in a heartbeat to get what they want. And what they want is an interview with me."

"If I did do it, there's nothing you can do to me." Stacia's expression went from worried to gloating in seconds. "It's not like what was printed was a lie. It was all the truth."

"You're right." Matt shoved his hands in the pockets of his jeans. He wanted badly to shake the shit out of her but there was no way he was going to put bruises on a woman ever again. "The story is out there. Nothing can change that. I guess you'll have to live with the fact that you're a bitter and spiteful woman."

"I think you should leave," Stacia said and took a step back to pull open the door.

"No problem," he said as he brushed past her and into the hallway where he turned to meet her icy gaze. "And by the way, Kelly has more heart, and more class than you could ever hope to have."

Stacia's reply was to slam the door in his face.

On the way back to his condo he called Kelly's cell phone but it went straight to voice mail. He left a brief message asking her to call him but didn't go into detail. This wasn't something he wanted to share with her over the phone. No, apologizing for being such an insensitive prick was something that had to be done in person. He just hoped it wasn't too late.

THE NEXT MORNING, it was eleven when Kelly finally got to her office. With hurried movements, she sat down at her desk and turned on her computer. After quickly scanning her emails, she sighed with relief when she didn't see anything labeled urgent.

"Where have you been?" Angie stood at the threshold. "I tried calling you but your phone kept going to voice mail. Katherine's been looking for you."

"I'm sorry." Kelly reached into her purse and pulled out her cell phone. "My battery died. I spent the night at my parents' house and didn't have my charger with me," she said as she connected the phone to the charger she kept plugged into her computer. "Is something going on I should know about?"

Angie moved into the office and braced her hands on the back of the visitor chair. "The word on the street is that Rick Taylor is quitting baseball."

Kelly's mouth gaped open. "What? Quitting forever, or just next season?"

Angie gestured with her hands. "No one knows. But everyone in accounting is buzzing about it. I think that's why Katherine's trying to find you."

"I was at the hospital visiting with Lily." Kelly leaned back in her chair and sighed. "Her surgery starts in about an hour."

"I didn't know that was today." Angie's eyes filled with sympathy. "I'll say a prayer."

"Thanks. She'll need all the prayers she can get." She rose to her feet. "I should go find Katherine."

"Will you keep me posted about Lily?" Angie asked as they walked out of the office.

"You bet," she said and then strode toward her boss's office while Angie headed back to accounting.

Half an hour later, Kelly walked out of Katherine's office with instructions to hold off on the press release regarding Rick Taylor's decision to stop playing professional baseball. Upper management believed that Rick was making a hasty decision in the wake of his grief, and after a period of mourning would change his mind.

But in case they were wrong, Doug would be placing a call to Matt's agent. The Blaze wanted him to stay. But would he? The tide had turned dramatically from a few months ago. Now Matt was in the driver's seat.

At one-fifteen, just after the singing of the national anthem, Kelly made her way down the steps of the lower level of the ballpark and plopped into the seat next to her father. Sweet man that he was, he always gave her the aisle seat—a gesture she greatly appreciated.

"I was wondering if you were going to make it before the first pitch. This is it, Peanut. One game, winner takes all," he said with a grin and then signaled to the vendor selling beer a couple of rows up.

Kelly couldn't help but smile. As usual, John Maxwell was decked out in his game-day attire of jeans, an orange-and-black Blaze T-shirt and a Blaze baseball cap turned backward on his head. He often joked about getting the Blaze logo tattooed on his arm but her mother had put the kibosh on that brilliant idea many moons ago.

"Do you want one?" he asked when the beer vendor stopped at their row.

"Hell, yes." She pulled out her phone and checked her missed calls. There were a ton of them, and as she scrolled through them her breath caught when she saw two of them were from Matt. Surprised, she looked up. Matt was on the pitcher's mound talking to Rizzo. He was even more imposing in his catcher's gear; she drank in the sight of him, missing him more than she thought it possible to miss anyone.

"Here you go."

She tore her gaze from Matt to find the beer vendor staring at her. "Sorry," she said with a smile and took the cup from his hand. She slipped her phone into her pocket. The voice mails could wait.

MATT SLAPPED ON his batting helmet and strode to the on-deck circle as Marquis Lopes stepped up to the plate. It was the bottom of the fourth inning and the score was tied at two apiece.

The noise in the ballpark was deafening, and everywhere he looked all he could see were the orange rally towels the fans waved and whipped around in an excited frenzy. The atmosphere was electric and fraught with tension—this was a do-or-die game and everyone in the entire park was on the edge of their seat.

This was what baseball was all about. That one game when everything was on the line, and one hit or one error could win or lose a ball game.

He took a few practice swings and then watched as Lopes swung and missed on a slider. The crowd let out a collective groan. Scanning the field, Matt felt only a slight stab of nostalgia at the sight of his former teammates. He was no longer one of them and he was fine with that—this was his home right now, and might be again next season if what his agent told him about Rick Taylor quitting baseball was true.

After the next pitch was called a ball, Matt glanced at the scoreboard and checked the time. It was after three. Lily's surgery had started at noon and he had no clue what was happening. His cell phone was in his locker. The skipper had a strict policy about cell phone usage during a game. Getting caught with one could result in a huge fine.

Lopes swung and hit a ball into foul territory. Matt took a few more swings and then stole a glance at the seats behind the dugout. Kelly was sitting with her father. At the moment they were both standing and enthusiastically waving their orange towels. Kelly hadn't returned either of his calls and when he'd gone to her office when he got to the ballpark it had been empty.

He understood why she hadn't called him back, but it was killing him not to be able to tell her about Stacia, and to apologize for his behavior.

The crowd groaned again. Lopes had struck out. It was the third out so Matt made his way back to the dugout. Just before going down the steps, he glanced up and met Kelly's gaze. She was in the first row behind the dugout, so close yet so far away.

For several seconds he stood there, unable to move, and although the crowd around them was loud and raucous all he could hear was the thundering of his heart as he stared into her beautiful eyes. For one insane moment he wanted to jump on top of the dugout and pull her into his arms but then he heard someone say his name and he was jolted back to reality. Tearing his gaze from hers, he stepped down into the dugout, stashed his bat and strapped on his gear. There were five innings left and he had a game to win.

AT THE TOP of the sixth inning, Kelly had just finished washing her hands in the women's restroom when her cell phone vibrated in her pocket. She pulled it out and quickly answered it when she saw Dorie's name on the small screen.

"How's Lily?" she asked as she exited the restroom and moved to a quieter area a few steps from the door. She watched people stroll by, all of them dressed in Blaze shirts and baseball caps. These fans adored their team.

"The surgery went well," Dorie said. "Lily's in recovery right now and her doctor is very optimistic."

Kelly put her hand to her heart. This was the best news she'd heard all day. "Oh, Dorie. I'm so relieved."

"You and me both." Dorie paused. "Hey, I know Matt's playing right now. Would you mind giving him the good news for me?"

"Not at all," she replied. "Lily told me about his visit last night and I know he'll want to know as soon as possible. I might even be able to get a message to him in the dugout."

"That would be great. I'll talk to you soon."

Once she was back in her seat, and with the outcome of Lily's surgery no longer weighing on her mind, Kelly thought she might be able to enjoy the game, but no such luck. Besides being a nail-biter with the score still tied, now all she could think about was getting a message to Matt. Yes, she was still angry at him, but he and Lily had forged a strong bond and he deserved to know she'd made it through the surgery.

At the top of the seventh inning she got the bright idea to go down to the clubhouse. Maybe Matt would use the extra time during the seventh inning stretch to use the restroom. It was a long shot, but usually the guys who weren't up at bat took a quick break to relieve themselves. She leaned toward her father and told him she'd return shortly and then left her seat and headed to the clubhouse.

After using her badge to enter, she bypassed the lounge and made her way to the locker room. It was empty save for the assistant equipment manager who gave her a nod and a smile and then hit the steps for the dugout.

As she waited, she paced the room. When she got tired of pacing, she sat on one of the benches and played with a loose thread on the cuff of her blazer. She heard the roar of the crowd, which probably meant one of the Dodgers had struck out. Her assumption was correct when about a minute later Marquis Lopes bounded down the stairs from the dugout. He stopped short, surprised to see her, and then gave her a friendly wave and continued on toward the restroom.

Tired of sitting, she got up and started pacing again. Maybe Matt wasn't coming down. That was okay, she'd ask Lopes to tell him about Lily. At least he would know and wouldn't worry anymore.

"Kelly?"

Startled, she spun around to find Matt standing at the base of the stairs. Although still wearing his knee and shin guards, he'd taken off his catcher's mask and chest protector. He moved toward her, and by the apprehensive expression on his face he probably thought she had bad news for him. "Is it Lily?" he asked, halting in front of her.

"She's okay," Kelly said. Relief flickered in his eyes. "The surgery is over and Dorie said the doctor is optimistic."

"Thank God." He ran a hand through his sweat-soaked hair, then wiped his palm on his thigh. "And thank you…for letting me know."

"You're welcome." Rattled by his masculine presence, she took a step back as Lopes returned from the restroom and took the steps up to the dugout. "I should get back—"

"Did you get my messages?"

"I haven't checked my voice mails yet. My battery died."

"We need to talk." His voice was as intense as his eyes; a tingle raced along her spine. She wasn't as immune to him as she'd like to be.

"Not now. You're in the middle of a game."

"I'm not due up this inning so we have at least ten

minutes." He looked around as two utility players came down from the dugout. "Let's go." He grabbed her hand.

"Where are we going?" she asked as he led her out of the locker room, past the restroom and opened the door to the large shower enclosure that had eight tiled bays—four to a side—each partitioned off for privacy. "Seriously? The shower?" she said as he shut the door behind them.

"It's the only place where we won't be disturbed." Matt let go of her hand and moved to the far end of the tiled room. He turned and put his hands on his hips. She tried not to stare at his powerful physique but it was hard not to. His uniform did nothing to disguise the muscles that shaped his rock-hard thighs. "It was Stacia. She's the one who contacted the tabloid and gave them the information about Joey."

"Stacia?" Kelly tilted her head and frowned. "That can't be right."

"Trust me. It's true. I saw her at Kamu's after you and I talked the other night. She offered her condolences, and in the course of the conversation she made a remark about Joey being buried in my Dodgers jersey. Only that fact wasn't mentioned in any of the television news reports or in the print articles. She was home the night I brought you dinner and she overheard us talking. I finally figured it out last night and went to your place to talk to you. Only you weren't there and she was."

"Did she admit it?" she asked, still having a hard time believing Stacia could be that cruel. While it was true that Stacia wasn't the most caring person in the world, she wouldn't stoop to something this low, would she?

"Not exactly. But when I told her I could get the tabloid to give me their source's name in exchange for an interview, it rattled her. She did it, Kelly. And she did it because she's pissed that I never hooked up with her. By the end of our conversation she was practically gloating that there wasn't a thing I could do about what she did."

"But…"

Matt raised his hand. "Look, I don't have a lot of time here, so I'm gonna cut right to the chase. I fucked up." He moved toward her. "I fucked up big-time, and I'm sorry. I'm sorry I accused you of leaking the story and even sorrier that I left bruises on your arms. Can you forgive me?"

Taken aback, Kelly wasn't sure how to respond to this turn of events. "I don't know," she finally said.

"What do you mean?" Matt asked with a slight trace of panic in his eyes. "Are you telling me there's no chance?"

"I'm not sure what I'm telling you." She brushed back a strand of hair that had escaped her ponytail. "All I know is you believed I could betray you. It was the first thought in your mind, and when I tried to talk to you, you wouldn't listen and you wouldn't return my calls."

"I was angry."

She scowled. "That's a lame excuse."

"It's the truth," he said, searching her face. "And the thought that you could betray me like that hurt far more than I ever could have imagined."

"That's still no excuse for what you did, Matt."

"You're right. What I did was inexcusable. And I know I've got a lot of nerve asking for your forgiveness, but I'm asking anyway. I made a mistake, Kelly. Please… don't walk away from me. I need you."

The desperation in his voice was almost her undoing. That and the fear she saw in his eyes. But her emotions were still raw from his actions. Could she ever forgive him? She wasn't sure. What she *was* sure of was she had a lot to think about, and she couldn't do it with him standing a foot away from her. No matter what he'd done, he still affected her as no other man ever had.

"I think we should table this discussion for now." Kelly turned and reached for the door handle but Matt moved to stand behind her and braced his hand on the door, preventing her from opening it.

"Do you know why it hurt?" The cadence of his low rough voice sent a jolt to the pit of her stomach. She felt his warm breath on her ear; a thrill raced up her spine.

"No." She fought the urge to lean back against him. He was so close she could feel the heat of him. She inhaled the combined scent of leather and his earthy maleness; it invaded her senses and brought back erotic memories of every single time he'd made love to her.

"Turn around," he commanded. Slowly, she turned to face him. Their bodies were almost touching. Her gaze was drawn to his; the raw need shimmering in their depths caused her heart to pound an erratic rhythm.

"It hurt because I'm in love with you." His husky words were so unexpected that her breath caught in her throat. "I love you, Kelly, but I didn't realize it until the thought of you betraying me almost killed me."

"That's a hell of way to figure it out," she whispered, blinking back sudden tears.

"Tell me about it." A wry smile quirked his lips. "This isn't how I imagined telling you how I feel, but I couldn't let you walk out of here without you knowing that I love you, and that I'll do whatever I have to do to earn your forgiveness. Do you think you can do that? Can you forgive me?"

"Matt…" she began and then shook her head as sanity prevailed. "We don't have time for this. The inning might be over. The team needs you."

He groaned. "Damn it. You're right. But I need to know one thing."

"What?"

His dark eyes roamed over her face as if committing it to memory. "Could you possibly love me too?"

"Scanlon. One out left. Get your ass back to the dugout," a deep male voice boomed from the locker room, startling them both.

"Shit." Matt lowered his hand from the door. "I've gotta go, but I want an answer to that question after the game. I need to know how you feel, and if you can forgive me."

"We'll talk after the game. I promise," she said, anxious for him to get back to the dugout.

Relief shone in his eyes. "Oh. There is one more thing," he said with a slow sexy grin.

"What now?"

"This." He slipped his arm around her waist, pulled her roughly against him and claimed her mouth. Without any protest whatsoever, she melted against him and instinctively parted her lips. Matt moaned and all but consumed her with a wet drugging kiss that shook her to her soul. She clutched at his broad shoulders and gave in to the passion only he'd been able to evoke in her. Time slowed to a stop as he slid his hands down to cup her ass and pull her even closer to his hard body. Hot desire pooled between her legs and threatened to erase the last bit of rational thought she possessed.

One of them finally remembered there was a really big game going on outside, but it wasn't her.

When Matt pulled back, his eyes gleamed with passion. "I dare you to forget that kiss," he said in a low, husky voice and then relinquished his hold on her.

After he'd left the room, she sagged against the door to catch her breath. How was she supposed to stay mad at him after a kiss like that? And to top it all off he'd had the nerve to go and tell her he was in love with her. That was *so* not fair.

Damn him.

TWENTY-THREE

THE ATMOSPHERE IN the ballpark crackled with electricity. Even in her confused state of mind Kelly couldn't help but feel it. From the moment she'd left her seat to go to the clubhouse to when she'd returned to sit next to her father only twenty minutes had elapsed, but what had happened in those twenty minutes was something she'd never forget.

Matt was in love with her. And after the game he was expecting her to tell him if she loved him too.

No pressure there, right?

It was the bottom of the eighth inning and the score was still tied. There were two outs and Rizzo, who was pitching a magnificent game, was up at bat. Kelly watched him take a couple of practice swings but her mind wasn't on the game. All she could think about was what she was going to say to Matt. She loved him, but could she trust him not to believe the worst of her again? His accusations had hurt her more than words could say and while his apology had been sincere, she might be taking a big risk if she forgave him.

Good Lord. She made difficult decisions just about every day at work, why couldn't she make one now?

Probably because this wasn't about media requests, personal appearance approvals or any of the other decisions she had to make on a daily basis. This was personal. This was about her heart.

"What's going on?" Her father's concerned voice penetrated her thoughts. "Ever since you came back from wherever you went you've been very quiet." He paused. "Where did you go anyway?"

"To the clubhouse," she said, then broke the bad news. "I'm probably going to be moving out of the condo."

"Why? You and Stacia have a sweet deal there."

"I found out something about her that really disturbs me."

Her father's brow furrowed. "Disturbing enough to give up living in a million-dollar condo right next to the ballpark?"

She leaned closer to him and said in a low voice, "Stacia's the one who leaked the story of Matt's son to the press."

"Why would she do that?"

"Because she's jealous of Matt and me."

"Whoa," he said, with genuine surprise on his face. "Back up there, Peanut. You and Matt?"

"We've been seeing each other," she said and wondered why he didn't already know. "Didn't Mom tell you?"

"No."

Wow. This was a surprise. She'd always assumed her mom told her dad everything. Evidently not.

Kelly lifted her feet and rested them on the rail in front of her. "You didn't know that I didn't come back to Kayla's house after the party until the next morning? That I was with Matt all night?"

"No. Sean and I played an early round of golf." He scratched his forehead and shot her a confused glance. "Is it serious between you and Matt?"

"He just told me he's in love with me. Is that serious?"

"That depends," he said as the crowd bellowed with disappointment. They both looked to the field to see Rizzo walking away from the batter's box, disgust evident on his face. He'd struck out and the Dodgers were running off the field toward their dugout. The ninth inning was about to begin. "Are you in love with him?" her father asked.

She turned to find him studying her solemnly. "Yes. I love him."

"Then why the long face?"

"He thought it was me, Dad." Remembering Matt's vicious accusations, she took a deep breath. "That I was the one who leaked the story. He said some awful things to me."

"I see." Her father looked to the field where Matt was now on the pitcher's mound conversing with Rizzo and Lopes. "Did he apologize?" he asked and swung his gaze back to hers. She nodded. "Do you feel the apology was sincere?" She nodded again. "Then as I see it you have two options. You can either tell him it's over, or you can accept his apology and give him another chance."

Kelly sighed, and glanced up at the crystal clear blue sky. That sky, combined with the warm temperature, made for a perfect day for baseball. "You make it sound so simple."

"Oh, it's not simple." Her father put his arm around her shoulders and gave her an affectionate hug. "Relationships aren't easy. Trust me, your mother and I have had our ups and downs over the years. It can be a challenge living with someone, and even more difficult to compromise, which is what relationships are all about."

"How did you make it work? Why aren't you and Mom another divorce statistic?"

"Because we never gave up when it got hard." He squeezed her shoulders gently. "Kelly, you've never given up on anything in your life. Even when you lost your way, you fought back and you recovered."

"Are you saying I shouldn't give up on Matt?"

"Only you can answer that. But if you give up the first time you hit a roadblock you'll never know if what you two have can stand the test of time."

She thought about that for a few seconds and then smiled. "I love you, Dad," she whispered and kissed his cheek. "Thanks for listening."

"Anytime, Peanut." He tugged at her ponytail and then looked at the scoreboard. "The heart of their batting order is up," he said. "Rizzo's got his work cut out for him. I hope he has enough gas left."

As Matt left the pitcher's mound and jogged back to home plate, Kelly watched him and thought about her father's words. There was one thing he was right about for sure, she'd never given up on anything in her life. Whether it was playing softball, going to college, chasing after her dream job or recovering from her eating disorder, she'd never given up. Giving up had never even been an option.

And it wasn't an option now. Anything worth having was never easy. She knew that better than anyone.

FROM HIS POSITION behind home plate, Matt could see Rizzo was thinking way too much. Not that he blamed the guy. It was the top of the ninth inning, the Dodgers had the bases loaded and one of their most feared hitters was striding toward the plate.

The upside was there were two outs.

There was only one thing to do, and that was to calm

Rizzo down any way he could. After signaling to the
umpire, he pushed up his catcher's mask and trotted toward Rizzo. Seeing that Lopes had also started toward
the mound, Matt waved him off. This particular convo
would be between pitcher and catcher only.

When he got to the mound, he did a quick scan of
the ballpark. The fans were on their feet chanting "Beat
L.A." over and over again. The tension, already high,
was now off the charts. Every single Blaze fan was saying a prayer right now, whether they believed in God or
not. It didn't get much better, or more nerve-racking,
than this.

Facing Rizzo, he lifted his glove to shield his mouth
so no one watching on television monitors could read
his lips.

"Look, I know this guy, he always swings at the first
pitch and when he's in a pressure situation he'll start
swinging at anything. Just keep it low and inside and
you'll own his ass," he said, noting the grim line of
Rizzo's mouth and the beads of sweat glistening on his
temples and brow.

"He might try to bunt. Squeeze in a run that way."
Rizzo took off his cap, dried the sweat with his forearm
and then slipped the cap back on his head.

"Let me worry about home plate. If he does bunt and
it comes your way, just do what you do best and fire it
at me." He handed Rizzo the ball and grinned. "You got
this. And by the way, the last time he was up he told me
he screwed your wife before you were married."

Rizzo's eyes narrowed and a vein popped out and
began to throb at his temple. "That little shit. Like Chantal would ever look twice at him." Rizzo slapped the

ball into his glove, hard. "Let's rock and roll. I'm gonna strike this motherfucker out."

Matt pulled his mask down and jogged back to home plate with a huge-ass grin on his face. So maybe the guy didn't actually say he'd fucked Chantal, but did it really matter? Now Rizzo had something else to think about and a score to settle.

God, he loved his job.

Ten minutes later, Matt took a long swig of his sports drink and leaned against the fence that protected the dugout. The Blaze centerfielder was at bat and Lopes was in the on-deck circle. He was up after Lopes and could possibly be the last batter in regular innings. Thanks to Rizzo's strikeout, the score was still tied and would go into extra innings if the Blaze couldn't put any runs on the board.

He drained the last of the liquid from the cup and lobbed it into a nearby trash receptacle. Behind him, Kelly was still watching the game with her father. He hadn't made eye contact with her since he'd returned from the clubhouse. Not because he didn't want to, but because he was afraid he might see something in her eyes that indicated she wasn't going to forgive him. Or that she didn't love him.

The apology he'd given her was rushed, but it couldn't be helped. He'd taken one look at her beautiful face and knew he had to tell her everything—no matter the outcome.

What would that outcome be? He'd know after the game.

After the center fielder hit a grounder straight to the Dodgers' first baseman and was called out, Matt grabbed his favorite bat from the cubby and strode to the on-deck circle as Lopes moved into the batter's box. As he looked around the ballpark it seemed as if he was engulfed in a sea of orange. Everyone in the stadium had one of those rally towels—and was using it. The fans were so loud he could barely hear himself think.

A few months ago he'd stood in this exact spot and felt like an outsider. Now all he felt was the love these fans had for their team, and by extension, for him. It was an amazing feeling, and one he would never take for granted again.

Matt swore softly as Lopes swung at the first pitch and hit a fly ball straight to the Dodgers' left fielder. It was caught easily, and as Lopes stalked toward the dugout Matt walked to the plate.

This was it. *Showtime.*

He took his stance and ignored the trash talk from his counterpart, the guy who'd replaced him. Instead he focused on the pitcher—the Dodgers' ace reliever. The first pitch came at him at about 95 mph, but it looked high so he laid off it. The umpire called it a ball and the crowd cheered. The second pitch fooled him. He swung, and missed, the outside slider. The crowd let out a collective groan. The next pitch he fouled off—the count was now one ball and two strikes.

As he took his stance one more time, he thought of Lily. Of the outlandish promise he'd made to her. Joey would never see another World Series, but Lily would, and more than anything he wanted her to wake up and know the Blaze had a shot at getting there.

The pitch came at him fast, but it was in his sweet spot, so he swung the bat as hard as he could.

The first thing that registered was the hard vibration of the bat in his hands, followed by the sound of the ball cracking off of the wood and, finally, the hopeful roar of the crowd as the ball shot, like a rocket, toward right field. Dropping his bat, he ran toward first base watching the ball's trajectory. The second it sailed over the bleachers, and almost 50,000 fans went batshit crazy, he pumped a triumphant fist in the air and rounded first base.

On the huge screen deep in center field, the words *HOME RUN* flashed wildly all over the screen and then a televised picture cut in and showed the kayakers in the cove fighting to get to the ball. It had landed in the bay. As he rounded third and headed for home, the foghorns blared loudly and he grinned like a damn fool at the sight of his teammates waiting for him at home plate. In about three seconds he was going to be at the bottom of the biggest and happiest dog pile in the National League.

And he couldn't wait.

The celebration was a joyous one and as Rizzo grasped his hand and pulled him up from the dirt, the pitcher was wearing a smile so wide Matt was reminded of the Cheshire cat from *Alice in Wonderland.* Before he knew it, Rizzo had pulled him into a bear hug and was slapping his back. For now their animosity was forgotten and all was right with the world.

"The champagne's waiting," Rizzo yelled after the hug. "Be prepared to get wet."

He felt a tap on his shoulder, turned and found J.T. standing behind him. "Way to go, man," his friend said and hugged him before being hauled off by Lopes to go God only knew where.

As the players, coaches and bat boys all milled around in varying degrees of euphoria, Matt pushed his way through them and headed for the dugout. Winning was amazing, but it would mean so much more if he could share it with Kelly.

In the stands, security guards had spread out around the perimeter to prevent any overzealous fans from storming the field. When he reached the dugout, he looked up and saw Kelly and John Maxwell crushed between some fans that had left their seats, itching to get closer to the celebration.

There was noise—so much noise, but when his eyes locked with Kelly's it all disappeared. For several heart-pounding seconds he waited for something—anything—that would indicate her feelings for him. He waited and prayed, hoping for a miracle.

And then it happened.

He couldn't hear her over the screaming of the fans, but he could read her lips. And what her lips were saying was what he'd been dying to hear.

I love you.

With a superhuman effort he didn't know he possessed, he used the railing for leverage and vaulted on top of the dugout. Two security guards turned and looked at him like he was a lunatic, while the fans in the vicinity cheered even louder. Some beckoned to him with outstretched arms while others took pictures with cameras and cell phones.

As he moved toward Kelly, her wide smile was eclipsed only by the love shining in her eyes. When he halted in front of her, he held out his hand. She hesitated long enough to look at her father who, surprisingly, appeared to be a little choked up. Then she took his hand and let him pull her onto the top of the dugout.

Matt's heart raced a mile a minute as he wrapped his arms around her waist and pulled her against him. Every camera in the place was likely trained on them, but he didn't care. The only thing that mattered was the beautiful sexy woman he was holding in his arms.

"You're crazy, you know that, right?" Kelly said, still smiling as she braced her hands on his shoulders.

"Say it again."

"You're crazy."

"Not that." He grinned. "Say it again. So I can hear it."

"I love you," she shouted happily.

"Thank God," Matt said, and then in front of the fans, the players and a national television audience of millions, he kissed the woman he loved.

* * * * *

Read on for a sneak peek from
STEALING SECOND by Alison Packard.

ONE

KATHERINE WHITTON DIDN'T believe in torturing herself. In her world—the world she created after leaving Dallas for Berkeley seventeen years ago—her very existence was perfectly arranged so she'd rarely be reminded of the past.

But there were days—days like this one—when even though she knew she shouldn't be standing at the large picture window of her office overlooking Blaze Field, she couldn't help herself. The draw was too powerful.

Today was Kids' Day at the ballpark. One of many the San Francisco Blaze held throughout the summer. Children of all ages were allowed onto the field to run the bases and get autographs from their favorite players.

She could almost feel their excitement at being able to step foot on the same field as their beloved team. The event, a dream come true for many of them, was one the players enjoyed as well. Every single Blaze player had once been a kid who loved baseball and who dreamed of meeting the baseball idol they revered and cheered for. And unlike some other public appearances the players were asked to attend, neither she nor her staff had to twist any arms.

Despite the heaviness in her heart, Katherine couldn't look away. At this moment the phrase "things happen for a reason" didn't comfort her. Actually, it never had. It was something she told herself to make sense of a life that hadn't turned out at all like the one she'd planned. She wasn't sure how long she stood there, but it was long enough to remind her of what she'd lost and what she'd chosen to live without.

Just after eleven, the phone on Katherine's uncharacteristically cluttered desk rang. She glanced at the number on the caller ID screen and quickly picked up the handset.

"Good morning, Doug," she said to her boss, as she pulled off her reading glasses and set them on top of the budget report she'd been reviewing. "What's up?" For as long as she'd worked for him, Doug Lowry had never been a micromanager. With his responsibilities as general manager he didn't have the time. He trusted his staff implicitly and rarely called any of them unless it was something that couldn't wait for their weekly staff meeting. And since the staff meeting was three days away, she could only surmise something important must have arisen.

"We may have a situation that I'll need you and your staff to jump on right away," Doug began, his cool, modulated tone the same as always. Even when he got upset, he never seemed to get ruffled. However, judging by the large bottle of antacids he kept on his desk, he appeared to be one of those people who internalized their stress rather than taking it out on those around him.

"Situation? What situation?" Katherine leaned forward and stared at the wall opposite her desk. A wall filled with artfully hung photographs that captured some of her favorite memories during her tenure with the Blaze. Her gaze rested on a framed photo of her and her father taken after she had accepted a prestigious Bay Area humanitarian award on behalf of the team's community outreach programs, several of which she'd initiated. The proud gleam in her father's eyes meant more to her than anything—Cal Whitton was her hero, not to mention the person she loved and respected most in the world.

"I received a call from Rick Taylor a couple of days ago. He led me to believe he may attempt to resurrect his career."

Katherine stifled a gasp. The president of the United States could have waltzed into her office and she would have been less surprised. "Are you serious? I thought he'd given up baseball for good."

"So did I. In fact, when I talked to Tom about it we both had the same reaction."

She lifted her brows as her fingers tightened on the phone. "Tom? He knows about this?"

"Yes. I called him right after I spoke to Rick."

"So he's known for a couple of days?" she asked, as her blood started to simmer.

"Yes. I'm surprised he hasn't shared it with you."

Katherine wasn't surprised. Not one damn bit. "I'm sure he meant to. He's busy," she said, trying to keep her tone pleasant. "When will we get a confirmation on Rick's status?"

"I'm not sure. He's trying to secure an agent. Be prepared for his decision at any time."

"I will," she said with a nod.

After she ended her conversation with Doug, it took less than ten minutes for her to leave her corner office and push through the double doors of the San Francisco Blaze clubhouse. Anger had a way of making her move a bit more quickly—even in stiletto heels.

Striding through the locker room portion of the clubhouse, Katherine ignored the players in various stages of undress and made her way down the long hallway that led to the staff offices. When she reached the last office on the right, she crossed the threshold, found the edge of the door with her palm and with the force of her ire, slammed it shut.

A perverse sense of satisfaction filled her as Tom Morgan visibly flinched and jerked his head up from the open laptop sitting on his scarred oak desk. In the space of a few seconds, his blue-green eyes went from startled to annoyed. No surprise there; it wasn't like she hadn't been on the receiving end of that particular reaction before.

"You always did know how to make an entrance." His lazy drawl still held a hint of Texas and never failed to heighten her pulse. A fact that irritated her beyond measure. "What's got your thong in a twist this time?"

"Rick Taylor." Katherine moved forward but didn't sit down in the chair opposite his desk. She didn't plan on staying long. And how did he know she wore a thong anyway? "Why am I the last one to know he's thinking about resuming his baseball career?"

Tom leaned back in his leather chair, a ghost of a smile hovering on his lips. "I doubt you're the last person to know, and I only found out two days ago."

"Why didn't you call me immediately? If Rick is trying to make a comeback, my department needs to be involved."

"It isn't my place to call you. It's Doug's." His enigmatic eyes briefly skimmed over her body, then lifted. There was no indication whether he liked what he saw. Not that it mattered. Not anymore. "Besides, aren't you the one who said you preferred I didn't contact you after hours?"

"When it comes to anything media-related, I'm on call 24/7. You know that."

Tom shrugged, drawing her attention to his broad shoulders. The Blaze T-shirt he wore didn't do much to disguise his muscular upper body. Although he didn't play anymore, he was still in excellent shape. Of course, he wouldn't be one of those ex-athletes who let themselves go after their playing days were over. He was still a perfect specimen. Not that she spent a lot of time thinking about him or his body.

Liar.

Okay, fine. Maybe she thought about his body once in a while. But only because it was an involuntary response.

"I assumed Doug would call you as soon as he got off the phone with me. Rick hasn't made it official. There's not much we can do until he does."

Katherine gave him a grudging nod. He was right, but she didn't have to like it. By all accounts, patience had never been one of her virtues. Starting from the moment she'd arrived into the world—three weeks premature. "I understand that. But I need to be kept abreast of the situation. I assume if he does intend to come back, he's going to one of our minor league affiliates?"

"At the moment, that's hard to predict," Tom said. "We have no idea what his fitness level is. He's basically missed two full seasons. If he's in top shape and his skills haven't diminished, he could be considered for one of the non-roster invitee slots at spring training with the Blaze. If not, he'll start out in the minors. At what level would depend on him."

"I'd appreciate it if you'd keep me in the loop. Due

to the circumstances, this is going to be a big story. I'd
like some advance warning so I can prep my staff and
make sure we keep the media circus as far away from
him as possible."

"Anything for you…Katie."

"Don't call me that," she snapped, annoyed that he
seemed incapable of using her given name whenever
they were alone together.

"Sorry." The grin that played at the corners of his
mouth indicated he wasn't sorry at all. "Force of habit."

She narrowed her eyes and gave him her best glacial
stare. Not that it would do any good. As always, Tom
would do as he damn well pleased. "Break the habit."

"I'll try, *Katherine*. But those fancy clothes and four-
inch heels can't change where you come from. You can
take the girl out of Texas, but you can't take Texas out
of the girl."

"You're wrong about that," she shot back with a scowl.
"I left Texas and…and everything that happened there
behind a long time ago."

Tom shook his head as amusement quirked the corners of his mouth. Years ago, when they were teens,
he'd worn his light brown hair long enough to brush
his shoulders. But now he kept it shorter and neatly
trimmed. That she remembered the silky texture of it
after so long irritated her. She'd lived without Tom longer than they'd been together. Little things, like the feel
of his hair and the taste of his skin, should be long forgotten.

"Katie, darlin'. We're Texans to the bone. Always
have been, always will be."

"Then why did you take the manager job with San
Francisco?" she asked, ignoring the endearment. Unlike

a few Texas men Katherine had known, Tom wasn't one
to call every woman he came into contact with *darlin'*.
He'd always saved it for her—back when she would have
sworn that nothing could ever tear them apart. "I have
it on good authority you were also offered the manager
position with the Rangers."

"The Blaze made me a better offer." Tom pushed up
from his chair and folded his arms over his chest. For
a moment she was distracted by his strong forearms,
tanned from the sun and covered with fine golden-brown
hair. What was wrong with her? She'd been doing a fairly
decent job of ignoring Tom Morgan and the bittersweet
memories seeing him evoked ever since he'd signed on
as manager two and a half years ago. Why, all of a sudden, was she responding to him in a manner not at all
professional?

"Did you know I worked for the Blaze when you accepted the job?" It was the one question she'd never gotten an answer to. Scratch that. One of two.

A scowl darkened his face. "It was the job I wanted,
so I took it."

"You didn't answer the question." Katherine's cheeks
grew warm under his intense scrutiny. Lifting a hand,
she fiddled with a tendril of hair that had escaped the
confines of her sleek bun. "Did you know?"

"Yes," Tom said tersely, then went silent. And in that
silence memories shimmered in the air between them.
Memories even seventeen years and his betrayal couldn't
erase.

She cleared her throat to break the tension that permeated the room. "What's the status on Rizzo's thumb?"

"Same as yesterday. But I'm optimistic he'll be off

the DL next week. I may give him a start in the Colorado series."

"That's good news. He's been missed in the rotation. We need both him *and* Gentry if we're going to have a shot at making it to the post-season."

"We're gonna need a lot more than Rizzo and Gentry." Tom sighed. "When we lost Lopes to free agency, we lost one of our best hitters. Scanlon isn't a miracle worker."

Despite the tense relationship between her and Tom, Katherine felt a certain degree of sympathy for him. The Blaze had won their first World Series almost two years ago, then fell to St. Louis last season in the National League Championship series. There was a lot of pressure on him to ensure the Blaze returned to the post-season and secured another World Series win. But with a weaker team than last year, the odds didn't seem to be in his favor.

"One game at a time." Katherine gave him a rueful smile. "Isn't that what you always say to the guys?"

"Yes." He inclined his head and fixed her with a speculative gaze. "Are you saying I should listen to my own advice?"

"You should. As advice goes, it's excellent."

A grin split his handsome face. Katherine's heart skipped a beat at the sight of it. Just like it had the first time she'd ever seen him—that long-ago day when Mrs. Raby had walked him into homeroom and introduced him to his new classmates.

"I think that's the most complimentary thing I've heard from you since I've been here," he said with a wry grin.

Despite herself, her lips quirked with amusement.

"Don't get used to it." She glanced past him to the credenza behind his desk and among the several framed photos on top of it, noted one of him and his sister, taken at the ESPY awards the year the Blaze won the World Series. "How's Sheila?"

Tom's eyes softened. They always did when the subject of his older sister came up. "I talked to her last night. She'll be in Phoenix on business the same week the team will be there. Even though we live in the same city during the season, I don't see as much of her as I'd like. It'll be good to connect with her in Phoenix. Even if it's only for dinner."

Katherine manufactured a smile, grateful she rarely accompanied the team on road trips. Being in such close proximity to Tom for days at a time would make their already-tense relationship even more strained. "Do you need me to arrange for some seats?"

"If it's no trouble."

"Not at all. I'll see what I can come up with and get back to you."

"Thanks, Katie."

Katherine waved a dismissive hand. "Don't thank me. I'd do the same for anyone on the team."

His eyes became flat and inscrutable. "Are we ever going to talk about it?"

She didn't have to ask what he was referring to. But talk about it? *Now?* Snow would fall in hell before *that* happened. "I don't see the point."

"Right." His tone was sarcastic. "No point at all."

Katherine stiffened and lifted her chin. Their past hung between them for a long, tense moment. "Don't call me Katie," she finally said, then turned and left his office.

TOM WATCHED KATIE walk out of his office, and not for the first time wondered why he'd accepted Doug Lowry's offer to manage the Blaze instead of the competing offer he'd received from the Rangers. It wasn't like he hadn't known Katie worked for the team—over the years, via a few of their mutual friends from high school, he'd learned that she'd interned for the Blaze during college, and when she graduated from UC Berkeley they'd hired her full-time. Thirteen years later, she held the position of senior vice president of communications and was damn good at her job. Tom wasn't surprised—in high school she was at the top of their graduating class and had been voted most likely to succeed.

Although he'd known working alongside Katie would be a challenge, given their past, he'd convinced himself that the opportunity to manage a major league club with the Blaze's potential was the chance of a lifetime. If he couldn't play anymore, he could manage, and as it turned out, he was better suited to leading a team than to the day-to-day grind of playing.

Not that managing wasn't a challenge. Dealing with the players and their massive egos required equal measures of authority, patience and restraint. Luckily, he was blessed with an abundance of all three—except when it came to dealing with Katie. She was still the only person who'd ever been able to get under his skin. Funny how he'd conveniently forgotten that when he accepted the position. Lately though, working with her had become more difficult. Her icy exterior was taking its toll on him in more ways than one.

Tom moved to the team's schedule taped to the wall and tried to banish Katie from his mind. It was mid-August and the Blaze had fallen to third place in the division. The Dodgers were five games ahead of them in the standings and were currently on a six-game winning streak. Maybe their archrivals would suffer a meltdown, and the Blaze could come from behind and take the division. If not, the wild-card slot was up for grabs, and given the win-loss records of the other teams in contention, realistically it was within reach. Tom hadn't given up on making it to the post-season—two years ago the Blaze's season had looked just as bleak but they'd gone on to win the World Series. There was no reason they couldn't do that again.

A sharp rap on the door pulled him from his thoughts. He turned to see the main reason the team had won that World Series championship standing at the threshold.

"Got a minute, Skipper?" Matt Scanlon asked, and respectfully waited to be invited in.

Tom waved him inside. "What's up?"

"There's a rumor going around the clubhouse that Taylor is coming back to the team," Matt said as he ambled into the spacious office. "Any truth to that?"

Tom scowled and returned to his desk. He wasn't surprised the word was out, just at how quickly it had made its way to the clubhouse. "Sit down," he said, as he sat in his own chair and closed his laptop.

Matt settled in the chair across from him. If he was concerned Taylor was coming back for the starting catcher position, it wasn't evident by his demeanor. But then again, Matt was still at the top of his game and had replaced Rick Taylor as the team's leader after Taylor quit baseball. Every guy on the team respected Matt, even the ones leery of him when he'd first arrived.

"When did the rumor start?"

"A couple of days ago. But it's picking up steam.

Some of the guys are still in touch with Taylor. Maybe he's said something to them." Matt leaned forward to rest his forearms on his knees. "Look, this might be the thing we need to boost morale. From the reaction I'm seeing in the clubhouse, the guys are stoked that Rick's trying to put his life back together. He's still young, and if he's half as good as he was when he decided to quit, then it wouldn't take much time in the minors to get him up to speed. And as much as I hate to say it, with J.T. gone, we need a quality backup."

Tom agreed. Losing J.T. Sawyer at the end of his contract had been a blow to the team. But he understood J.T.'s decision. In San Francisco, he'd been the second-string catcher behind Matt, but in San Diego, with the second-place Padres, he was the starter and having an All Star–caliber season. Unfortunately, J.T.'s replacement wasn't living up to expectations.

"I don't confirm or deny rumors, you know that. But as soon as I know something definite, the team will be advised as soon as possible." After Katie, of course. Otherwise she'd have him skewered on a spit over a crackling fire before sundown.

"That's fair." Matt nodded and pushed up from the chair. "I'll say 'no comment' if I'm asked about it in the media room tonight after the game."

After Scanlon left his office, Tom swiveled his chair around to face the credenza and let his gaze rest on the smiling image of his sister. Sheila Morgan was one of the reasons he'd landed in San Francisco. Two years older than him, Sheila had left for college when he was a junior in high school. She attended USF and after graduating decided to stay in San Francisco. There weren't many people he felt comfortable confiding in, but his big sister was one of them. As much as he loved his parents, there were some things he couldn't talk to either of them about.

The other reason he'd accepted the job with the Blaze rather than staying in Texas and managing the Rangers wasn't a mystery. He was certifiably crazy. Why else would he subject himself to working so closely with the woman who'd walked away from him seventeen years ago without a backward glance?

At first, the pain of losing Katie had been unbearable. Then he'd found a way to live with it. Only that solution had created a whole other set of problems, and by the time he'd figured it out, he was damn lucky he hadn't completely ruined his career...or killed someone in the process.

JUST PAST ONE O'CLOCK, Katherine sipped her raspberry iced tea and looked into the bluest eyes she'd ever seen. Adam Logan's penetrating gaze was mesmerizing, and rumor had it his movie-star good looks had left a trail of broken hearts from Los Angeles to San Francisco. Although Adam was cofounder of one of the top sports management agencies in California, and their lunch today at Kamu's was strictly professional, feminine instinct told her that Adam wouldn't be averse to a more personal relationship if she were so inclined. And lately, she'd been thinking she might be. She was tired of bringing a different date to the various social functions she attended. Maybe it was time to find someone a little more...permanent.

"Thanks for meeting me on such short notice," she said as she set her glass on the table. "I'll cut to the chase. I believe Leah Porter is an excellent fit for the position we have open. Not only is she an excellent writer, she knows baseball and looks great on camera."

"I spoke to Leah about the position and she's definitely interested, but she's concerned that online reporting, even for the Blaze, will be limiting," Adam said, then paused as their server returned to the table to fill his water glass. With an amiable nod, he thanked the young woman, who'd been extraordinarily attentive ever since they'd sat down, then looked back at Katherine. "Her goal is television."

Katherine nodded. "I understand and frankly, after meeting with her, I think she's got what it takes to make it on the national level. If she accepts our offer, she'll be the dedicated reporter for the Blaze. Not only will she be responsible for posting articles on the team's website, she'll be the face of the team for the majority of the video segments we run on the site, as well as the human-interest pieces we release to the local sports affiliates. It's valuable exposure and an opportunity that doesn't come along every day."

A charming smile curved his lips, revealing a dimple on his cheek that softened his handsomely chiseled features. "I can't disagree. I'll call her when I get back to the office. If she decides to accept your offer, I'll contact you regarding compensation and we can go from there."

"Wonderful." She smiled and picked up her fork. "I look forward to hearing from you."

They ate in companionable silence for almost a minute until Adam's phone chimed. "Excuse me. I've been expecting an important text." He picked up his phone and studied the screen.

Katherine took the opportunity to survey the room. Kamu's, located across from Blaze Field, was a popular spot for the Blaze players, coaches and front office staff. It was also a place where the fans could mingle with the players—as long as it was done respectfully. The owner, a longtime Blaze fan, had no qualms about tossing out any fans who harassed the players.

As she took a bite of Kamu's grilled salmon, she wasn't surprised to see Kelly Maxwell enter the restaurant and head straight for the mahogany bar. Kelly and her boyfriend, Matt Scanlon, now lived together in a luxury condo nearby, and were regulars at Kamu's. Since she was positive Kelly didn't drink during working hours, Katherine assumed her number one employee was waiting for takeout. Kelly turned, as if sensing she was being watched, and then smiled and waved when her gaze connected with Katherine's. Kelly's attention quickly shifted to Adam and her smile grew even wider. No doubt Kelly was thinking there was more to Katherine's lunch than just lunch.

"There's something else we need to discuss."

Katherine returned her attention to Adam. "Regarding Leah?" she asked.

"No. Rick Taylor." He returned his phone to the table. "He's signed with Logan-Johnson and wants to return to baseball. To the Blaze, to be precise."

"So it's official," she said, and despite her best efforts not to let it affect her, a wave of emotion threatened to engulf her. Rick Taylor had been through hell, and many, including her, believed there was no chance he'd ever play pro ball again. Never had she been so happy to be wrong. She glanced toward the bar, her stomach plunging at the sight of Kelly motioning to Tom, who was standing in the vestibule near the entrance. For a moment he hesitated, then strode toward Kelly and slid onto a stool next to her.

As she watched Tom and Kelly's easy familiarity, Katherine tamped down her jealousy. There was nothing romantic going on between Tom and Kelly. Kelly had eyes only for Matt, and as for Tom, well, she had no clue if he was seeing anyone and she didn't *want* to know. After all this time, the thought of him with anyone shouldn't bother her, but it did.

Damn it all.

Why hadn't he stayed in Texas and left her in peace?

TWO

THE WORDS COMING OUT of Kelly Maxwell's mouth could have been Latin, or even Chinese, for all Tom knew. It wasn't until she said Rick Taylor's name that he forced himself to look away from the mirror behind Kamu's polished wood bar. "What have you heard about Rick?" he asked her.

"Only what Matt has told me. Rumor has it that Rick is determined to reclaim his place on the team." Kelly swiveled on her stool and rested her elbow on the bar. She was wearing black pants and a matching blazer with a white shirt underneath—pretty much her standard workday attire. Tom figured he could count on one hand the number of times he'd seen her in a dress. "Is it true?"

"It's only speculation at this point. And that's exactly what I told your boss this morning."

He grinned as Kelly gave him a sheepish smile.

"You can't blame me for trying."

"You and Katherine should know better than to tag-team me." He made sure to use Katie's given name. It didn't suit her, but ever since he'd been in San Francisco she'd insisted on it. It was yet another tactic to distance herself from her past. "Y'all act like I never share any information with you, and that's just not true. The fact is, Doug is the only one we know of who's spoken directly to Rick. All I was told is that Rick is mulling it over."

"I hope he comes back." Kelly pushed her long ponytail over her shoulder and sighed. "After everything that's happened to him, he deserves it."

"That's big of you, considering he'd be competing with Matt for the starting catcher position."

"Matt can take care of himself. And he's not worried."

"No reason for him to be."

Not yet anyway. Everything depended on Taylor's physical conditioning and skills. He'd been well on his way to a Rookie of the Year season before his motorcycle accident. His rehab had progressed much better than expected, and he'd been due to return to the team a year ago last spring. But then, tragically, his wife and unborn child had been killed in a car accident and he'd decided to quit baseball for good.

But now that his grief had eased, Taylor was having second thoughts. That was what Doug said, anyway. It remained to be seen if Rick would actually stage a comeback. That the team would take him back wasn't in question. Rick was a part of the Blaze family and he'd get a chance to make the roster. What *was* in question was whether he still had what it took to play pro ball. Tom hoped he did. Rick Taylor was a fine young man *and* he was from Texas. A Texan would fight to the end, or die trying. The Alamo was proof of that.

Kelly nudged his arm and gave him a sly grin. "Did you notice Katherine is here?"

Damn straight, he'd noticed. That was who he'd been staring at in the mirror. Katie, and one of the country's top sports agents, Adam Logan, were sitting in a booth in the back and looked a little too friendly for his liking. Tom pressed his lips together as the sound of Katie's full-bodied laughter rose above the quiet chatter in

the room. She hadn't laughed like that in his presence
since the summer after high school.

"Is she?" he said with feigned innocence and turned
to look in the same direction as Kelly. "Business meeting?" he asked, hoping to get the lowdown on Katie's
private life.

"Probably. But a part of me hopes it's more."

Tom fought off a scowl. "Why do you say that?"

Kelly offered him a wistful smile. "Because all she
does is work. She needs to get out and have some fun."
She turned toward the bar as the server set her take-out
order in front of her. "Gotta run. I'm swamped. I'll see
you in the media room after the game." She slid from
her stool, grabbed her lunch, then strode toward the exit.

Kelly was right about one thing. Katie was a helluva
hard worker, but Tom found it difficult to believe she
didn't find time for fun, and he knew for a fact she
wasn't living like a cloistered nun. She'd brought a different man to just about every single Blaze social function Tom had attended since he'd signed on as manager.
Obviously, she wasn't lacking for dates.

It shouldn't bother him. Not after so long. But there
were still nights when the thought of anyone else touching her was enough to make him want to take a drink.

Ten minutes later, he was still waiting for his take-
out order, and instead of keeping tabs on the booth in
the back, he forced himself to watch the latest sports
news on one of the flat panels hung over the bar. Seeing Katie with Logan had killed his appetite, but with
a game tonight it was going to be a long day and he'd
be starving later.

So far there were no reports of Rick Taylor's impend-
ing decision, but it wouldn't take long for the gossip in

the clubhouse to spread to the media. He'd probably have to field those questions tonight. He hoped for a definitive answer soon. Most sports reporters were like a dog with a bone once they got wind of a story. Dealing with them wasn't one of his favorite parts of the job, but it was unavoidable. More than once he'd wanted to tell them to go to hell, but as hard as it was, he'd managed to restrain himself. The last thing he needed was an antagonistic relationship with the press.

Despite his best intentions, he couldn't help but look in the mirror. His gut tightened as he saw Katie and Logan navigating around the tables in the middle of the room and heading his way. He'd met Adam Logan a few times—Adam's firm, Logan-Johnson, represented the Blaze's star pitcher, Trey Gentry. Logan was a bit too citified for Tom's taste, but he didn't hold it against the guy. Not everyone was lucky enough to hail from Texas.

What *did* irritate Tom was Logan's proprietary hand on the small of Katie's back. Was Kelly right? Could there be something more going on between Katie and Logan than business? The guy had been named one of the most eligible bachelors in the city several times and had a reputation for dating supermodels and actresses. Katie was as beautiful as any model or actress, but her looks weren't her only asset. She was smarter than hell, and that combination of beauty and brains was both alluring and addictive. He knew that better than anyone.

As the couple passed behind him, Katie glanced at him and his gaze collided with hers in the mirror. She inclined her head but didn't pause, and then she and Logan made their exit. Two minutes later, with his takeout order in hand, he left Kamu's and was surprised to find her standing alone near the entrance.

"Where's your date?" he asked, surprised that Logan wasn't in sight. "He could have at least walked you back to the ballpark."

Katie's pale blue eyes narrowed on him. "It's across the street. I think I can handle it."

"How long have you been dating him?" Tom asked, then almost wished he hadn't. Since arriving in San Francisco he'd made it a point not to ask Katie about the past, or her personal life. She'd firmly set those boundaries his first week as manager, and until this morning he'd adhered to them. Her aloofness during his tenure with the Blaze had put a burr under his saddle, until he'd found that the best way break her icy facade was to find subtle ways to annoy her. He found her anger and irritation more to his liking than her remoteness.

"Who says I'm dating him?"

"Aren't you?"

"Whom I date is none of your business." She adjusted the strap of her purse over her shoulder as they moved to the side of the entrance to allow an elderly couple to enter the restaurant. The light breeze from the bay ruffled the wisps of auburn hair that had escaped her bun, and he had to physically restrain himself from brushing it away from her eyes. Touching Katie wasn't allowed. Not anymore.

"But Adam did share something with me that you need to know about," she continued.

"What? Is it about Gentry?" The young pitcher was phenomenal, but dealing with his rapidly expanding ego was becoming more trouble than it was worth.

"No. We didn't discuss Trey at all. While we were having lunch, Adam got a text from his firm. Rick Taylor signed with Logan-Johnson this morning."

Although not surprised, Tom let the news percolate in his brain for a few seconds. "That means he's serious about resuming his career."

Katie nodded. "It appears so. However, until we get the official word, we can't say much. Unless you hear otherwise, deflect any questions with the usual response. Once I get the go-ahead I'll schedule a press conference." She glanced at the watch that encircled her slim wrist. "I have a feeling I'll be meeting with Doug sometime today. I'm almost positive Adam is on the phone to him right now."

"Spring training should be interesting," Tom commented as they, by unspoken agreement, moved to the corner of Second and King to wait for the light. "Whatever town Taylor rolls into, they won't know what hit 'em."

"It'll be a zoo. Everyone loves a comeback story."

Tom ran a hand over his jaw. "I hope this doesn't blow up in Rick's face. He's been out of the sport for almost two years. If he isn't in top shape, I don't think he's got a whisker of a chance of getting a non-roster invitation. I have no doubt he could do well in the minors, but I doubt that would satisfy him."

"Knowing Rick, he wouldn't have started the ball rolling if he didn't believe he could make it back to the majors."

"I hope you're right," he said as the light changed and they stepped off the curb. The sudden blaring of a horn caused his heart to almost burst out of his chest, and he turned just in time to see a low-slung sports car bearing down on them. Instinctively, he dropped his take-out bag and snaked his arms around Katie's waist to pull her back to safety. The speeding driver made a right turn and, with its tires squealing, the car sped quickly out of sight.

A nearby pedestrian yelled out an obscenity, then, shaking her head in disgust, she crossed the street, but Tom couldn't seem to move. The only thing he was aware of was Katie's soft, trembling body pressed against his.

"Are you okay?" he asked as he caught the light but intoxicating scent of her perfume and inhaled deeply. Primal desire played havoc with his senses—holding her again after so many years was like coming home.

"Yes." She nodded, but made no attempt to pull away. "Where's a cop when you need one?" she joked, with a shaky laugh.

The same place a cold shower was when *he* needed one. Nowhere to be found. Before Katie could feel how much she affected him, he let go of her and bent over to pick up his lunch. Luckily, the bag and its contents didn't seem the worse for wear.

Unfortunately, he couldn't say the same for himself.

ACKNOWLEDGMENTS

TO MY AMAZING FRIENDS, Chrissie Humphrey and Jennifer Vincent: Thank you for reading every chapter I sent your way and, in return, giving me the unvarnished truth.

To my family: Thank you for your support and encouragement. I love you!

And to my editor, Angela James, and everyone at Carina Press: I couldn't ask for a more supportive editor or a nicer group of people to work with. Thank you all for everything you do.

ABOUT THE AUTHOR

ALISON FELL IN love with reading at a very early age. Her favorite grandmother worked for Scholastic Books, and every Friday would bring home a box filled with books she was able to buy for a nickel apiece because they were slightly irregular. In her early teens, Alison discovered Harlequin Presents romance novels at the library and read them voraciously. What she liked most about them? The exotic locales and happy endings, of course!

When Alison isn't working at the day job that pays the bills, keeps a roof over her head, and supports her book and chocolate habit, she spend most of her free time writing. But when she takes a break, she enjoys reading and spending time with her family and friends.